you're Thinking About Tomatoes

ILLUSTRATED BY **COLE HENLEY**

MICHAEL ROSEN

You're Thinking About Tomatoes

unbound

First published in 2022

Unbound
Level 1, Devonshire House, One Mayfair Place, London W1J 8AJ
www.unbound.com

A CIP record for this book is available from the British Library

ISBN 978-1-80018-144-1 (hardback)
ISBN 978-1-80018-145-8 (ebook)

Printed in Slovenia by DZS

1 3 5 7 9 8 6 4 2

Michael:
For Joe and Eddie

Cole:
To the ongoing work of the Colonial Countryside
project and all the voiceless who shaped the landscapes
we inhabit and enjoy

With special thanks to Peadar O'Dwyer
for generously supporting this book

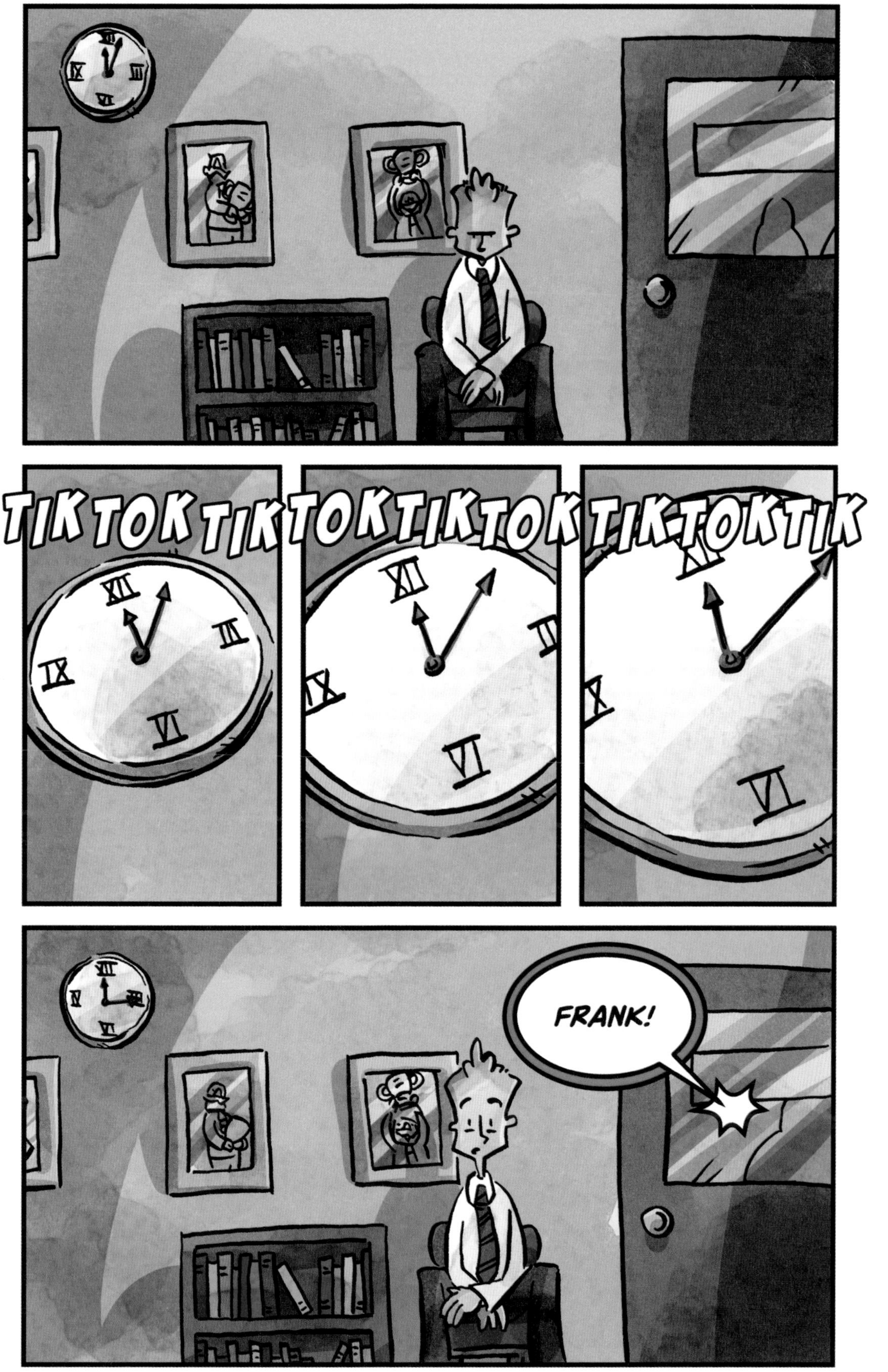
TIK TOK TIK TOK TIK TOK TIK TOK TIK
FRANK!

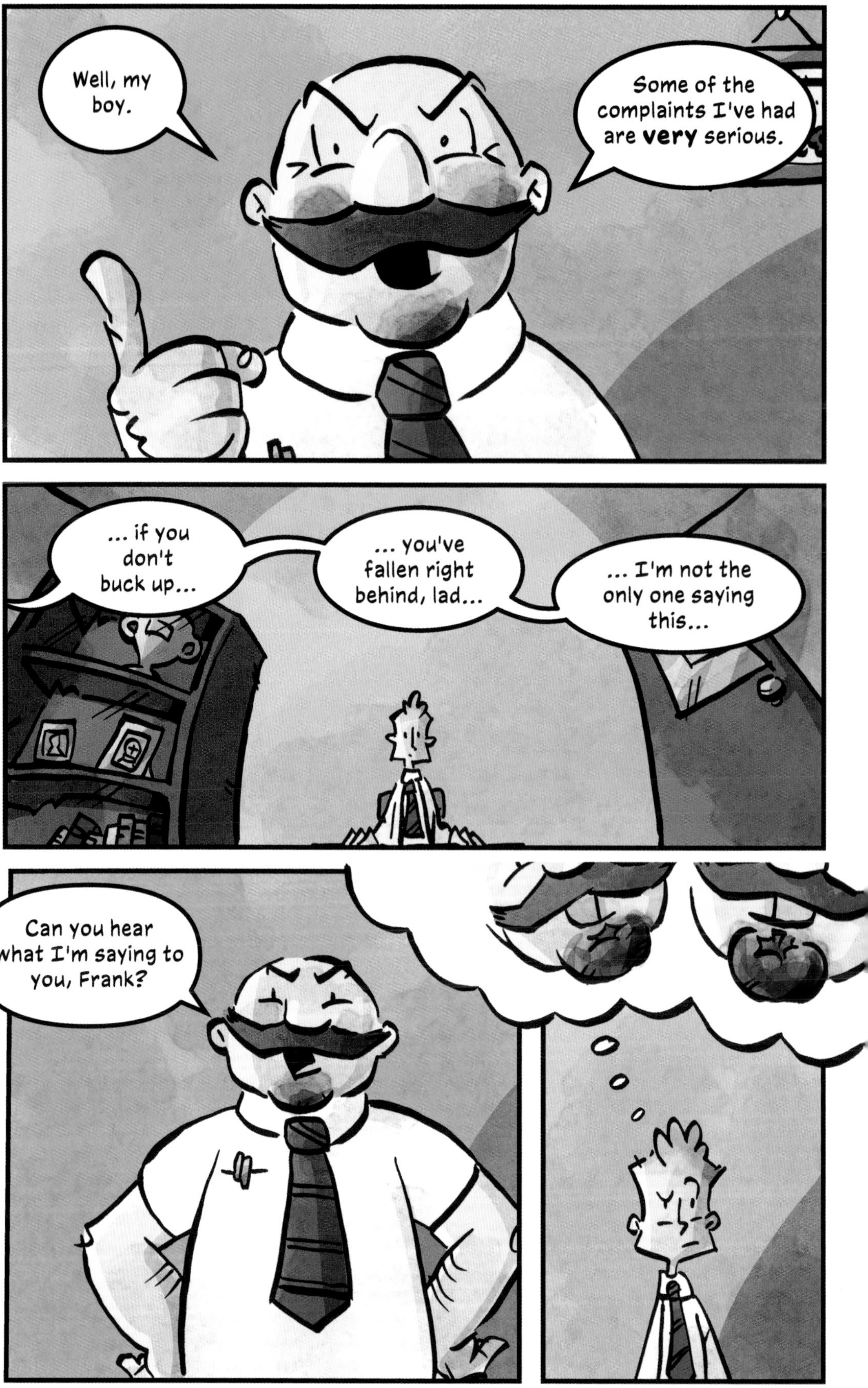
Well, my boy.
Some of the complaints I've had are **very** serious.
... if you don't buck up...
... you've fallen right behind, lad...
... I'm not the only one saying this...
Can you hear what I'm saying to you, Frank?

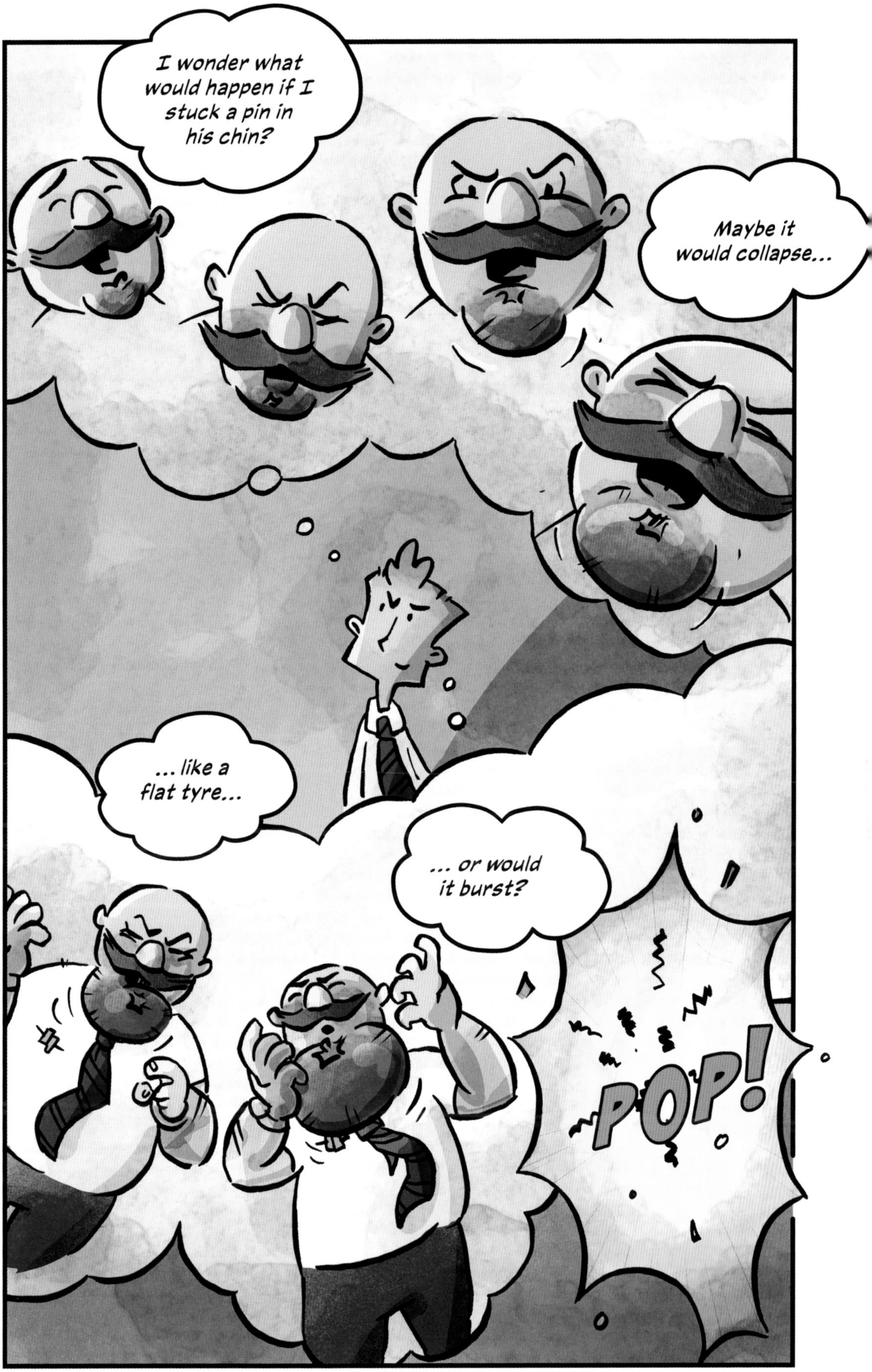
I wonder what would happen if I stuck a pin in his chin?
Maybe it would collapse...
... like a flat tyre...
... or would it burst?
POP!

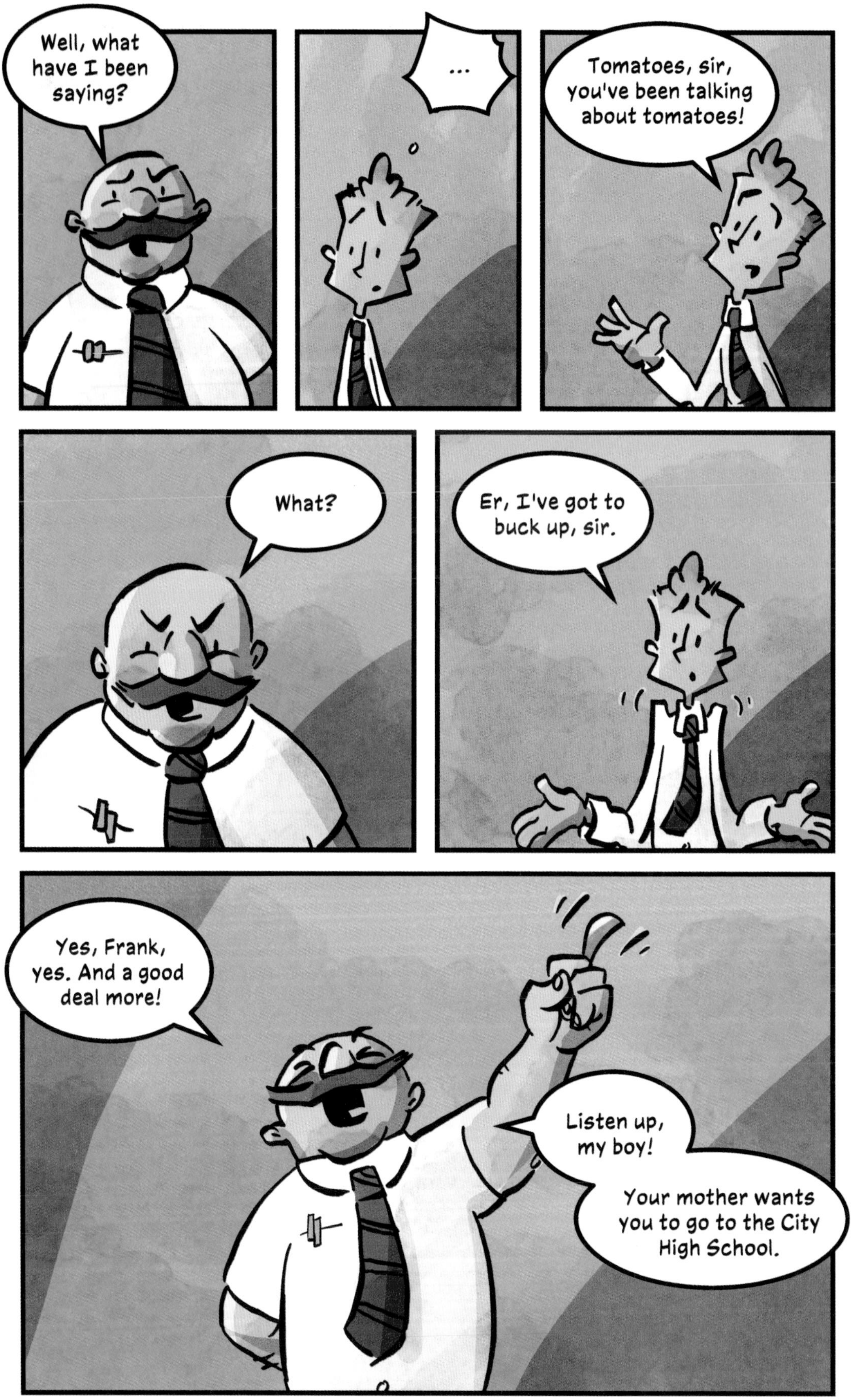
Well, what have I been saying?
...
Tomatoes, sir, you've been talking about tomatoes!
What?
Er, I've got to buck up, sir.
Yes, Frank, yes. And a good deal more!
Listen up, my boy!
Your mother wants you to go to the City High School.

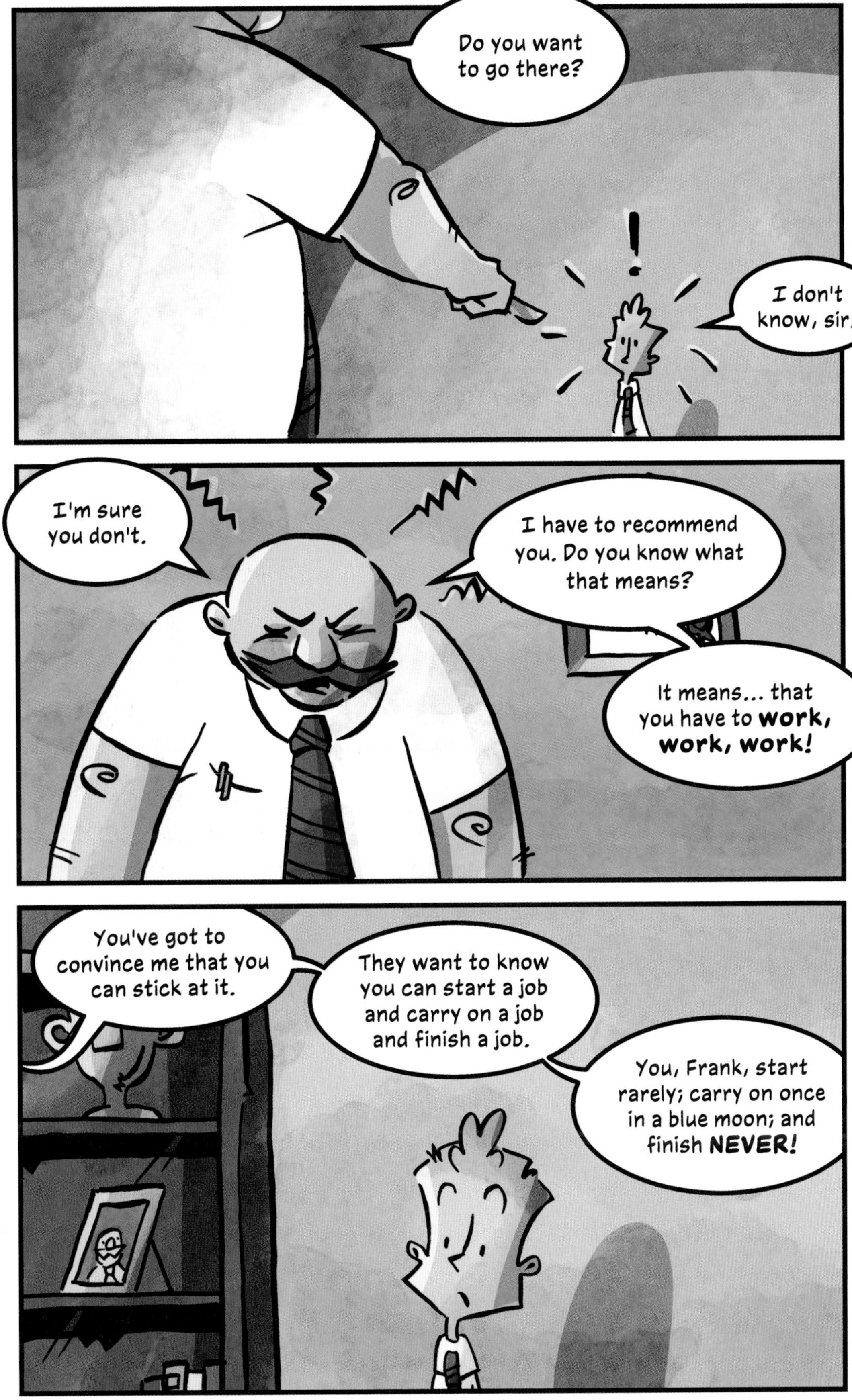
Do you want to go there?
I don't know, sir.
I'm sure you don't.
I have to recommend you. Do you know what that means?
It means... that you have to **work, work, work!**
You've got to convince me that you can stick at it.
They want to know you can start a job and carry on a job and finish a job.
You, Frank, start rarely; carry on once in a blue moon; and finish **NEVER!**

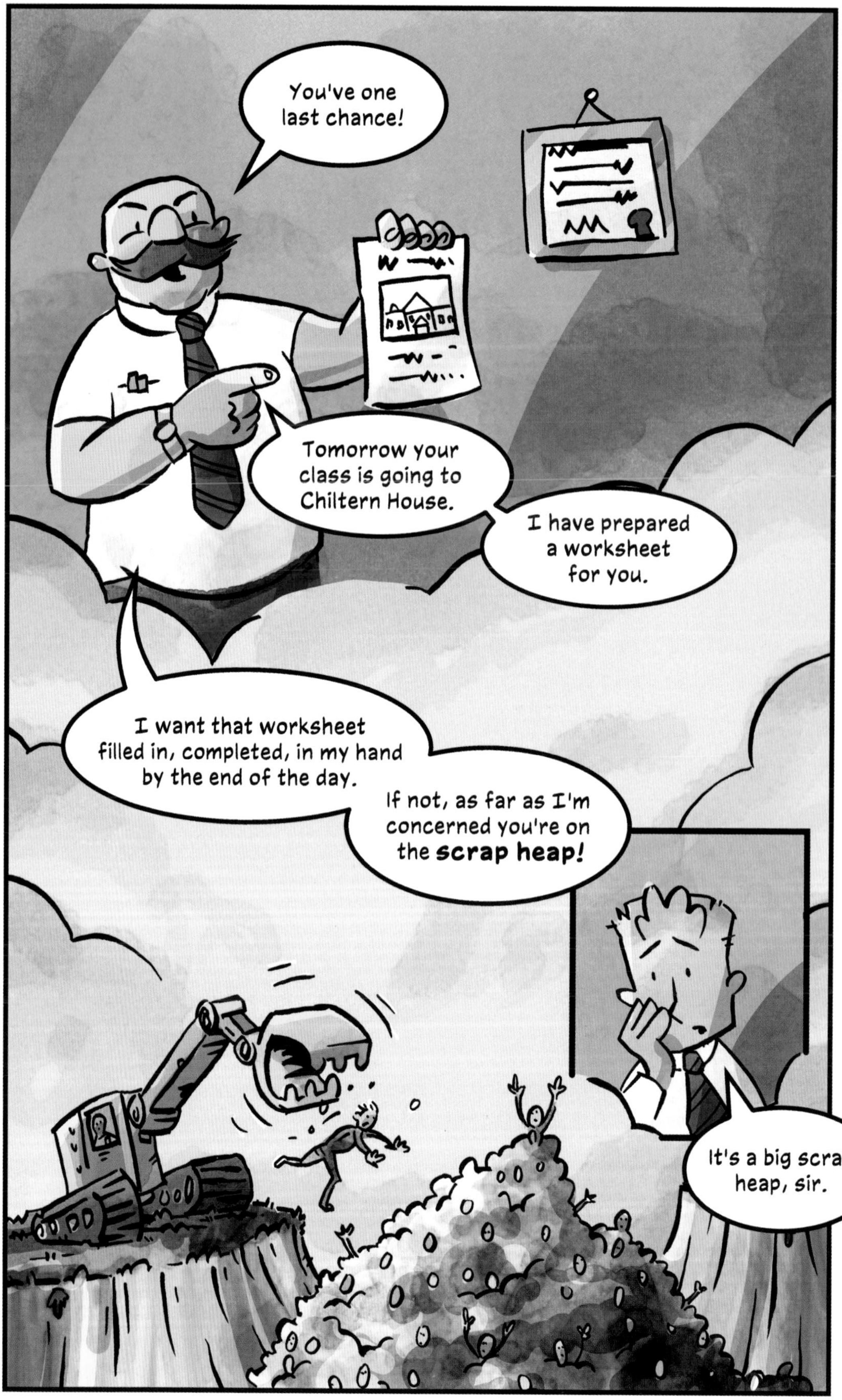
You've one last chance!
Tomorrow your class is going to Chiltern House.
I have prepared a worksheet for you.
I want that worksheet filled in, completed, in my hand by the end of the day.
If not, as far as I'm concerned you're on the **scrap heap!**
It's a big scrap heap, sir.

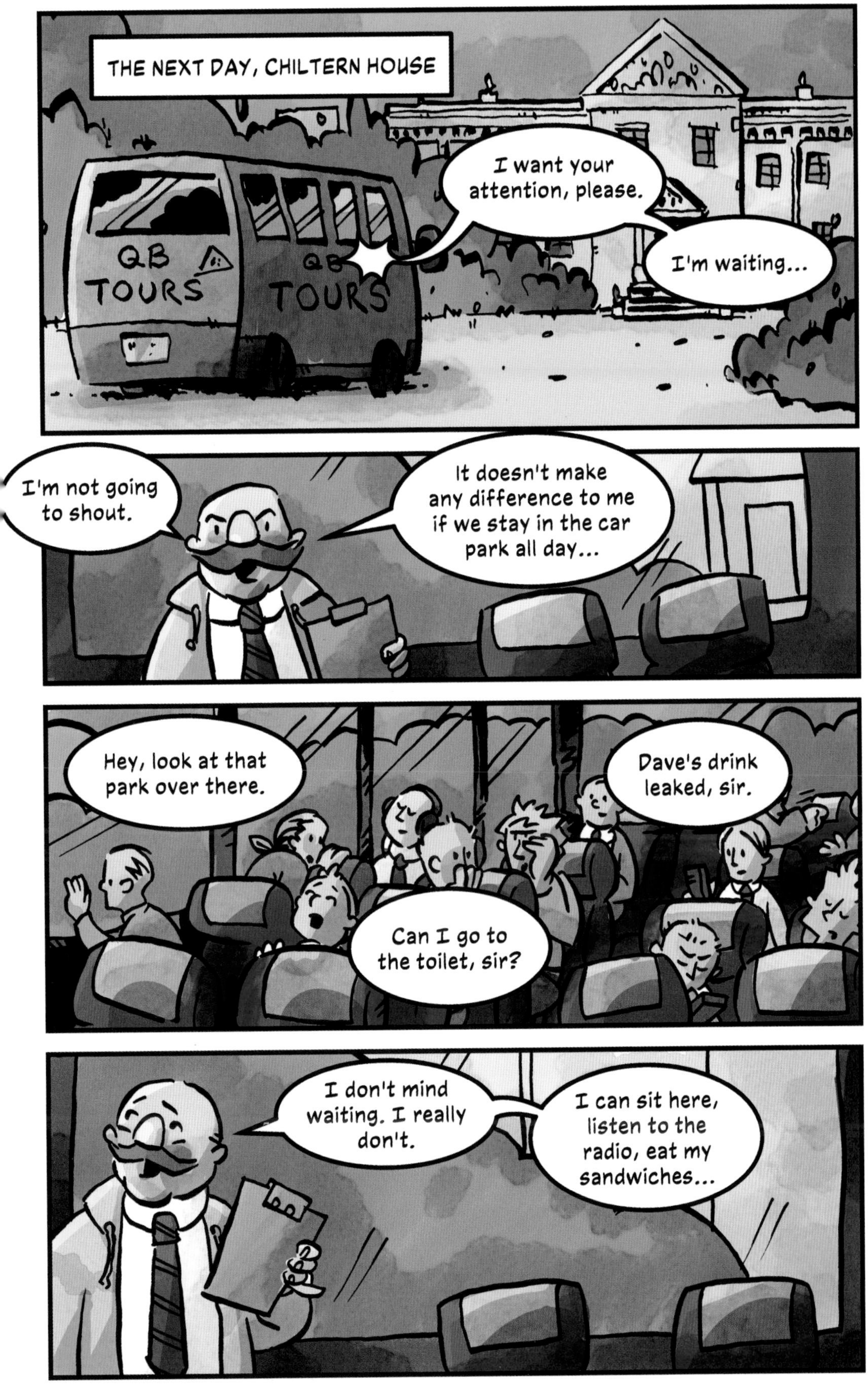
THE NEXT DAY, CHILTERN HOUSE
QB TOURS
QB TOURS
I want your attention, please.
I'm waiting...
I'm not going to shout.
It doesn't make any difference to me if we stay in the car park all day...
Hey, look at that park over there.
Dave's drink leaked, sir.
Can I go to the toilet, sir?
I don't mind waiting. I really don't.
I can sit here, listen to the radio, eat my sandwiches...

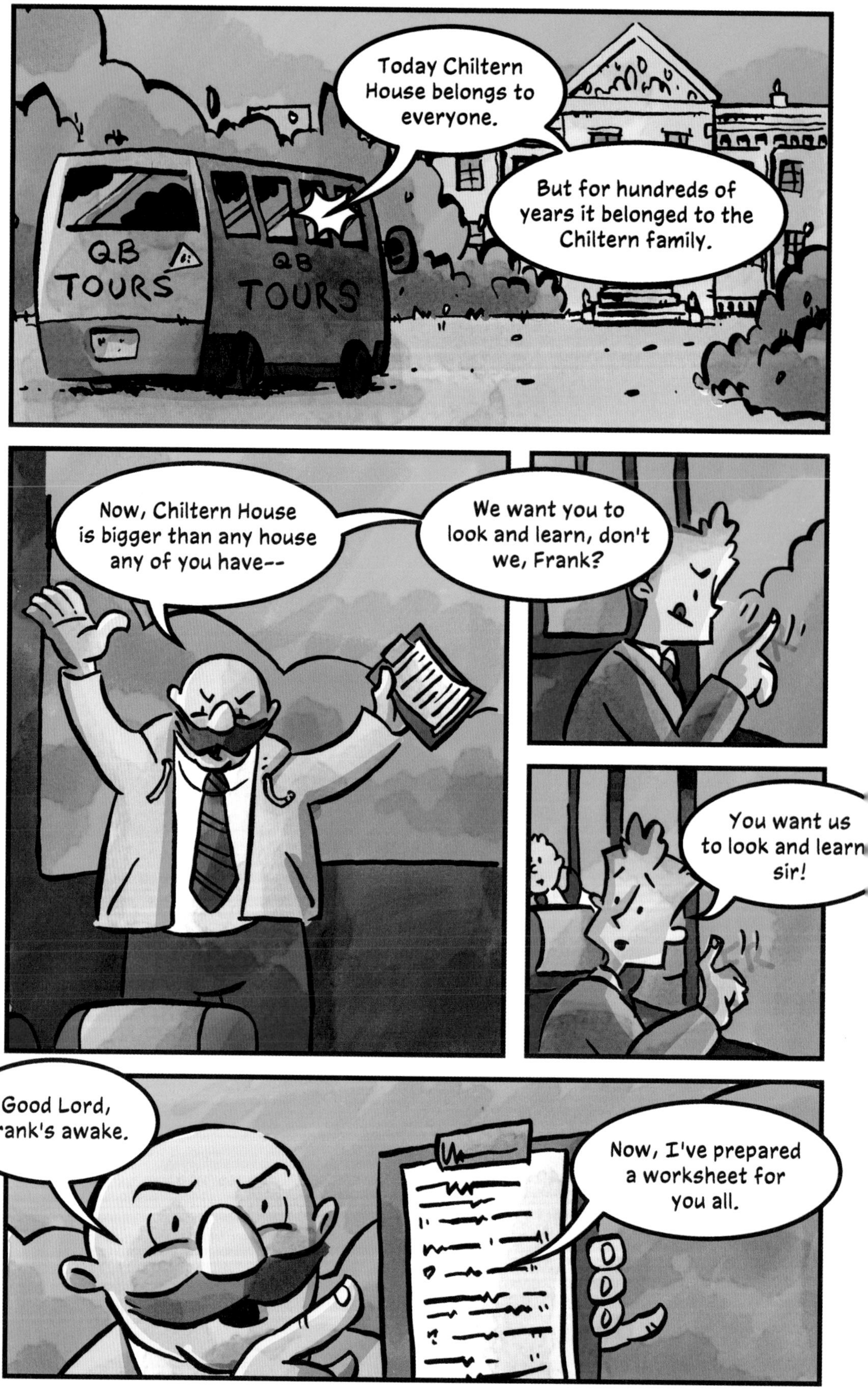
Today Chiltern House belongs to everyone.
But for hundreds of years it belonged to the Chiltern family.
QB TOURS
QB TOURS
Now, Chiltern House is bigger than any house any of you have--
We want you to look and learn, don't we, Frank?
You want us to look and learn sir!
Good Lord, Frank's awake.
Now, I've prepared a worksheet for you all.

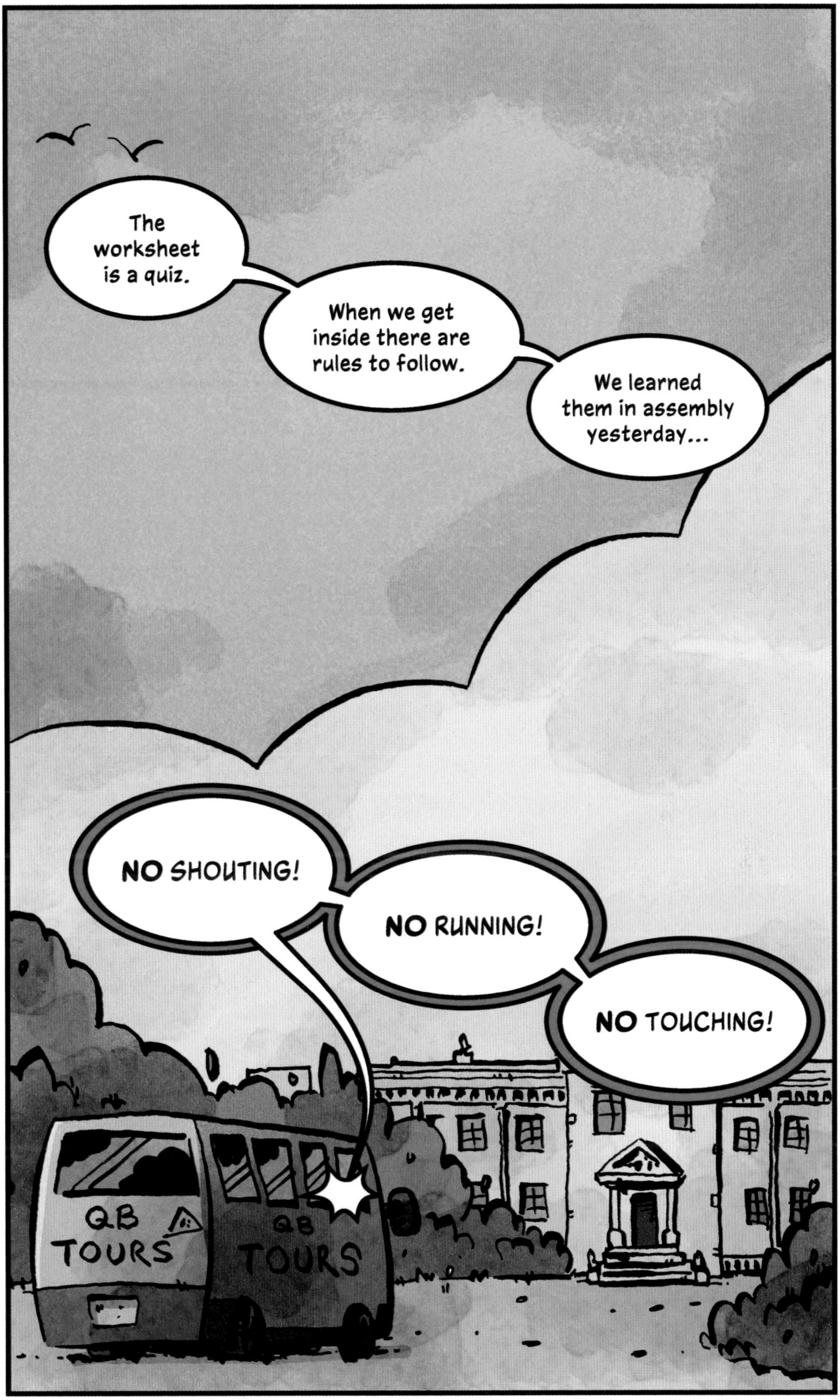
The worksheet is a quiz.
When we get inside there are rules to follow.
We learned them in assembly yesterday...
NO SHOUTING!
NO RUNNING!
NO TOUCHING!
QB TOURS
QB TOURS

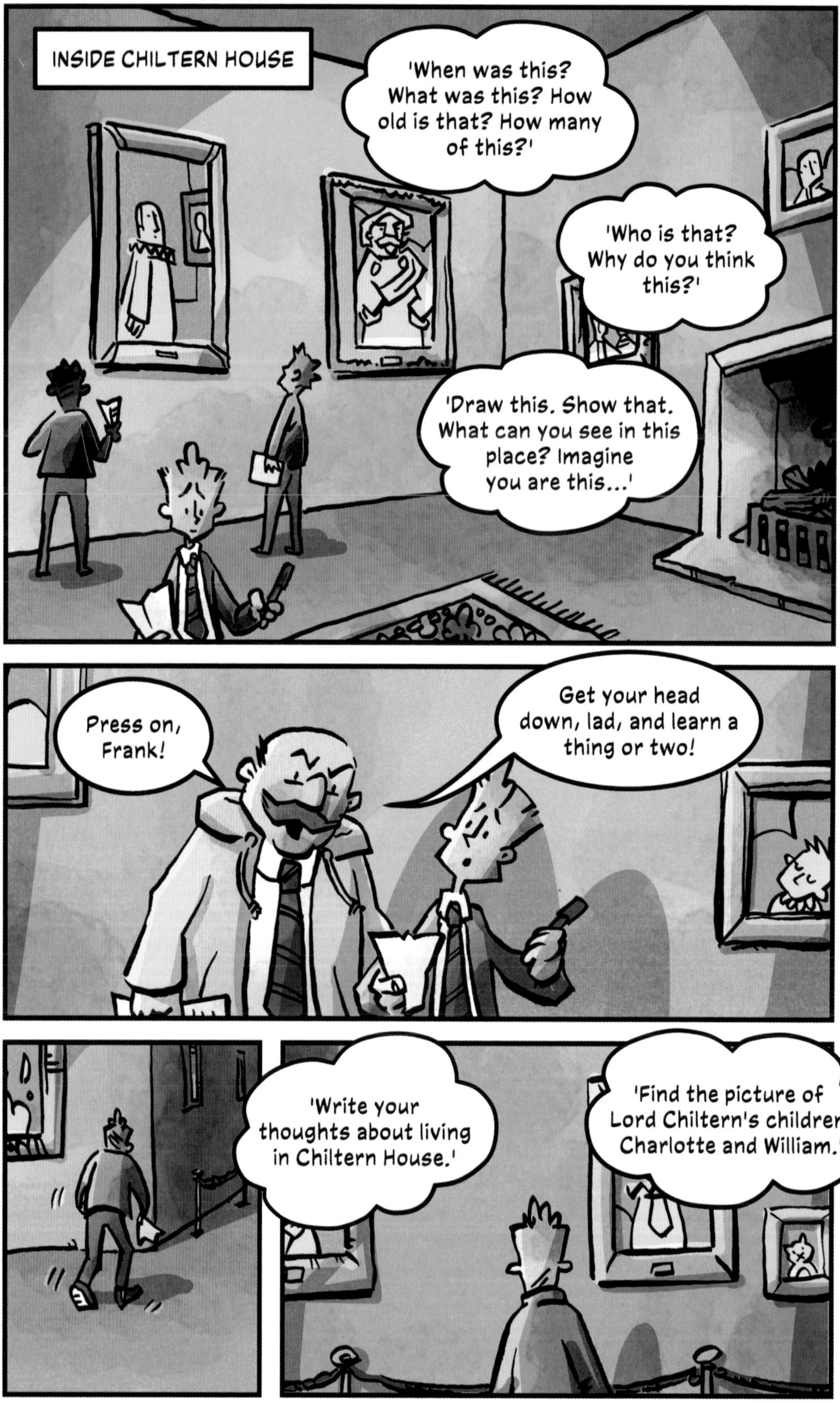
INSIDE CHILTERN HOUSE
'When was this? What was this? How old is that? How many of this?'
'Who is that? Why do you think this?'
'Draw this. Show that. What can you see in this place? Imagine you are this...'
Press on, Frank!
Get your head down, lad, and learn a thing or two!
'Write your thoughts about living in Chiltern House.'
'Find the picture of Lord Chiltern's children, Charlotte and William.'

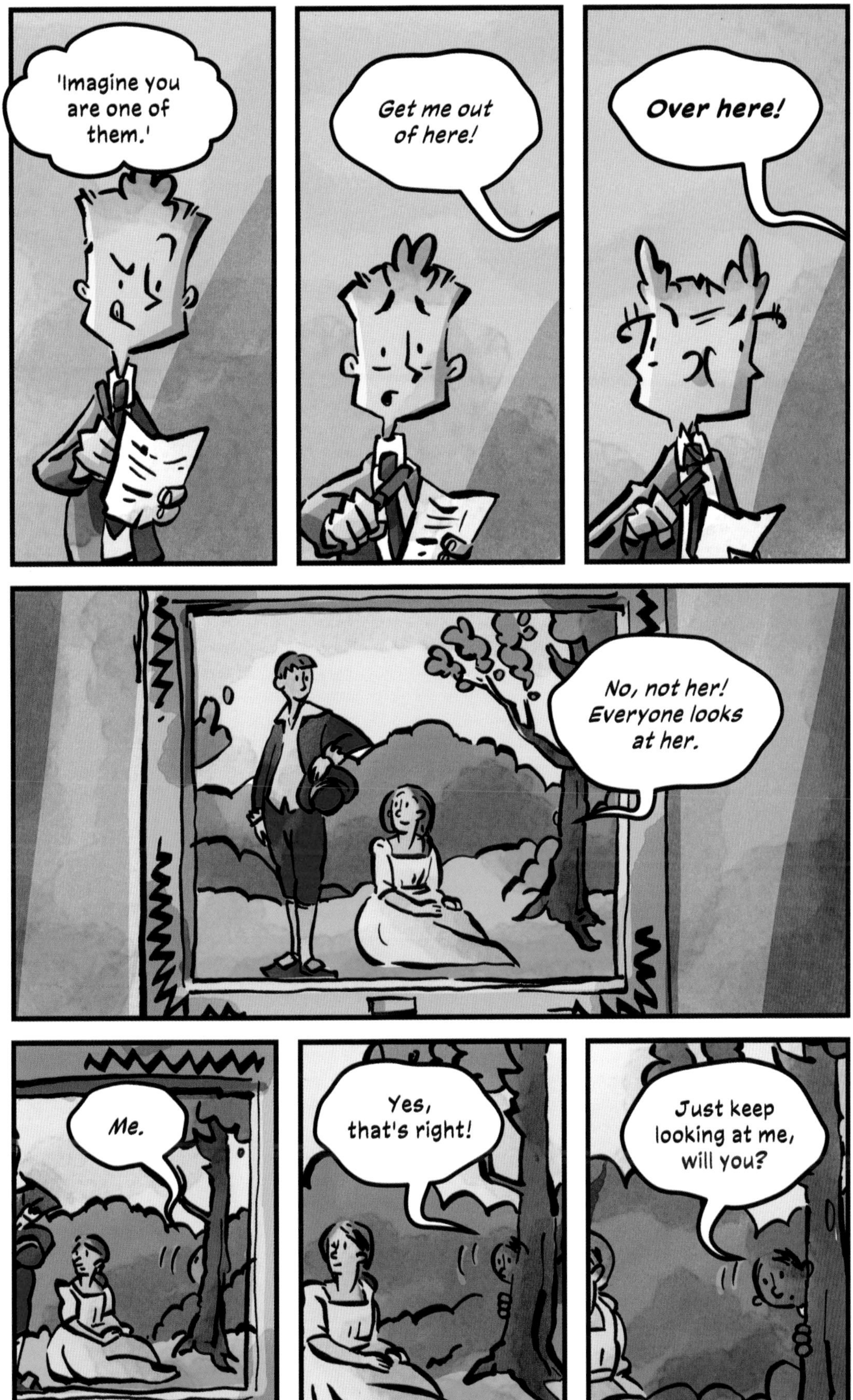
'Imagine you are one of them.'
Get me out of here!
Over here!
No, not her! Everyone looks at her.
Me.
Yes, that's right!
Just keep looking at me, will you?

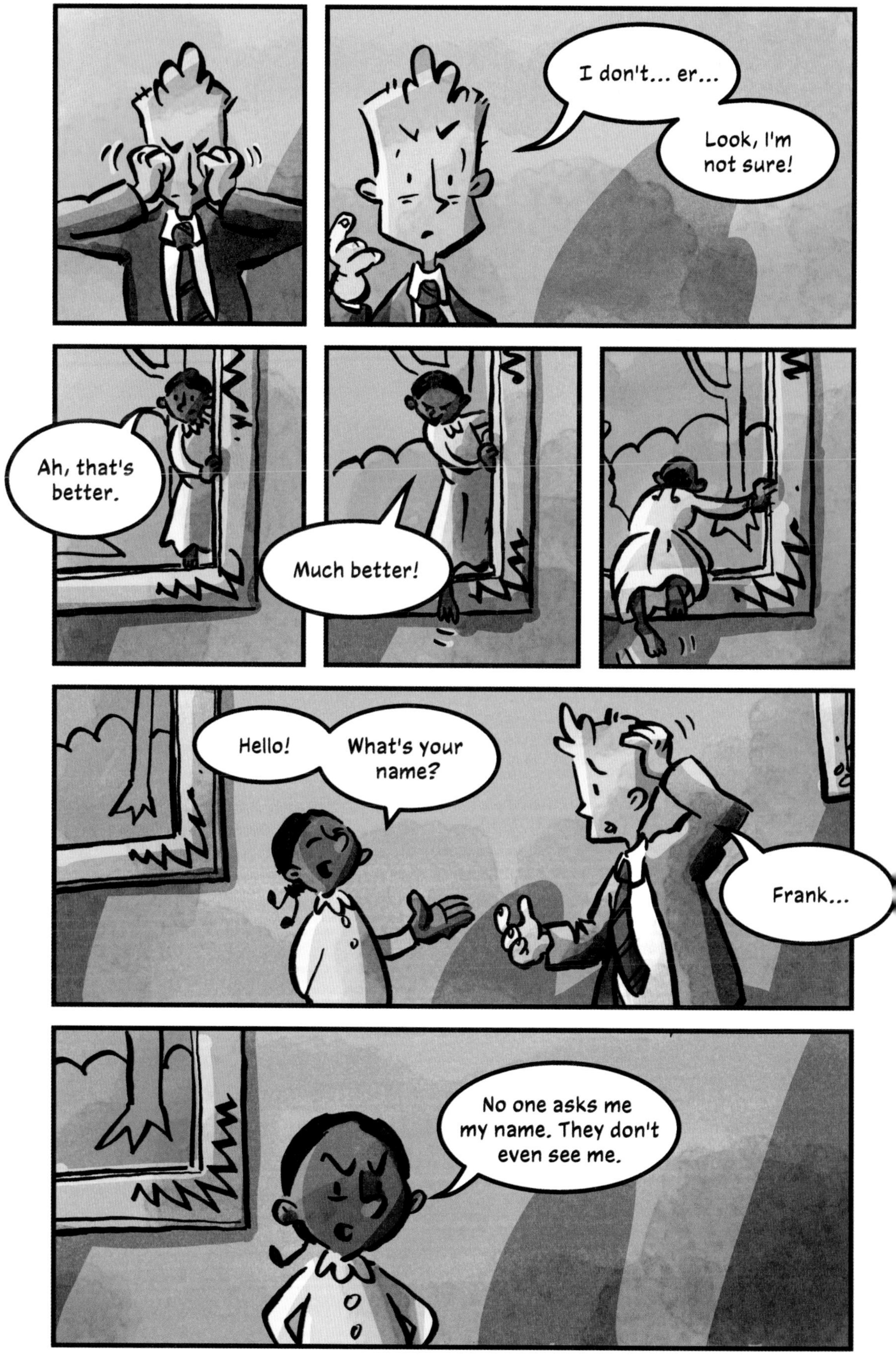
I don't... er...
Look, I'm not sure!
Ah, that's better.
Much better!
Hello!
What's your name?
Frank...
No one asks me my name. They don't even see me.

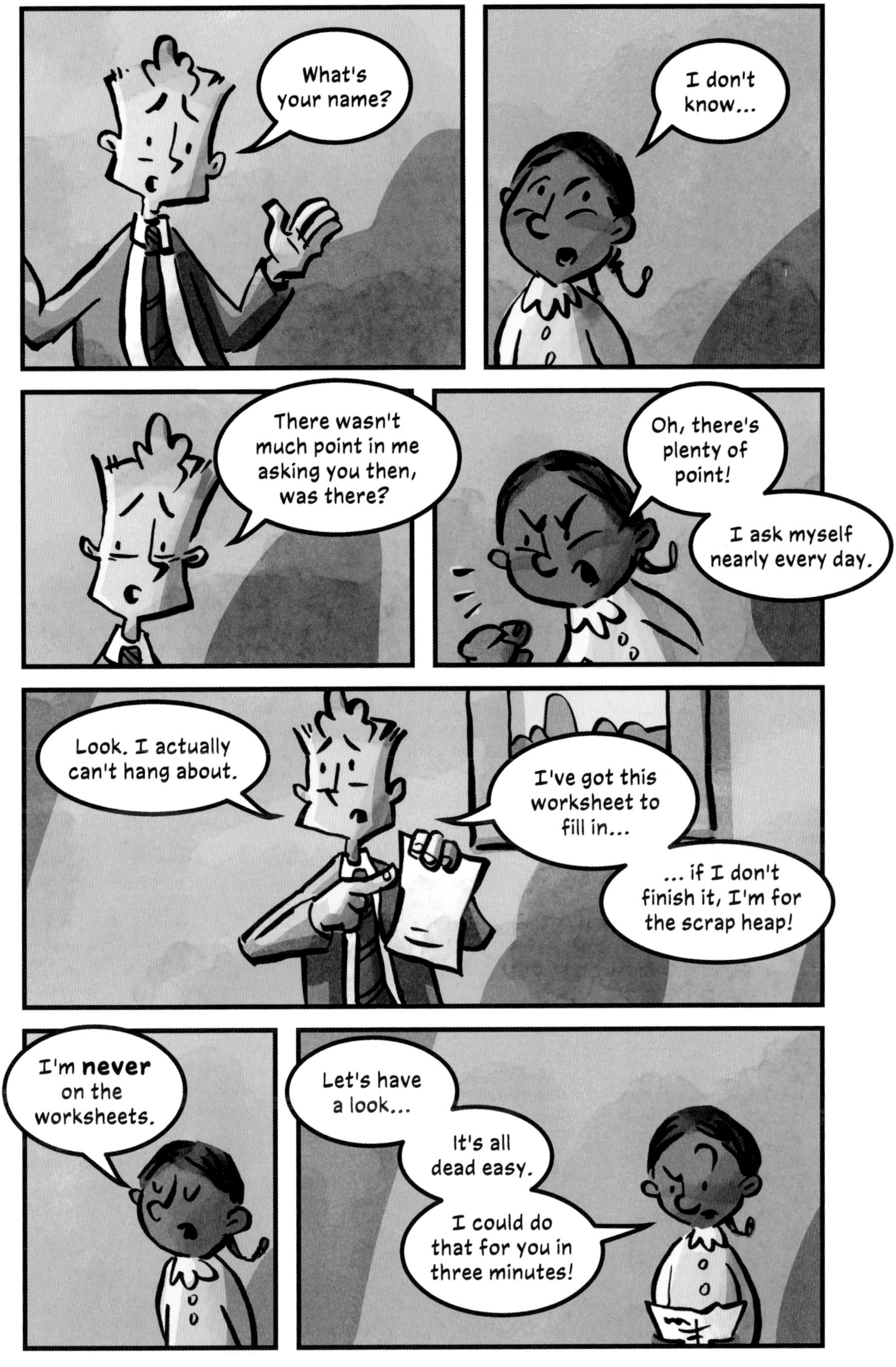
What's your name?
I don't know...
There wasn't much point in me asking you then, was there?
Oh, there's plenty of point!
I ask myself nearly every day.
Look. I actually can't hang about.
I've got this worksheet to fill in...
... if I don't finish it, I'm for the scrap heap!
I'm **never** on the worksheets.
Let's have a look...
It's all dead easy.
I could do that for you in three minutes!

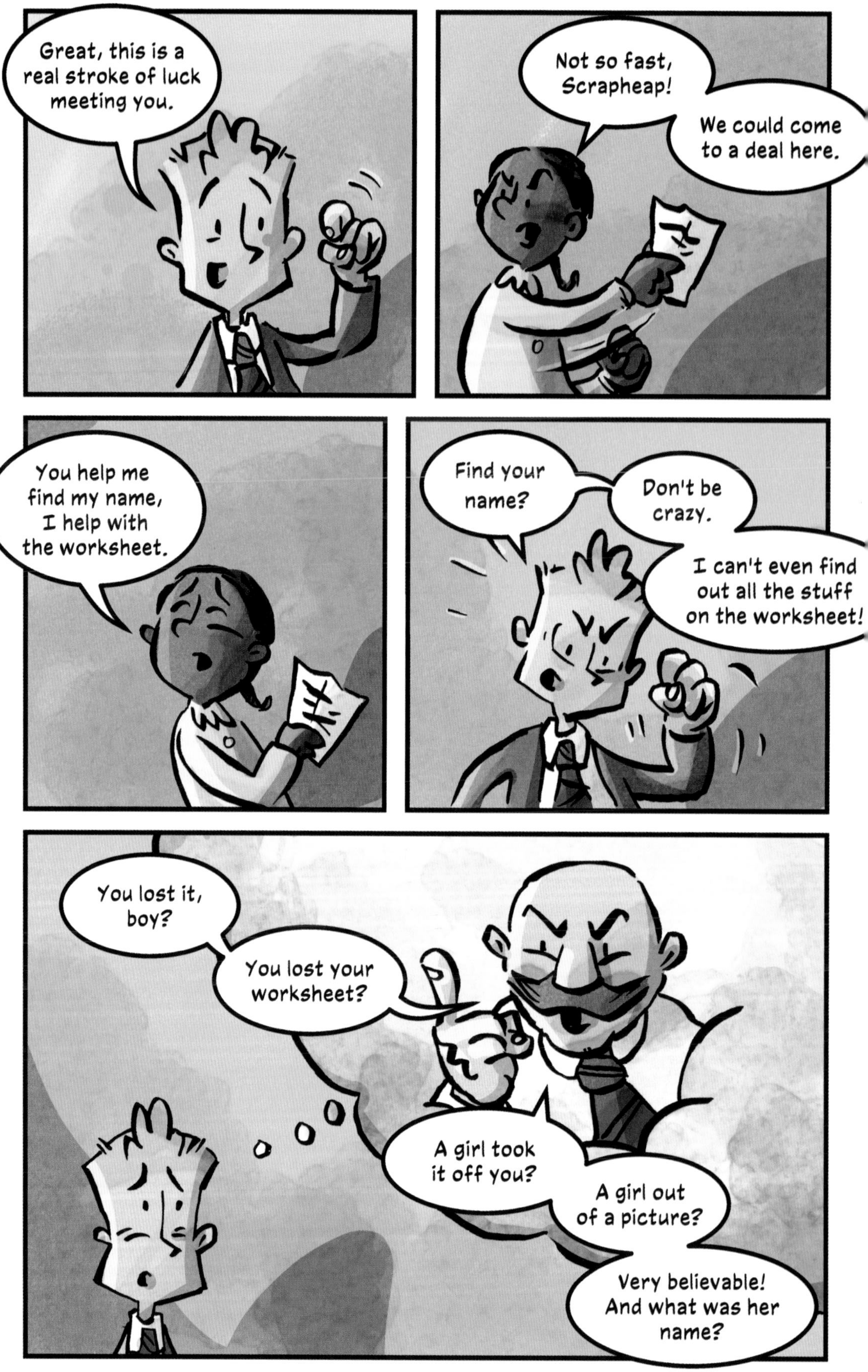
Great, this is a real stroke of luck meeting you.
Not so fast, Scrapheap!
We could come to a deal here.
You help me find my name, I help with the worksheet.
Find your name?
Don't be crazy.
I can't even find out all the stuff on the worksheet!
You lost it, boy?
You lost your worksheet?
A girl took it off you?
A girl out of a picture?
Very believable! And what was her name?

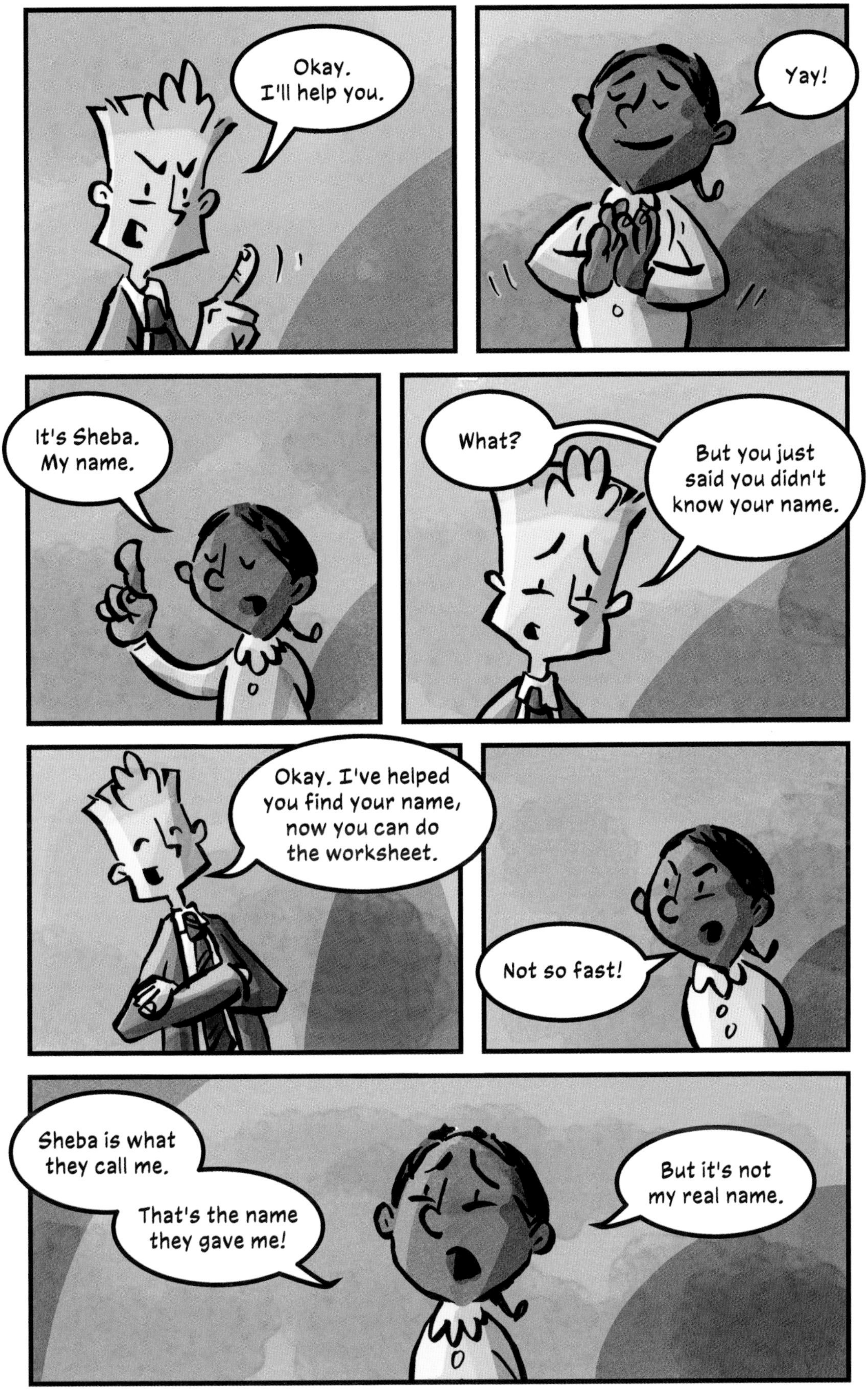
Okay.
I'll help you.
Yay!
It's Sheba.
My name.
What?
But you just
said you didn't
know your name.
Okay. I've helped
you find your name,
now you can do
the worksheet.
Not so fast!
Sheba is what
they call me.
That's the name
they gave me!
But it's not
my real name.

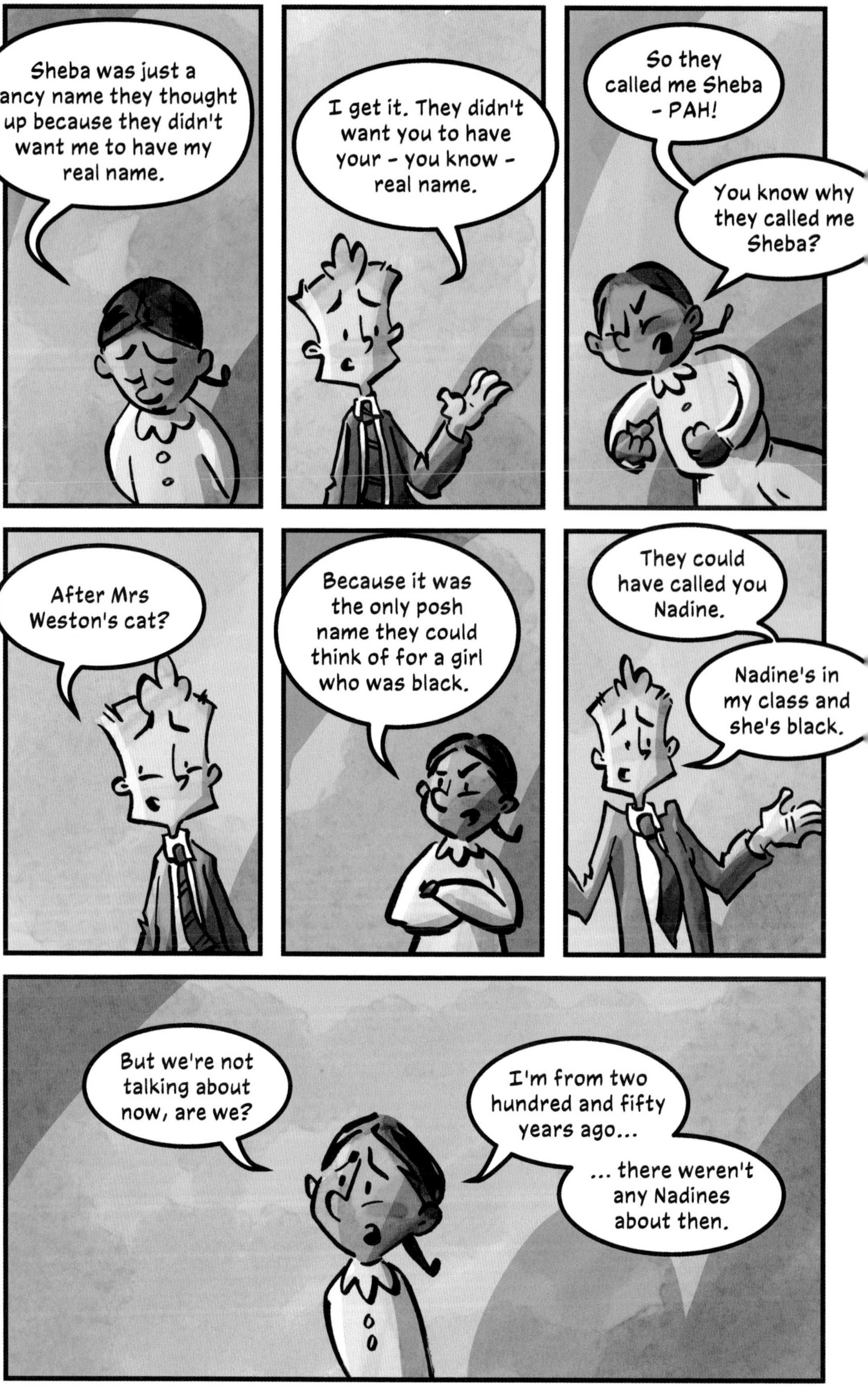
Sheba was just a fancy name they thought up because they didn't want me to have my real name.
I get it. They didn't want you to have your - you know - real name.
So they called me Sheba - PAH!
You know why they called me Sheba?
After Mrs Weston's cat?
Because it was the only posh name they could think of for a girl who was black.
They could have called you Nadine.
Nadine's in my class and she's black.
But we're not talking about now, are we?
I'm from two hundred and fifty years ago...
... there weren't any Nadines about then.

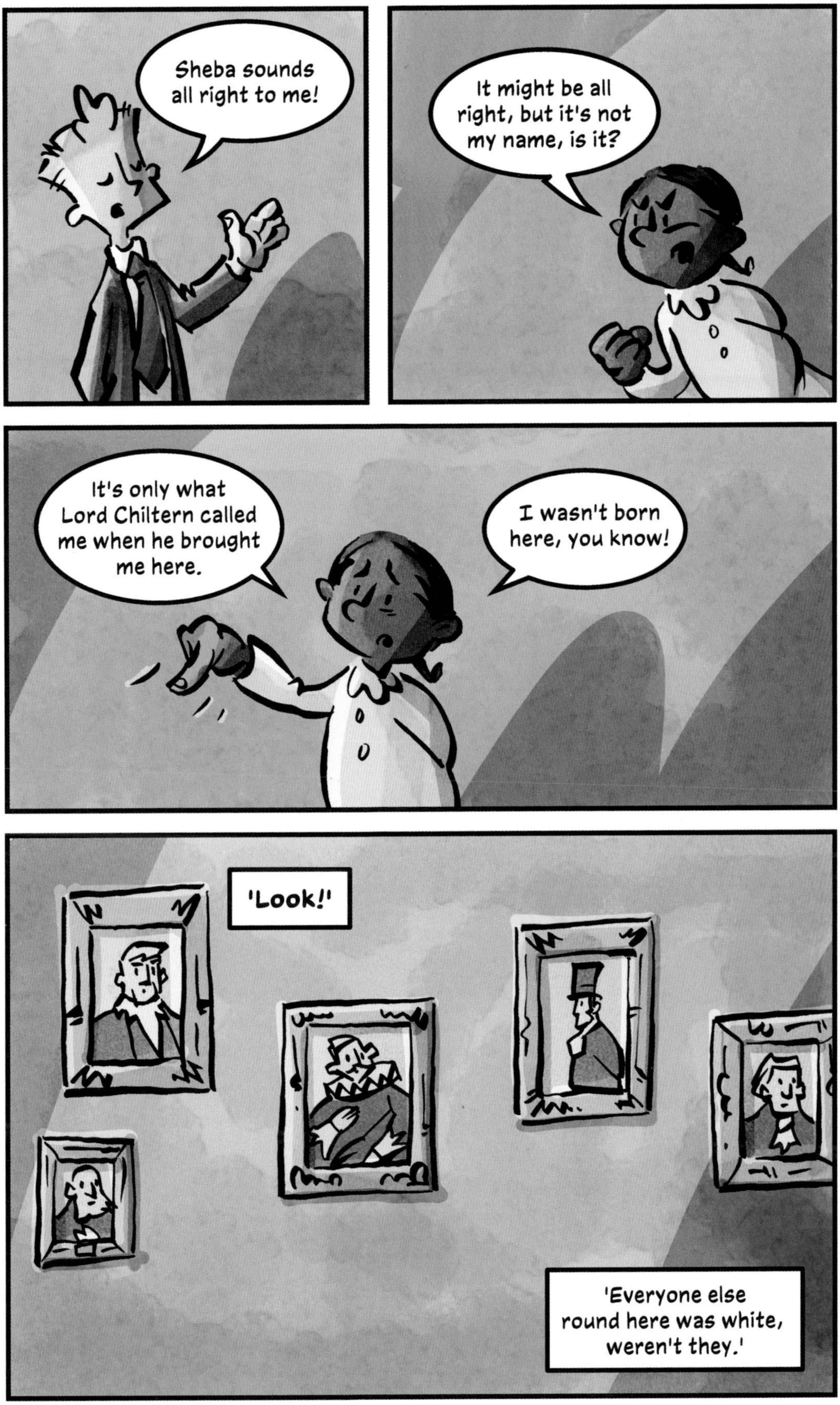
Sheba sounds all right to me!
It might be all right, but it's not my name, is it?
It's only what Lord Chiltern called me when he brought me here.
I wasn't born here, you know!
'Look!'
'Everyone else round here was white, weren't they.'

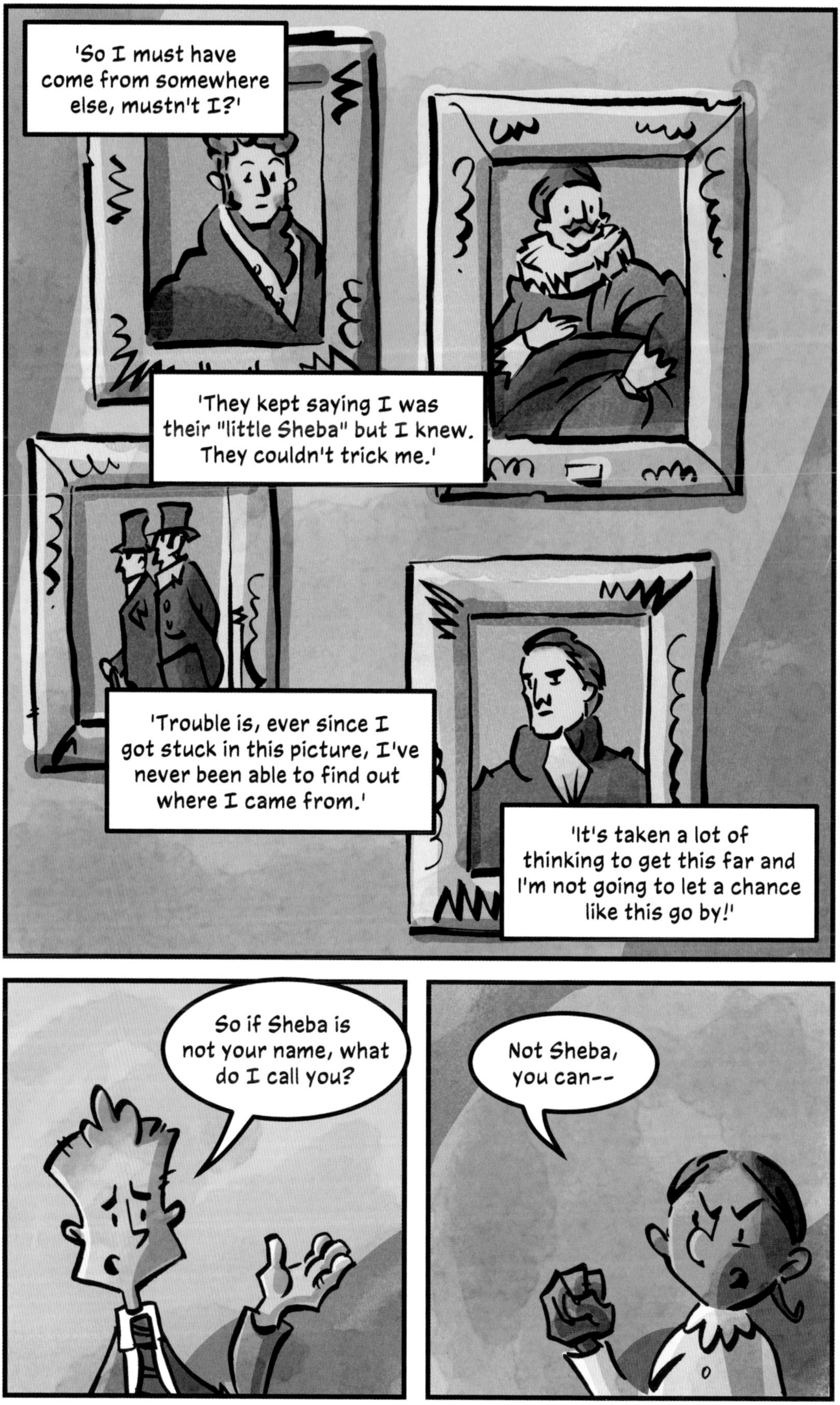
'So I must have come from somewhere else, mustn't I?'
'They kept saying I was their "little Sheba" but I knew. They couldn't trick me.'
'Trouble is, ever since I got stuck in this picture, I've never been able to find out where I came from.'
'It's taken a lot of thinking to get this far and I'm not going to let a chance like this go by!'
So if Sheba is not your name, what do I call you?
Not Sheba, you can--

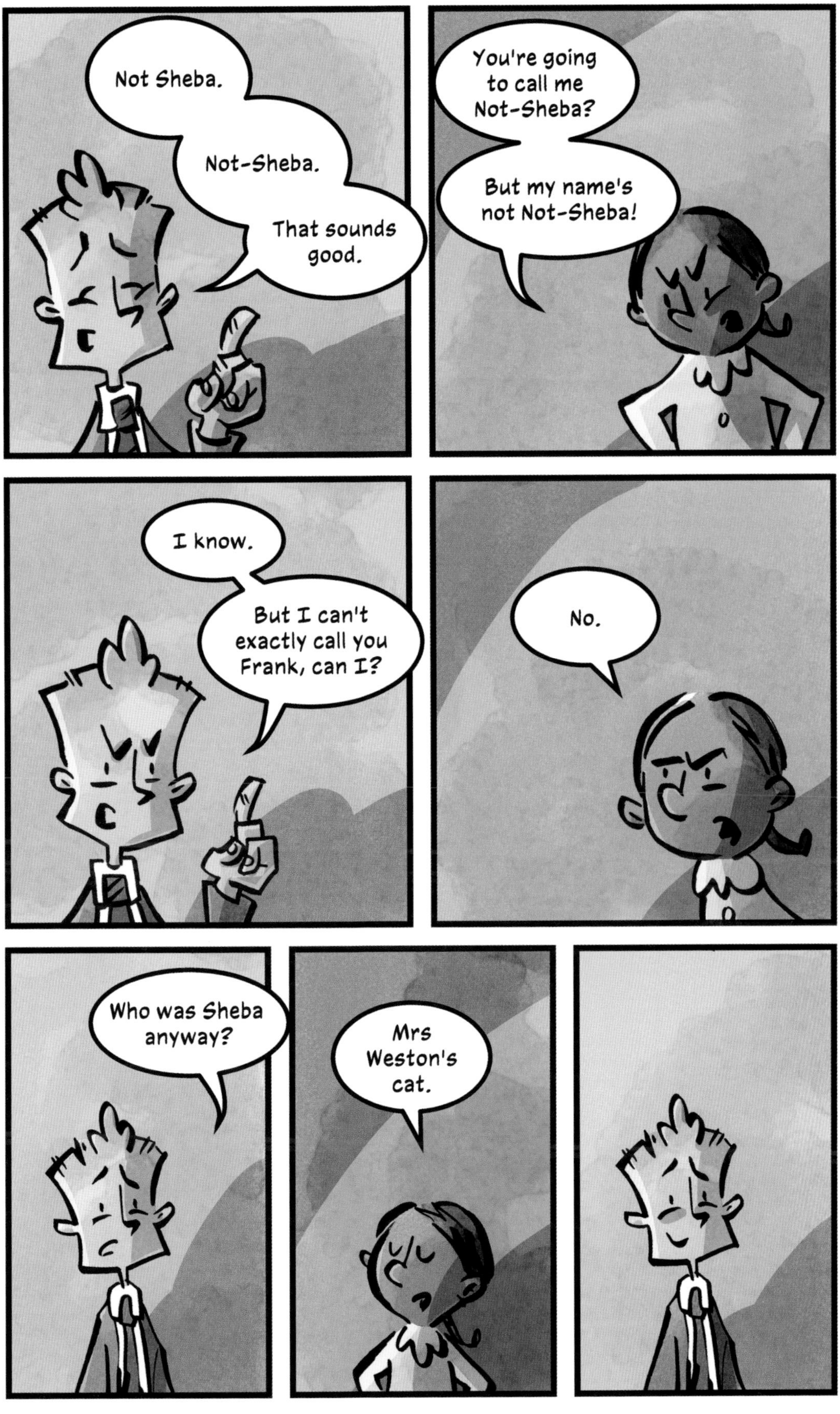
Not Sheba.
Not-Sheba.
That sounds good.
You're going to call me Not-Sheba?
But my name's not Not-Sheba!
I know.
But I can't exactly call you Frank, can I?
No.
Who was Sheba anyway?
Mrs Weston's cat.

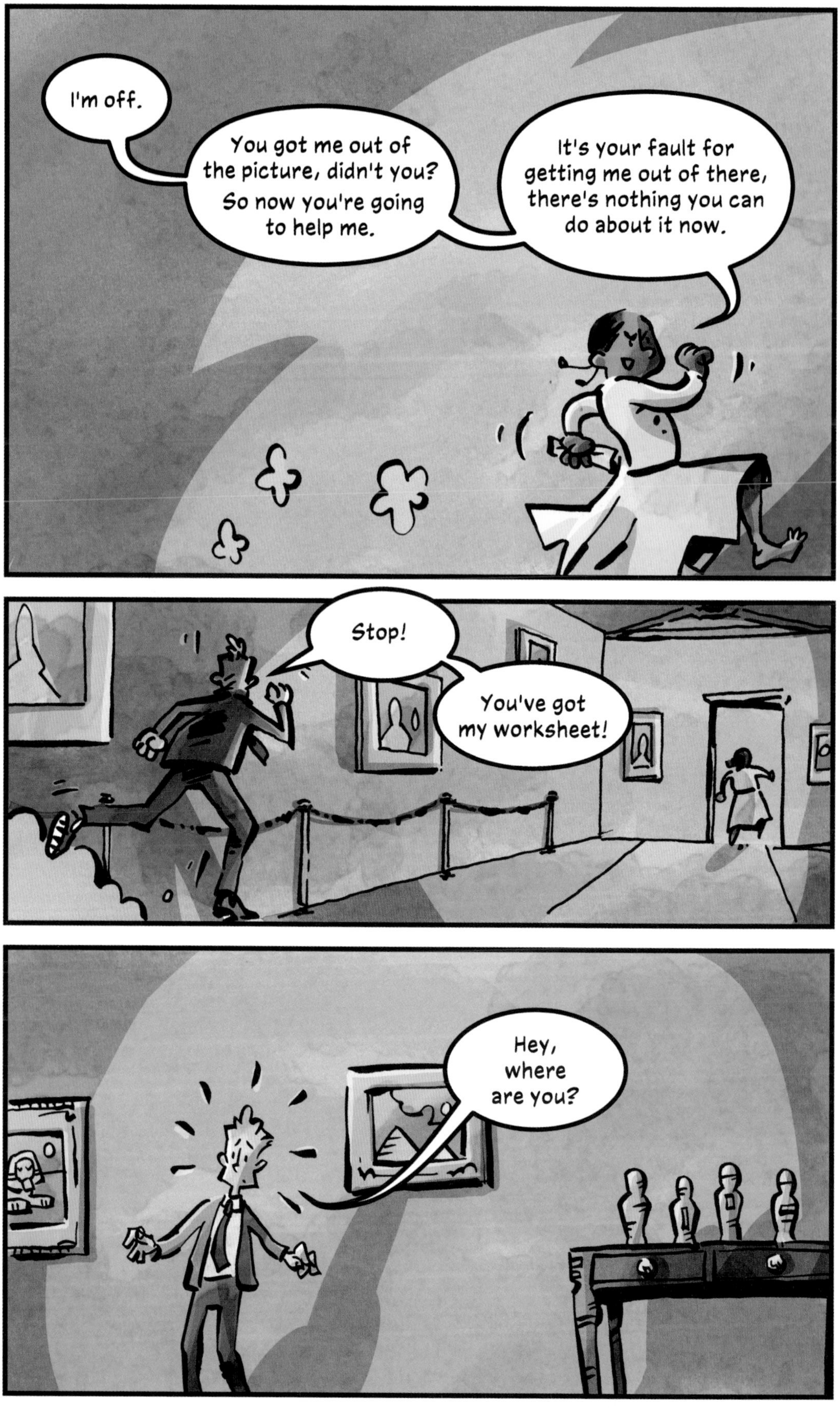
I'm off.
You got me out of the picture, didn't you? So now you're going to help me.
It's your fault for getting me out of there, there's nothing you can do about it now.
Stop!
You've got my worksheet!
Hey, where are you?

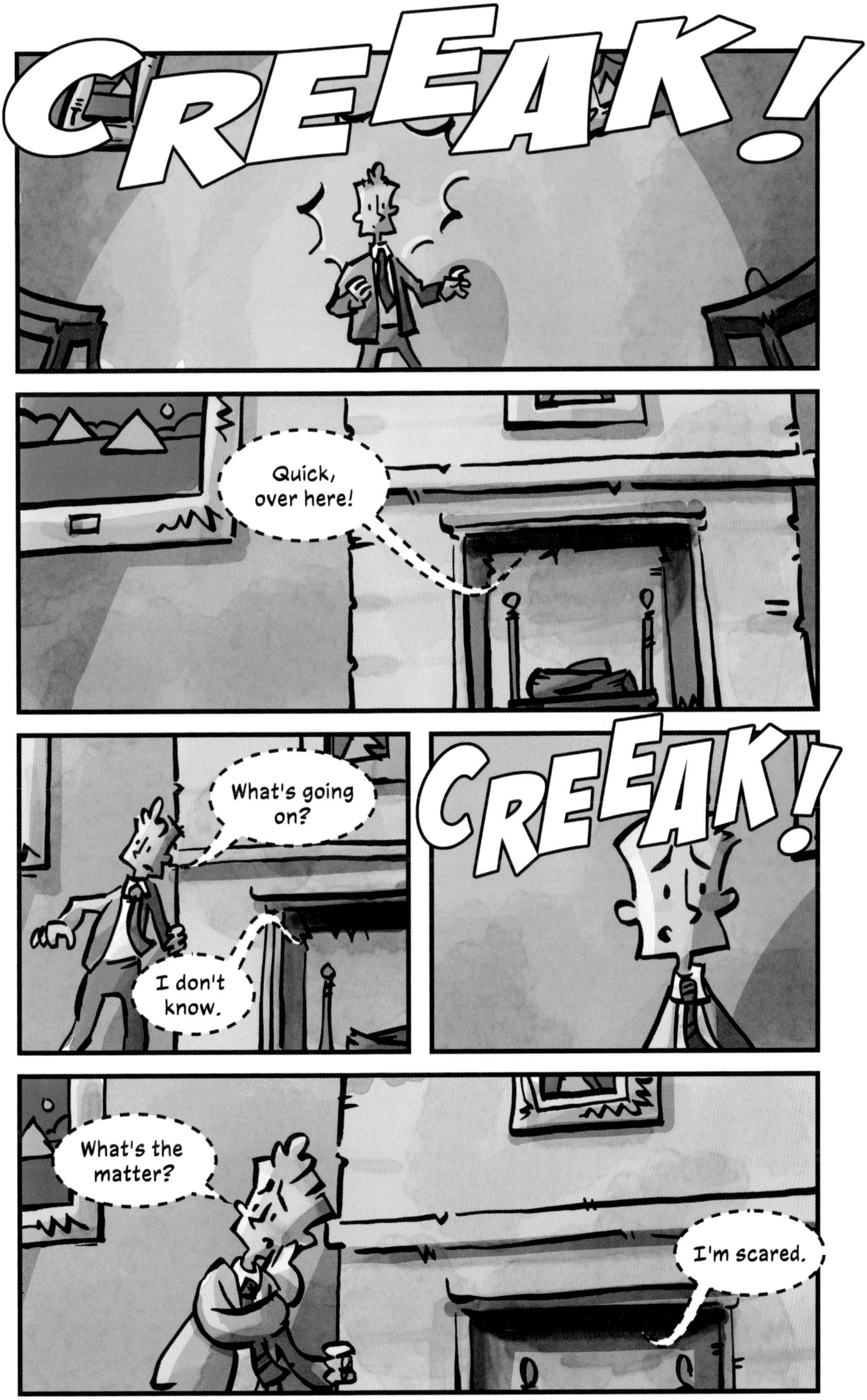
CREEAK!
Quick, over here!
What's going on?
I don't know.
CREEAK!
What's the matter?
I'm scared.

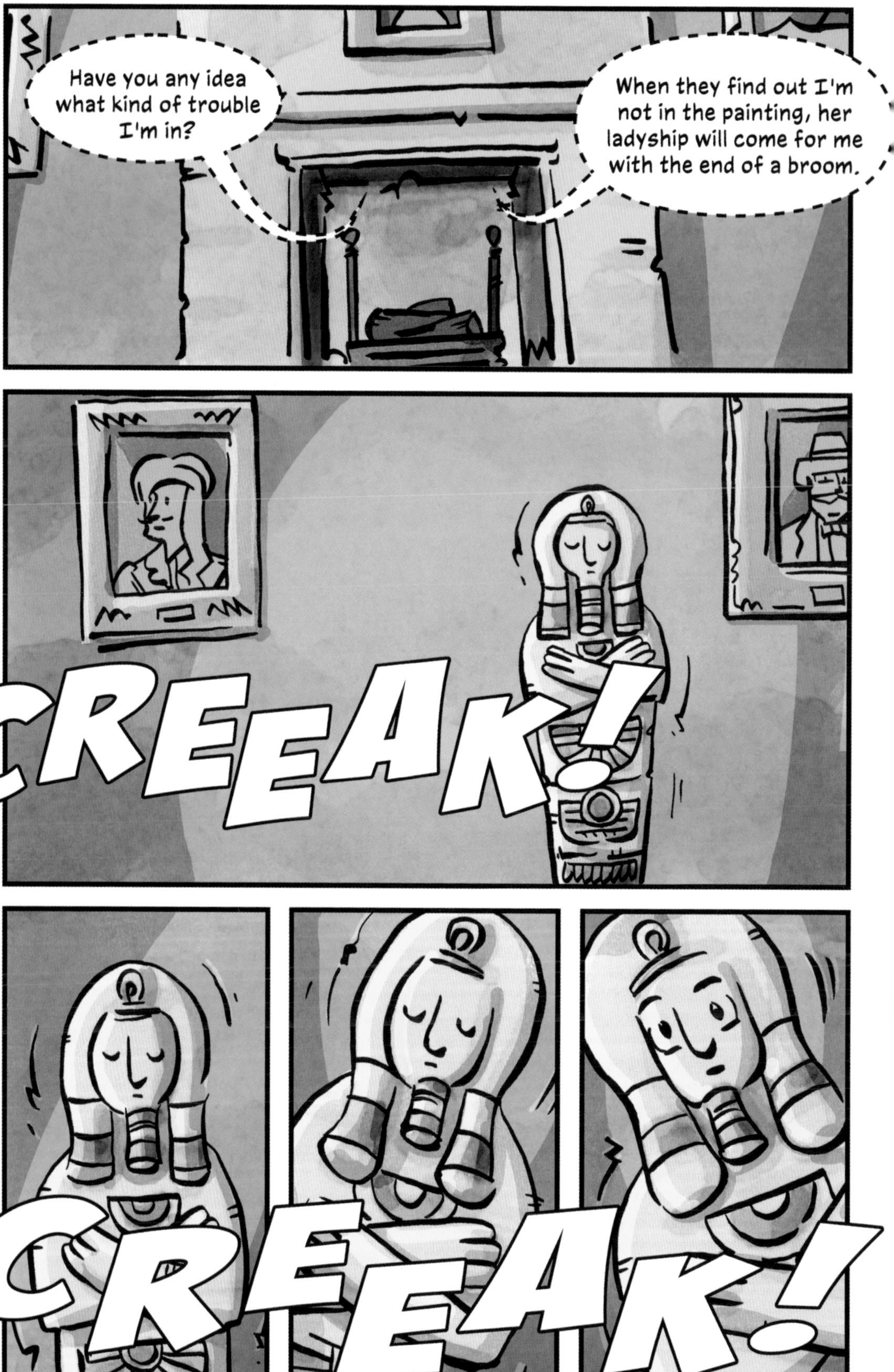
Have you any idea what kind of trouble I'm in?
When they find out I'm not in the painting, her ladyship will come for me with the end of a broom.
CREEAK!
CREEAK!

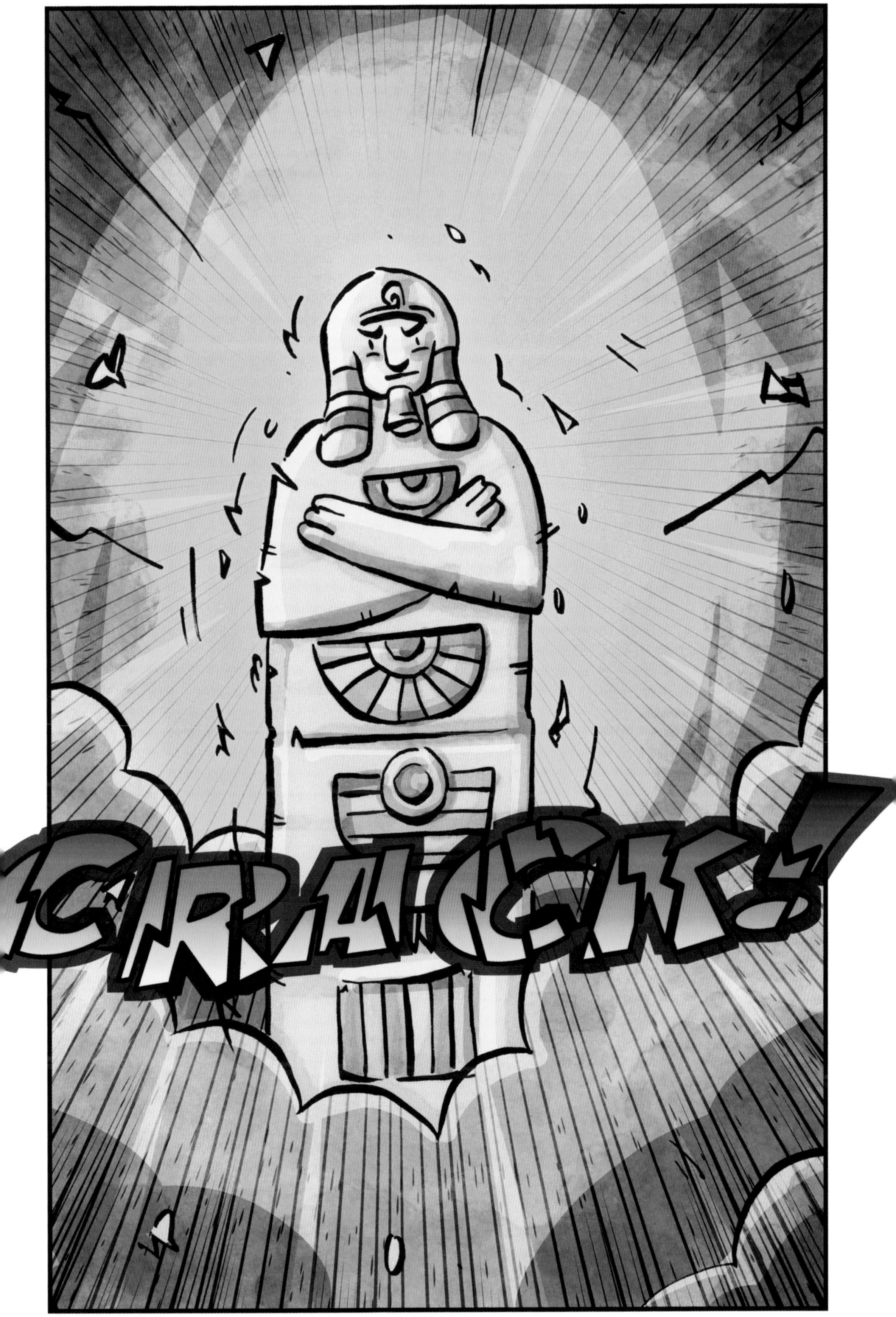
CRACK!

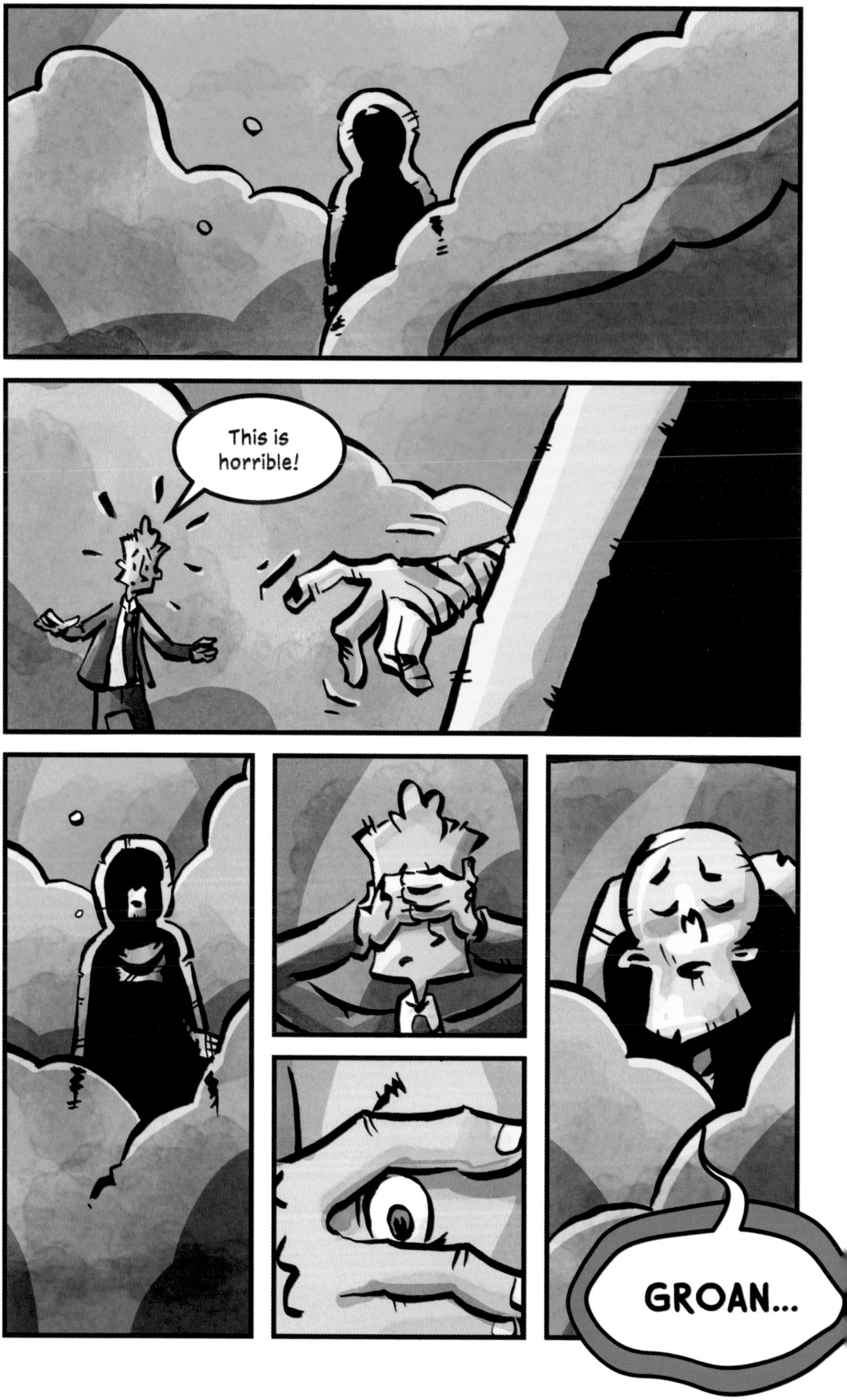
This is horrible!
GROAN...

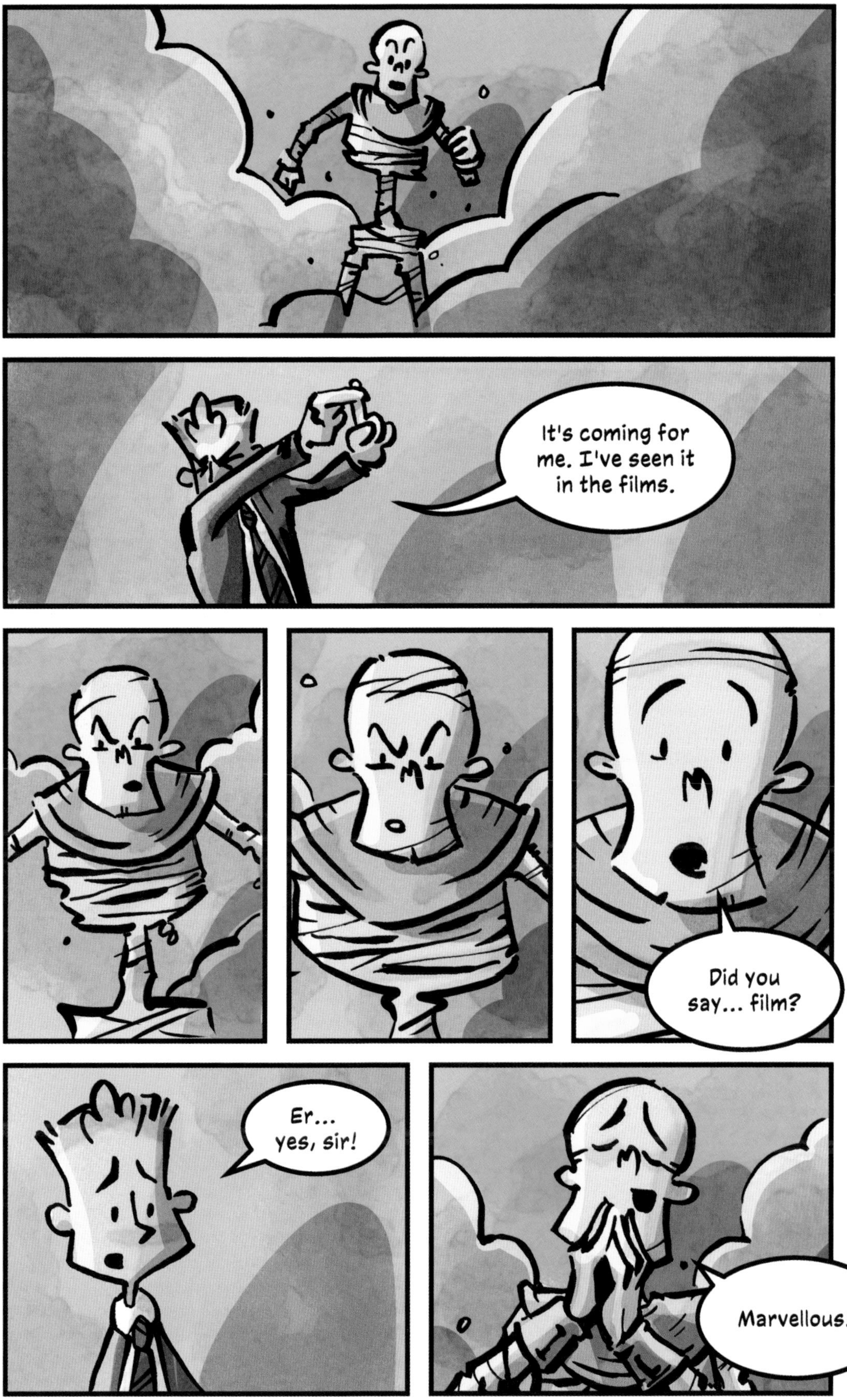
It's coming for me. I've seen it in the films.
Did you say... film?
Er... yes, sir!
Marvellous!

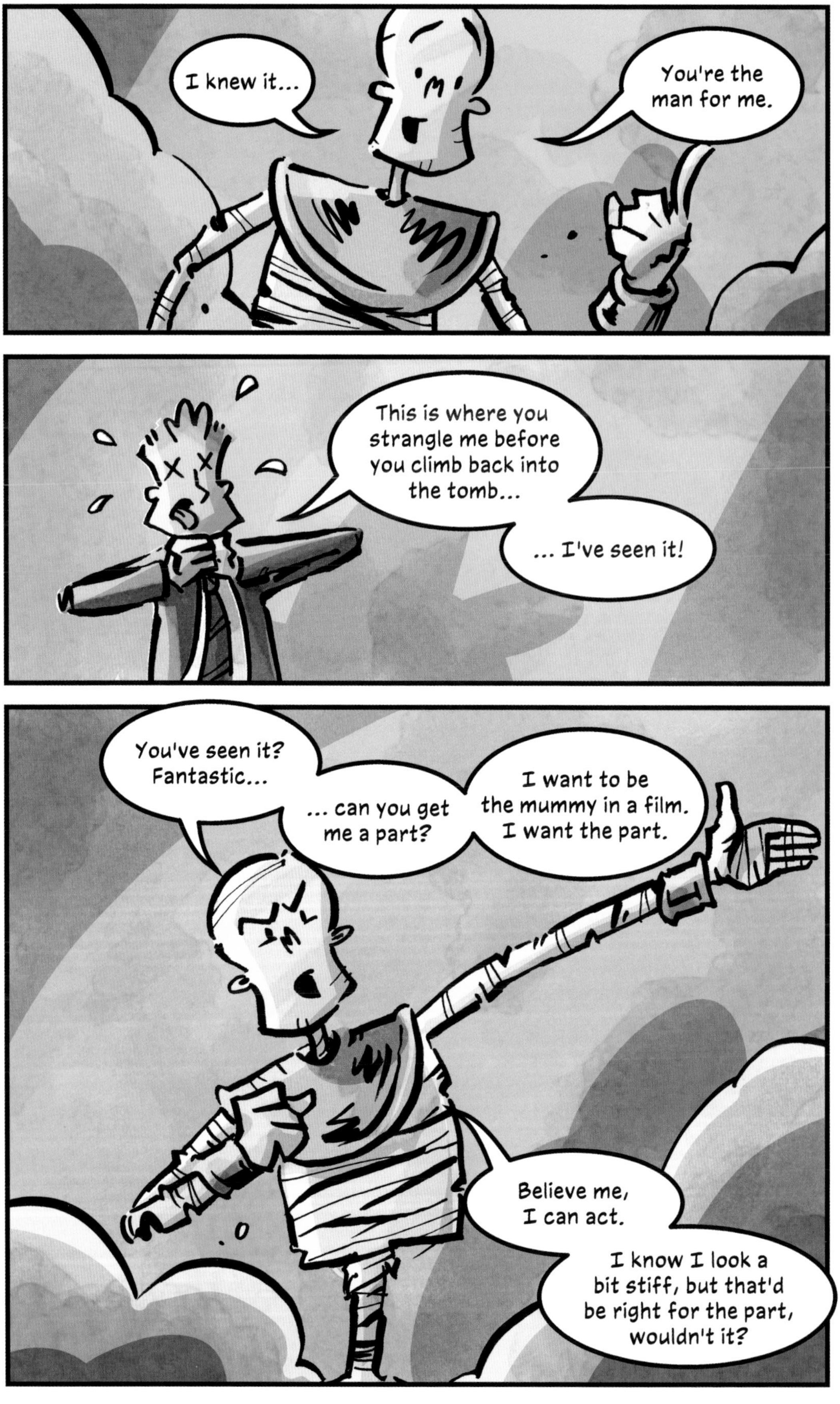
I knew it...
You're the man for me.
This is where you strangle me before you climb back into the tomb...
... I've seen it!
You've seen it? Fantastic...
... can you get me a part?
I want to be the mummy in a film. I want the part.
Believe me, I can act.
I know I look a bit stiff, but that'd be right for the part, wouldn't it?

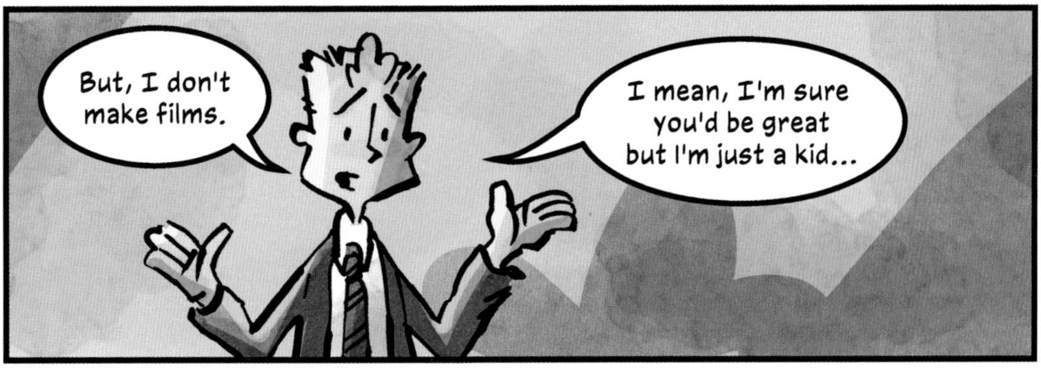
But, I don't make films.
I mean, I'm sure you'd be great but I'm just a kid...

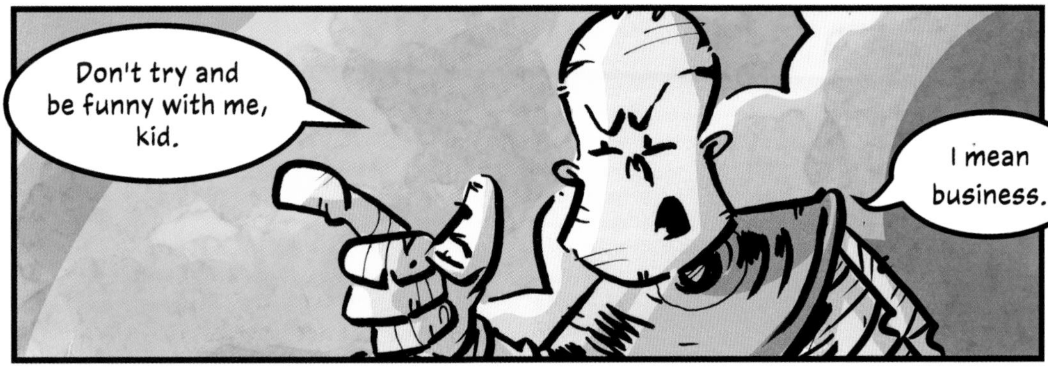
Don't try and be funny with me, kid.
I mean business.

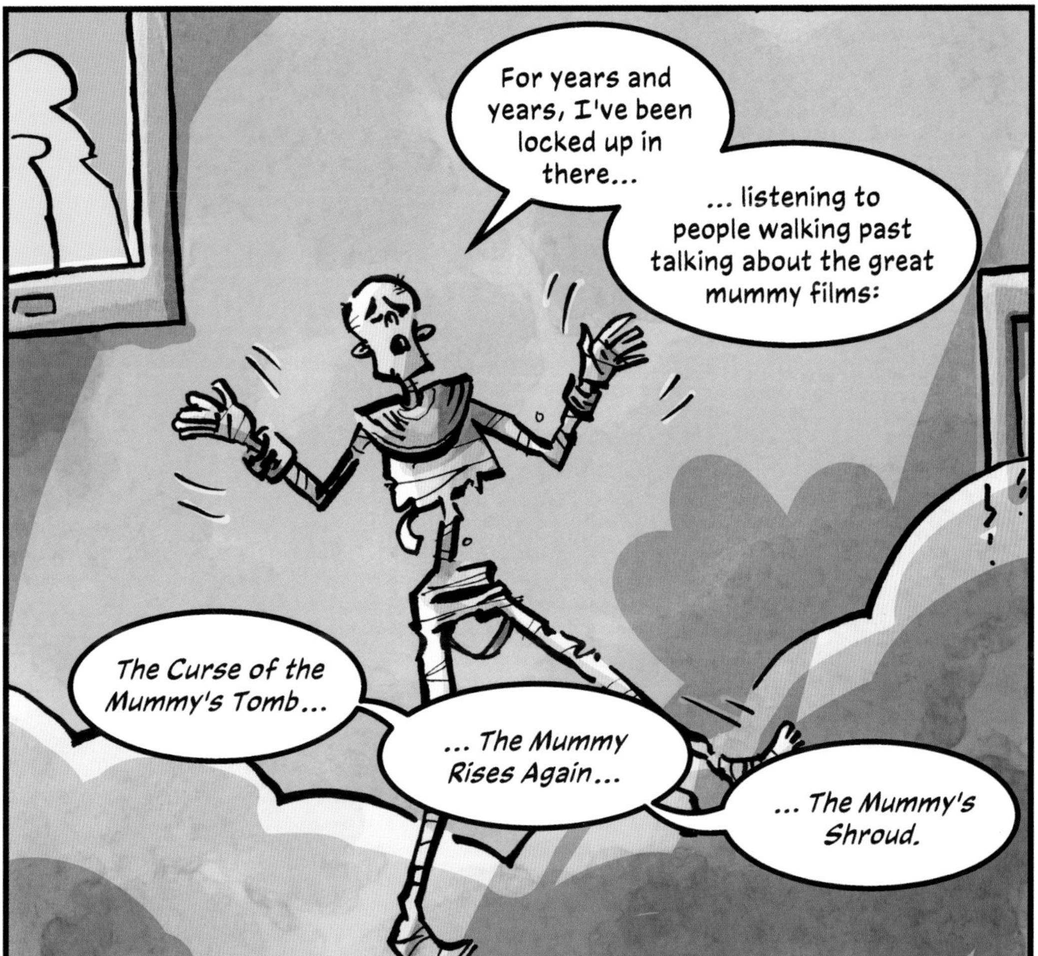
For years and years, I've been locked up in there...
... listening to people walking past talking about the great mummy films:
The Curse of the Mummy's Tomb...
... The Mummy Rises Again...
... The Mummy's Shroud.

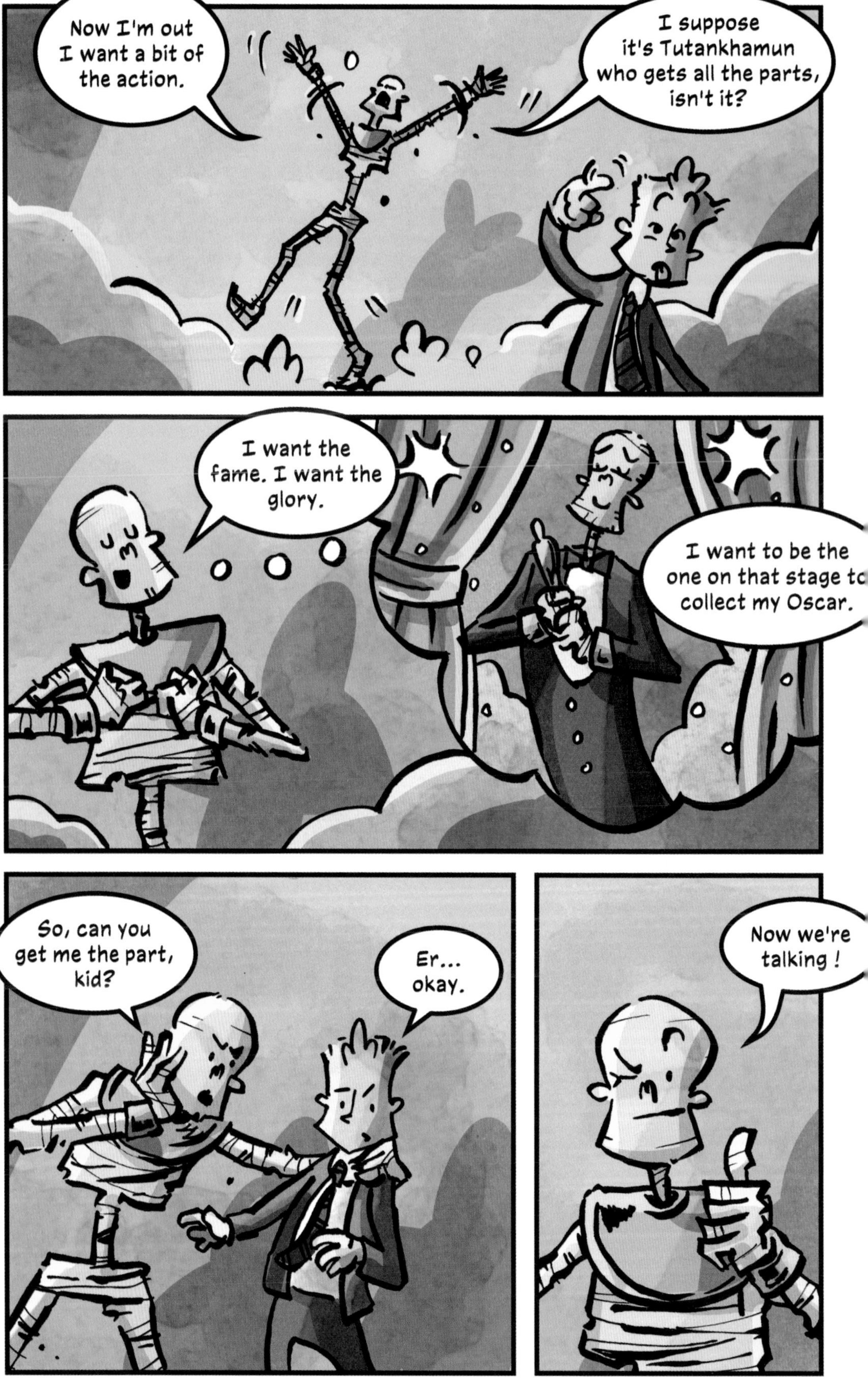
Now I'm out I want a bit of the action.
I suppose it's Tutankhamun who gets all the parts, isn't it?
I want the fame. I want the glory.
I want to be the one on that stage to collect my Oscar.
So, can you get me the part, kid?
Er... okay.
Now we're talking !

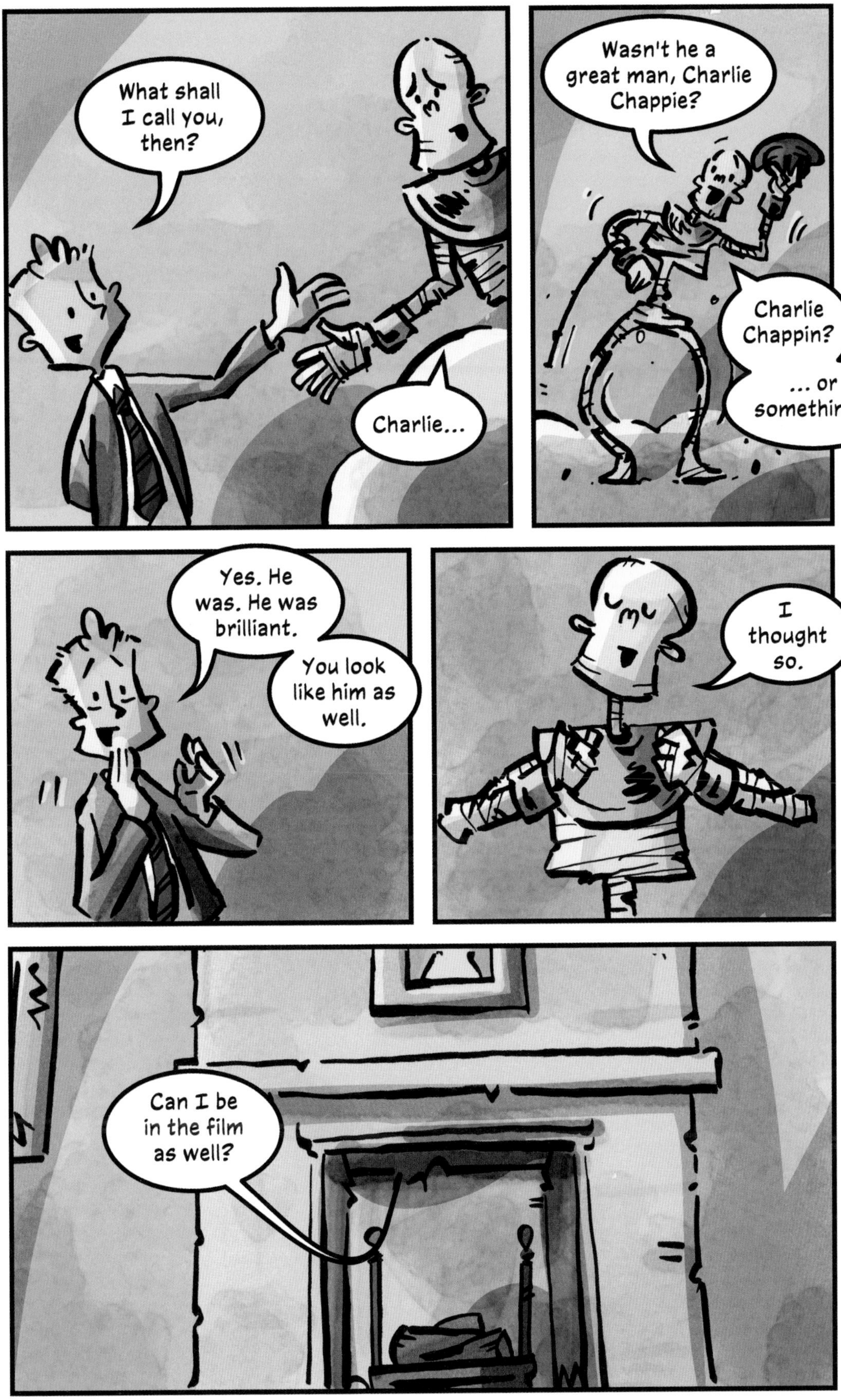
What shall I call you, then?
Charlie...
Wasn't he a great man, Charlie Chappie?
Charlie Chappin?
... or something?
Yes. He was. He was brilliant.
You look like him as well.
I thought so.
Can I be in the film as well?

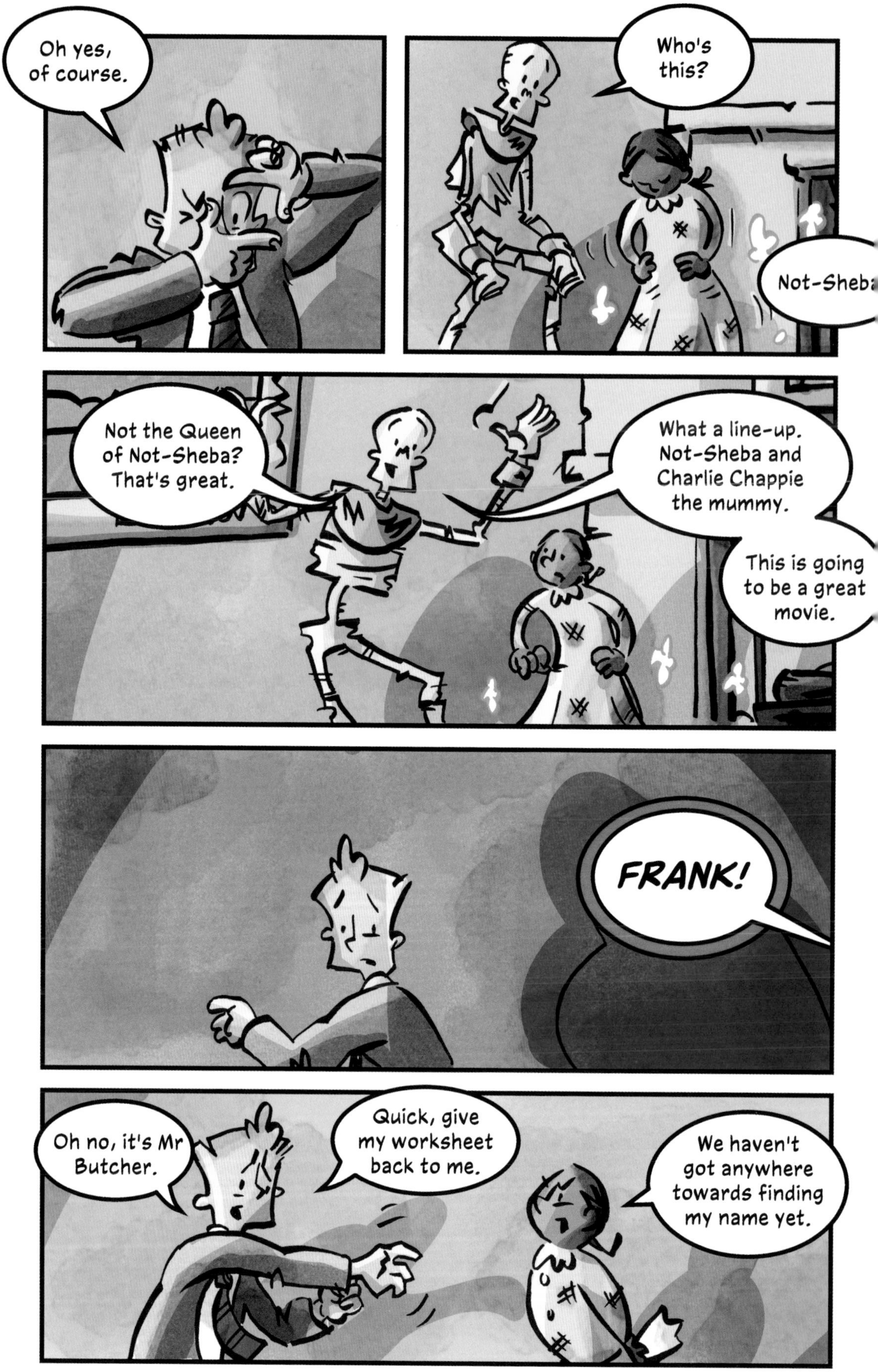

Oh yes, of course.
Who's this?
Not-Sheba
Not the Queen of Not-Sheba? That's great.
What a line-up. Not-Sheba and Charlie Chappie the mummy.
This is going to be a great movie.
FRANK!
Oh no, it's Mr Butcher.
Quick, give my worksheet back to me.
We haven't got anywhere towards finding my name yet.

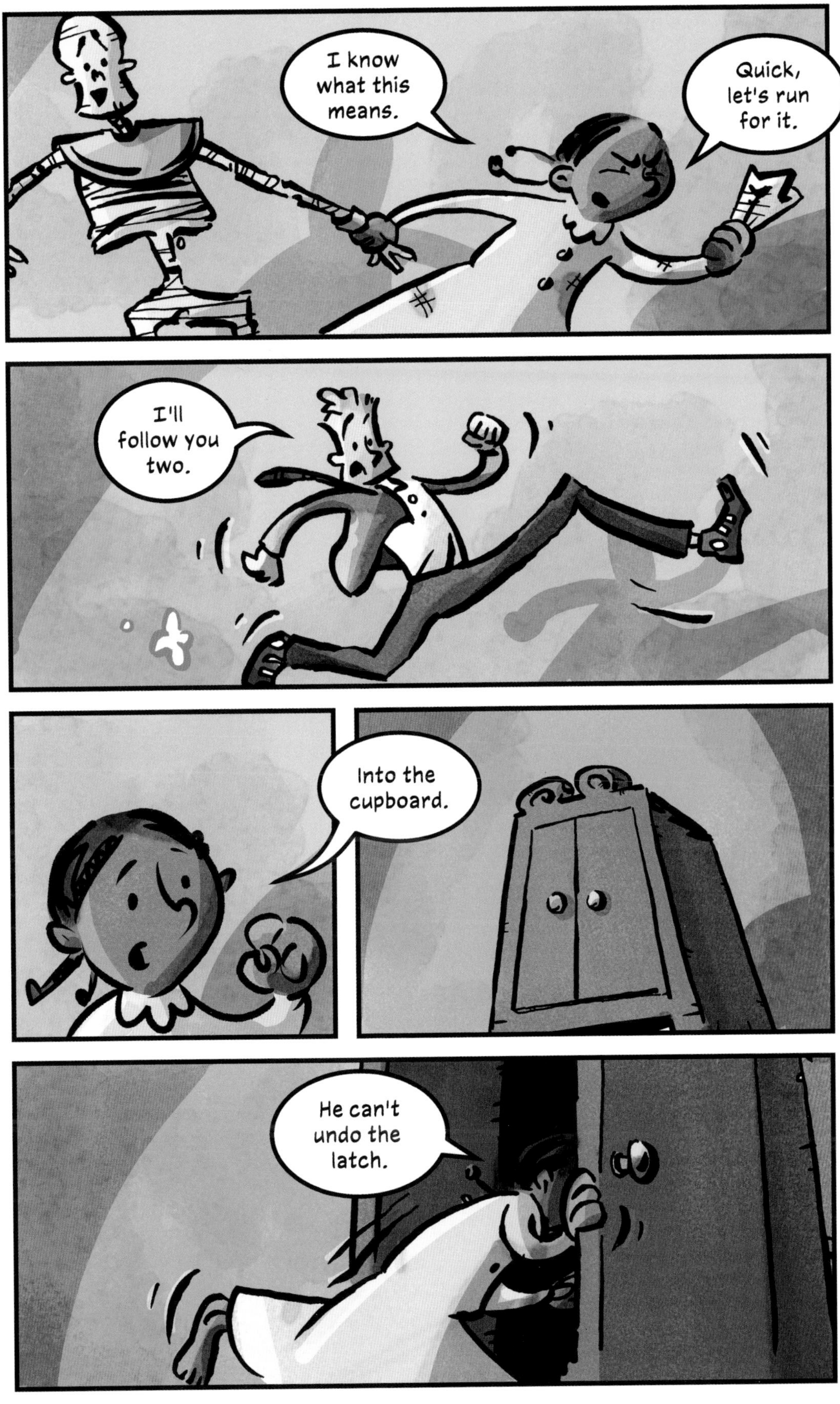
I know what this means.
Quick, let's run for it.
I'll follow you two.
Into the cupboard.
He can't undo the latch.

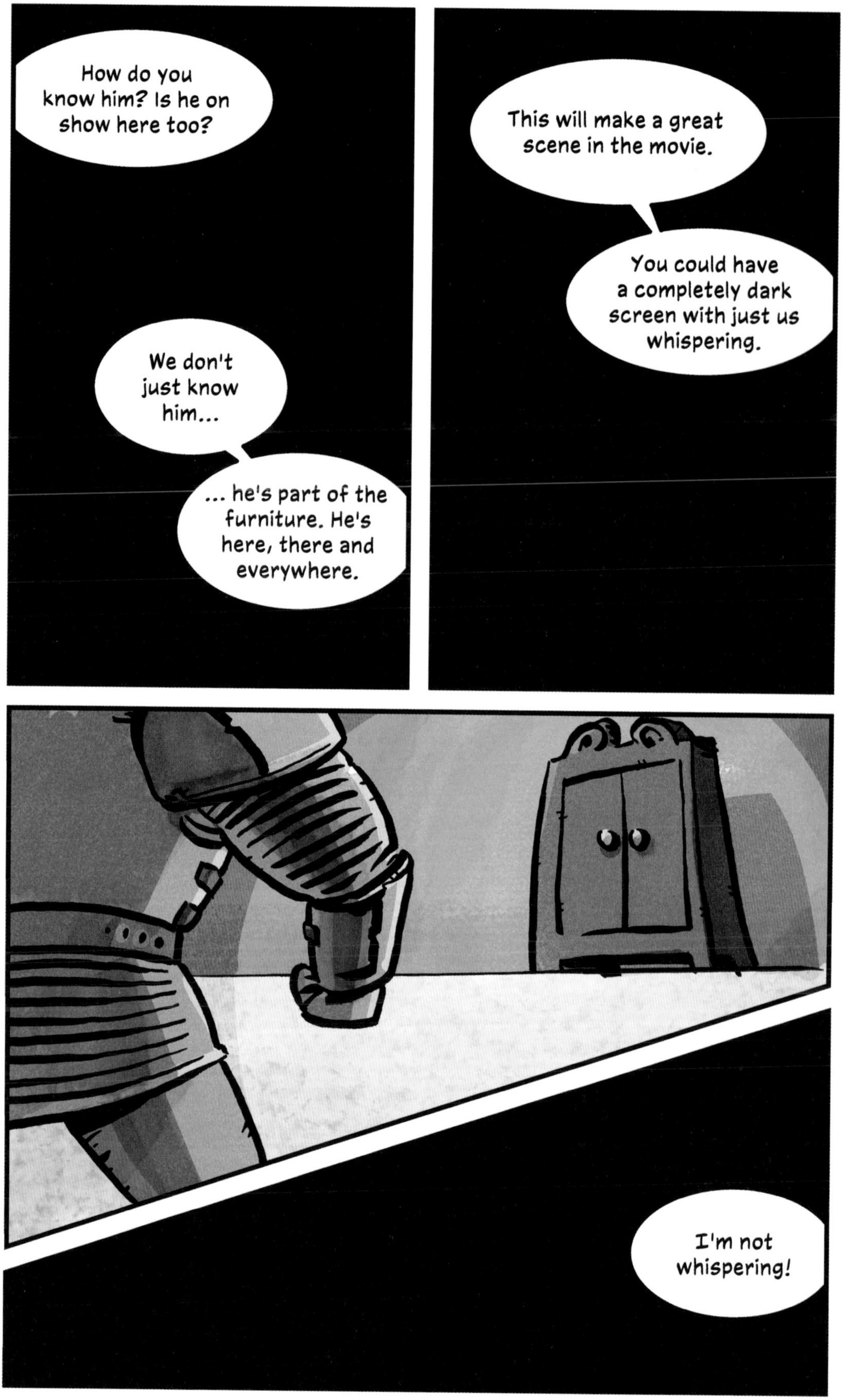
How do you know him? Is he on show here too?
We don't just know him...
... he's part of the furniture. He's here, there and everywhere.
This will make a great scene in the movie.
You could have a completely dark screen with just us whispering.
I'm not whispering!

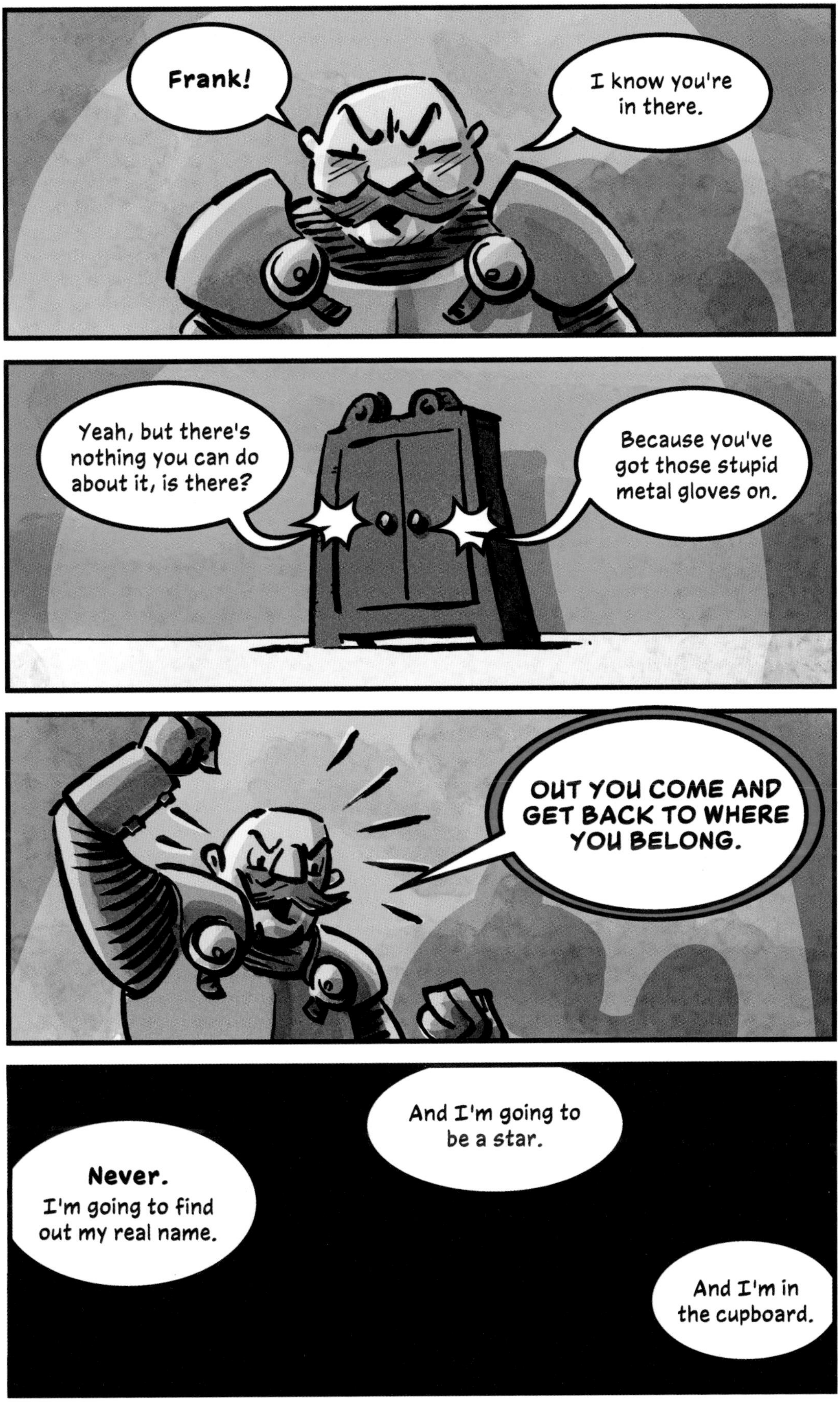
Frank!
I know you're in there.
Yeah, but there's nothing you can do about it, is there?
Because you've got those stupid metal gloves on.
OUT YOU COME AND GET BACK TO WHERE YOU BELONG.
Never. I'm going to find out my real name.
And I'm going to be a star.
And I'm in the cupboard.

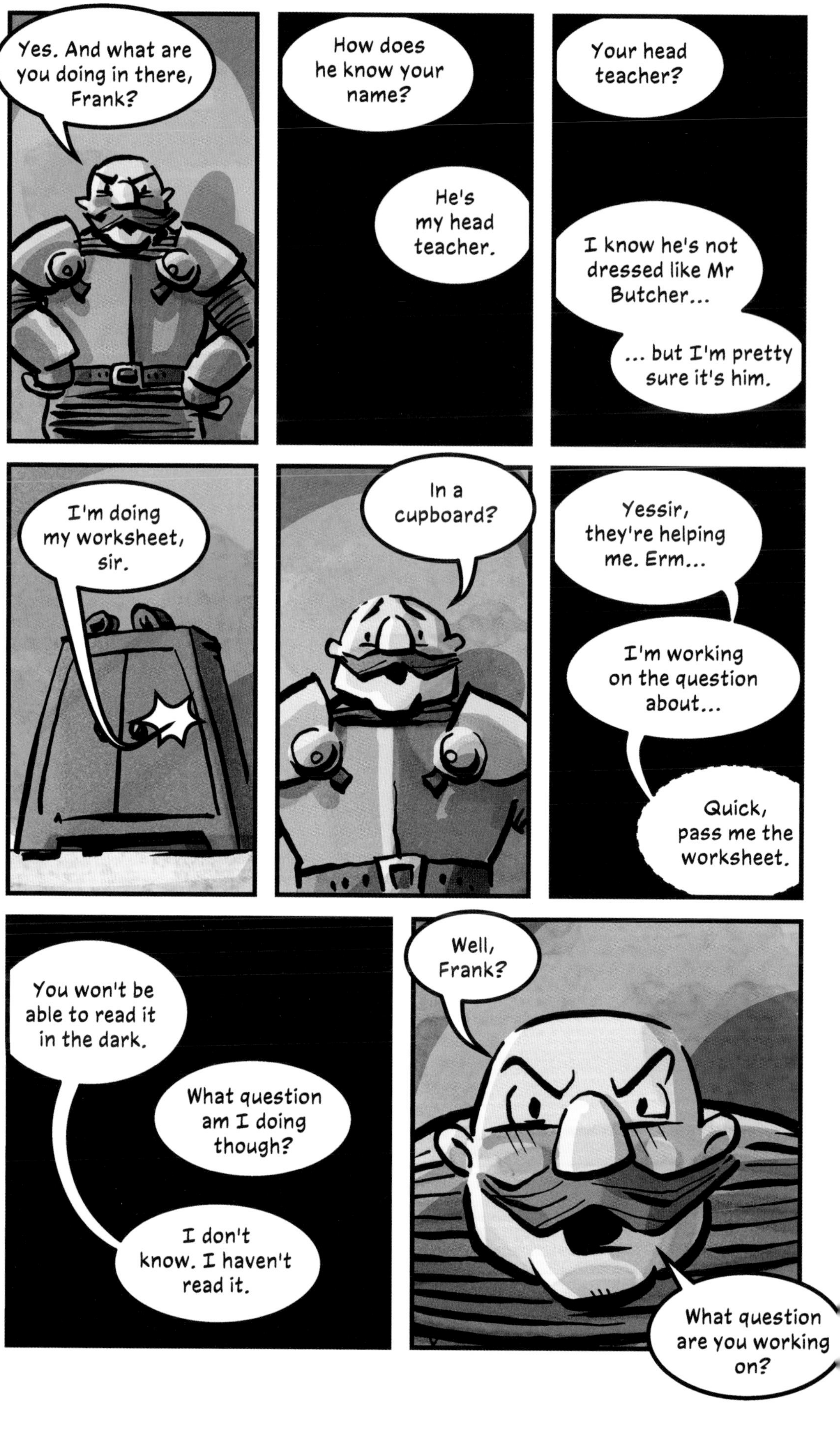
Yes. And what are you doing in there, Frank?
How does he know your name?
He's my head teacher.
Your head teacher?
I know he's not dressed like Mr Butcher...
... but I'm pretty sure it's him.
I'm doing my worksheet, sir.
In a cupboard?
Yessir, they're helping me. Erm...
I'm working on the question about...
Quick, pass me the worksheet.
You won't be able to read it in the dark.
What question am I doing though?
I don't know. I haven't read it.
Well, Frank?
What question are you working on?

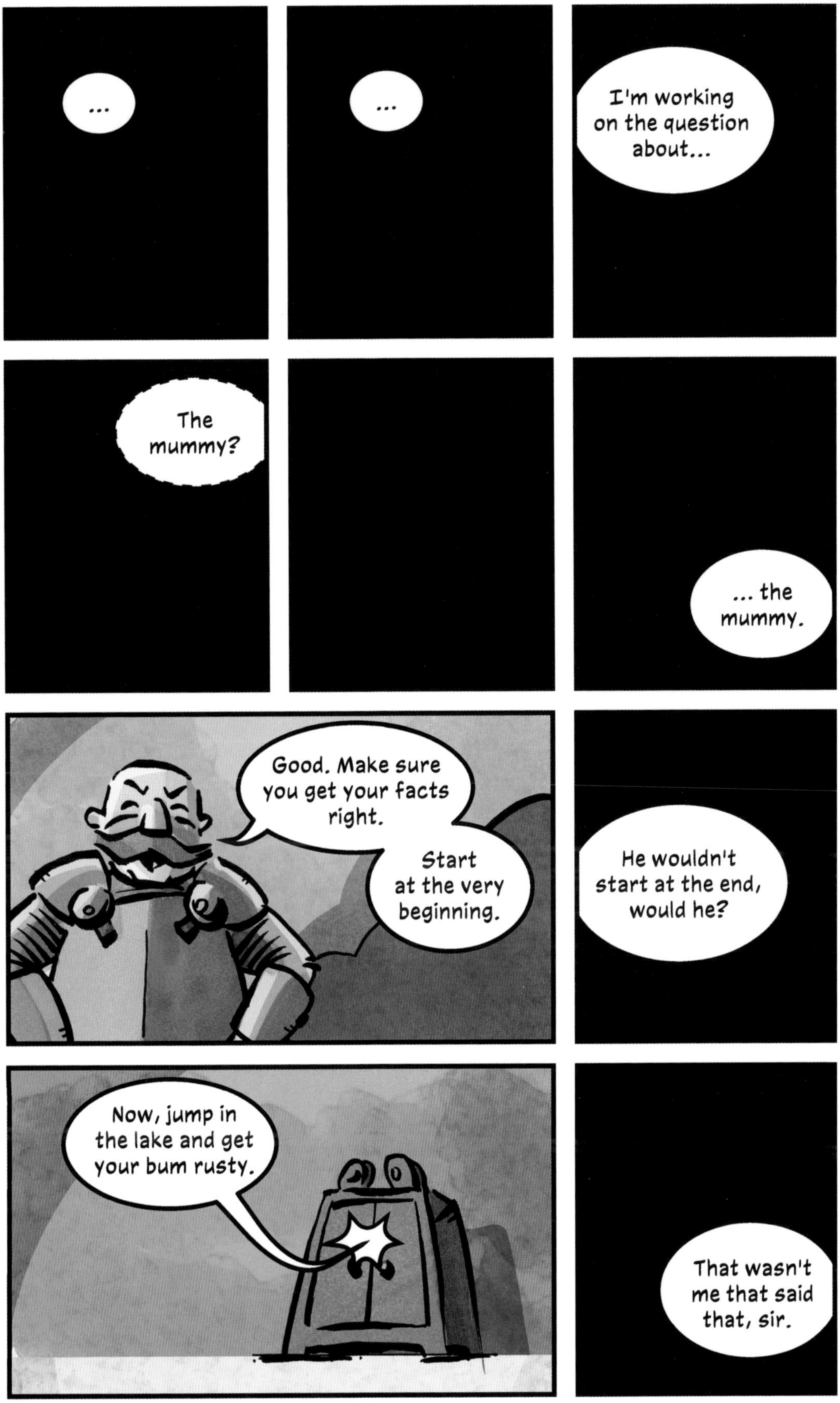
...
...
I'm working on the question about...
The mummy?
... the mummy.
Good. Make sure you get your facts right.
Start at the very beginning.
He wouldn't start at the end, would he?
Now, jump in the lake and get your bum rusty.
That wasn't me that said that, sir.

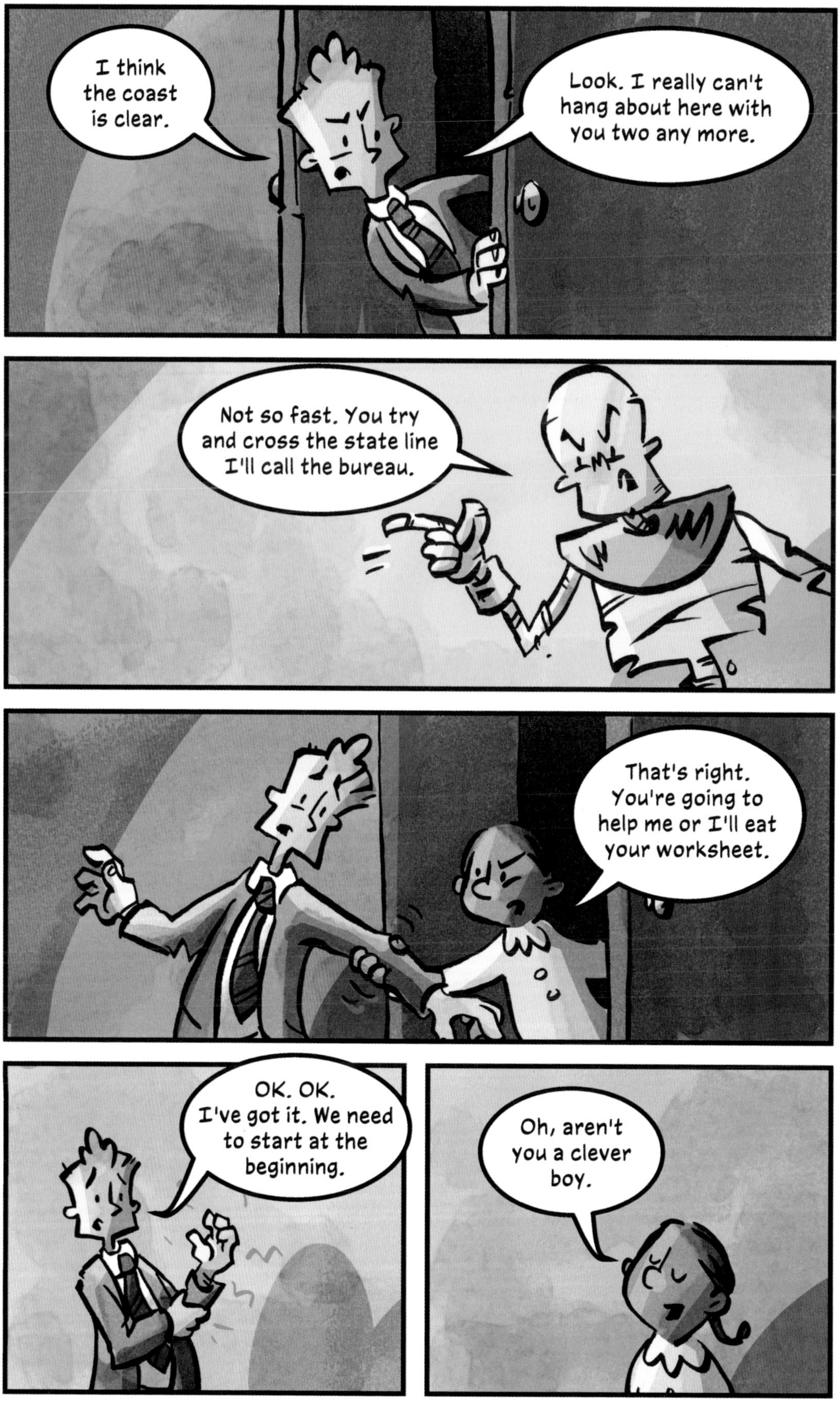
I think the coast is clear.
Look. I really can't hang about here with you two any more.
Not so fast. You try and cross the state line I'll call the bureau.
That's right. You're going to help me or I'll eat your worksheet.
OK. OK. I've got it. We need to start at the beginning.
Oh, aren't you a clever boy.

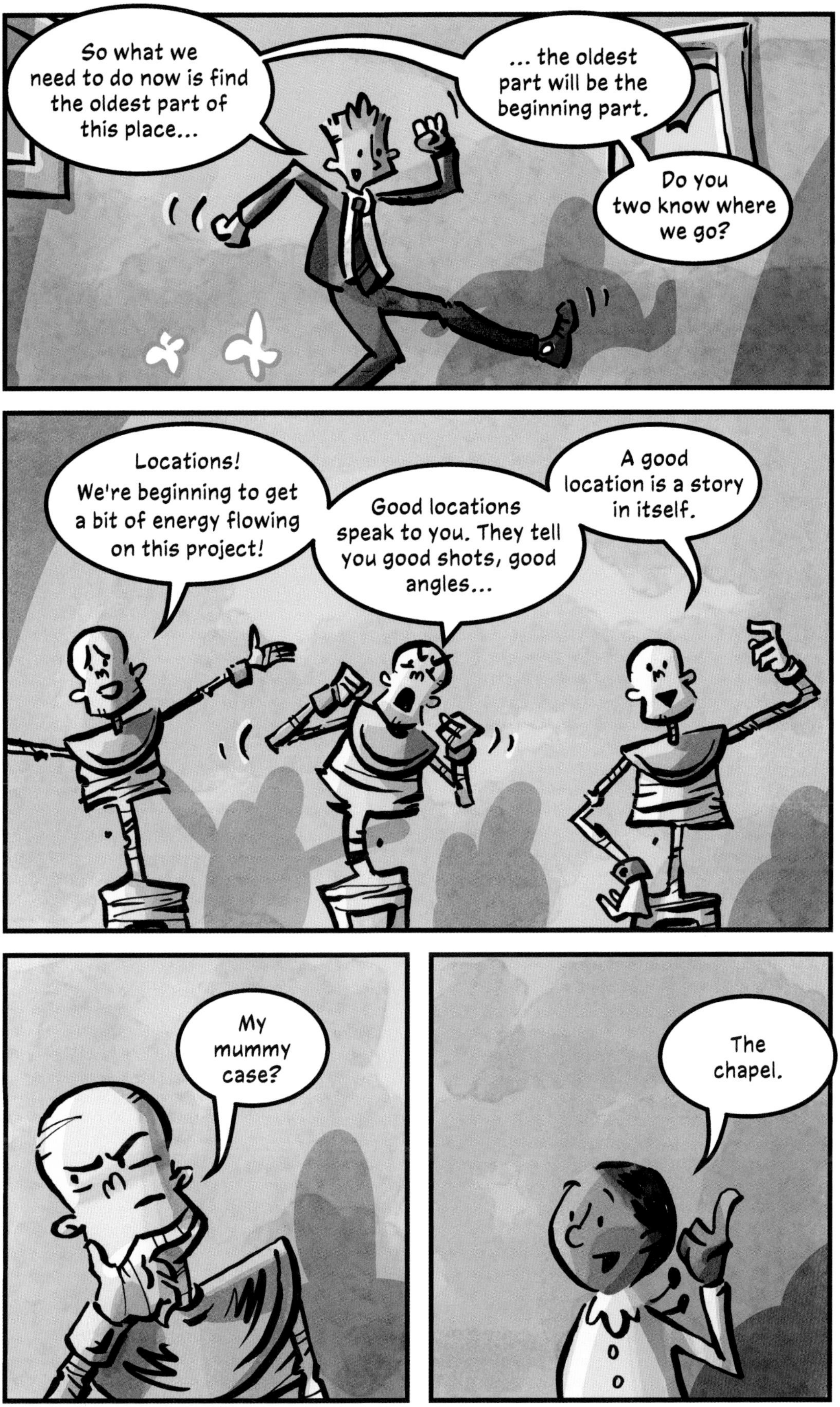
So what we need to do now is find the oldest part of this place...
... the oldest part will be the beginning part.
Do you two know where we go?
Locations! We're beginning to get a bit of energy flowing on this project!
Good locations speak to you. They tell you good shots, good angles...
A good location is a story in itself.
My mummy case?
The chapel.

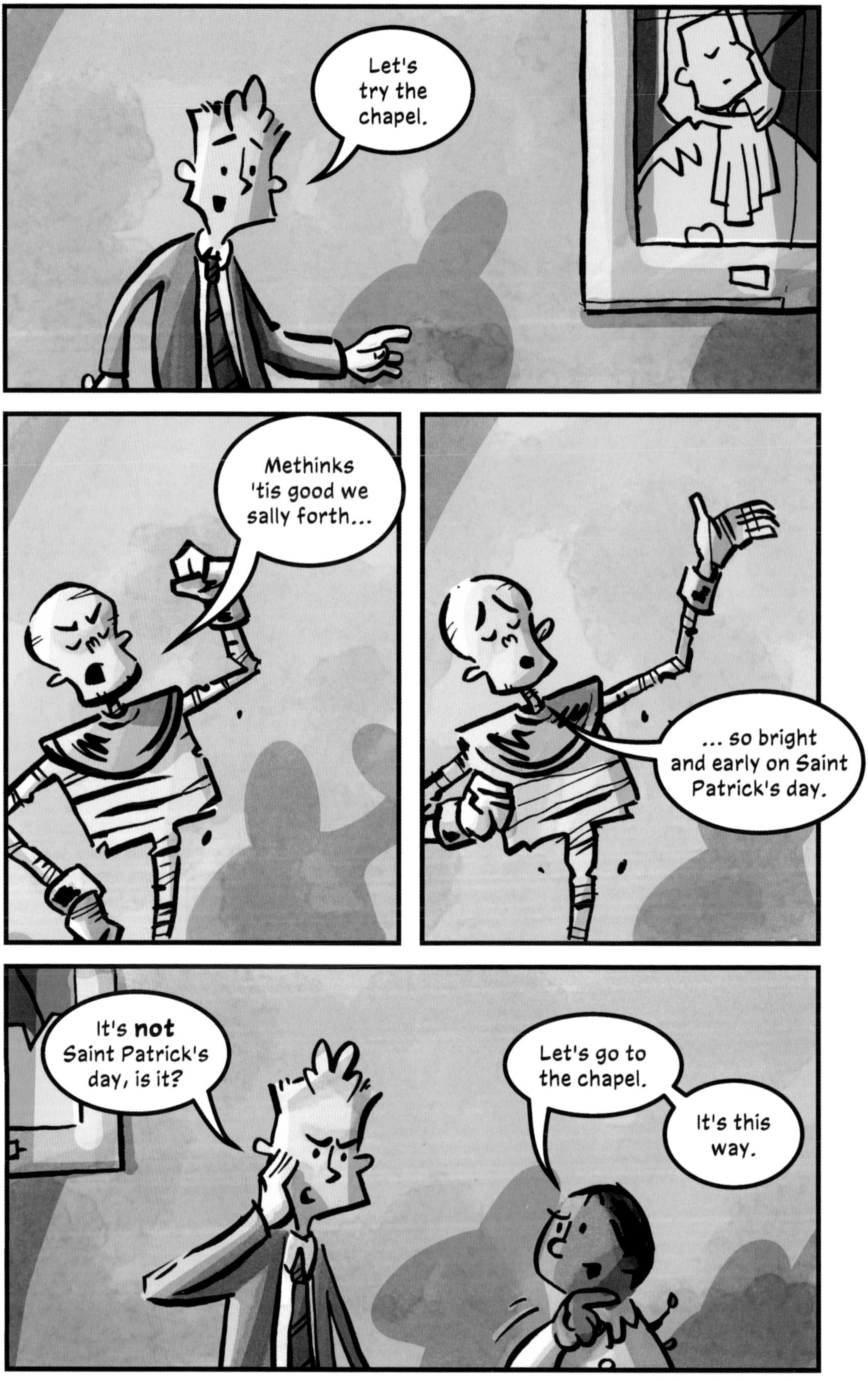
Let's try the chapel.
Methinks 'tis good we sally forth...
... so bright and early on Saint Patrick's day.
It's **not** Saint Patrick's day, is it?
Let's go to the chapel.
It's this way.

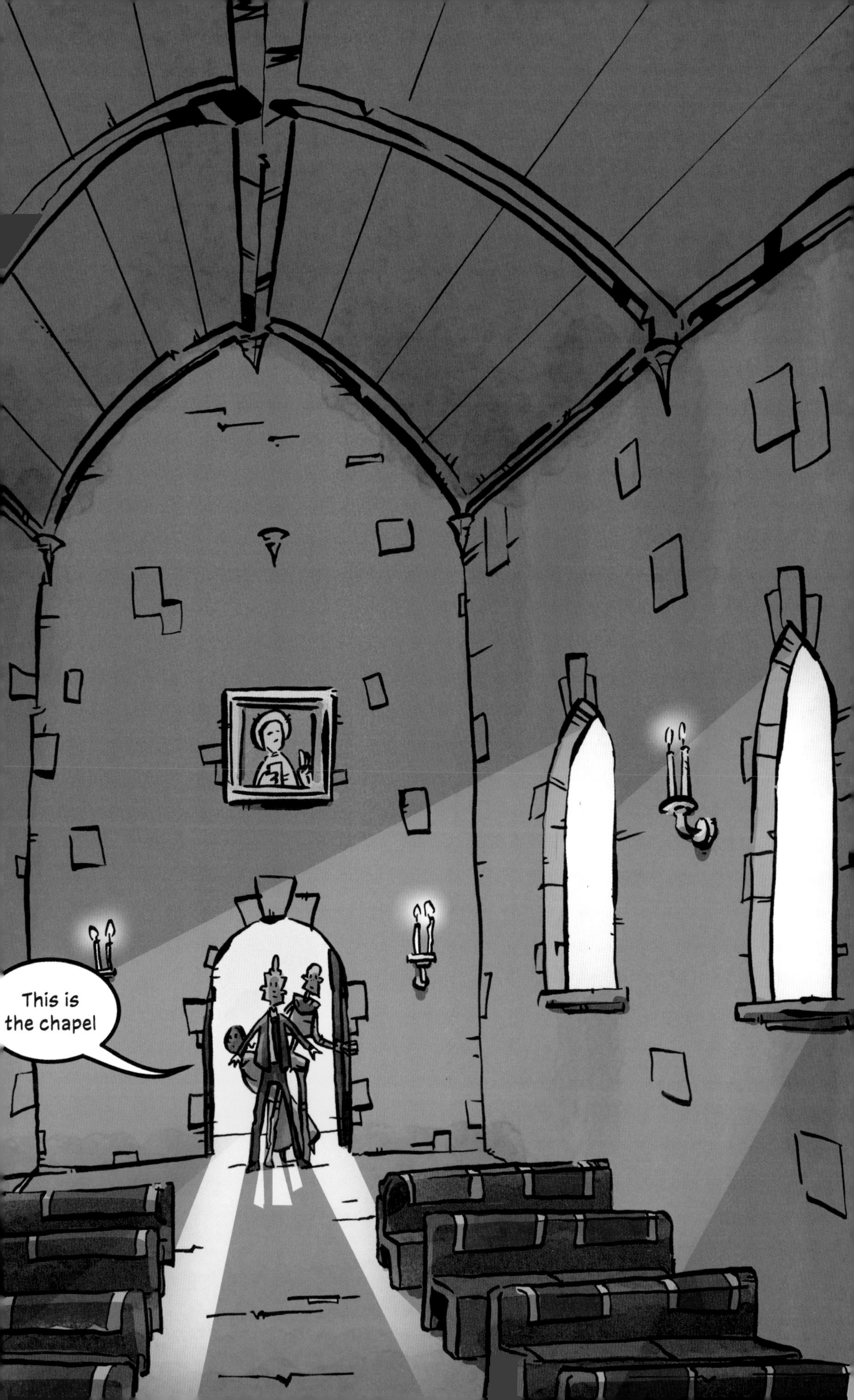
This is the chapel

WOOOOOOOOOOOOOOOOOOOO

That noise. That's what grave robbers do...

WOOOOOOOOOOOOOOOOOO

What are grave robbers?

People who rob graves, silly!

Look!

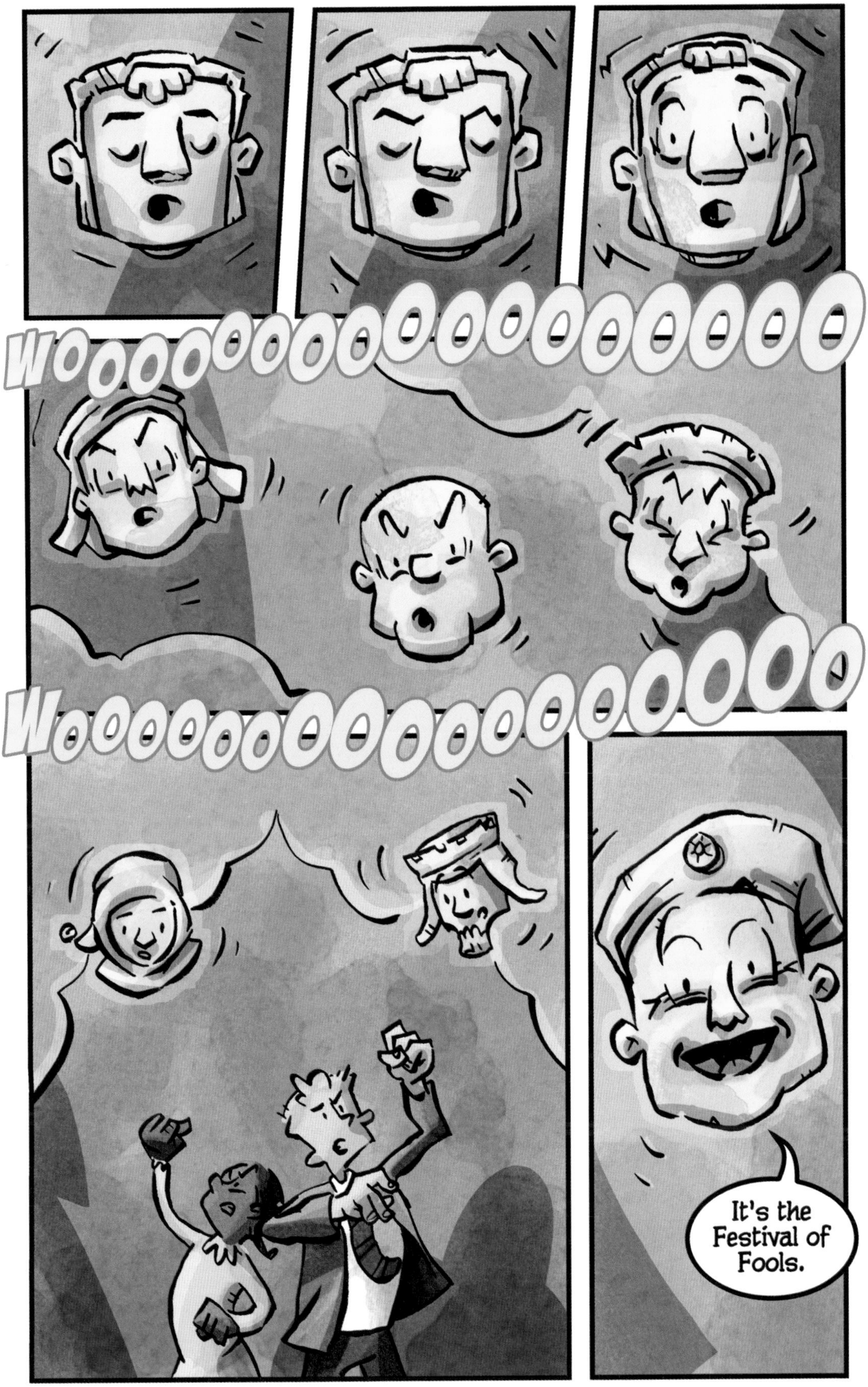
WOOOOOOOOOOOOOOOOOOOO
WOOOOOOOOOOOOOOOOOOOO
It's the Festival of Fools.

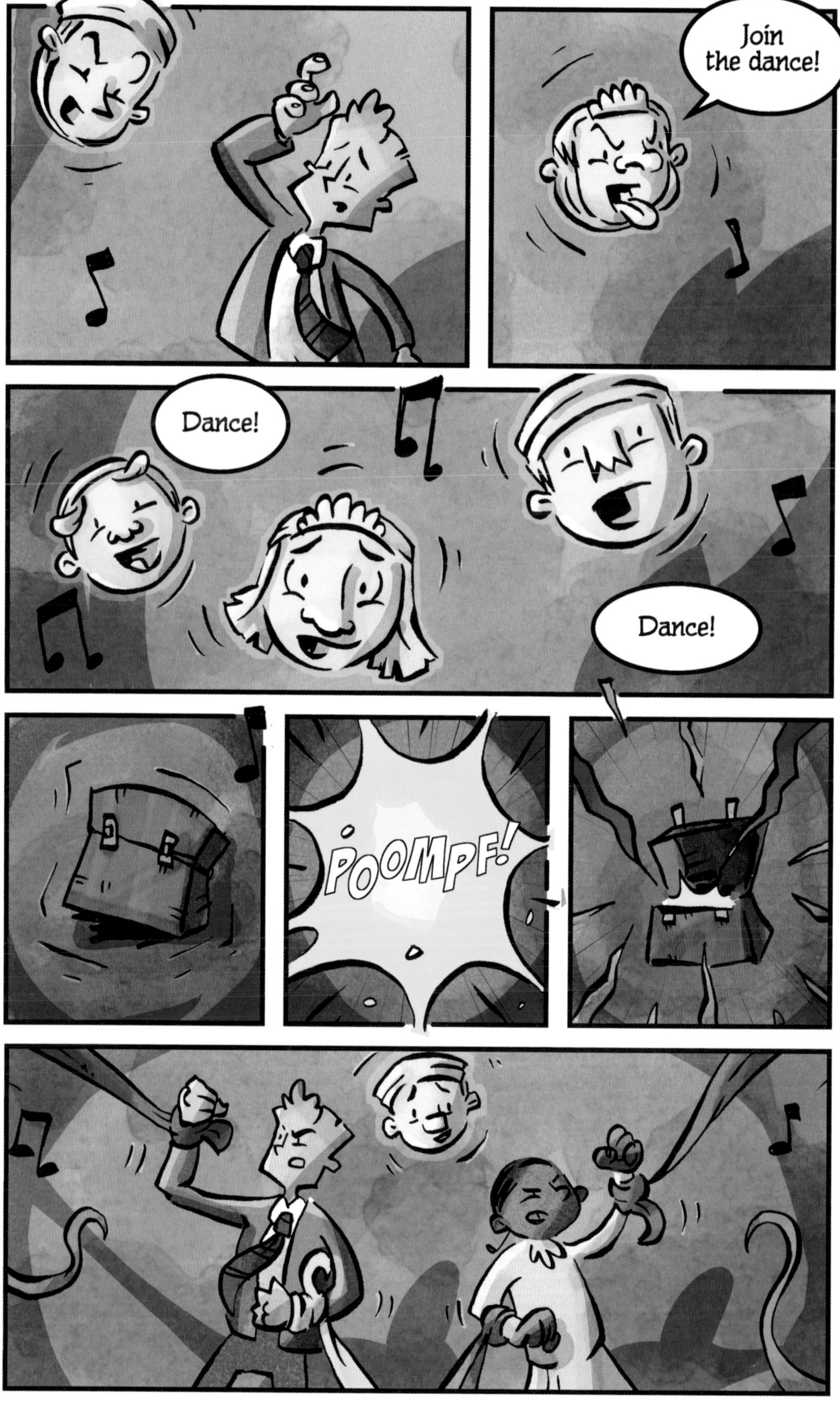
Join the dance!
Dance!
Dance!
POOMPF!

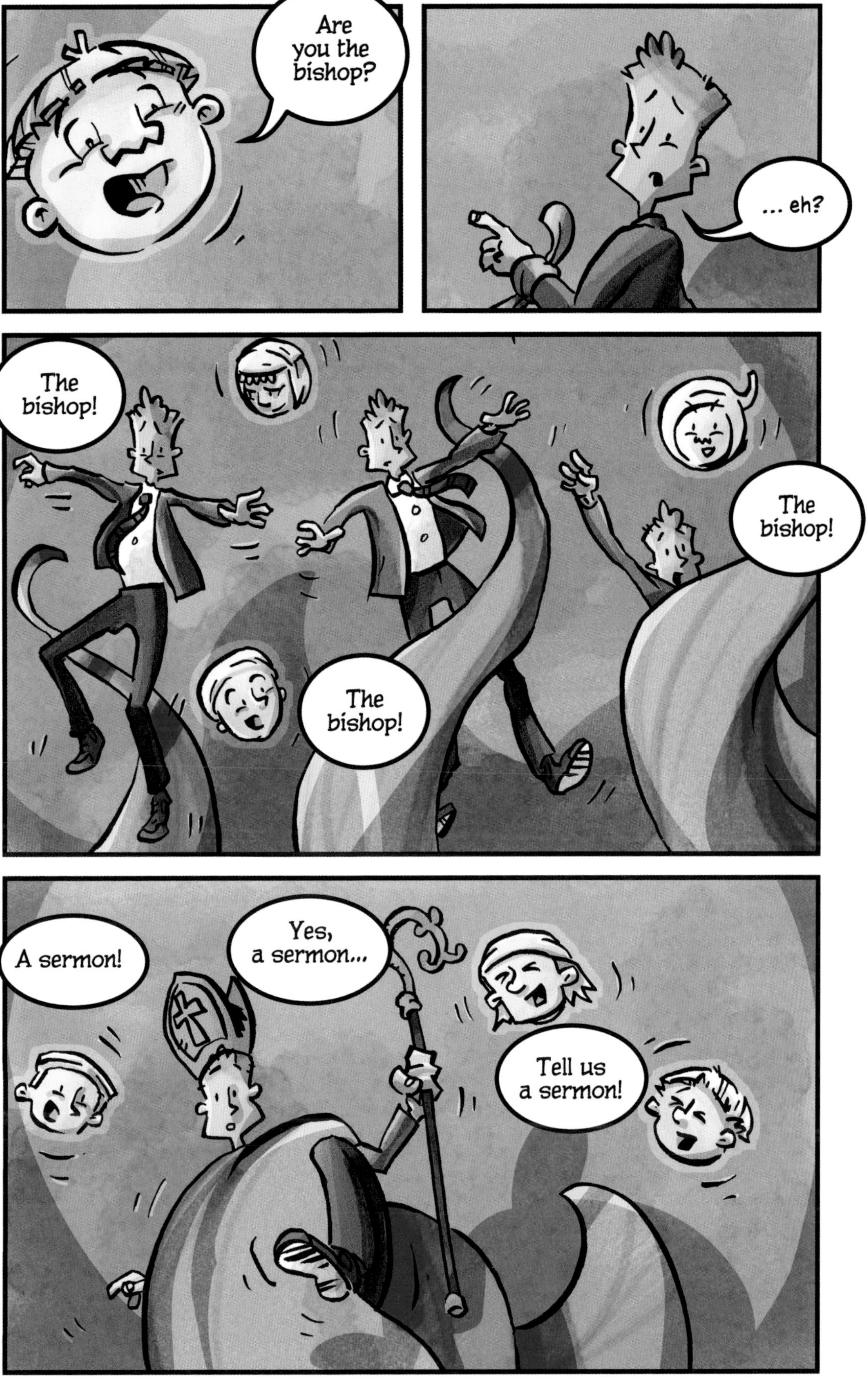
Are you the bishop?
... eh?
The bishop!
The bishop!
The bishop!
A sermon!
Yes, a sermon...
Tell us a sermon!

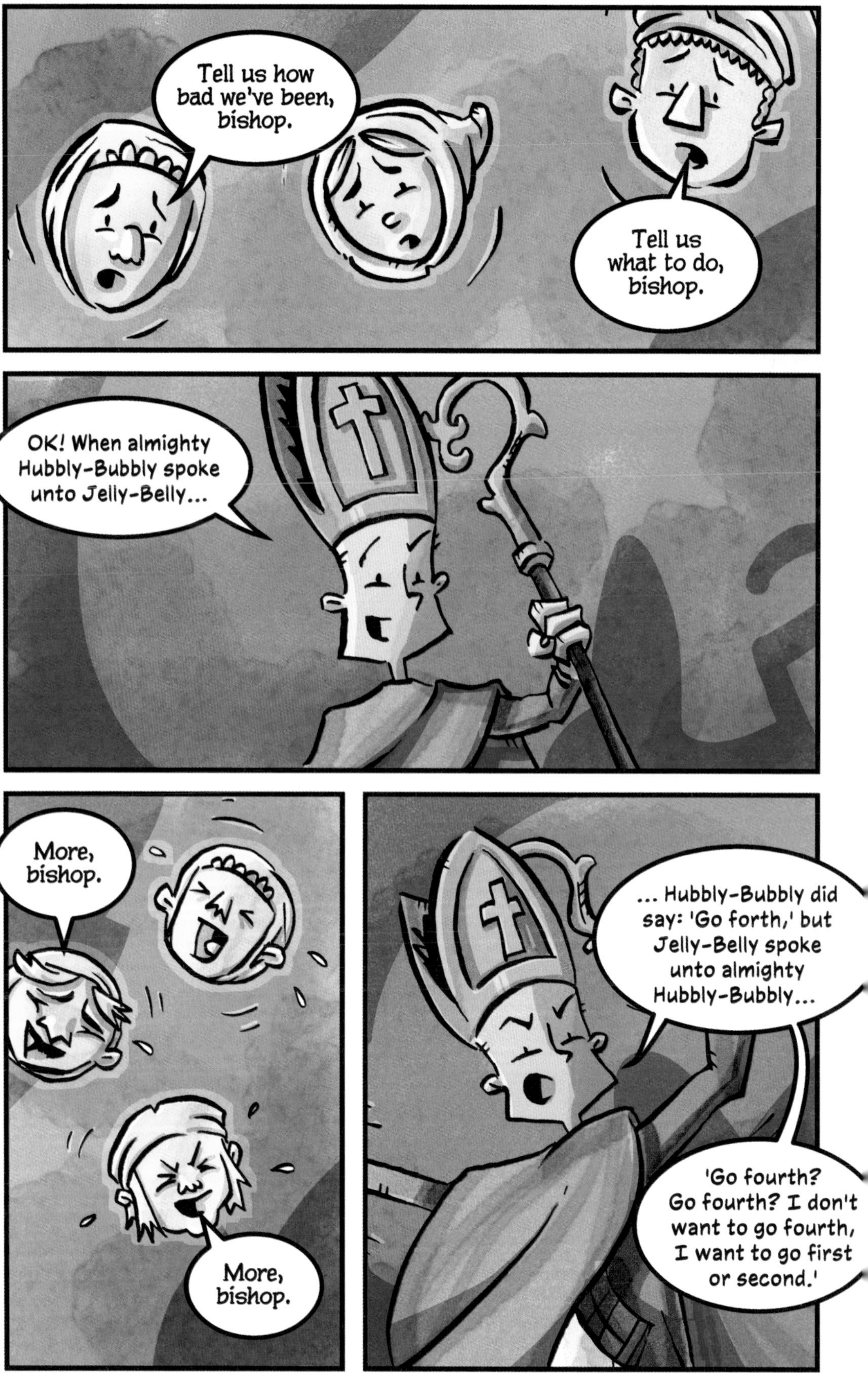
Tell us how bad we've been, bishop.
Tell us what to do, bishop.
OK! When almighty Hubbly-Bubbly spoke unto Jelly-Belly...
More, bishop.
More, bishop.
... Hubbly-Bubbly did say: 'Go forth,' but Jelly-Belly spoke unto almighty Hubbly-Bubbly...
'Go fourth? Go fourth? I don't want to go fourth, I want to go first or second.'

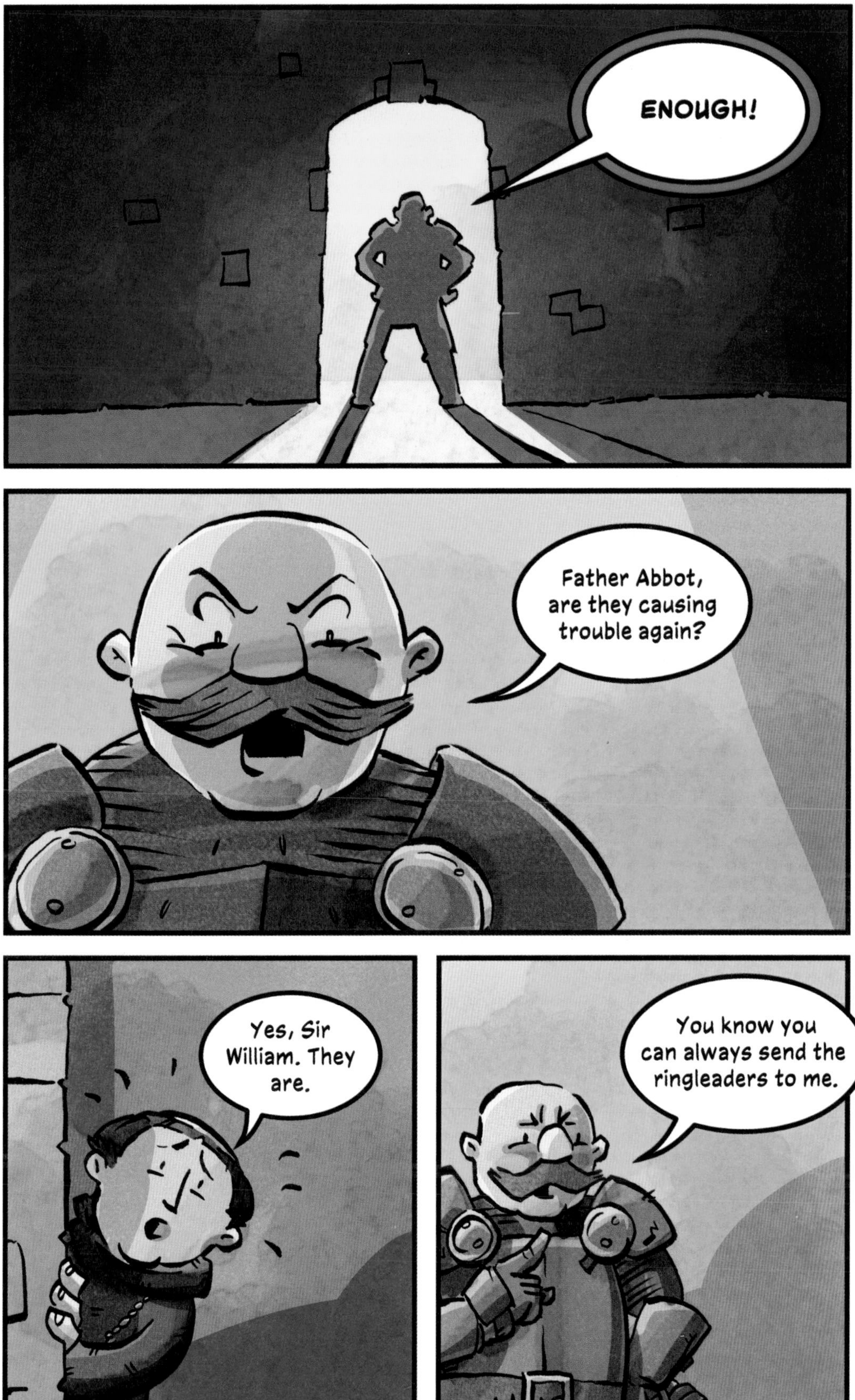
ENOUGH!
Father Abbot, are they causing trouble again?
Yes, Sir William. They are.
You know you can always send the ringleaders to me.

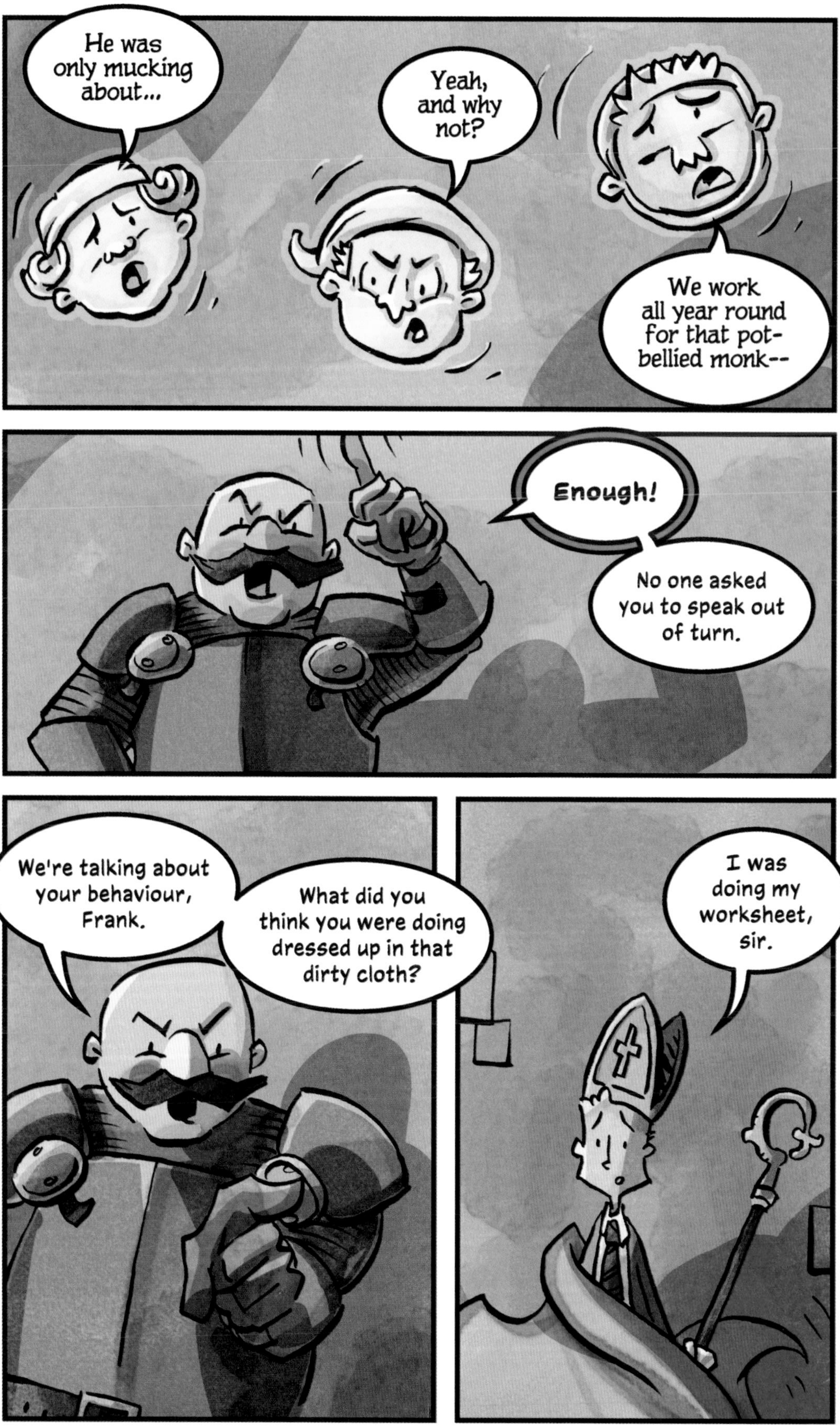
He was only mucking about...
Yeah, and why not?
We work all year round for that pot-bellied monk--
Enough!
No one asked you to speak out of turn.
We're talking about your behaviour, Frank.
What did you think you were doing dressed up in that dirty cloth?
I was doing my worksheet, sir.

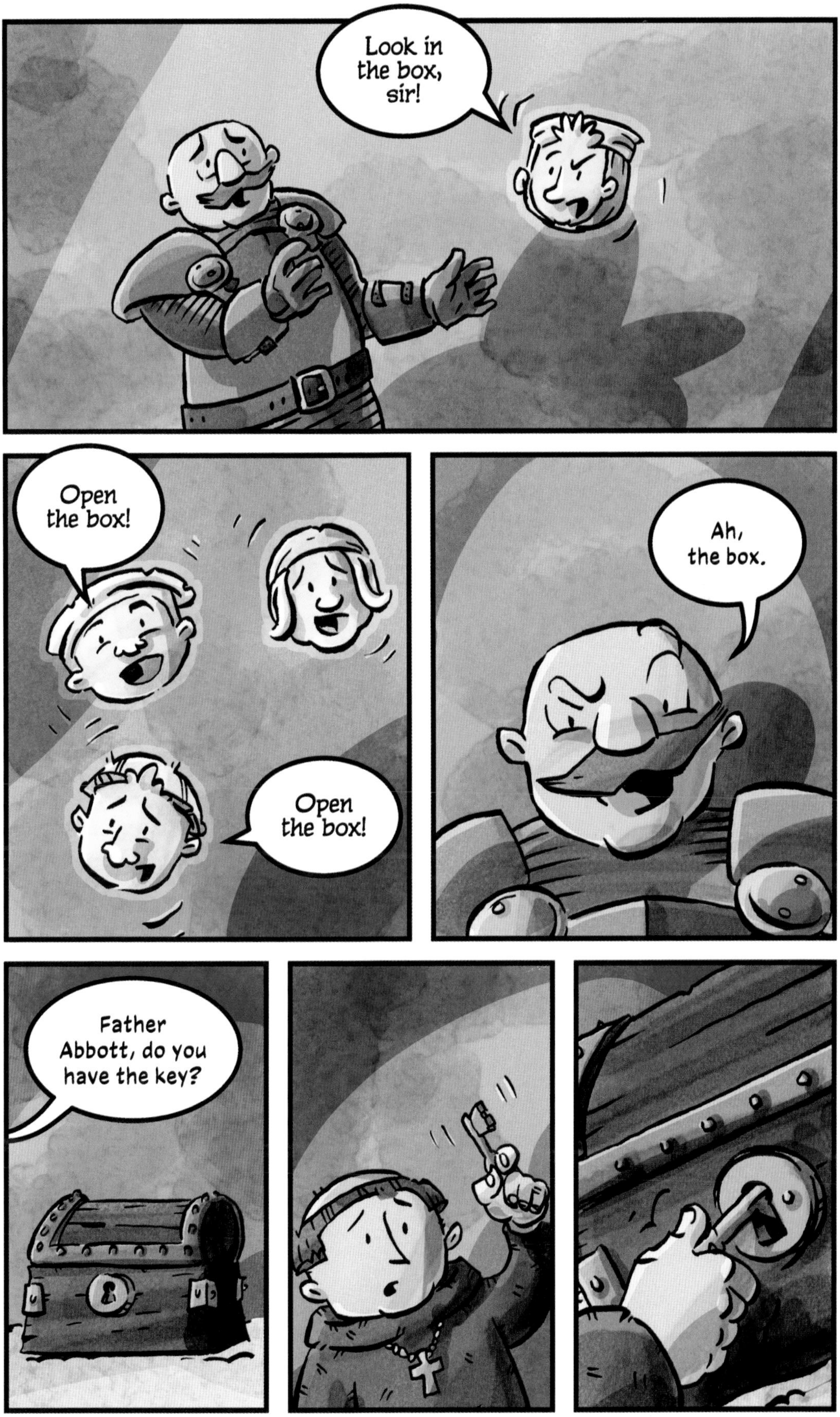
Look in the box, sir!
Open the box!
Open the box!
Ah, the box.
Father Abbott, do you have the key?

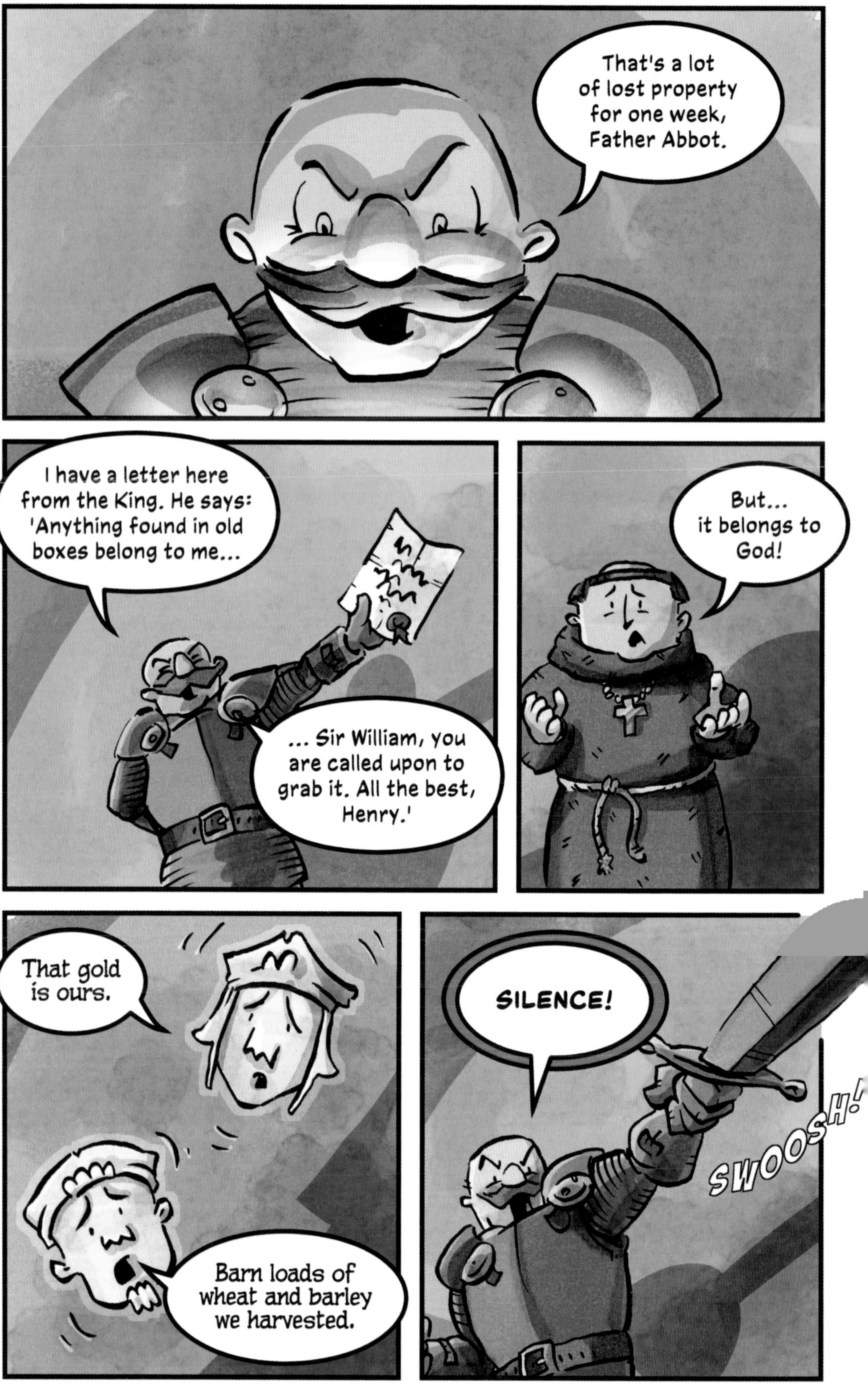
That's a lot of lost property for one week, Father Abbot.
I have a letter here from the King. He says: 'Anything found in old boxes belong to me...
... Sir William, you are called upon to grab it. All the best, Henry.'
But... it belongs to God!
That gold is ours.
Barn loads of wheat and barley we harvested.
SILENCE!
SWOOSH!

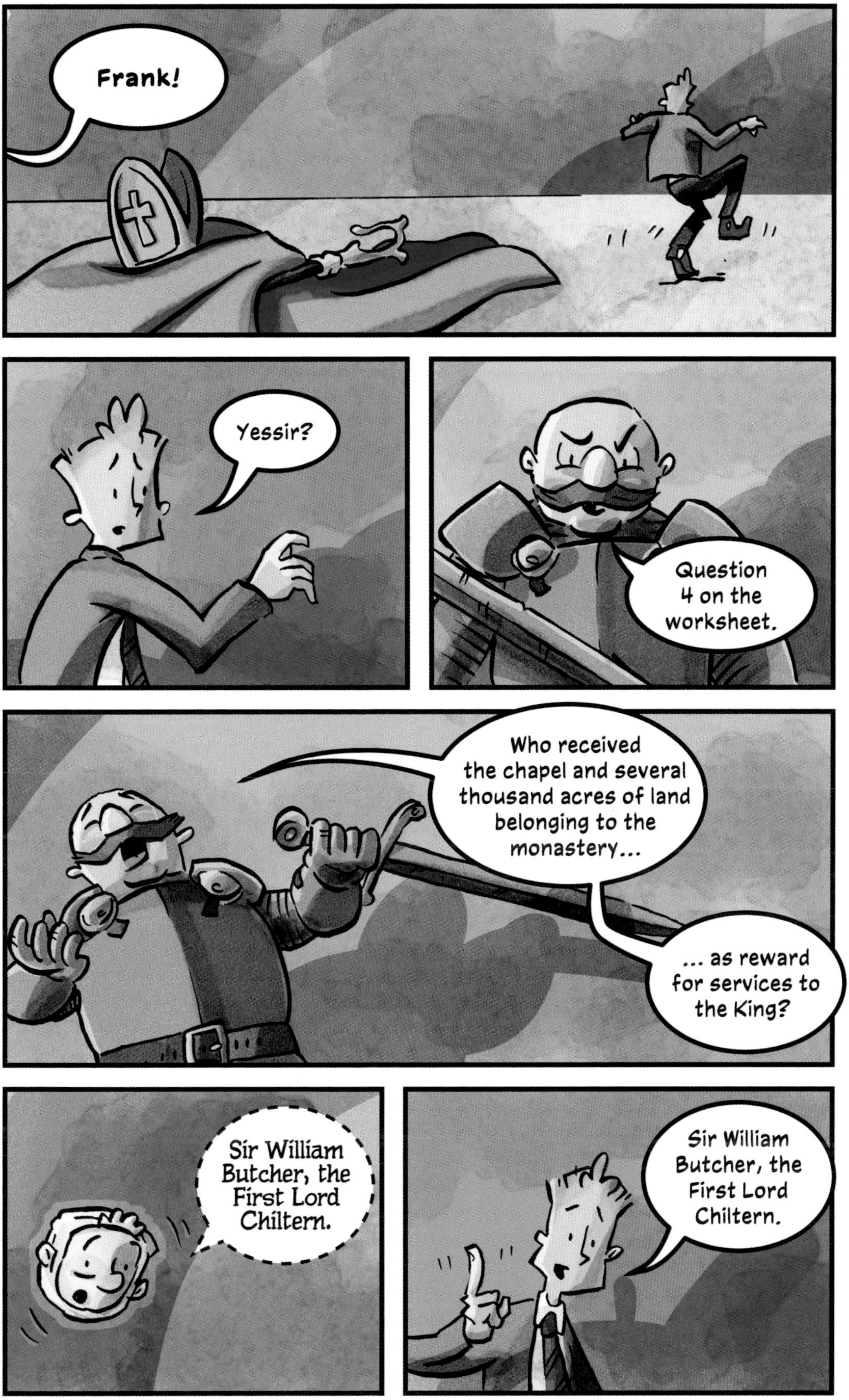
Frank!
Yessir?
Question 4 on the worksheet.
Who received the chapel and several thousand acres of land belonging to the monastery...
... as reward for services to the King?
Sir William Butcher, the First Lord Chiltern.
Sir William Butcher, the First Lord Chiltern.

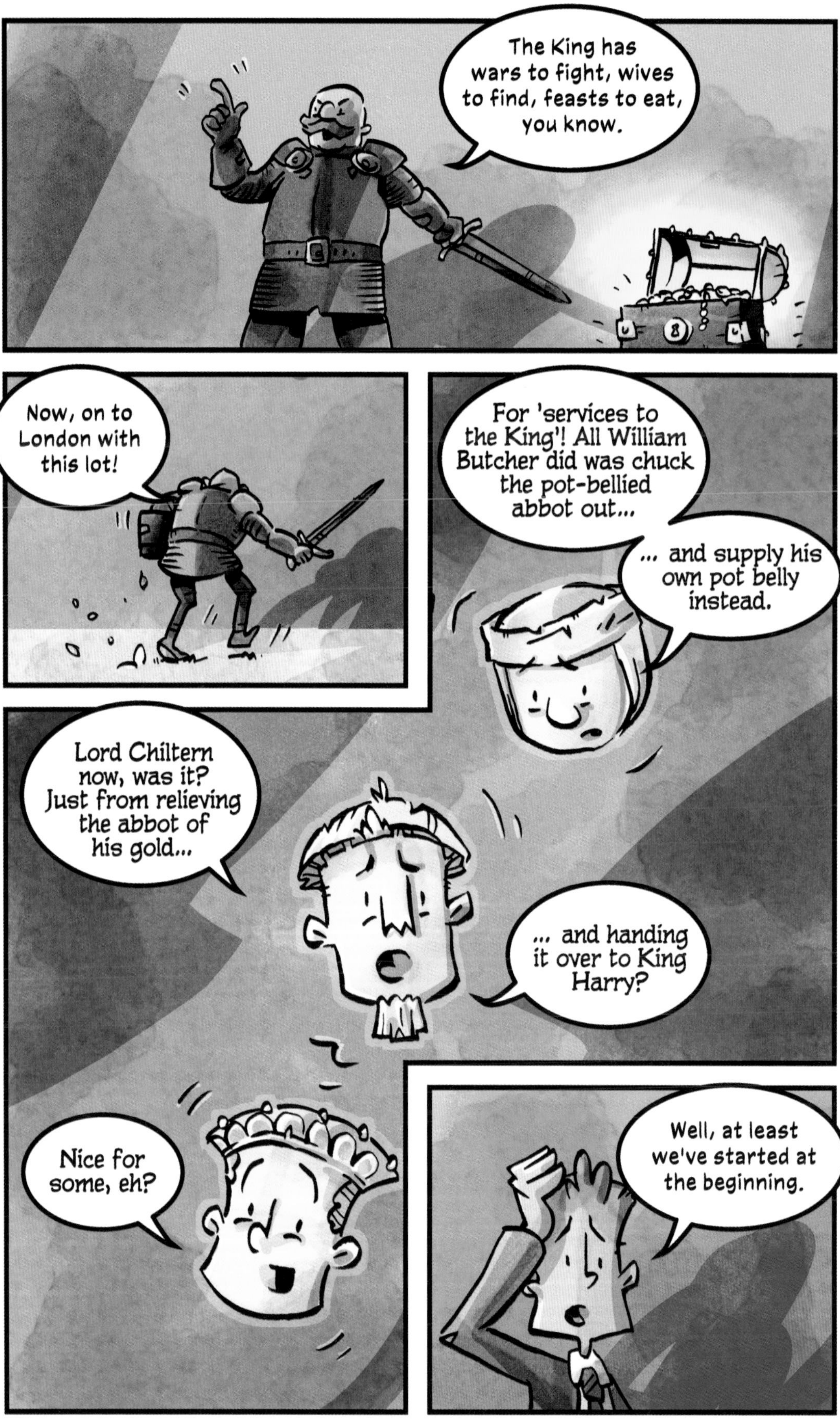
The King has wars to fight, wives to find, feasts to eat, you know.
Now, on to London with this lot!
For 'services to the King'! All William Butcher did was chuck the pot-bellied abbot out...
... and supply his own pot belly instead.
Lord Chiltern now, was it? Just from relieving the abbot of his gold...
... and handing it over to King Harry?
Nice for some, eh?
Well, at least we've started at the beginning.

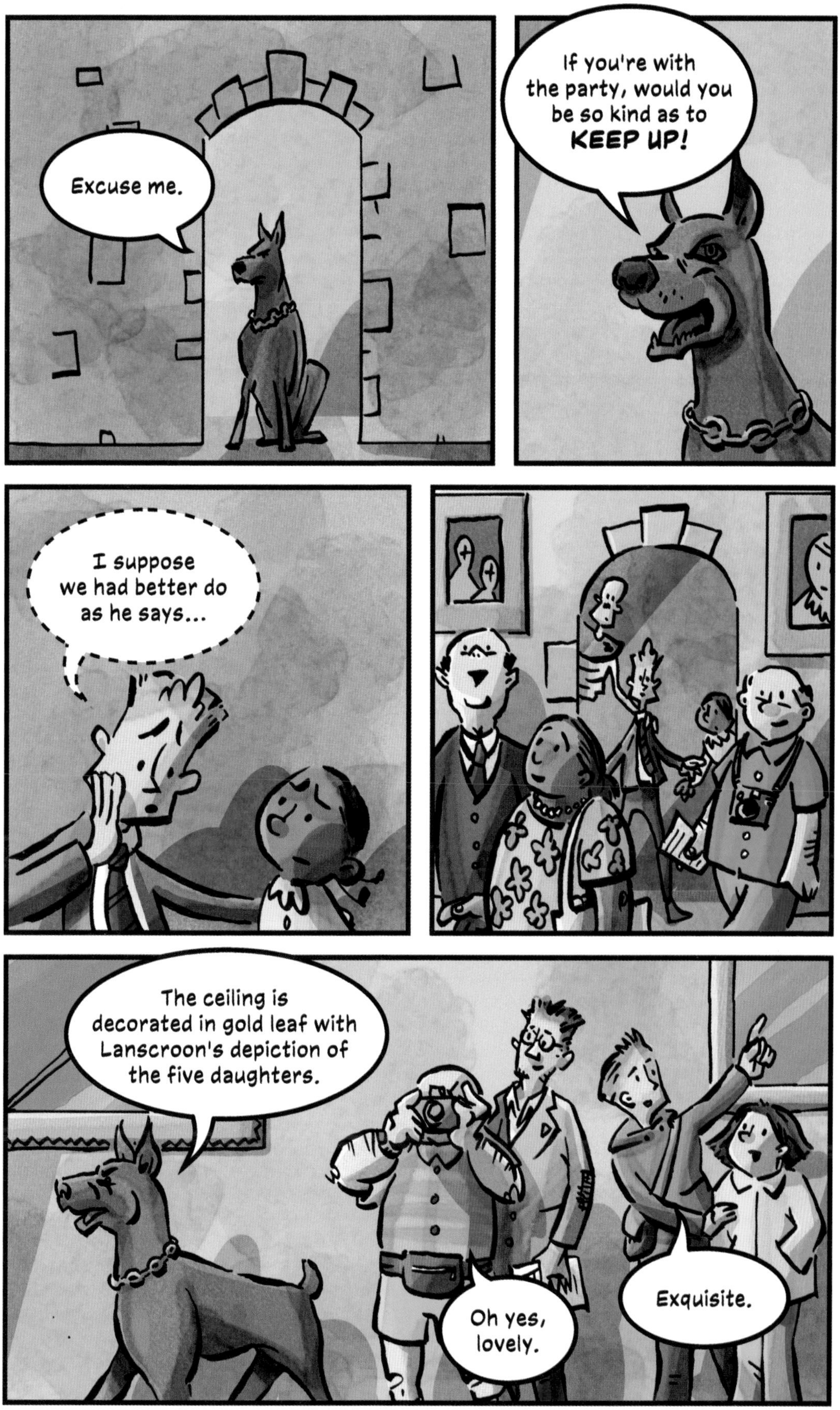

Excuse me.
If you're with the party, would you be so kind as to **KEEP UP!**
I suppose we had better do as he says...
The ceiling is decorated in gold leaf with Lanscroon's depiction of the five daughters.
Oh yes, lovely.
Exquisite.

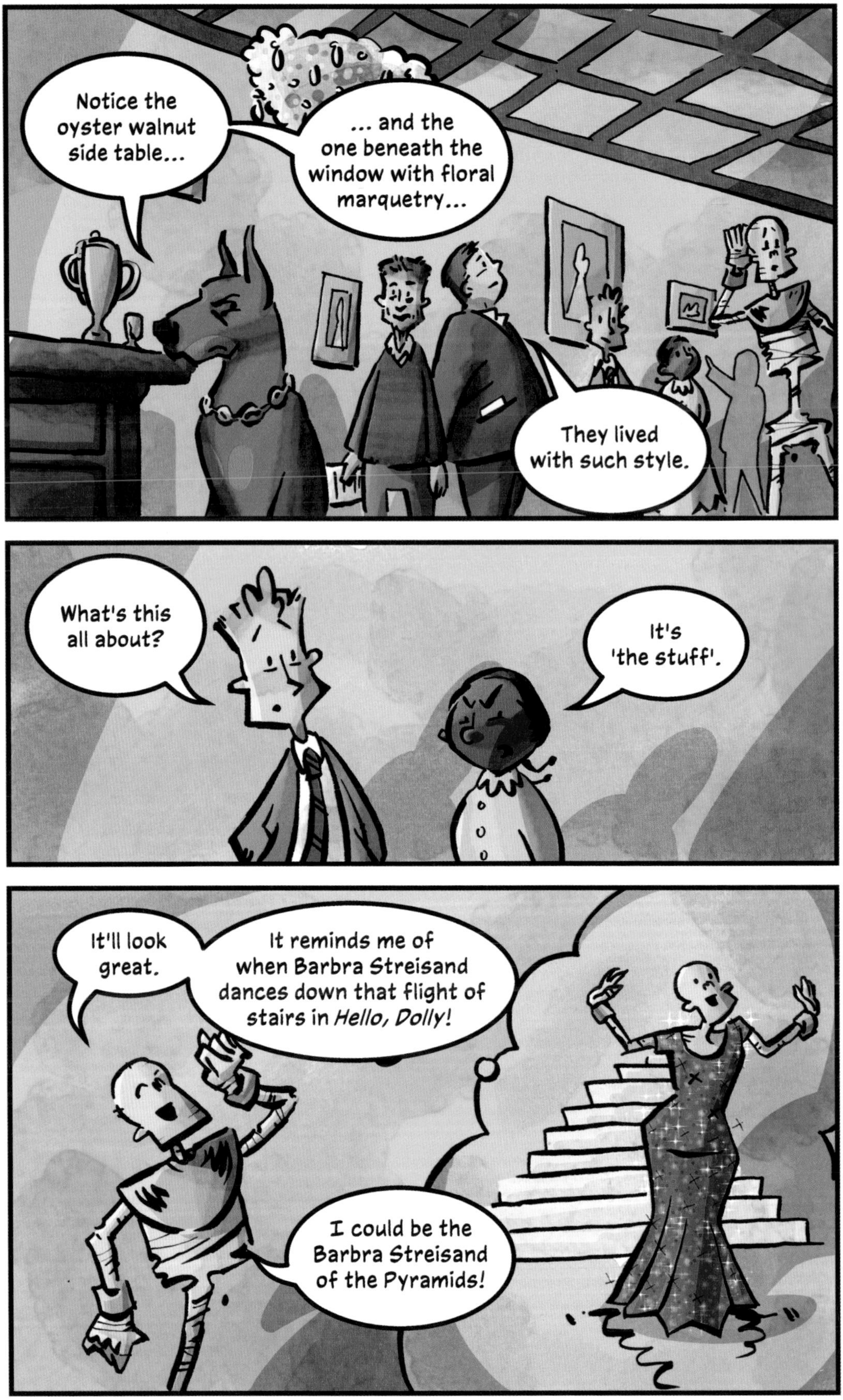
Notice the oyster walnut side table...
... and the one beneath the window with floral marquetry...
They lived with such style.
What's this all about?
It's 'the stuff'.
It'll look great.
It reminds me of when Barbra Streisand dances down that flight of stairs in *Hello, Dolly*!
I could be the Barbra Streisand of the Pyramids!

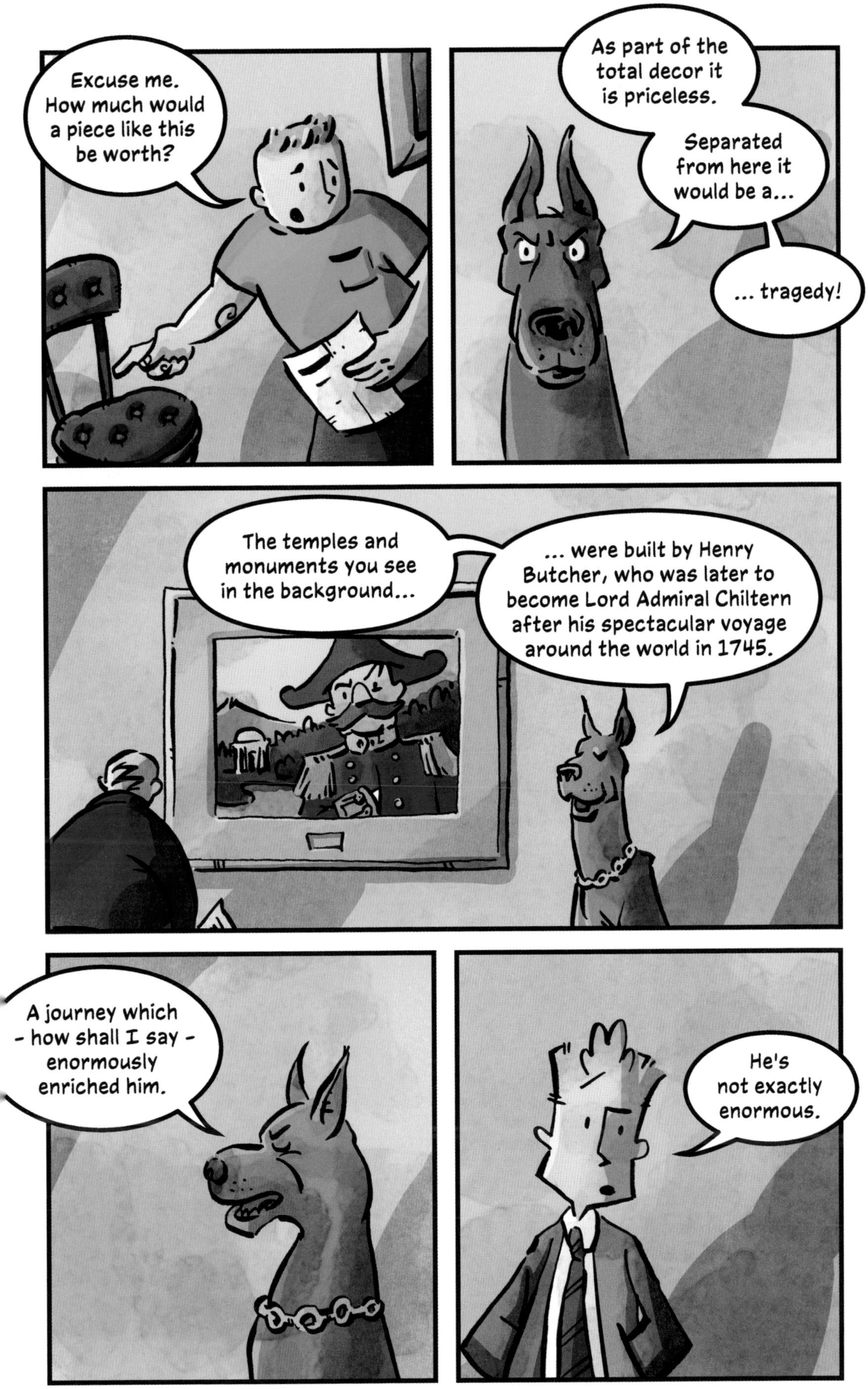
Excuse me. How much would a piece like this be worth?
As part of the total decor it is priceless.
Separated from here it would be a...
... tragedy!
The temples and monuments you see in the background...
... were built by Henry Butcher, who was later to become Lord Admiral Chiltern after his spectacular voyage around the world in 1745.
A journey which - how shall I say - enormously enriched him.
He's not exactly enormous.

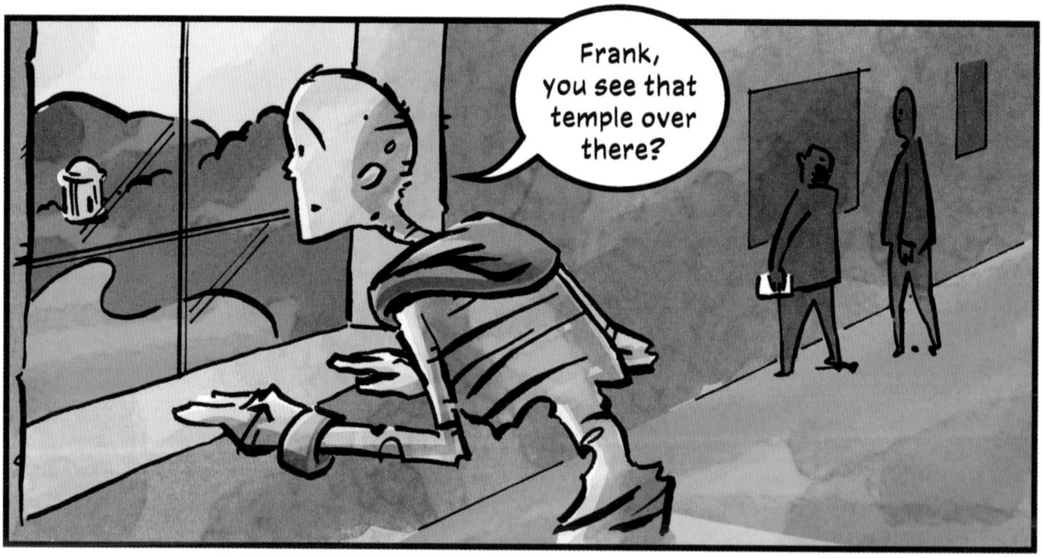
Frank, you see that temple over there?

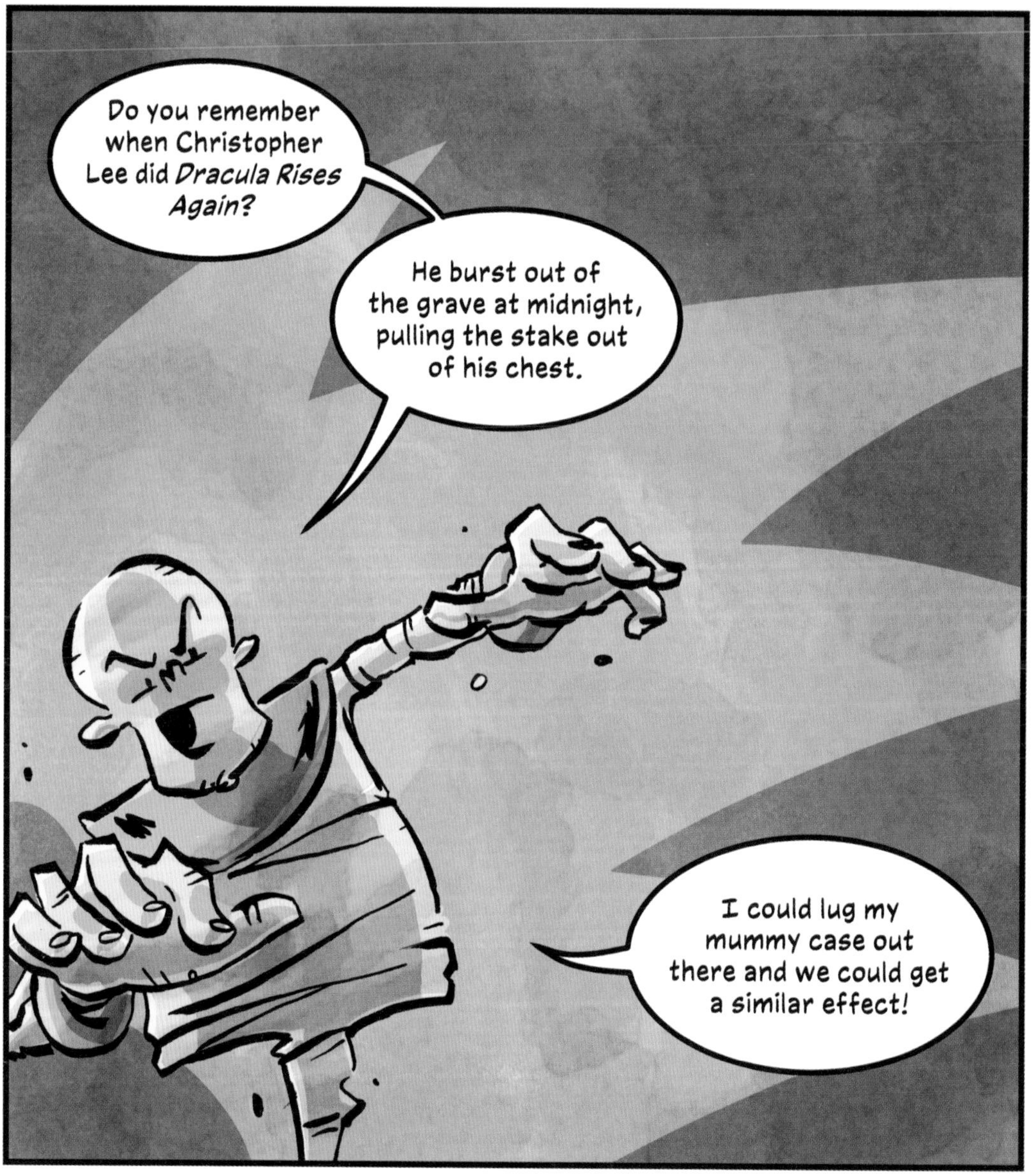
Do you remember when Christopher Lee did *Dracula Rises Again*?
He burst out of the grave at midnight, pulling the stake out of his chest.
I could lug my mummy case out there and we could get a similar effect!

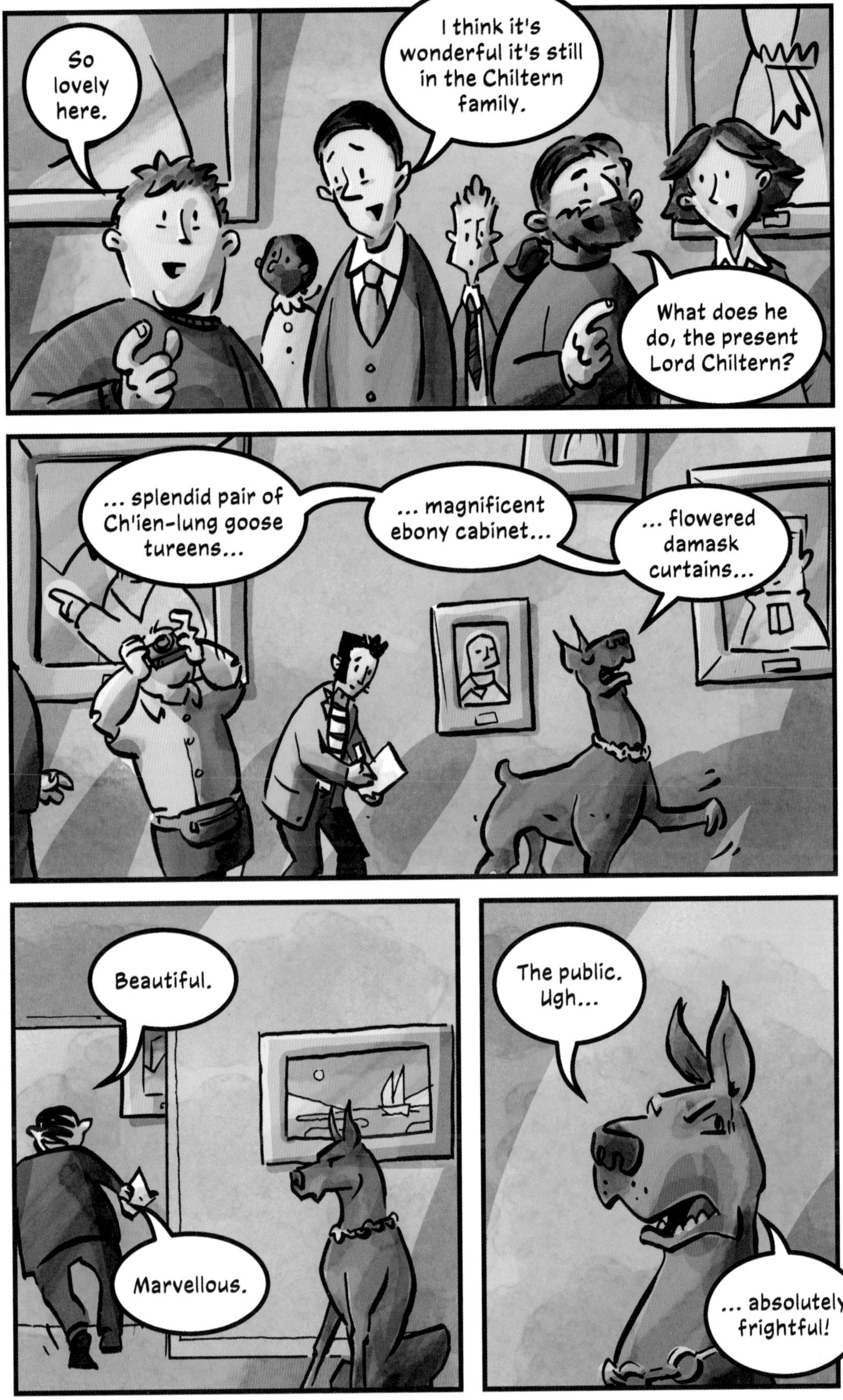
So lovely here.
I think it's wonderful it's still in the Chiltern family.
What does he do, the present Lord Chiltern?
... splendid pair of Ch'ien-lung goose tureens...
... magnificent ebony cabinet...
... flowered damask curtains...
Beautiful.
Marvellous.
The public. Ugh...
... absolutely frightful!

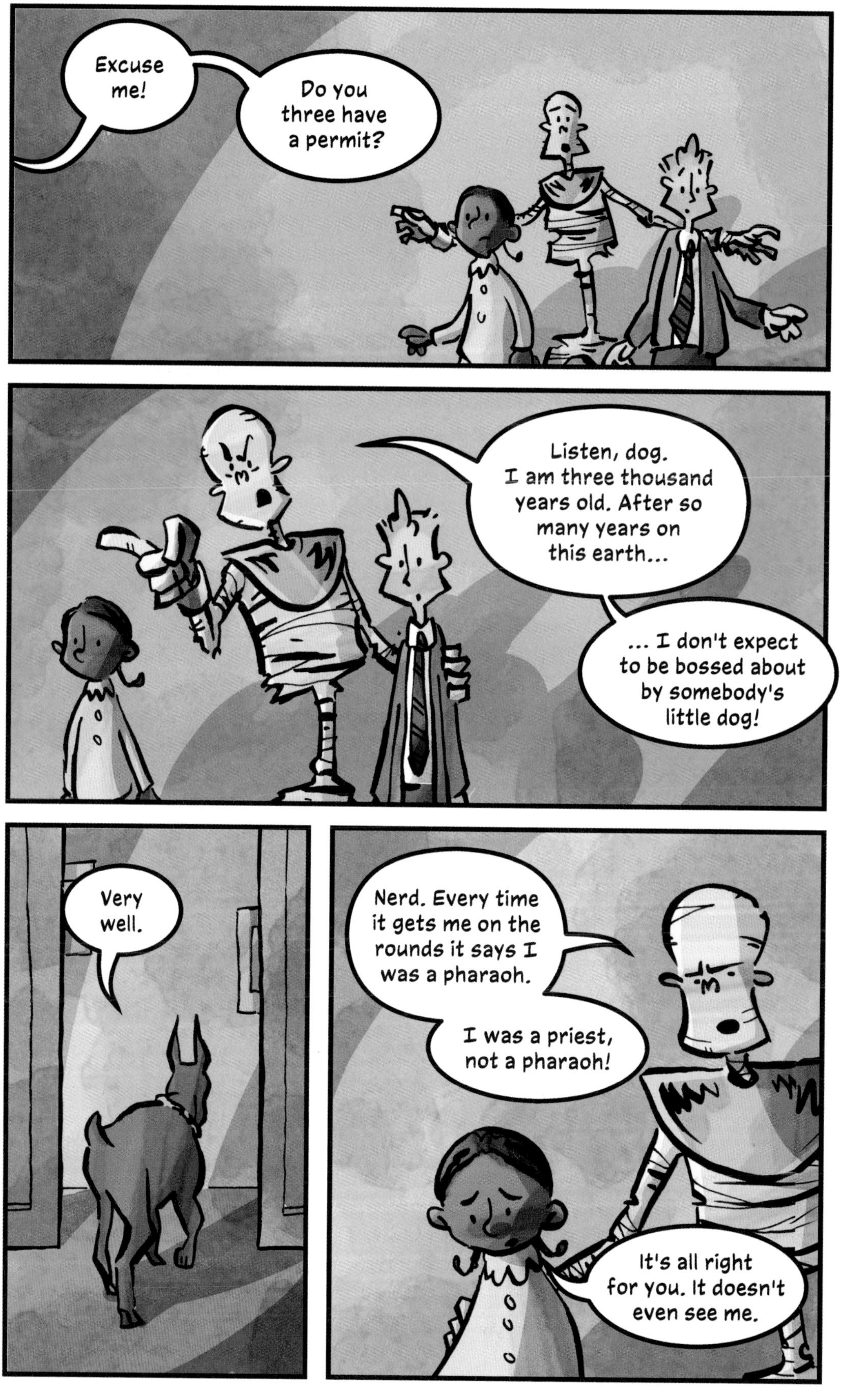
Excuse me!
Do you three have a permit?
Listen, dog. I am three thousand years old. After so many years on this earth...
... I don't expect to be bossed about by somebody's little dog!
Very well.
Nerd. Every time it gets me on the rounds it says I was a pharaoh.
I was a priest, not a pharaoh!
It's all right for you. It doesn't even see me.

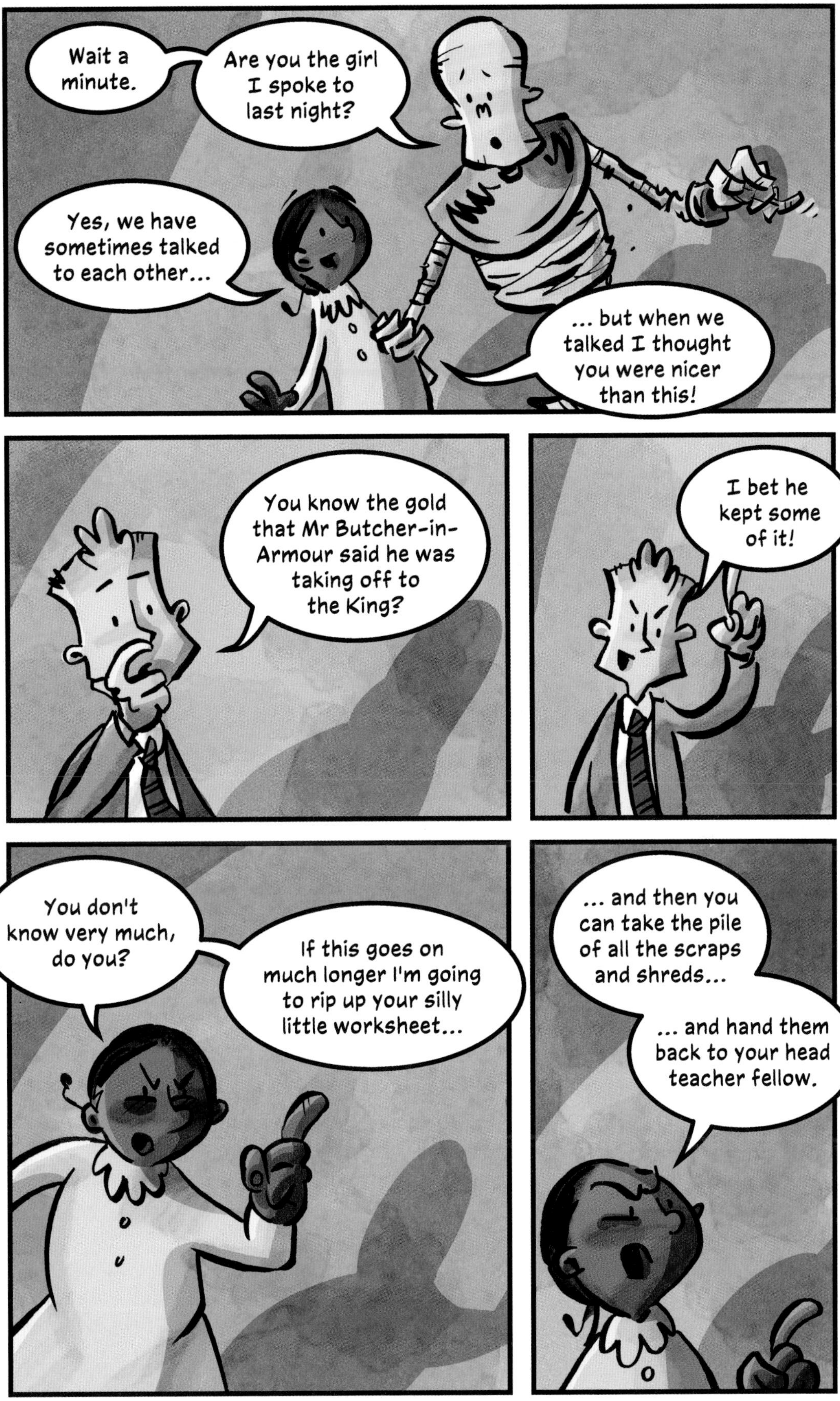
Wait a minute.
Are you the girl I spoke to last night?
Yes, we have sometimes talked to each other...
... but when we talked I thought you were nicer than this!
You know the gold that Mr Butcher-in-Armour said he was taking off to the King?
I bet he kept some of it!
You don't know very much, do you?
If this goes on much longer I'm going to rip up your silly little worksheet...
... and then you can take the pile of all the scraps and shreds...
... and hand them back to your head teacher fellow.

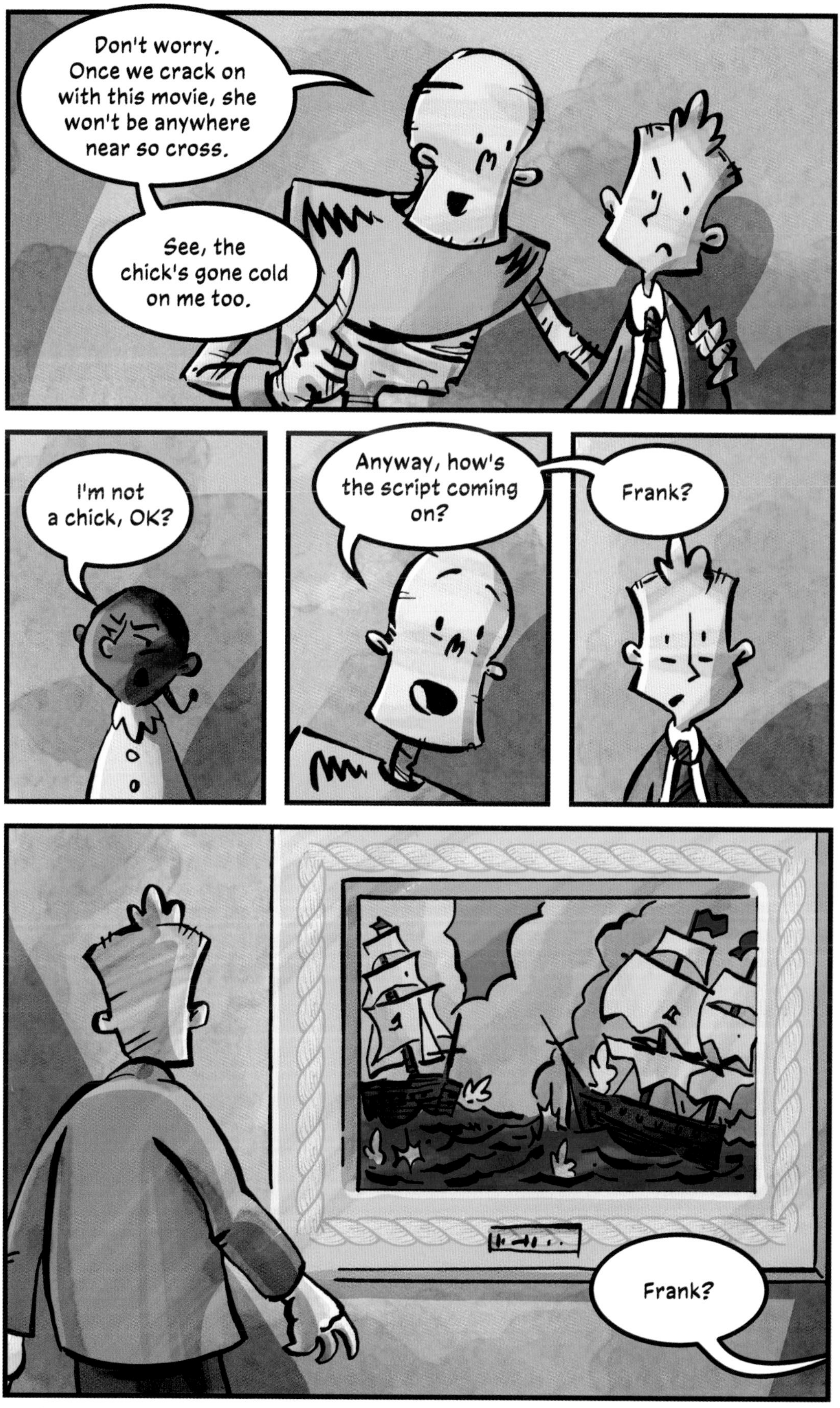
Don't worry. Once we crack on with this movie, she won't be anywhere near so cross.
See, the chick's gone cold on me too.
I'm not a chick, OK?
Anyway, how's the script coming on?
Frank?
Frank?

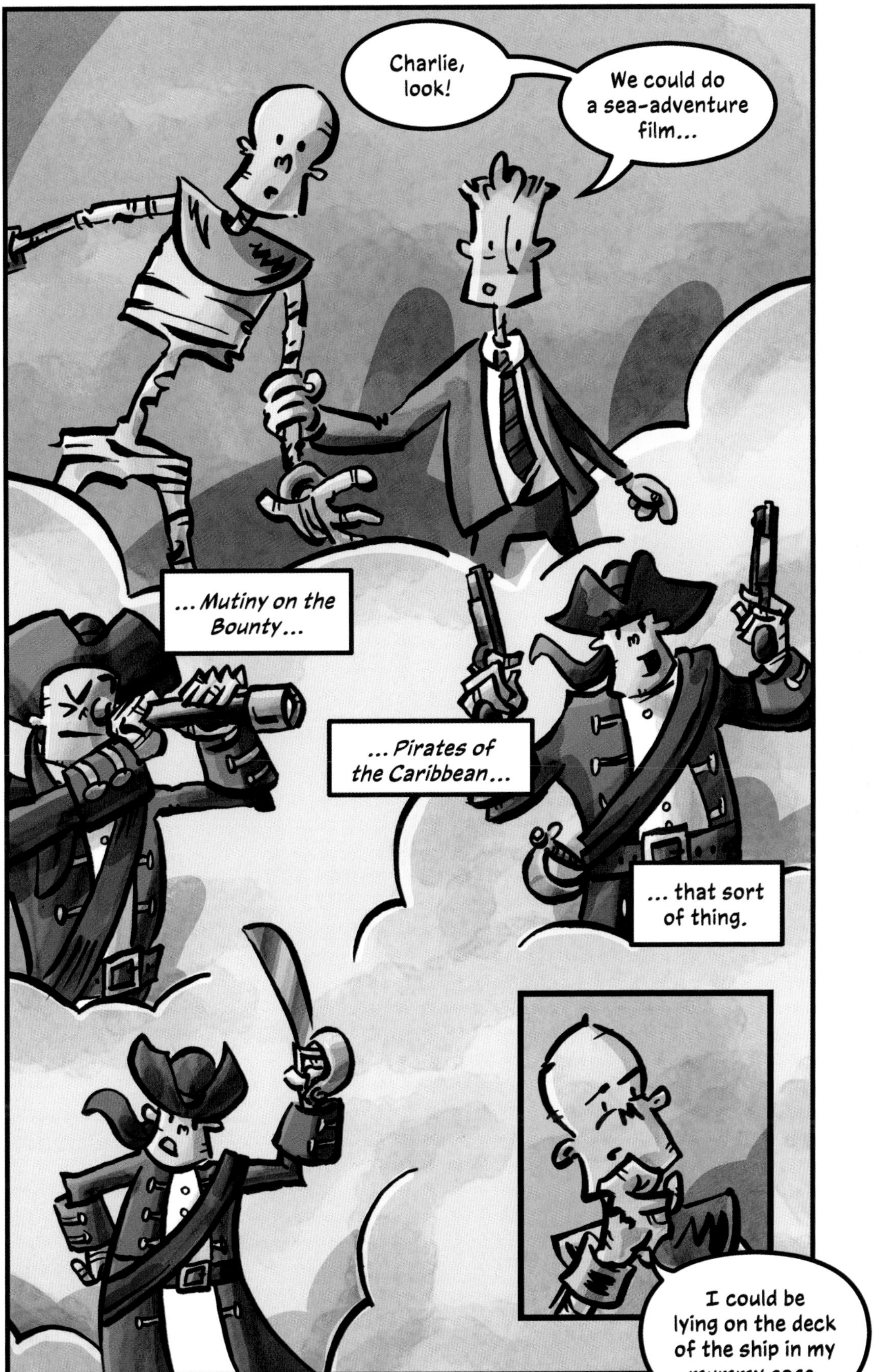

Charlie, look!
We could do a sea-adventure film...
... Mutiny on the Bounty...
... Pirates of the Caribbean...
... that sort of thing.
I could be lying on the deck of the ship in my mummy case.

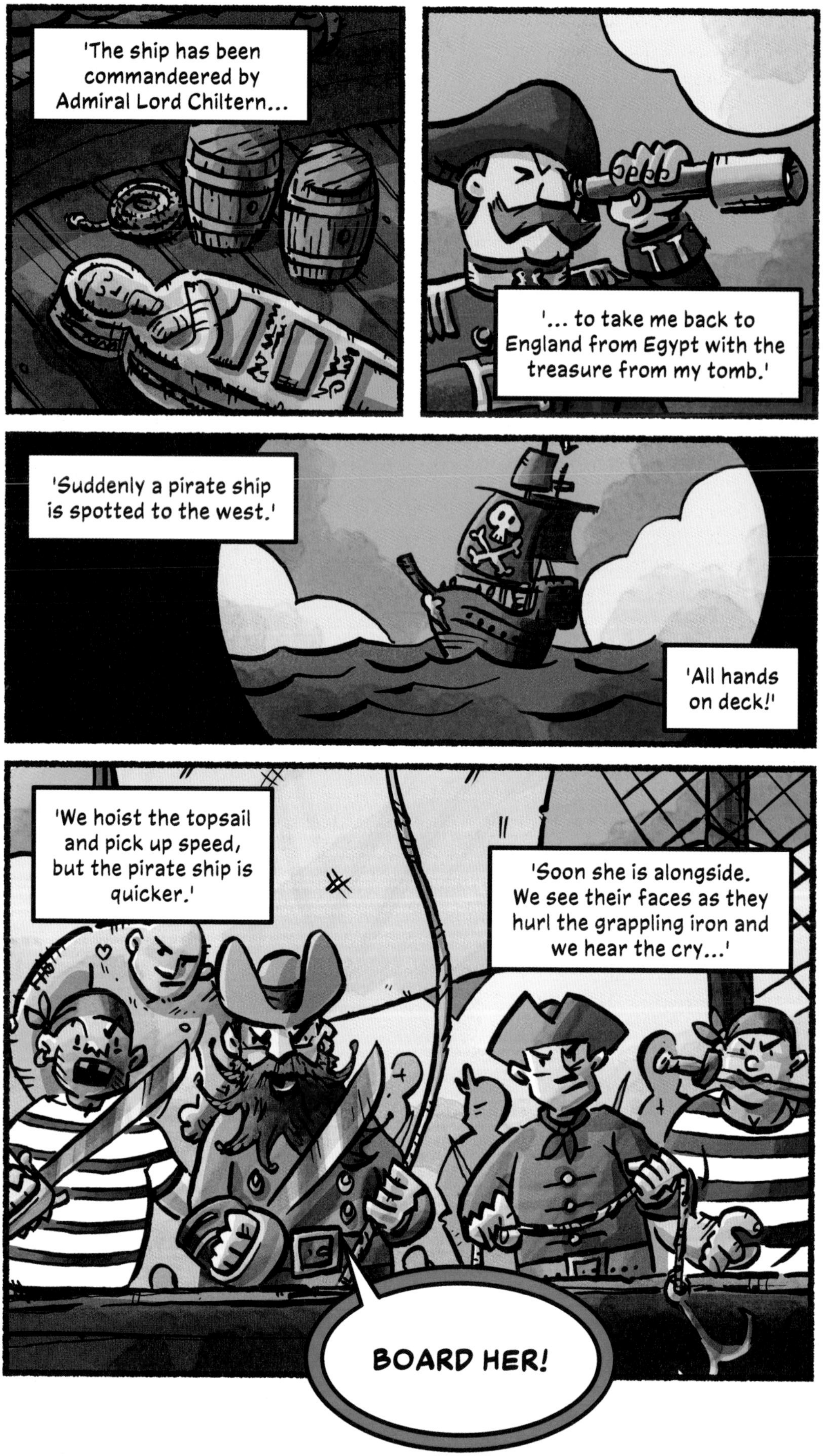
'The ship has been commandeered by Admiral Lord Chiltern...
'... to take me back to England from Egypt with the treasure from my tomb.'
'Suddenly a pirate ship is spotted to the west.'
'All hands on deck!'
'We hoist the topsail and pick up speed, but the pirate ship is quicker.'
'Soon she is alongside. We see their faces as they hurl the grappling iron and we hear the cry...'
BOARD HER!

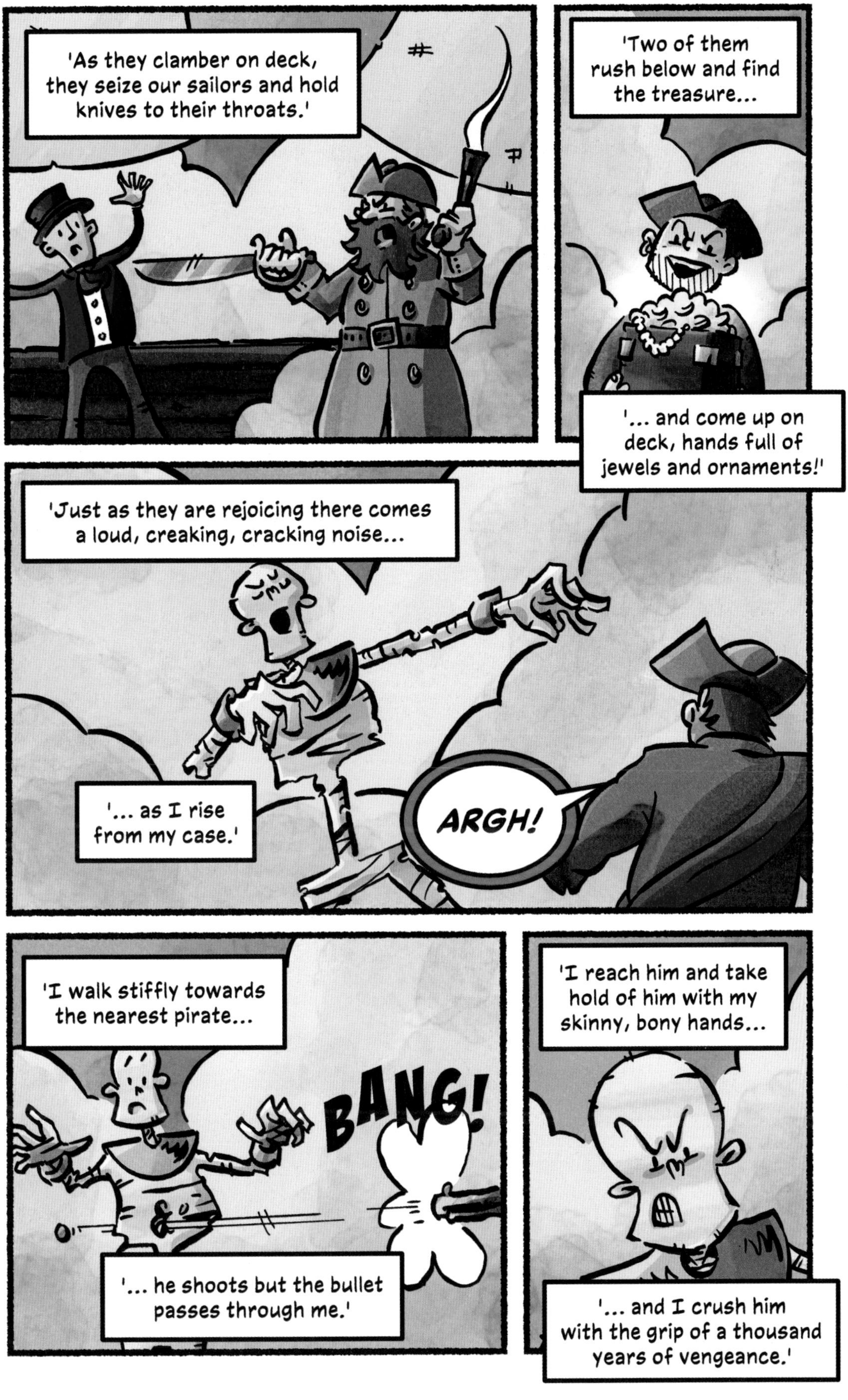
'As they clamber on deck, they seize our sailors and hold knives to their throats.'
'Two of them rush below and find the treasure...
'... and come up on deck, hands full of jewels and ornaments!'
'Just as they are rejoicing there comes a loud, creaking, cracking noise...
'... as I rise from my case.'
ARGH!
'I walk stiffly towards the nearest pirate...
BANG!
'... he shoots but the bullet passes through me.'
'I reach him and take hold of him with my skinny, bony hands...
'... and I crush him with the grip of a thousand years of vengeance.'

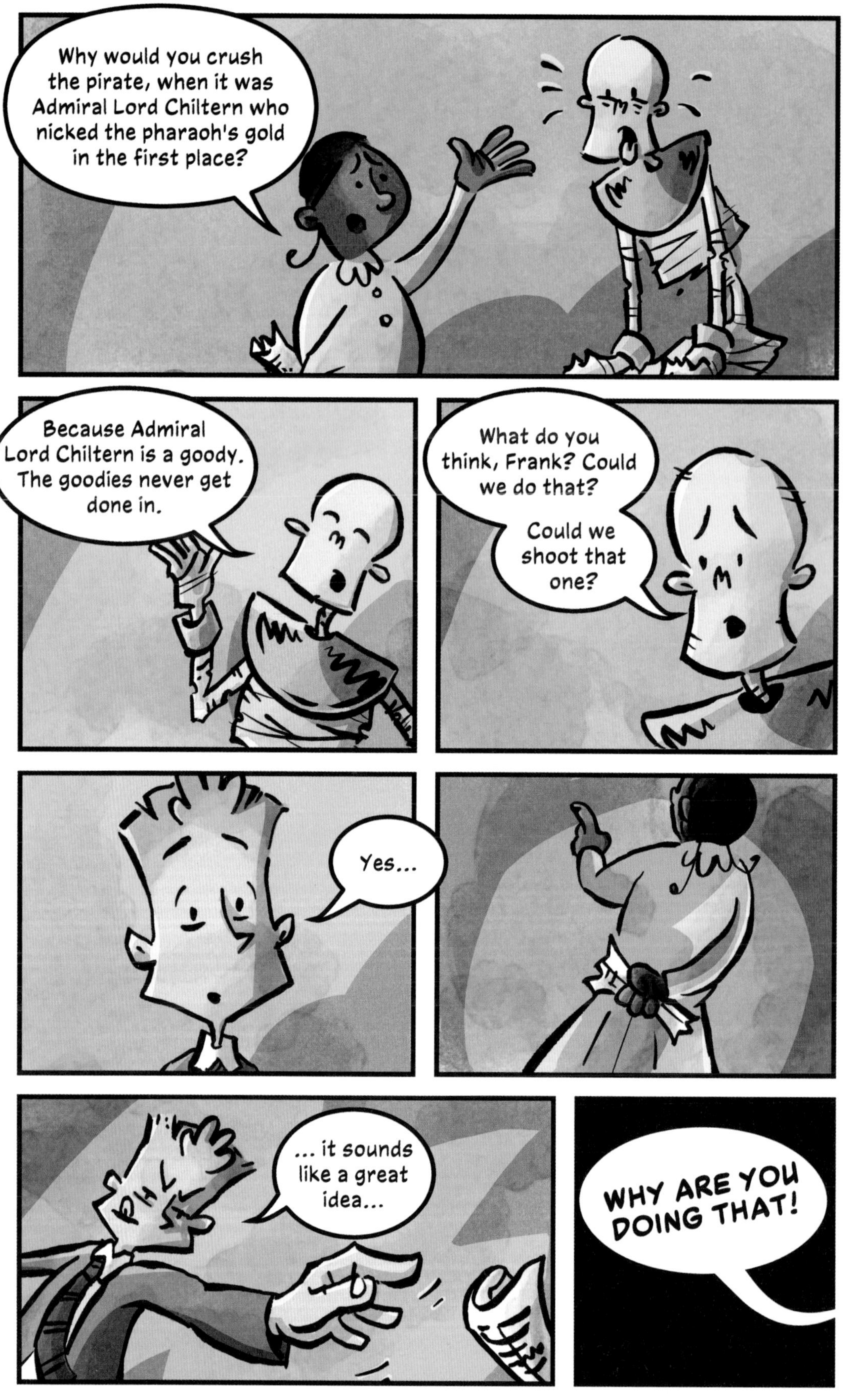
Why would you crush the pirate, when it was Admiral Lord Chiltern who nicked the pharaoh's gold in the first place?
Because Admiral Lord Chiltern is a goody. The goodies never get done in.
What do you think, Frank? Could we do that?
Could we shoot that one?
Yes...
... it sounds like a great idea...
WHY ARE YOU DOING THAT!

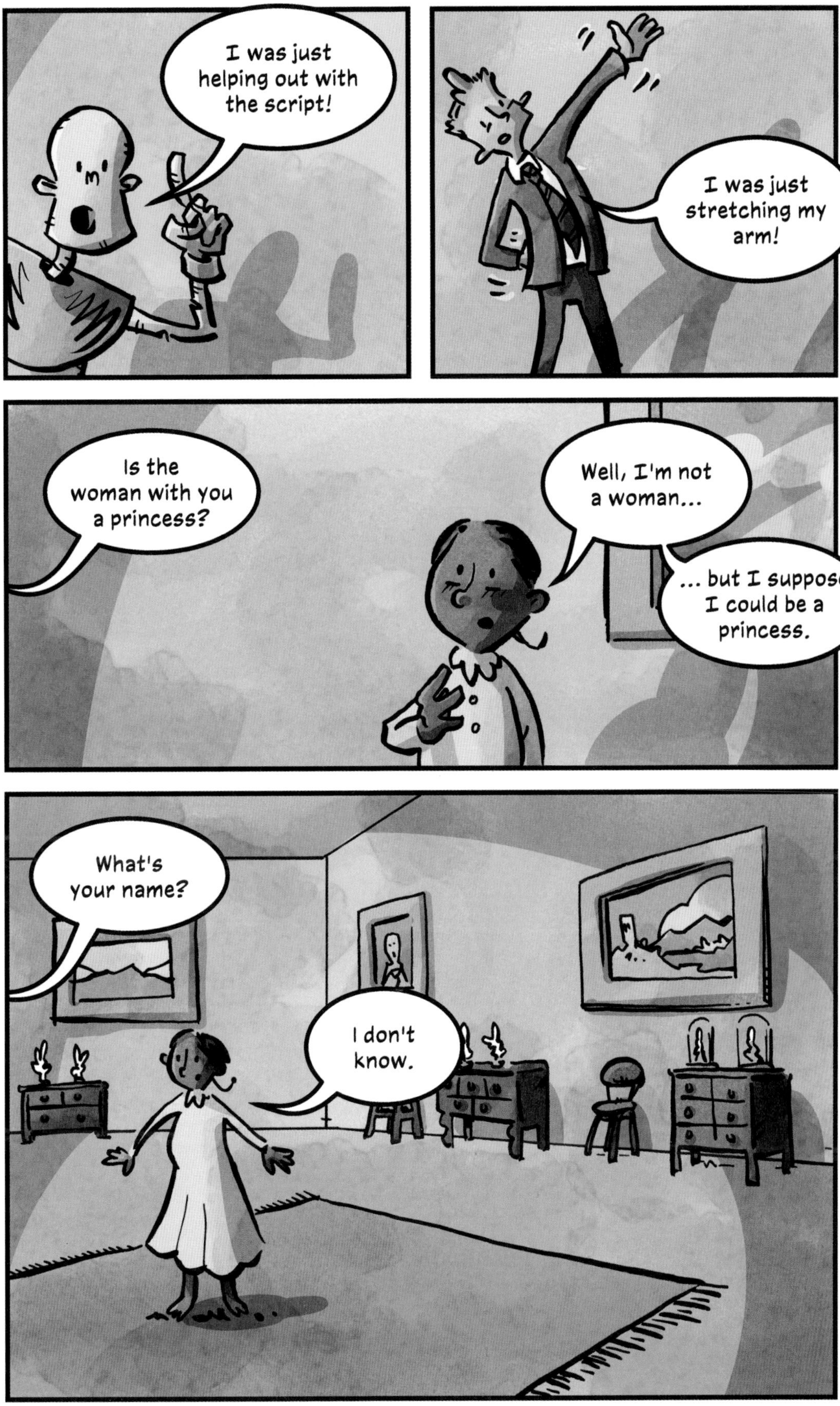
I was just helping out with the script!
I was just stretching my arm!
Is the woman with you a princess?
Well, I'm not a woman...
... but I suppose I could be a princess.
What's your name?
I don't know.

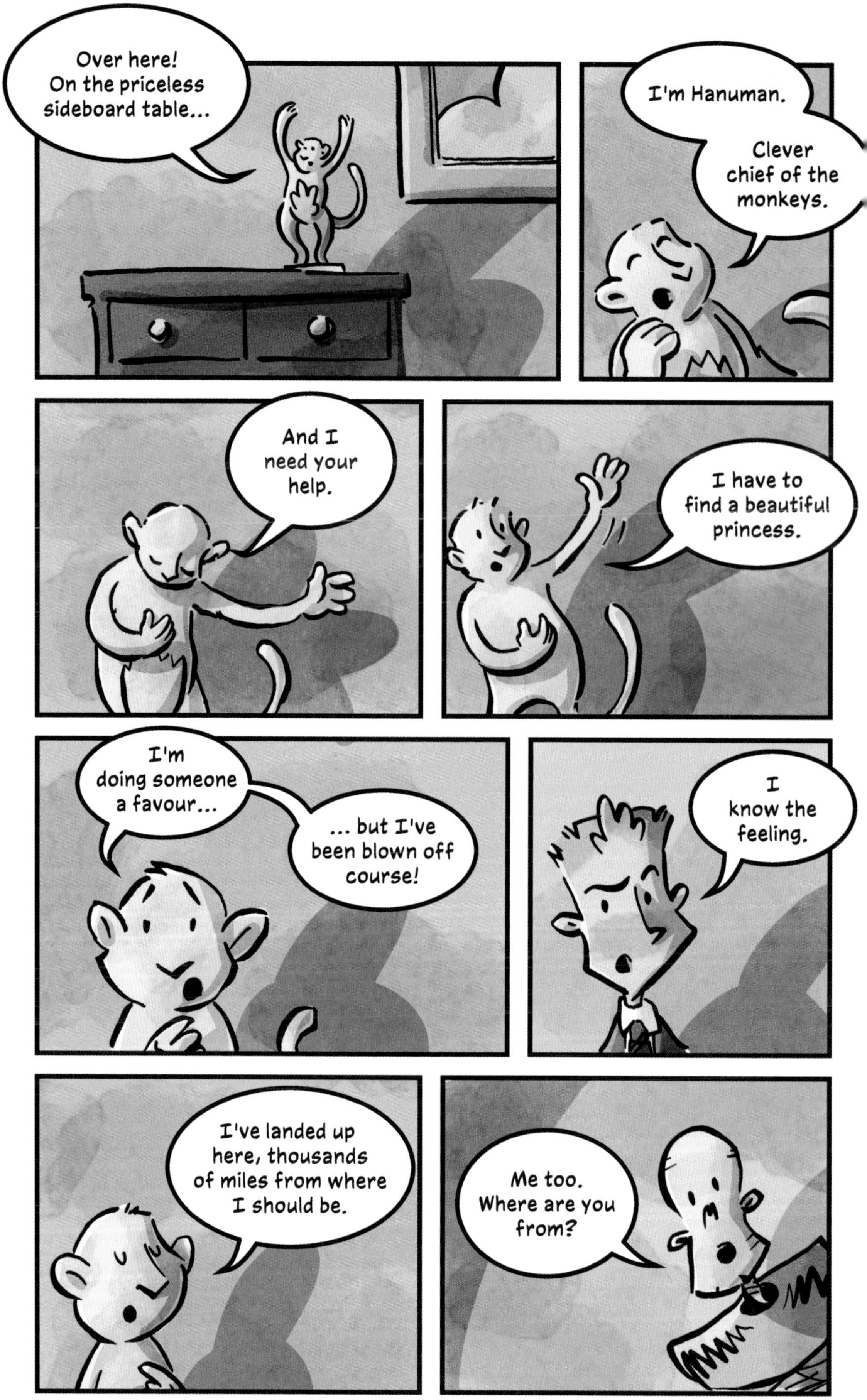
Over here! On the priceless sideboard table...
I'm Hanuman.
Clever chief of the monkeys.
And I need your help.
I have to find a beautiful princess.
I'm doing someone a favour...
... but I've been blown off course!
I know the feeling.
I've landed up here, thousands of miles from where I should be.
Me too. Where are you from?

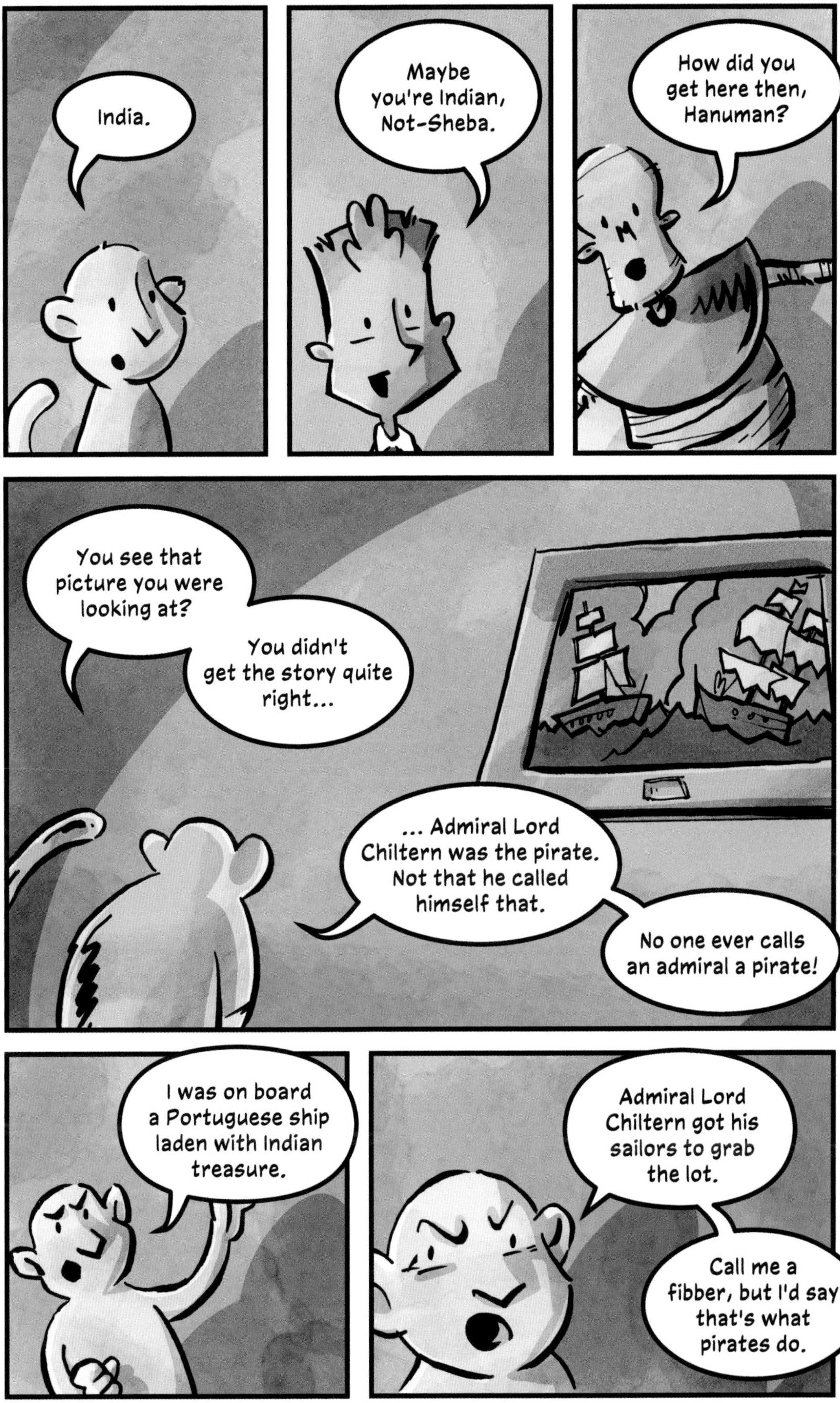
India.
Maybe you're Indian, Not-Sheba.
How did you get here then, Hanuman?
You see that picture you were looking at?
You didn't get the story quite right...
... Admiral Lord Chiltern was the pirate. Not that he called himself that.
No one ever calls an admiral a pirate!
I was on board a Portuguese ship laden with Indian treasure.
Admiral Lord Chiltern got his sailors to grab the lot.
Call me a fibber, but I'd say that's what pirates do.

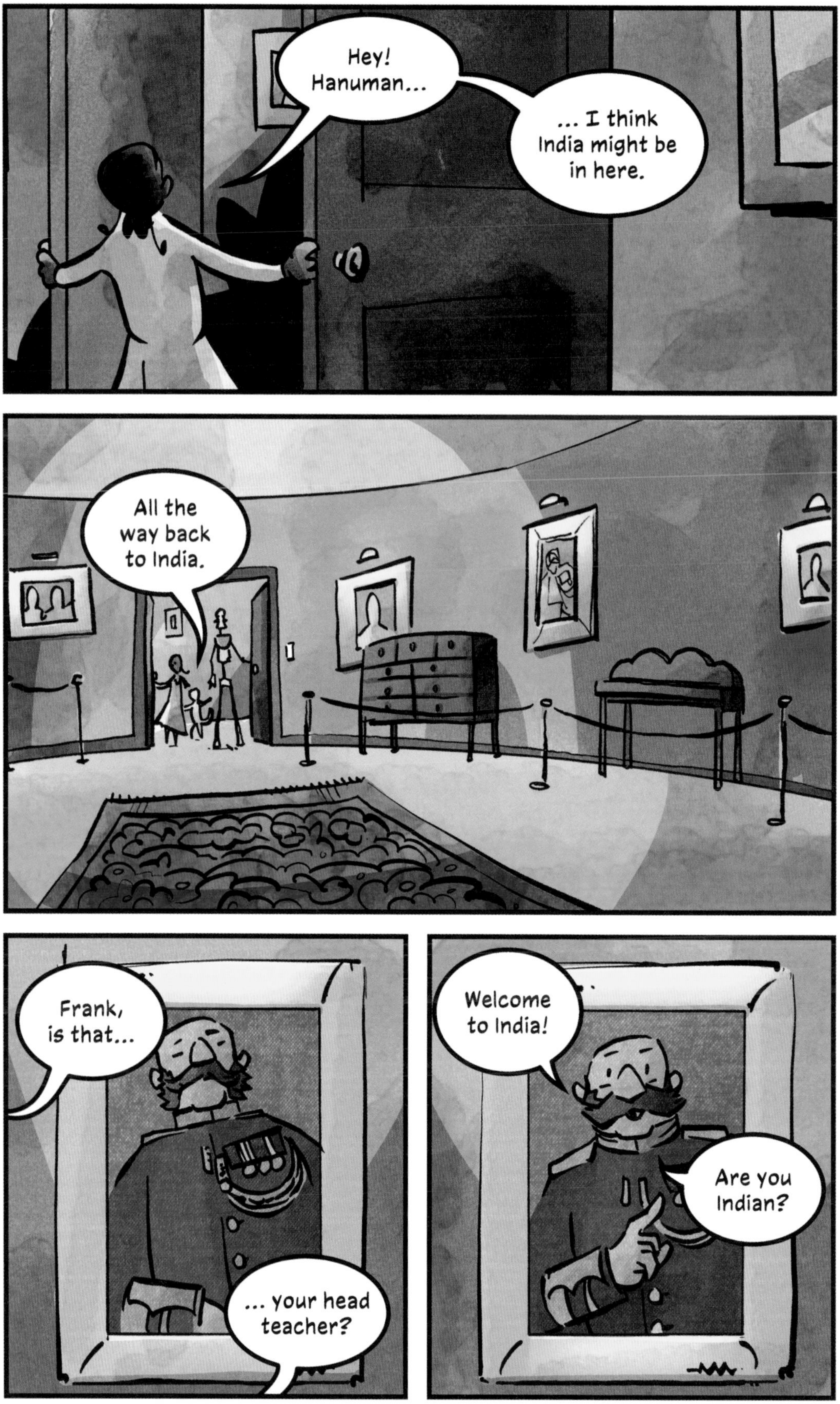
Hey! Hanuman...
... I think India might be in here.
All the way back to India.
Frank, is that...
... your head teacher?
Welcome to India!
Are you Indian?

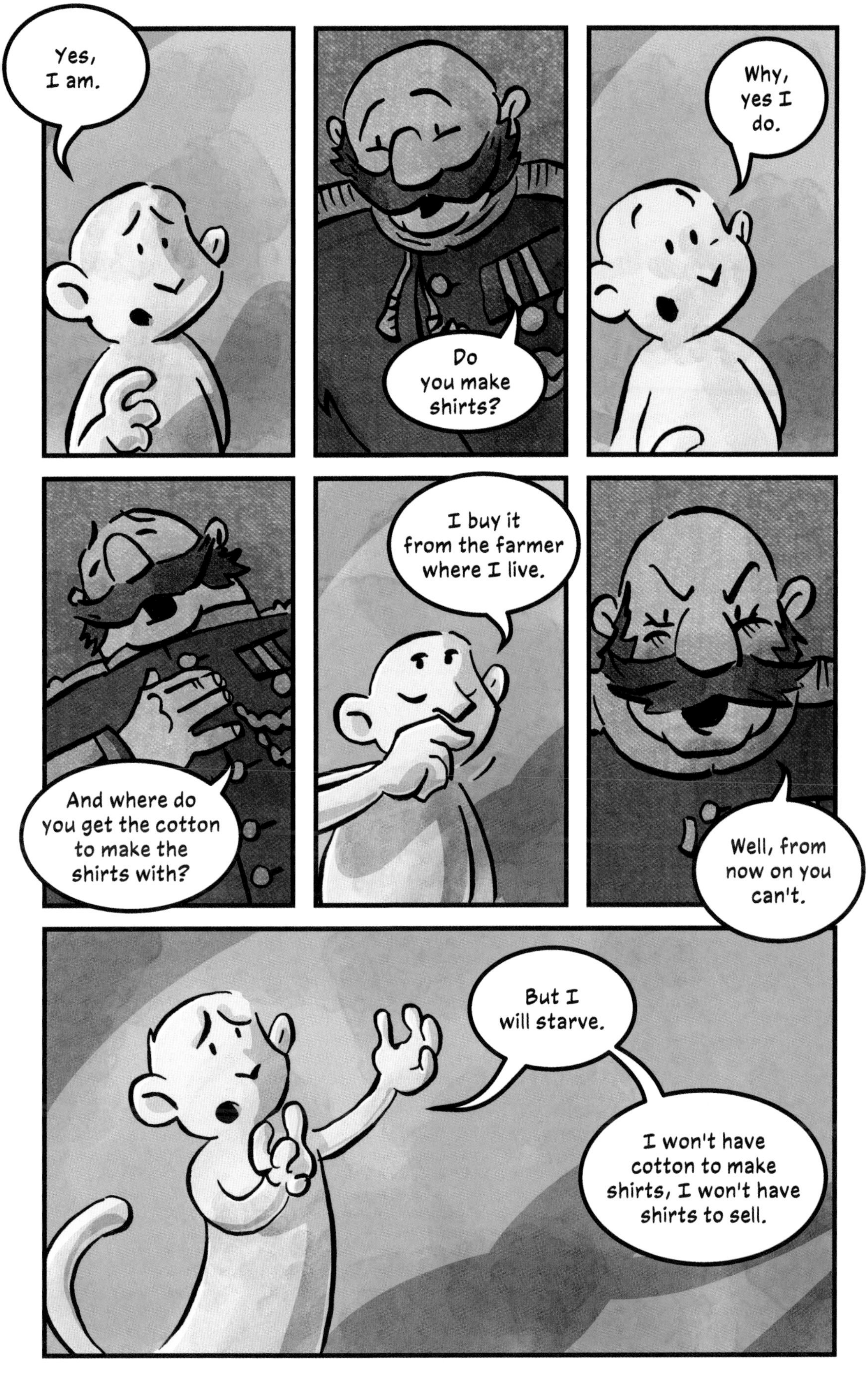
Yes, I am.
Do you make shirts?
Why, yes I do.
And where do you get the cotton to make the shirts with?
I buy it from the farmer where I live.
Well, from now on you can't.
But I will starve.
I won't have cotton to make shirts, I won't have shirts to sell.

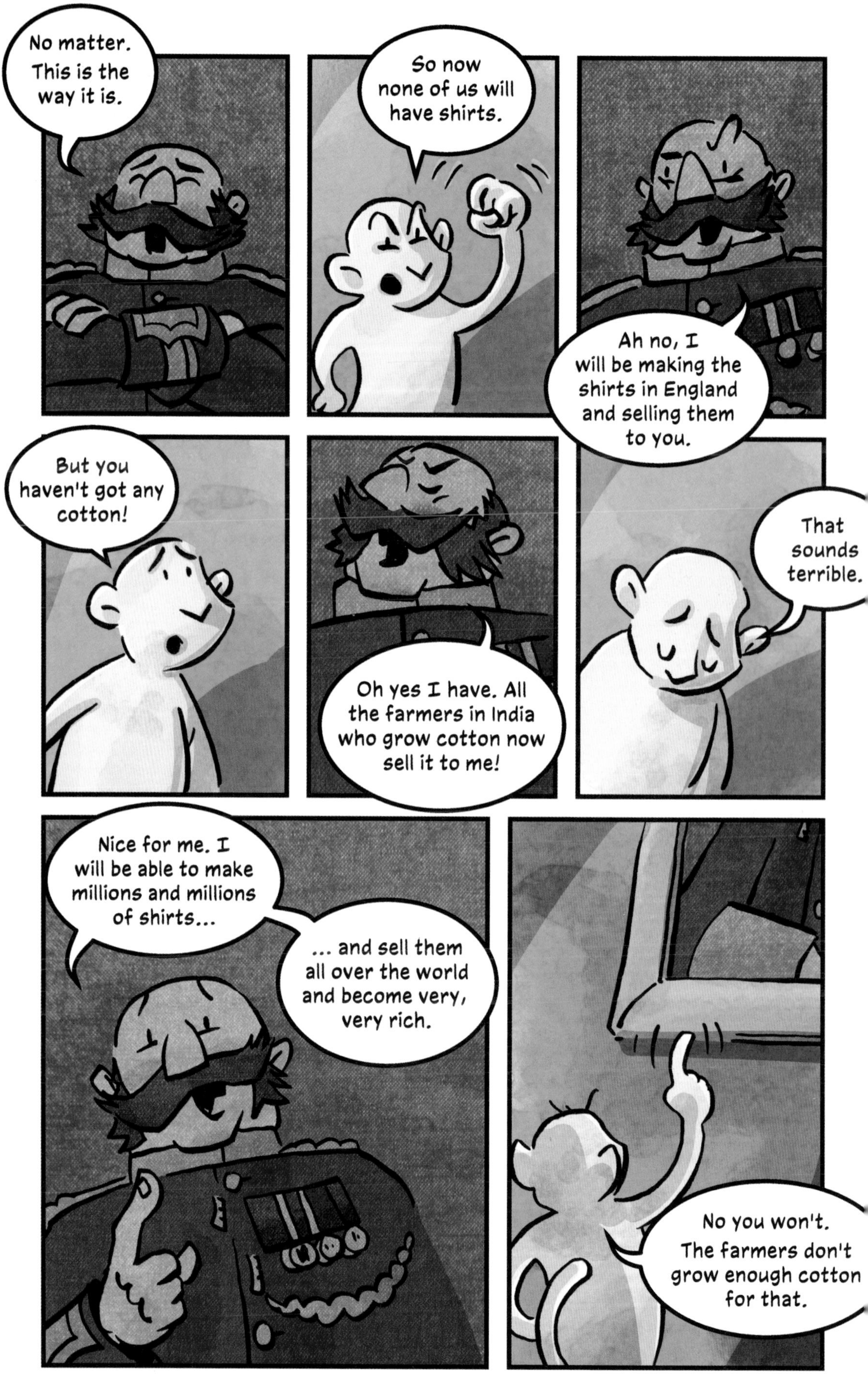
No matter. This is the way it is.
So now none of us will have shirts.
Ah no, I will be making the shirts in England and selling them to you.
But you haven't got any cotton!
Oh yes I have. All the farmers in India who grow cotton now sell it to me!
That sounds terrible.
Nice for me. I will be able to make millions and millions of shirts...
... and sell them all over the world and become very, very rich.
No you won't. The farmers don't grow enough cotton for that.

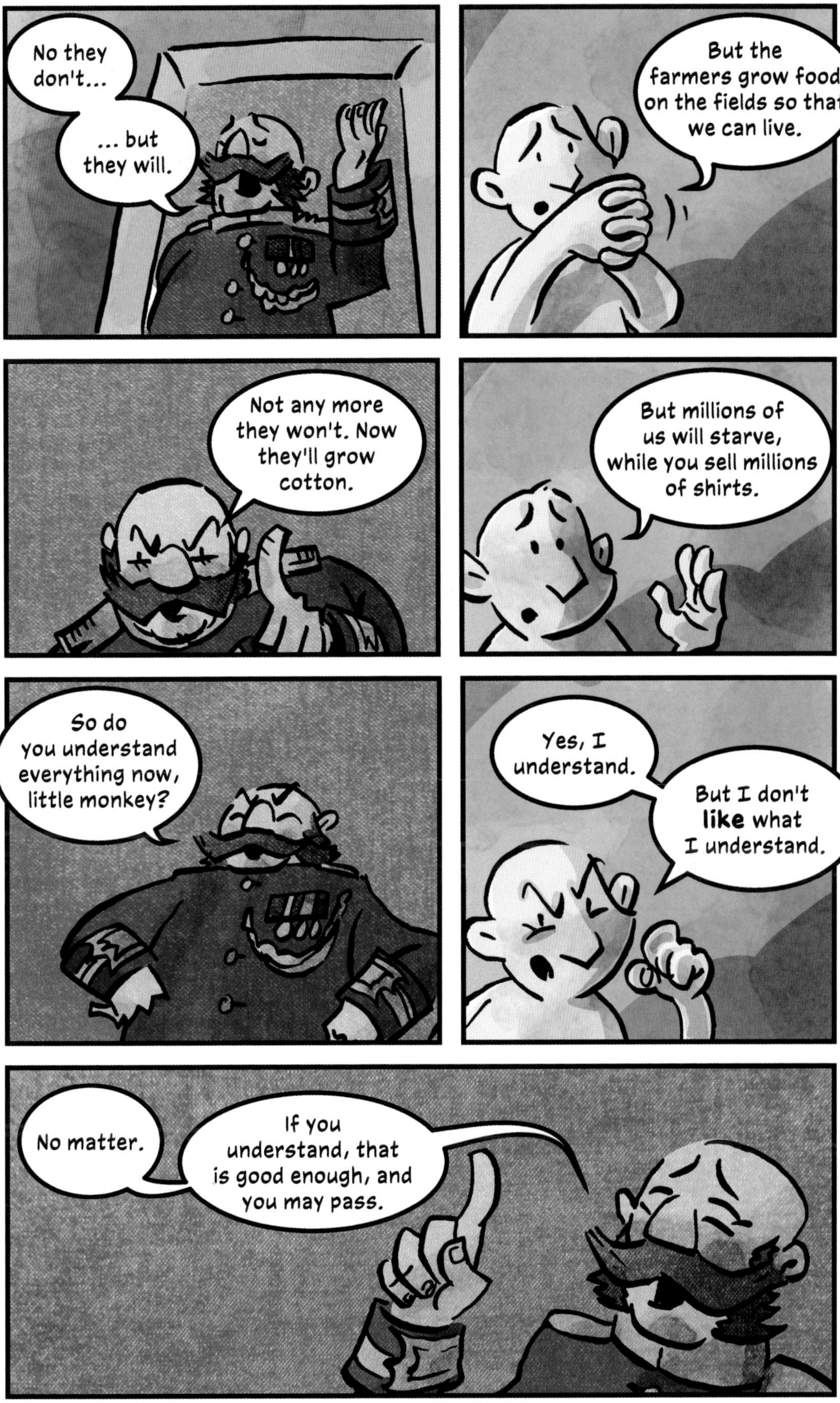
No they don't...
... but they will.
But the farmers grow food on the fields so that we can live.
Not any more they won't. Now they'll grow cotton.
But millions of us will starve, while you sell millions of shirts.
So do you understand everything now, little monkey?
Yes, I understand.
But I don't **like** what I understand.
No matter.
If you understand, that is good enough, and you may pass.

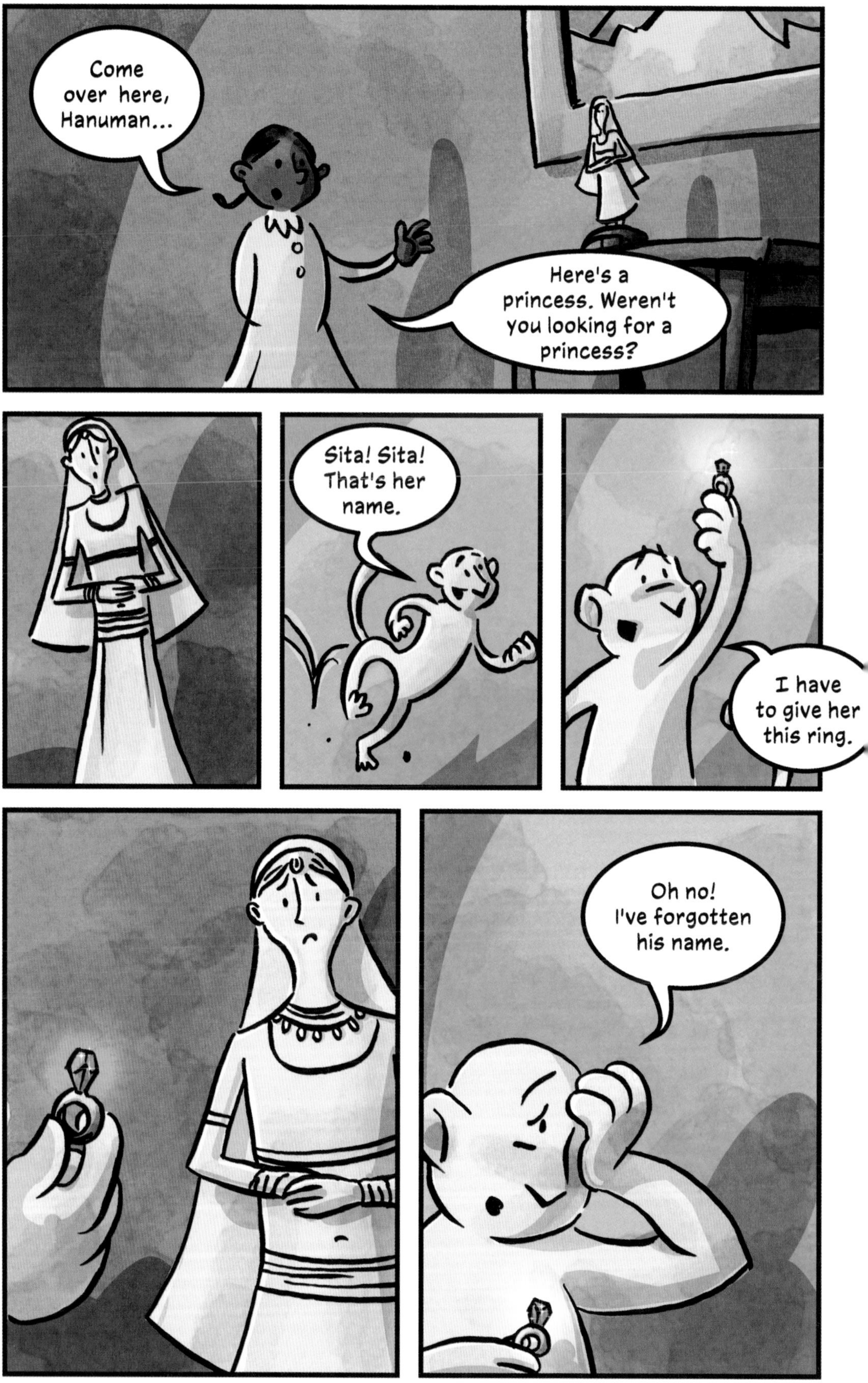
Come over here, Hanuman...
Here's a princess. Weren't you looking for a princess?
Sita! Sita! That's her name.
I have to give her this ring.
Oh no! I've forgotten his name.

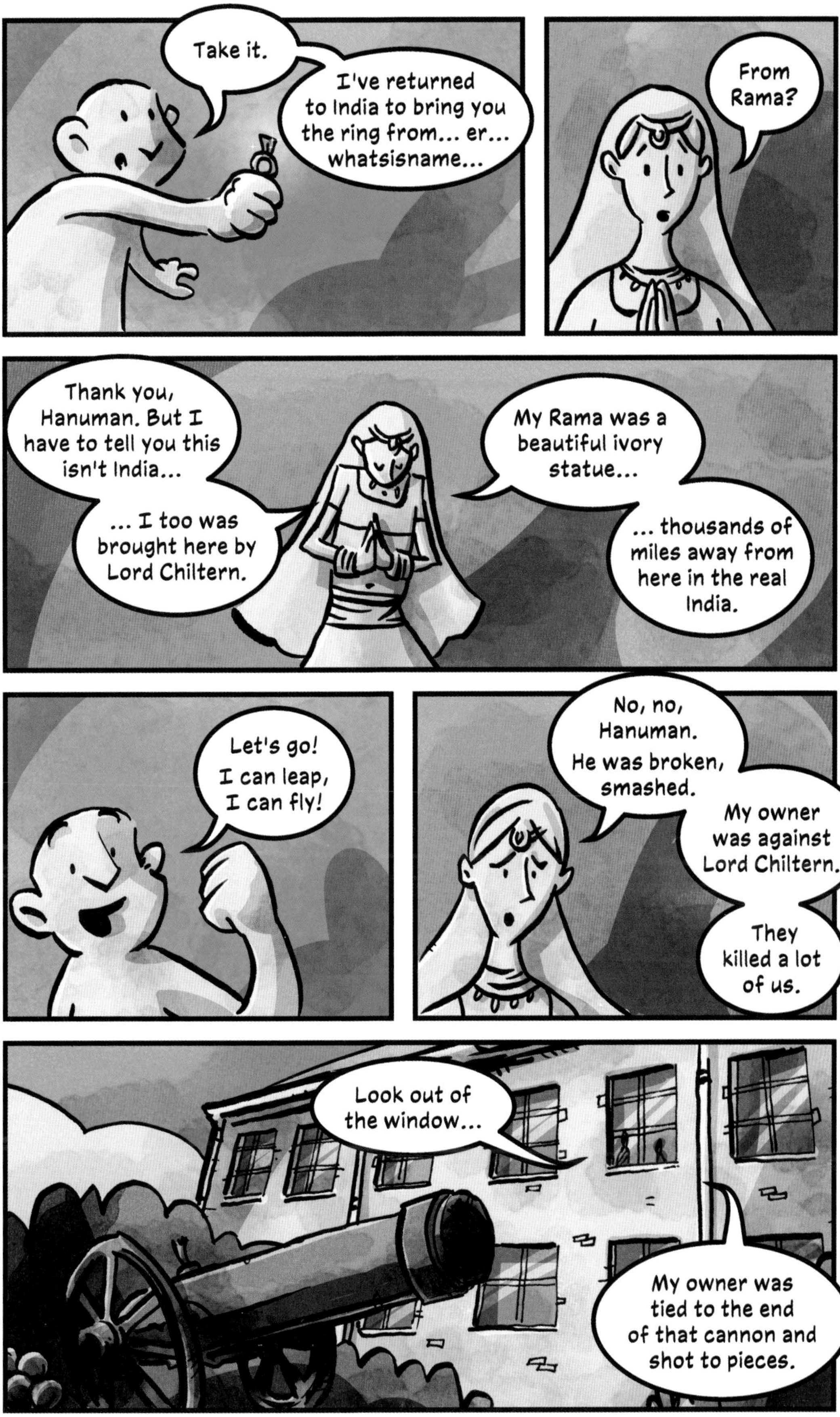
Take it.
I've returned to India to bring you the ring from... er... whatsisname...
From Rama?
Thank you, Hanuman. But I have to tell you this isn't India...
... I too was brought here by Lord Chiltern.
My Rama was a beautiful ivory statue...
... thousands of miles away from here in the real India.
Let's go! I can leap, I can fly!
No, no, Hanuman.
He was broken, smashed.
My owner was against Lord Chiltern.
They killed a lot of us.
Look out of the window...
My owner was tied to the end of that cannon and shot to pieces.

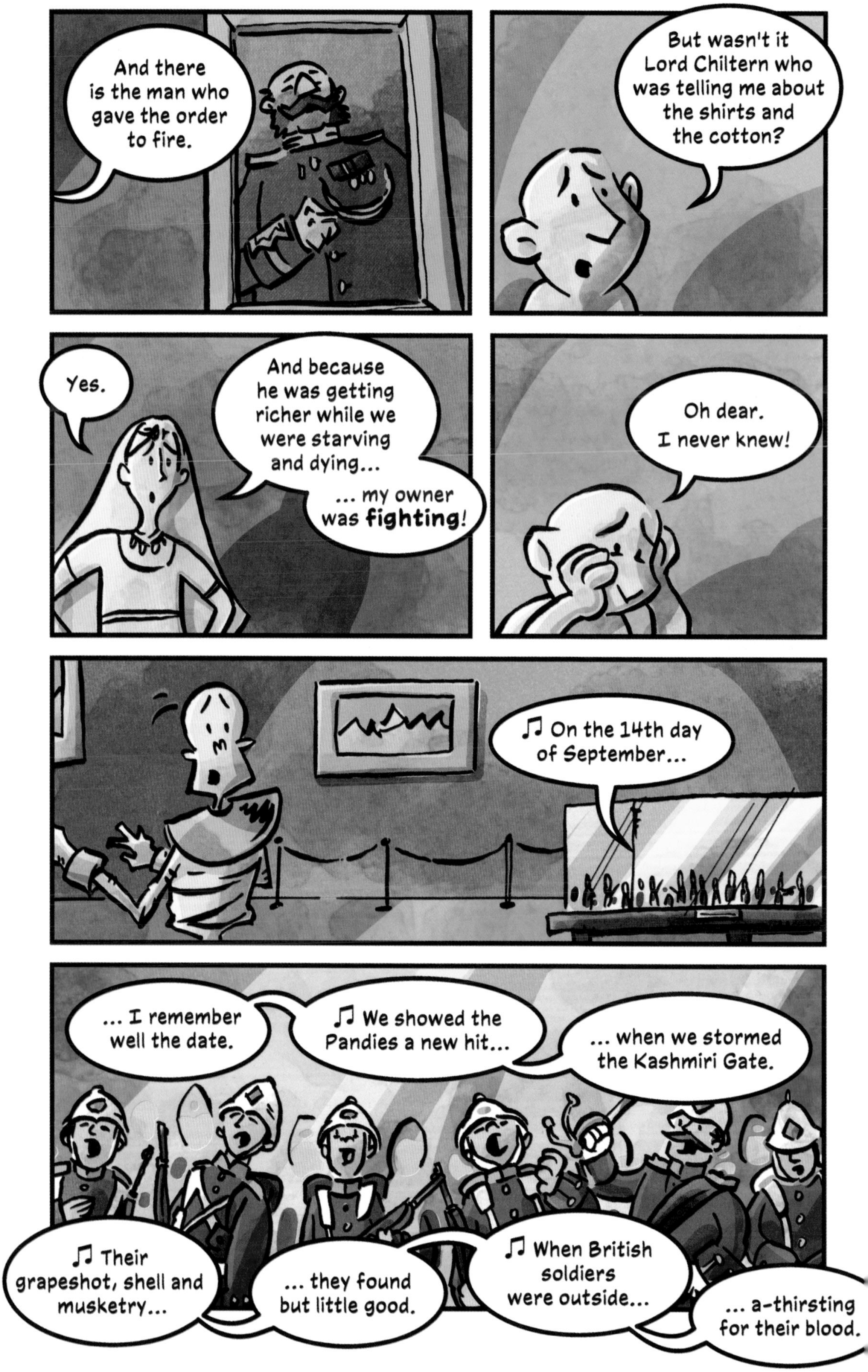
And there is the man who gave the order to fire.
But wasn't it Lord Chiltern who was telling me about the shirts and the cotton?
Yes.
And because he was getting richer while we were starving and dying...
... my owner was **fighting**!
Oh dear. I never knew!
♫ On the 14th day of September...
... I remember well the date.
♫ We showed the Pandies a new hit...
... when we stormed the Kashmiri Gate.
♫ Their grapeshot, shell and musketry...
... they found but little good.
♫ When British soldiers were outside...
... a-thirsting for their blood.

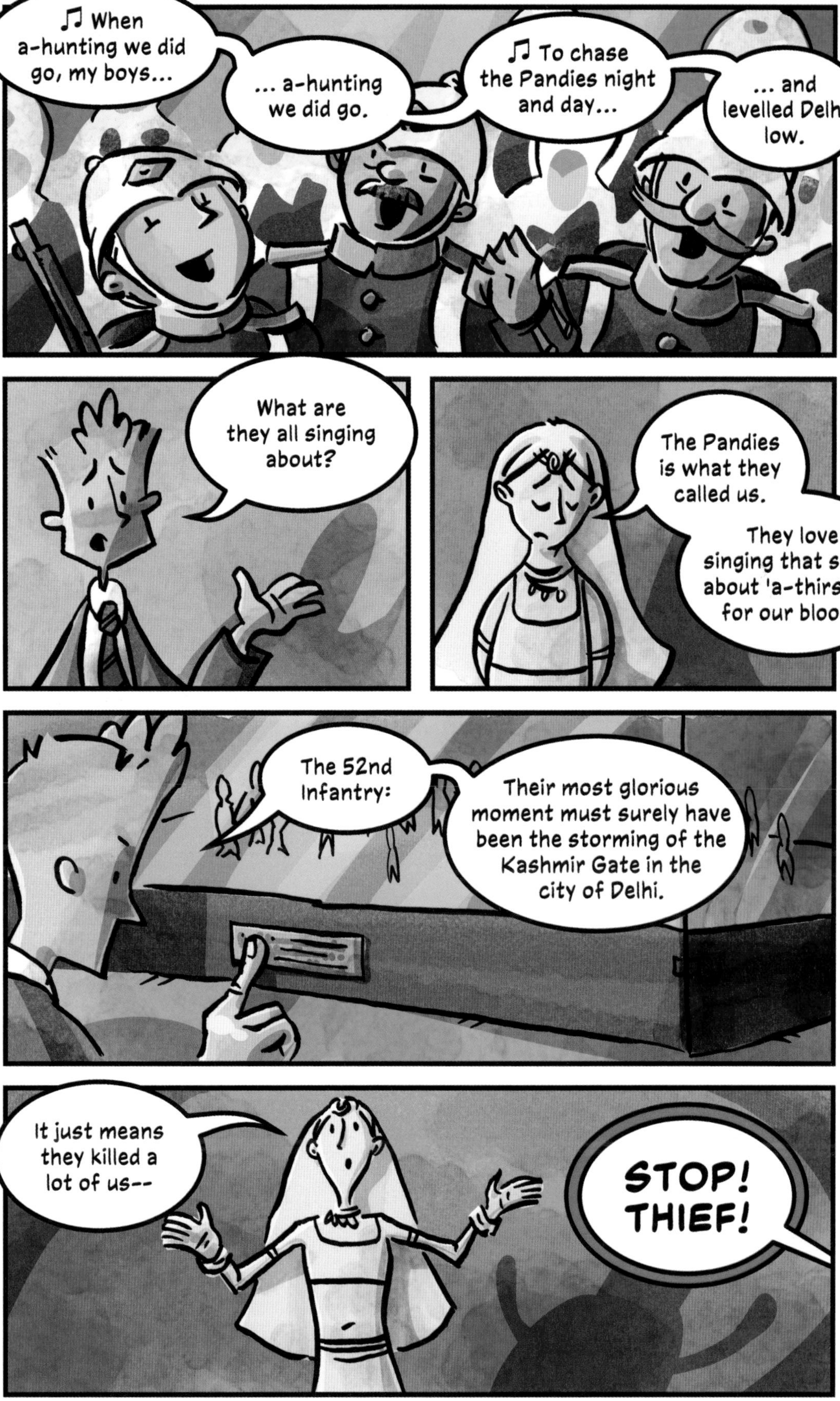
♫ When a-hunting we did go, my boys...
... a-hunting we did go.
♫ To chase the Pandies night and day...
... and levelled Delhi low.
What are they all singing about?
The Pandies is what they called us.
They love singing that stuff about 'a-thirsting for our blood'.
The 52nd Infantry:
Their most glorious moment must surely have been the storming of the Kashmir Gate in the city of Delhi.
It just means they killed a lot of us--
STOP! THIEF!

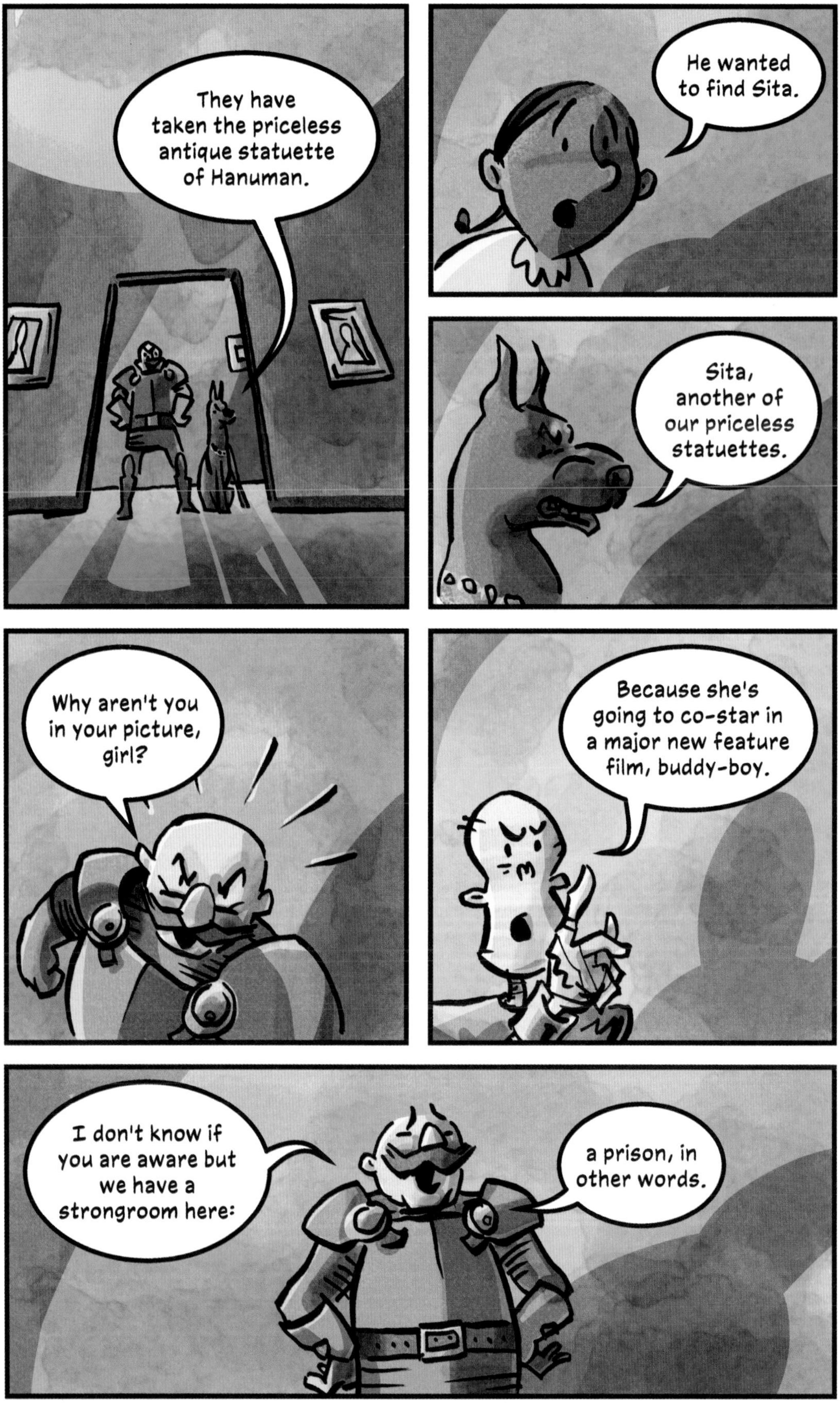
They have taken the priceless antique statuette of Hanuman.
He wanted to find Sita.
Sita, another of our priceless statuettes.
Why aren't you in your picture, girl?
Because she's going to co-star in a major new feature film, buddy-boy.
I don't know if you are aware but we have a strongroom here:
a prison, in other words.

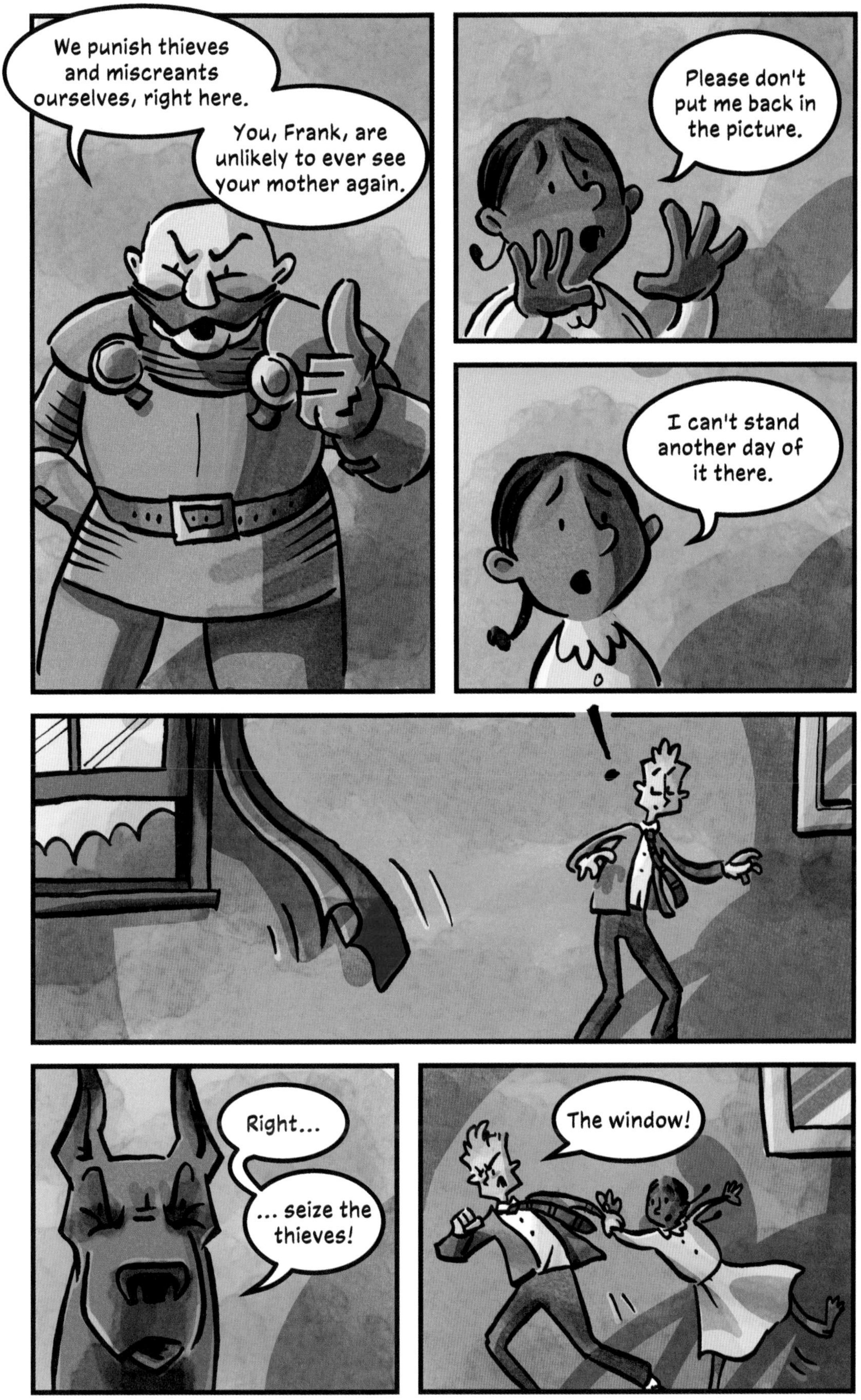

We punish thieves and miscreants ourselves, right here.
You, Frank, are unlikely to ever see your mother again.
Please don't put me back in the picture.
I can't stand another day of it there.
!
Right...
... seize the thieves!
The window!

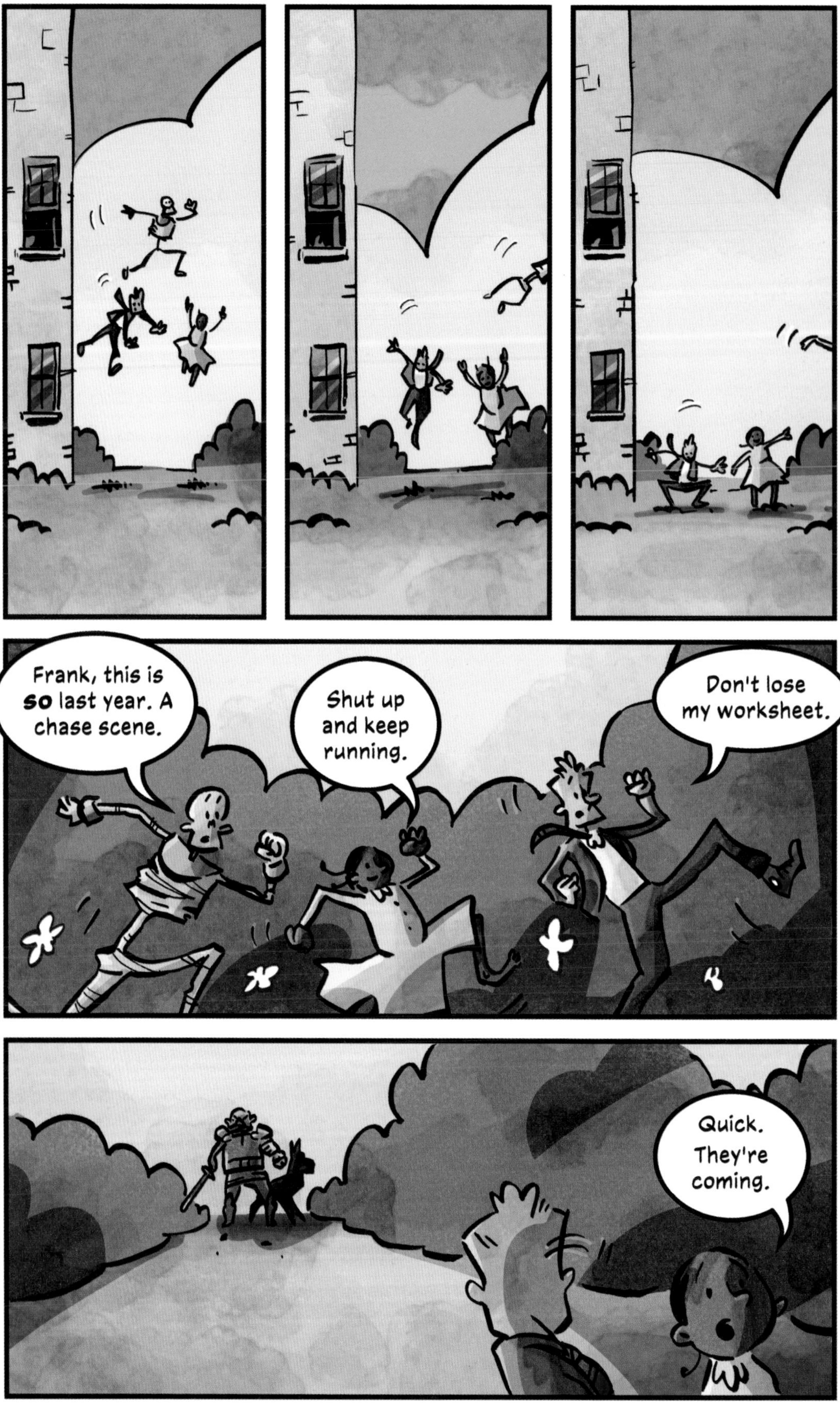
Frank, this is **so** last year. A chase scene.
Shut up and keep running.
Don't lose my worksheet.
Quick. They're coming.

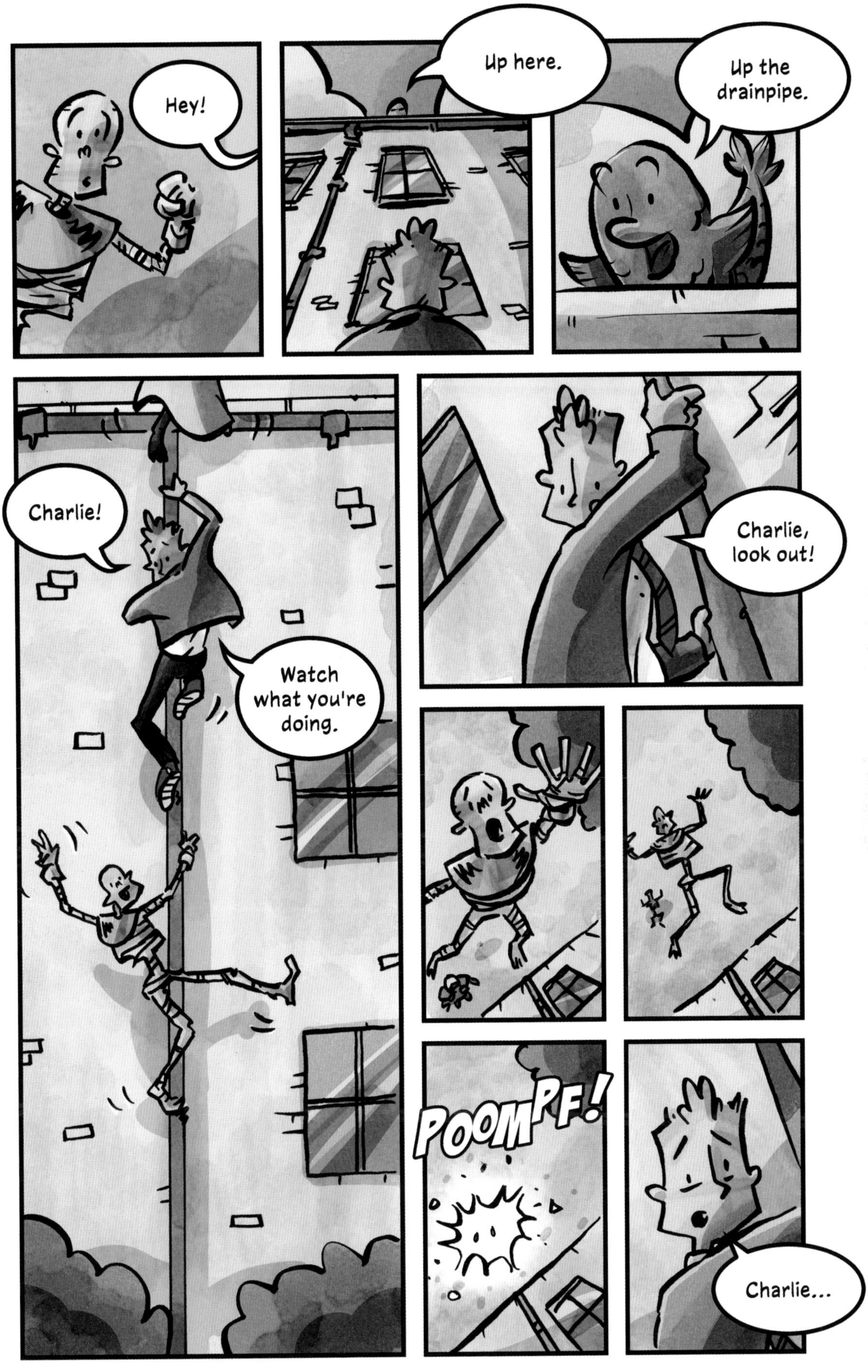
Hey!
Up here.
Up the drainpipe.
Charlie!
Watch what you're doing.
Charlie, look out!
POOMPF!
Charlie...

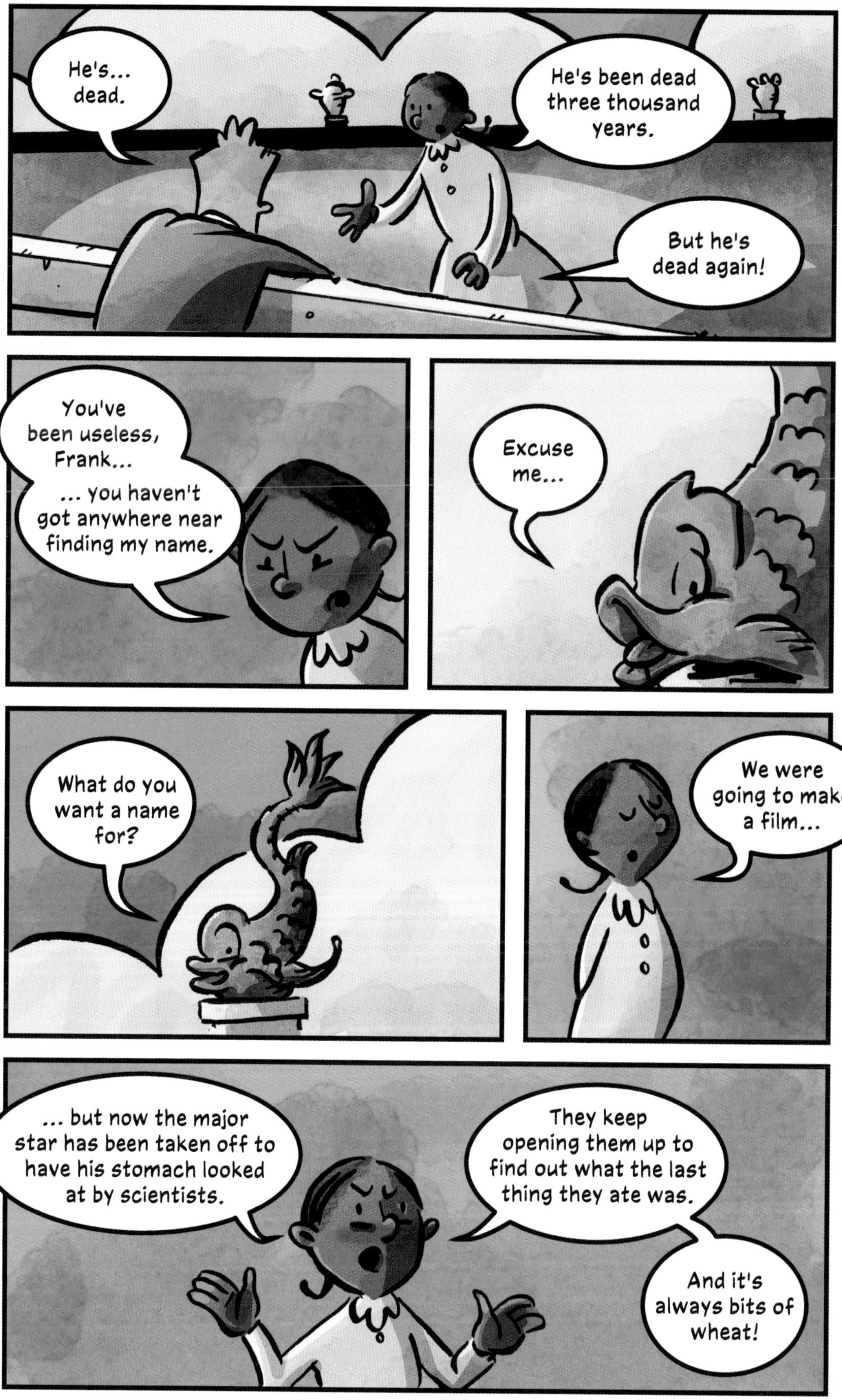
He's... dead.
He's been dead three thousand years.
But he's dead again!
You've been useless, Frank...
... you haven't got anywhere near finding my name.
Excuse me...
What do you want a name for?
We were going to make a film...
... but now the major star has been taken off to have his stomach looked at by scientists.
They keep opening them up to find out what the last thing they ate was.
And it's always bits of wheat!

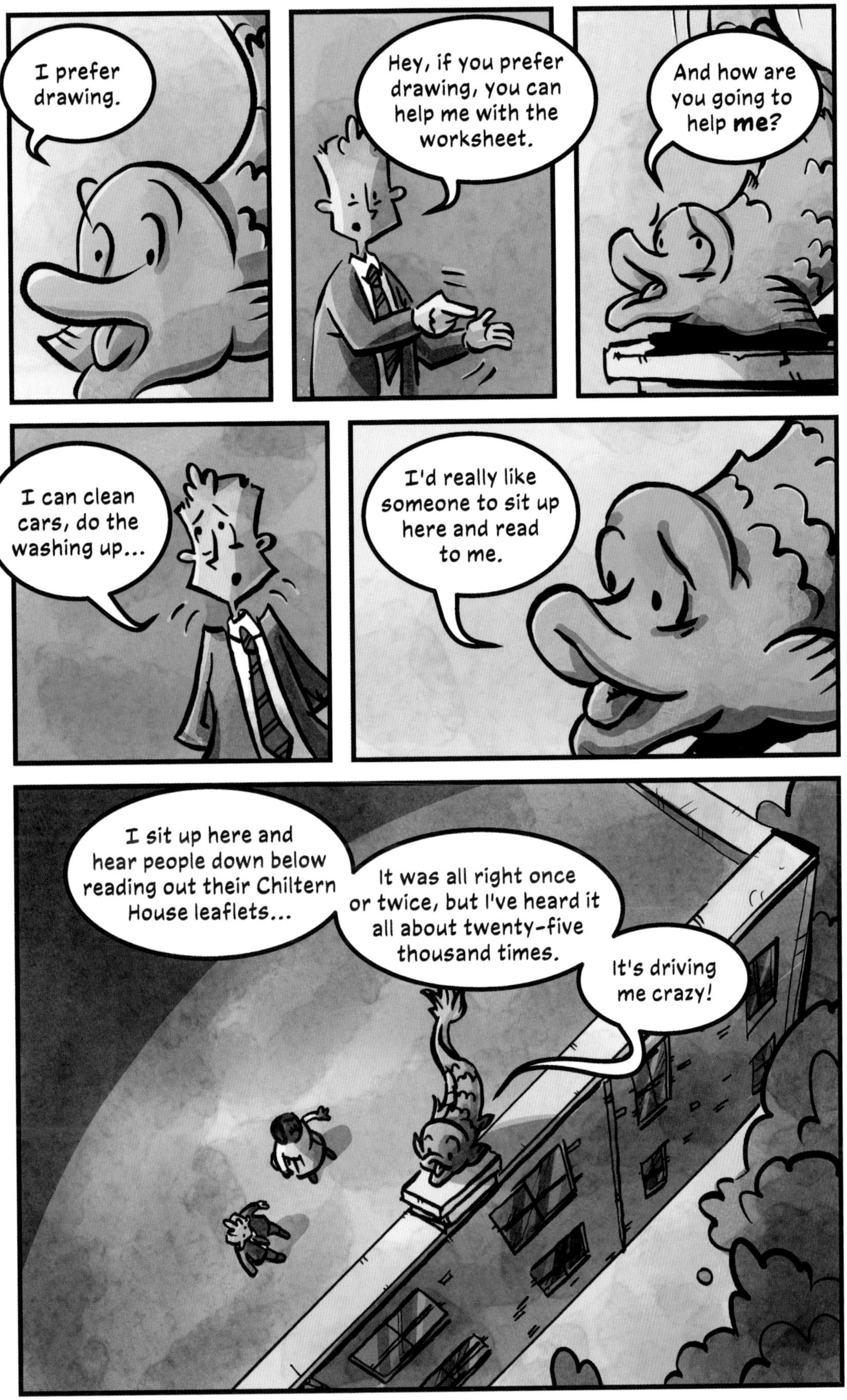
I prefer drawing.
Hey, if you prefer drawing, you can help me with the worksheet.
And how are you going to help **me**?
I can clean cars, do the washing up...
I'd really like someone to sit up here and read to me.
I sit up here and hear people down below reading out their Chiltern House leaflets...
It was all right once or twice, but I've heard it all about twenty-five thousand times.
It's driving me crazy!

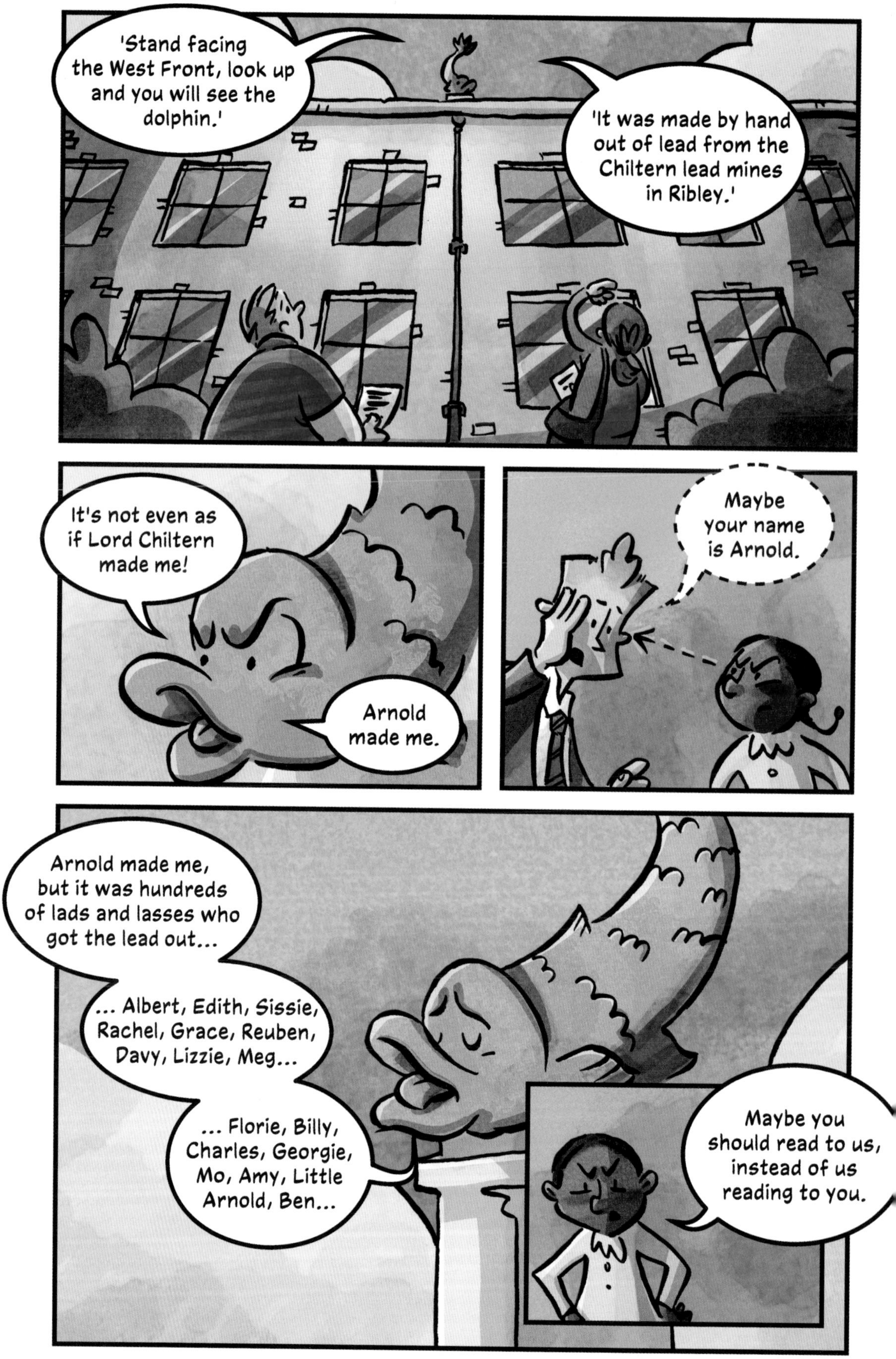
'Stand facing the West Front, look up and you will see the dolphin.'
'It was made by hand out of lead from the Chiltern lead mines in Ribley.'
It's not even as if Lord Chiltern made me!
Arnold made me.
Maybe your name is Arnold.
Arnold made me, but it was hundreds of lads and lasses who got the lead out...
... Albert, Edith, Sissie, Rachel, Grace, Reuben, Davy, Lizzie, Meg...
... Florie, Billy, Charles, Georgie, Mo, Amy, Little Arnold, Ben...
Maybe you should read to us, instead of us reading to you.

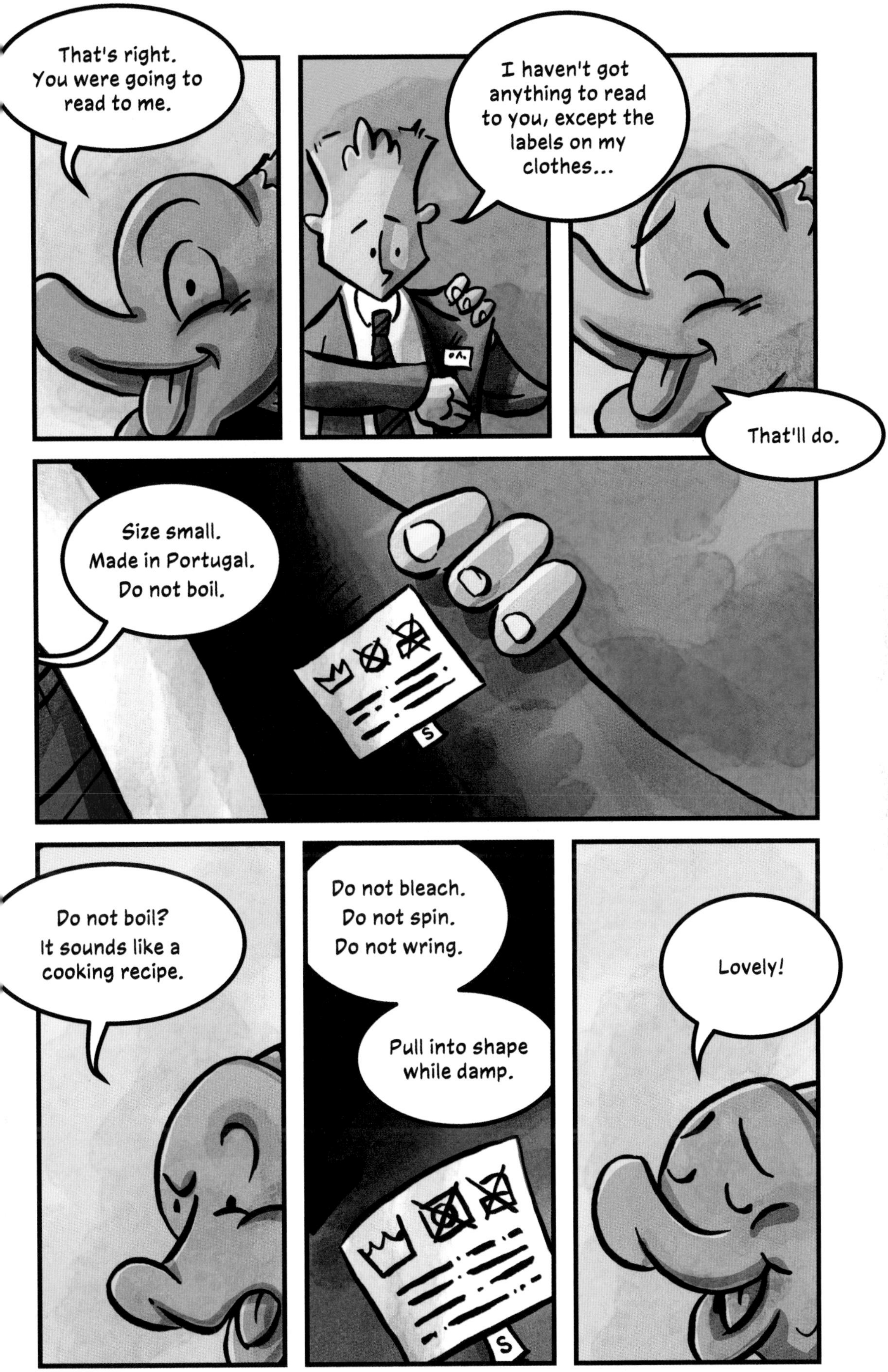
That's right. You were going to read to me.
I haven't got anything to read to you, except the labels on my clothes...
That'll do.
Size small. Made in Portugal. Do not boil.
S
Do not boil? It sounds like a cooking recipe.
Do not bleach. Do not spin. Do not wring.
Pull into shape while damp.
S
Lovely!

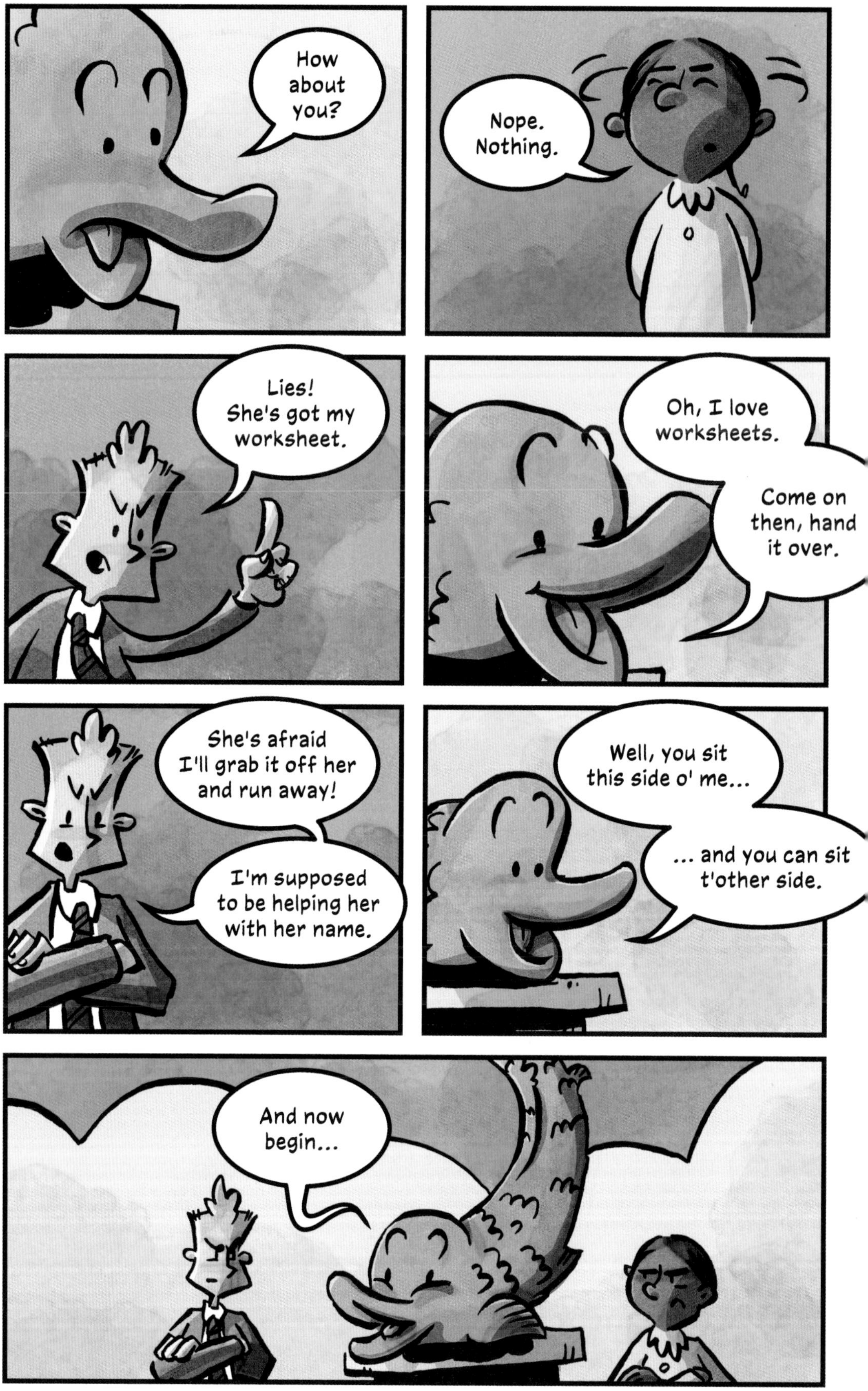
How about you?
Nope. Nothing.
Lies! She's got my worksheet.
Oh, I love worksheets.
Come on then, hand it over.
She's afraid I'll grab it off her and run away!
I'm supposed to be helping her with her name.
Well, you sit this side o' me...
... and you can sit t'other side.
And now begin...

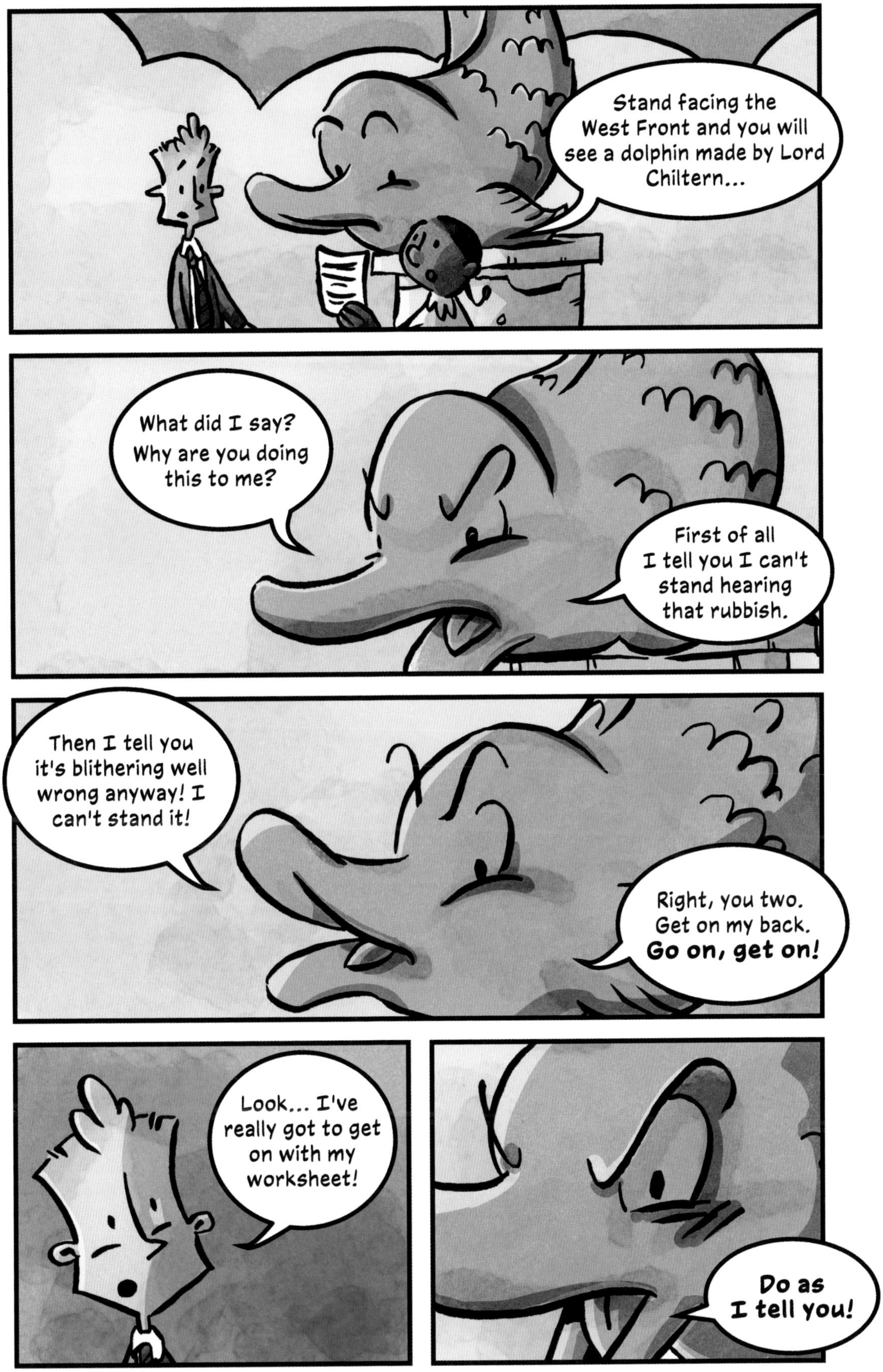
Stand facing the West Front and you will see a dolphin made by Lord Chiltern...
What did I say? Why are you doing this to me?
First of all I tell you I can't stand hearing that rubbish.
Then I tell you it's blithering well wrong anyway! I can't stand it!
Right, you two. Get on my back. **Go on, get on!**
Look... I've really got to get on with my worksheet!
Do as I tell you!

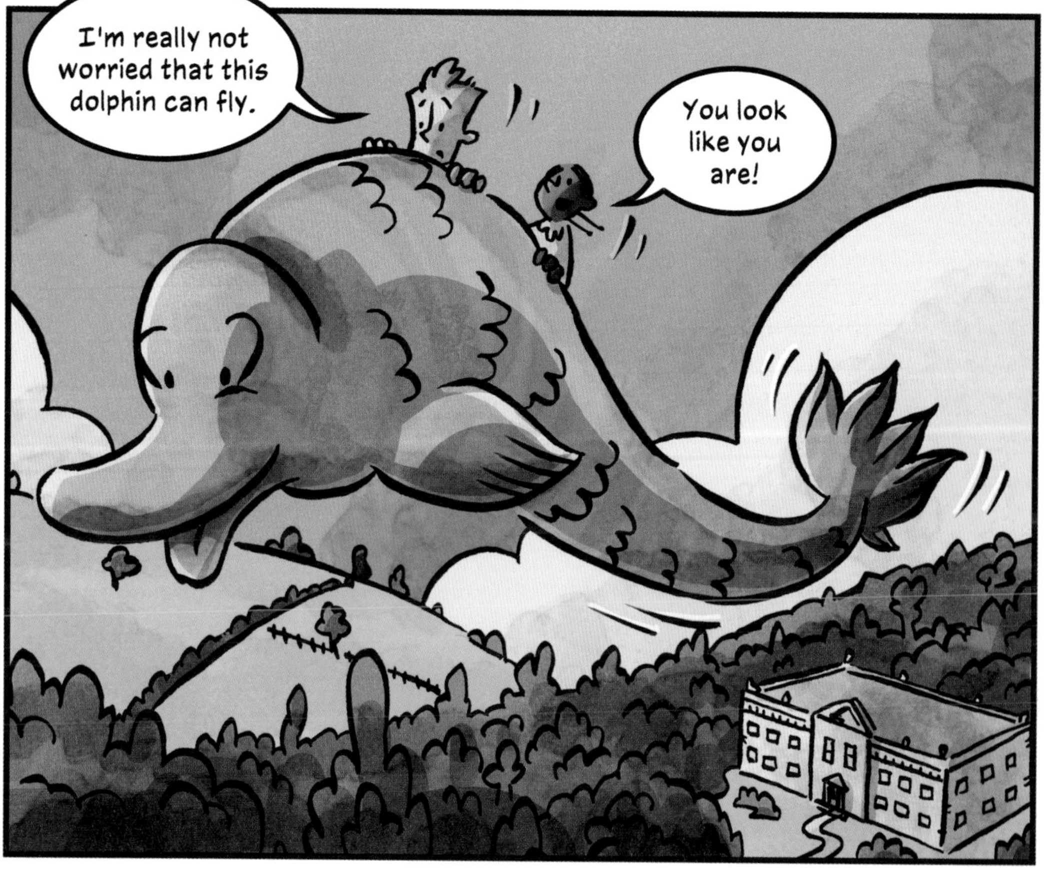
I'm really not worried that this dolphin can fly.
You look like you are!

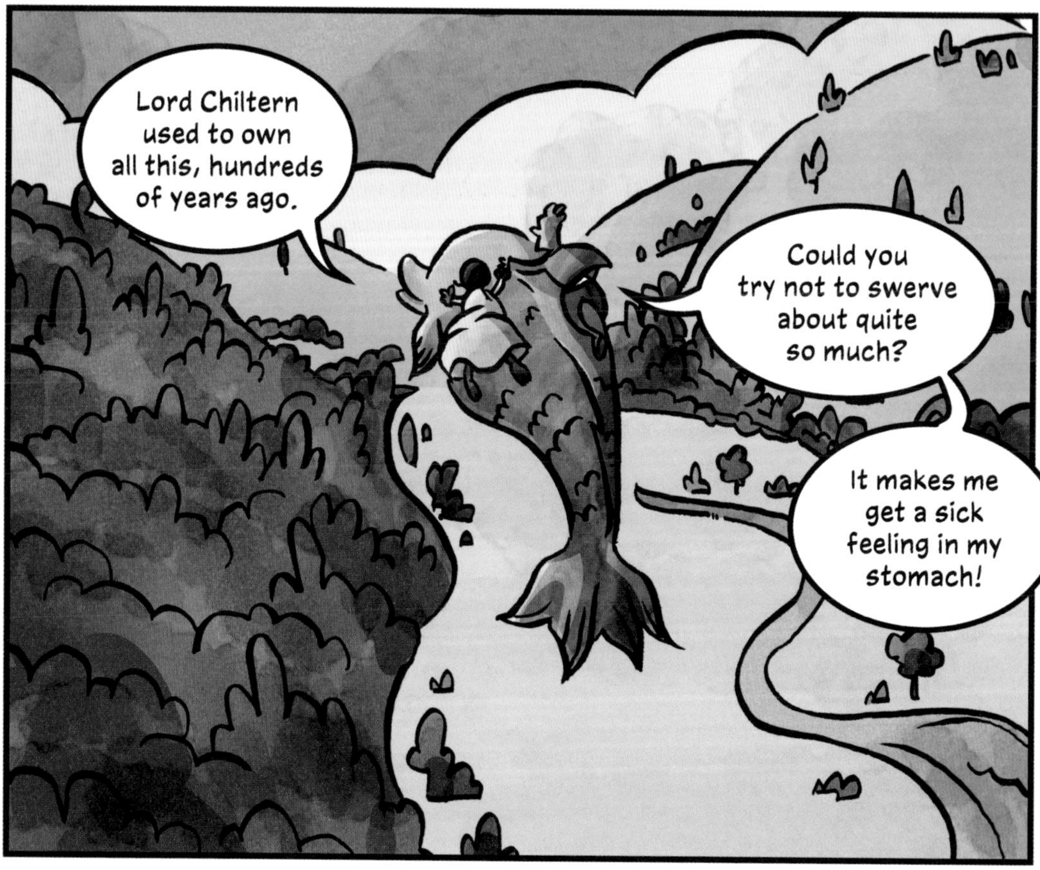
Lord Chiltern used to own all this, hundreds of years ago.
Could you try not to swerve about quite so much?
It makes me get a sick feeling in my stomach!

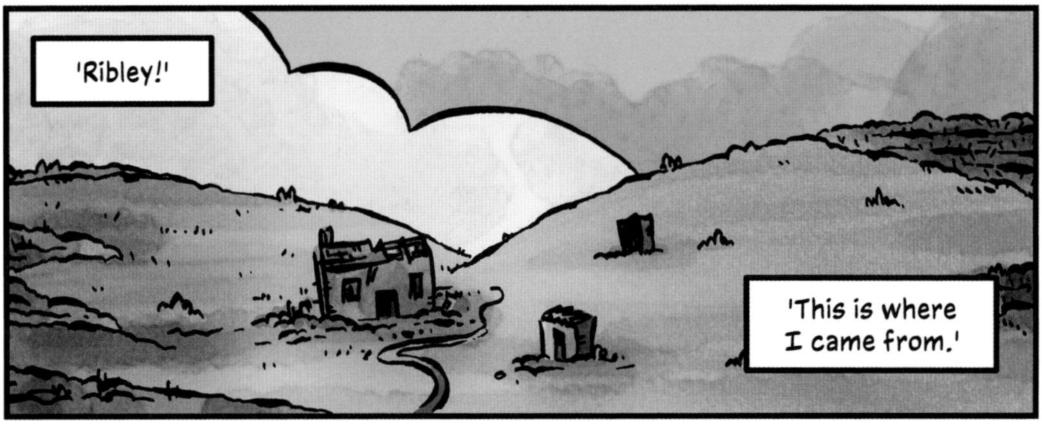
'Ribley!'
'This is where I came from.'

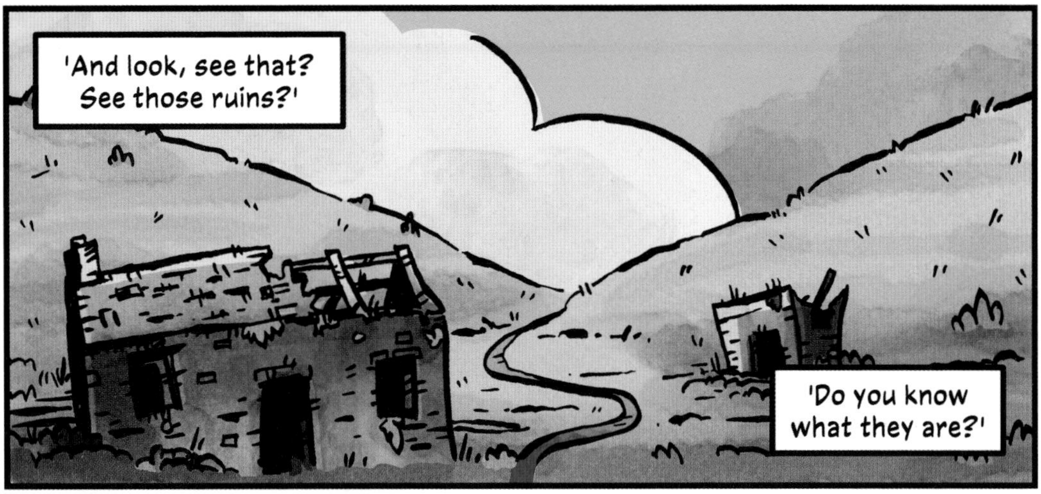
'And look, see that? See those ruins?'
'Do you know what they are?'

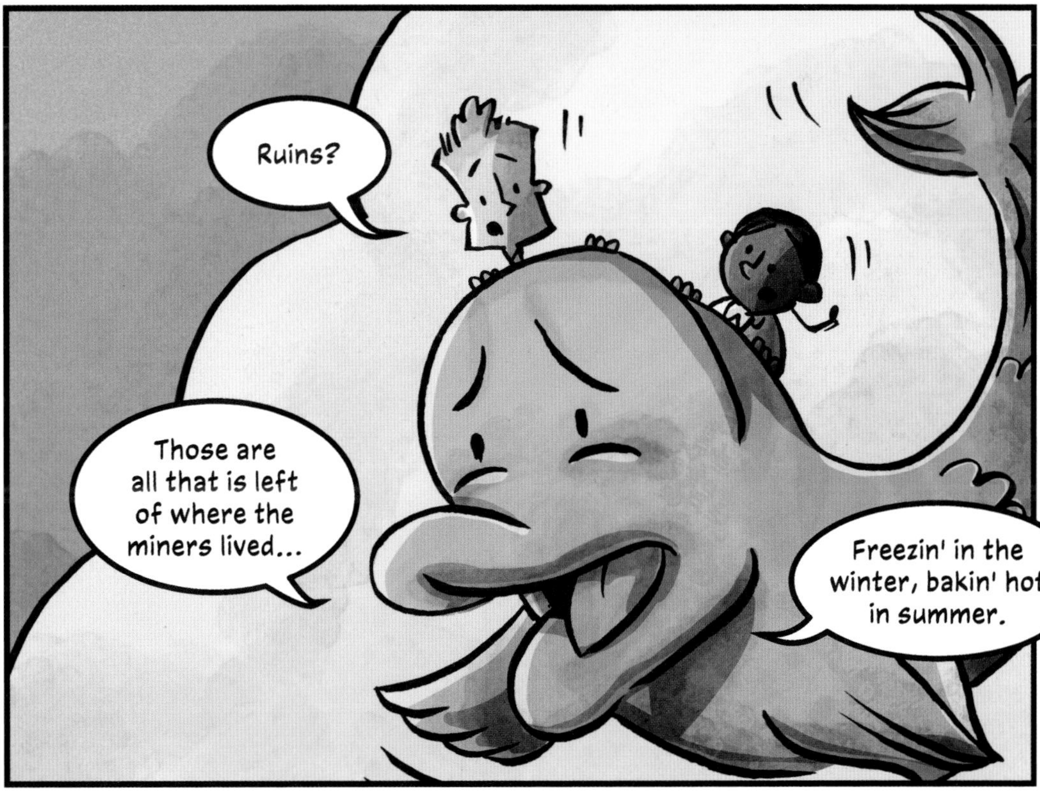
Ruins?
Those are all that is left of where the miners lived...
Freezin' in the winter, bakin' hot in summer.

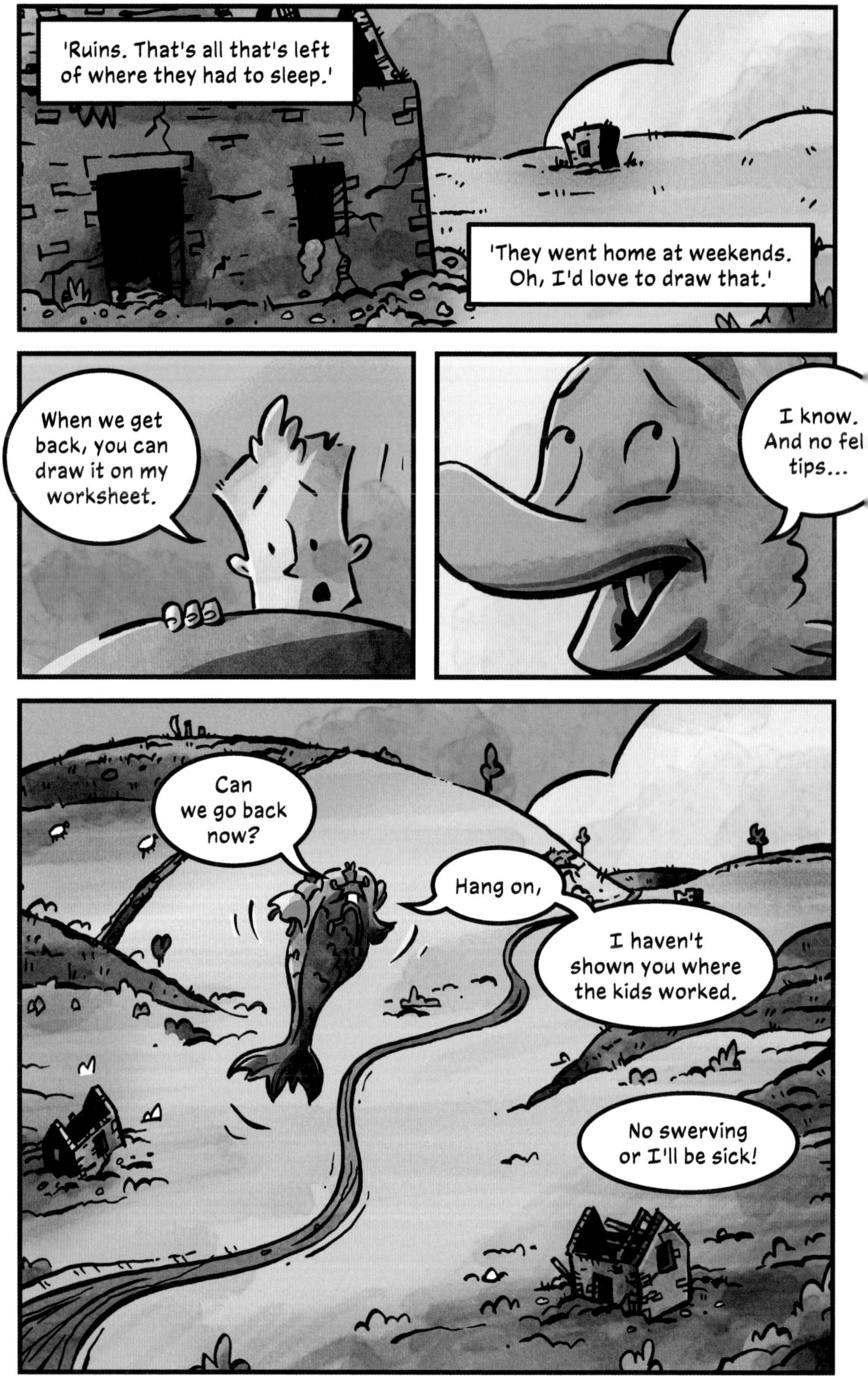
'Ruins. That's all that's left of where they had to sleep.'
'They went home at weekends. Oh, I'd love to draw that.'
When we get back, you can draw it on my worksheet.
I know. And no fel tips...
Can we go back now?
Hang on,
I haven't shown you where the kids worked.
No swerving or I'll be sick!

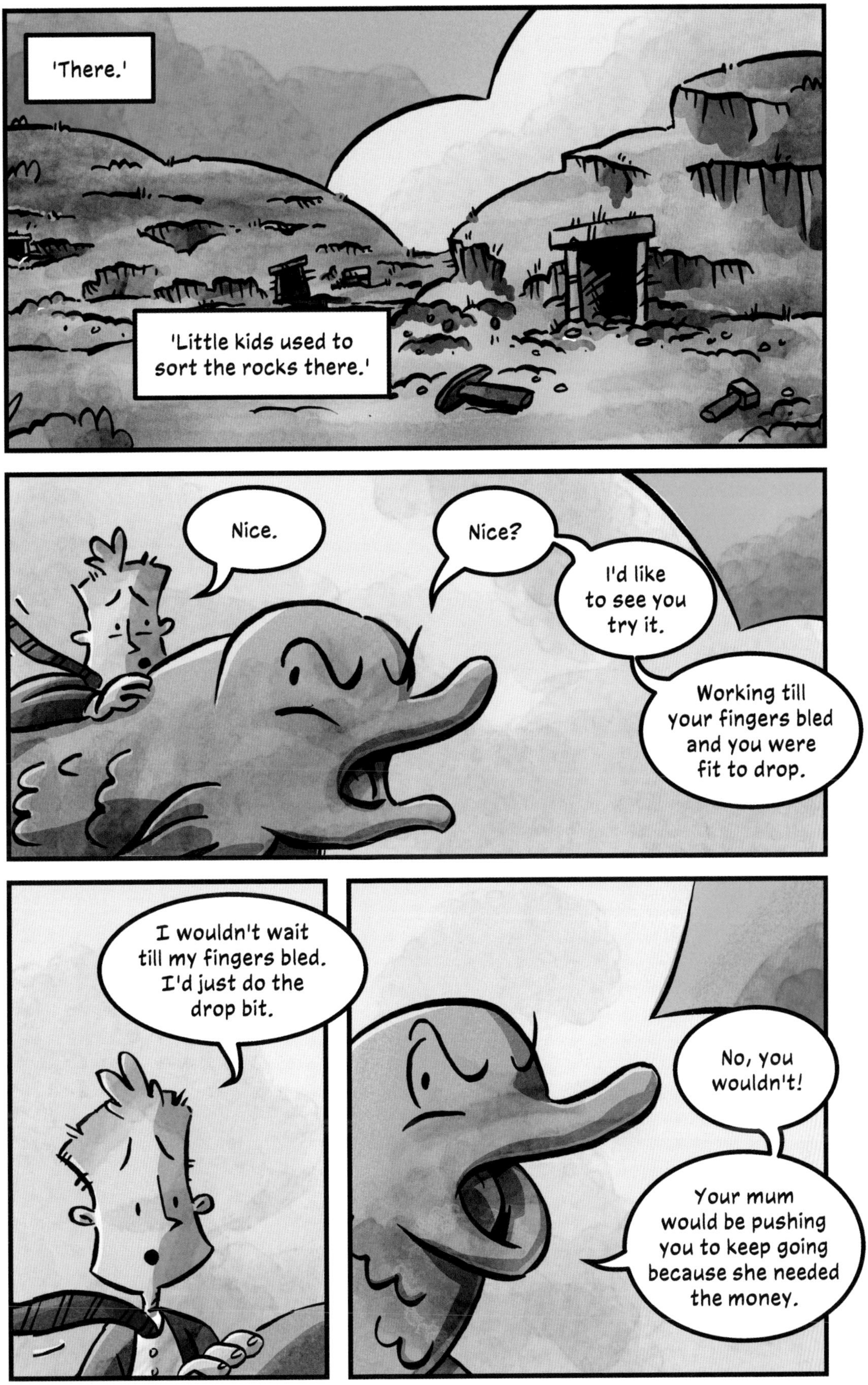
'There.'
'Little kids used to sort the rocks there.'
Nice.
Nice?
I'd like to see you try it.
Working till your fingers bled and you were fit to drop.
I wouldn't wait till my fingers bled. I'd just do the drop bit.
No, you wouldn't!
Your mum would be pushing you to keep going because she needed the money.

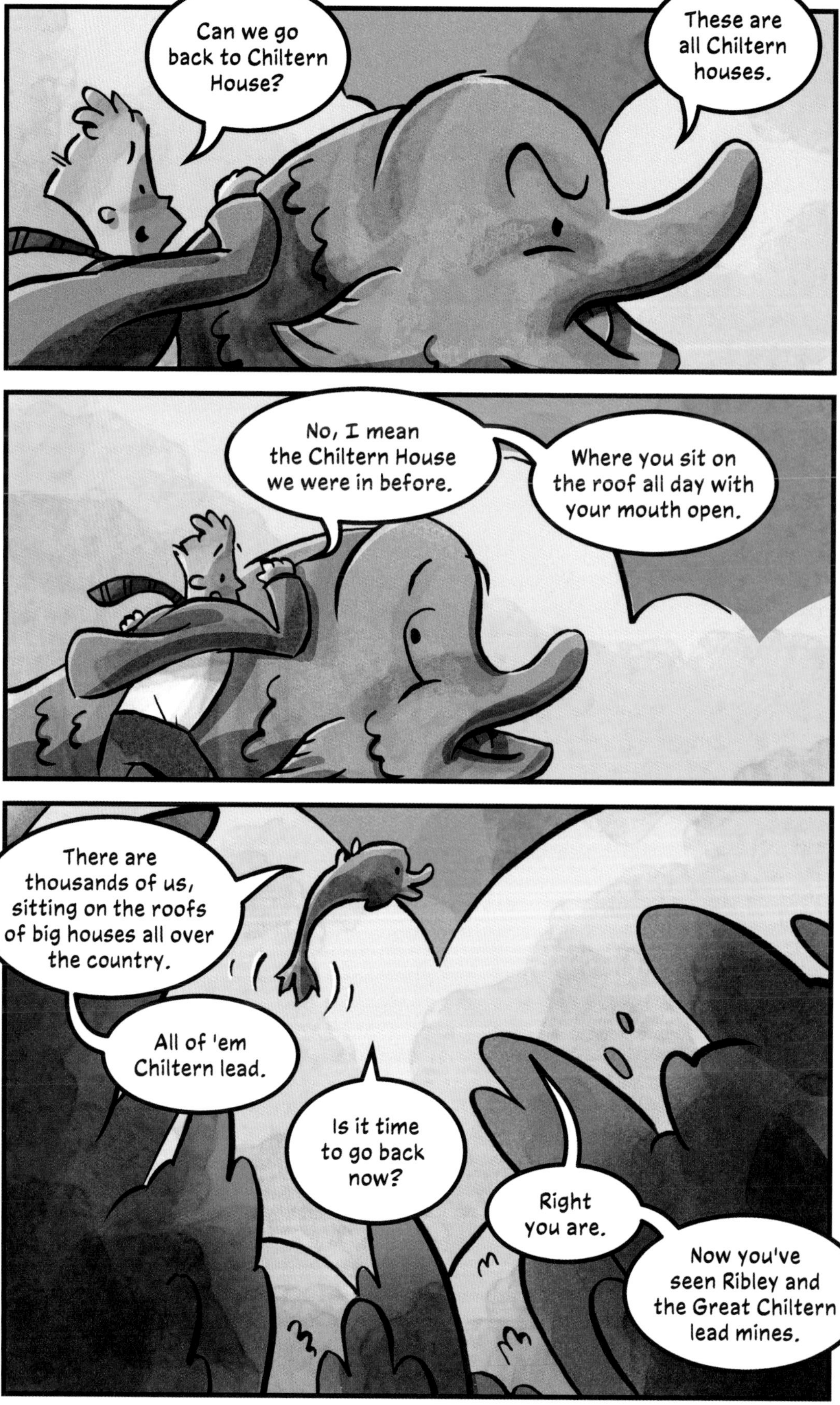
Can we go back to Chiltern House?
These are all Chiltern houses.
No, I mean the Chiltern House we were in before.
Where you sit on the roof all day with your mouth open.
There are thousands of us, sitting on the roofs of big houses all over the country.
All of 'em Chiltern lead.
Is it time to go back now?
Right you are.
Now you've seen Ribley and the Great Chiltern lead mines.

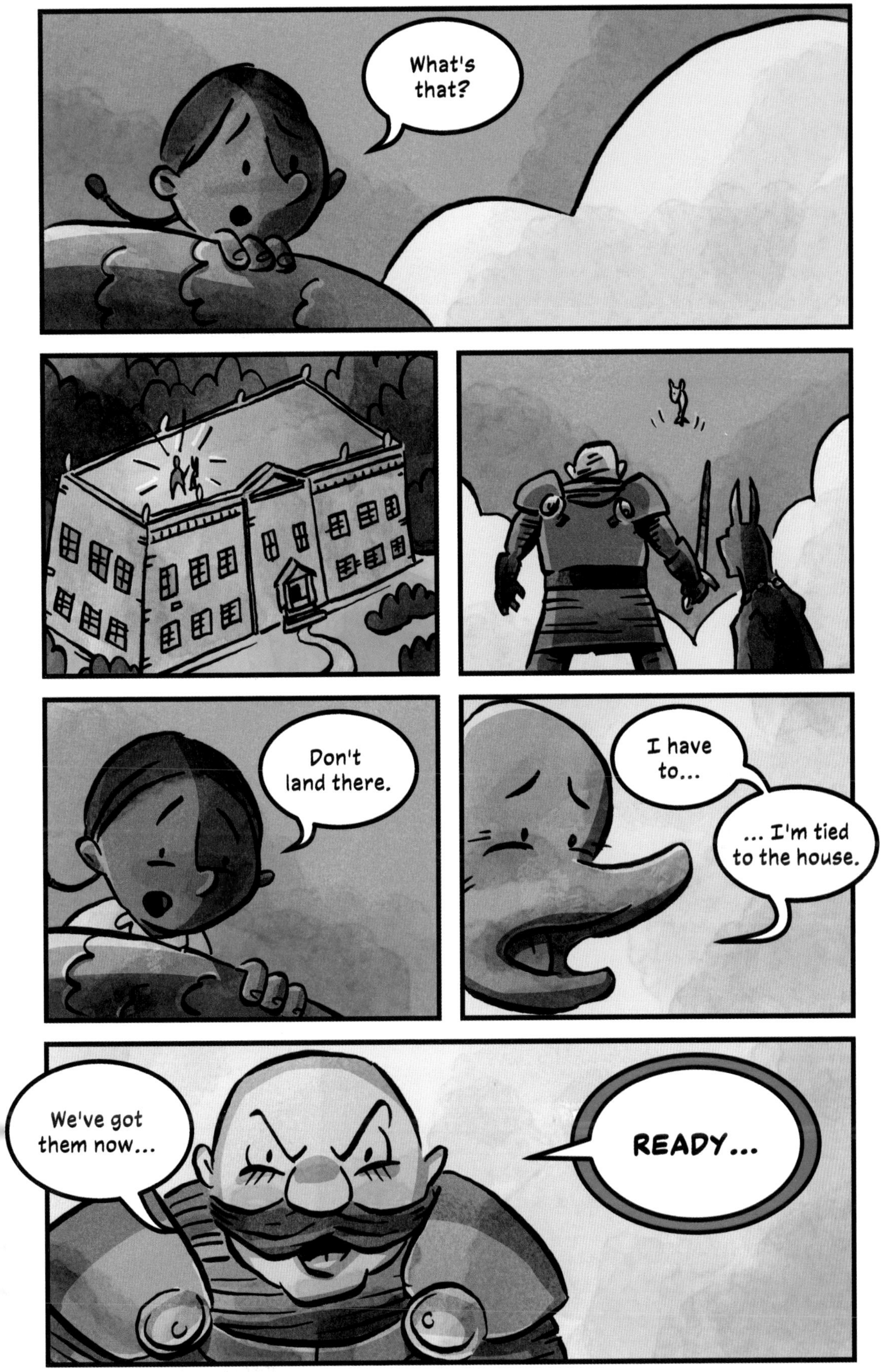
What's that?
Don't land there.
I have to...
... I'm tied to the house.
We've got them now...
READY...

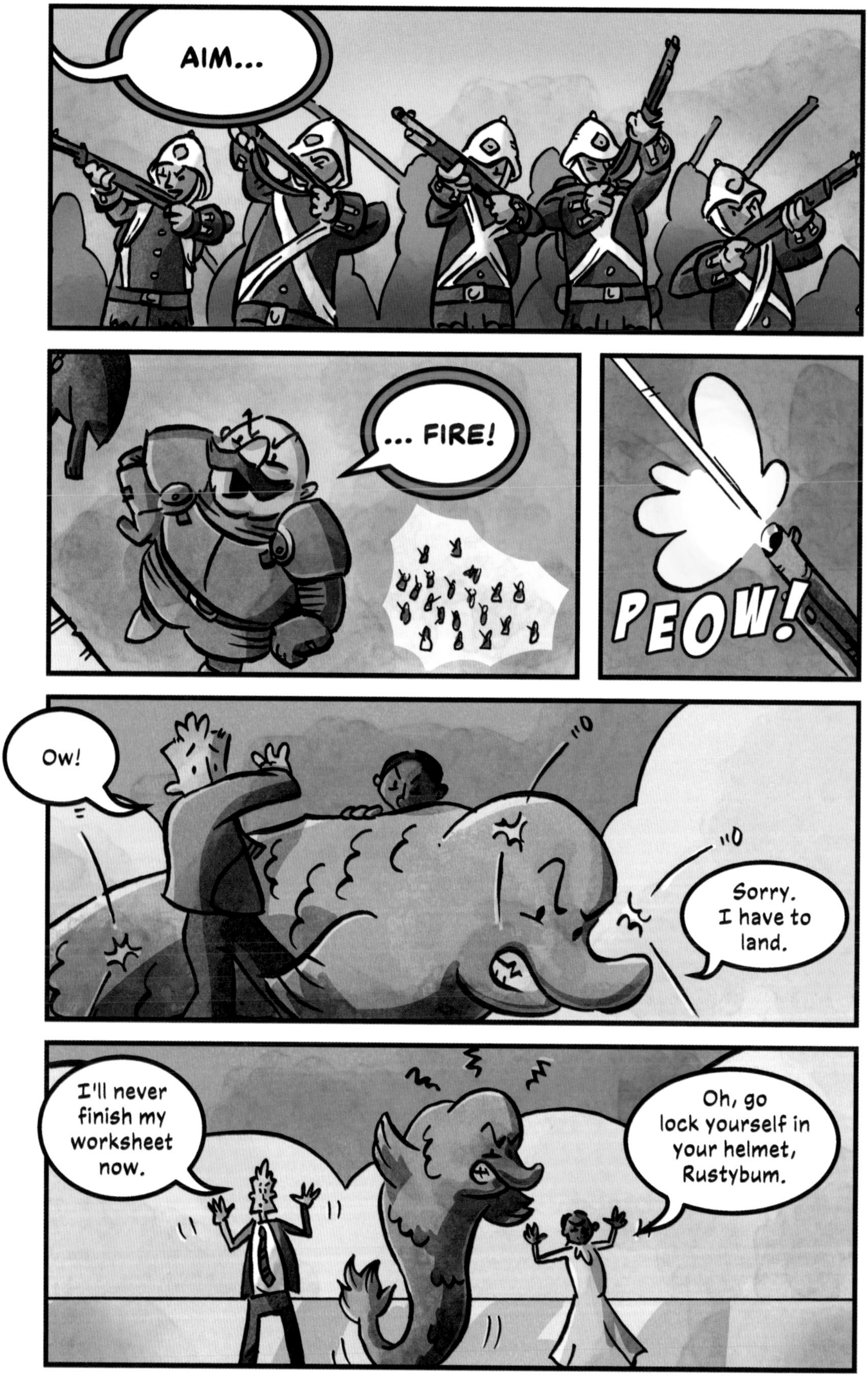
AIM...
... FIRE!
PEOW!
Ow!
Sorry. I have to land.
I'll never finish my worksheet now.
Oh, go lock yourself in your helmet, Rustybum.

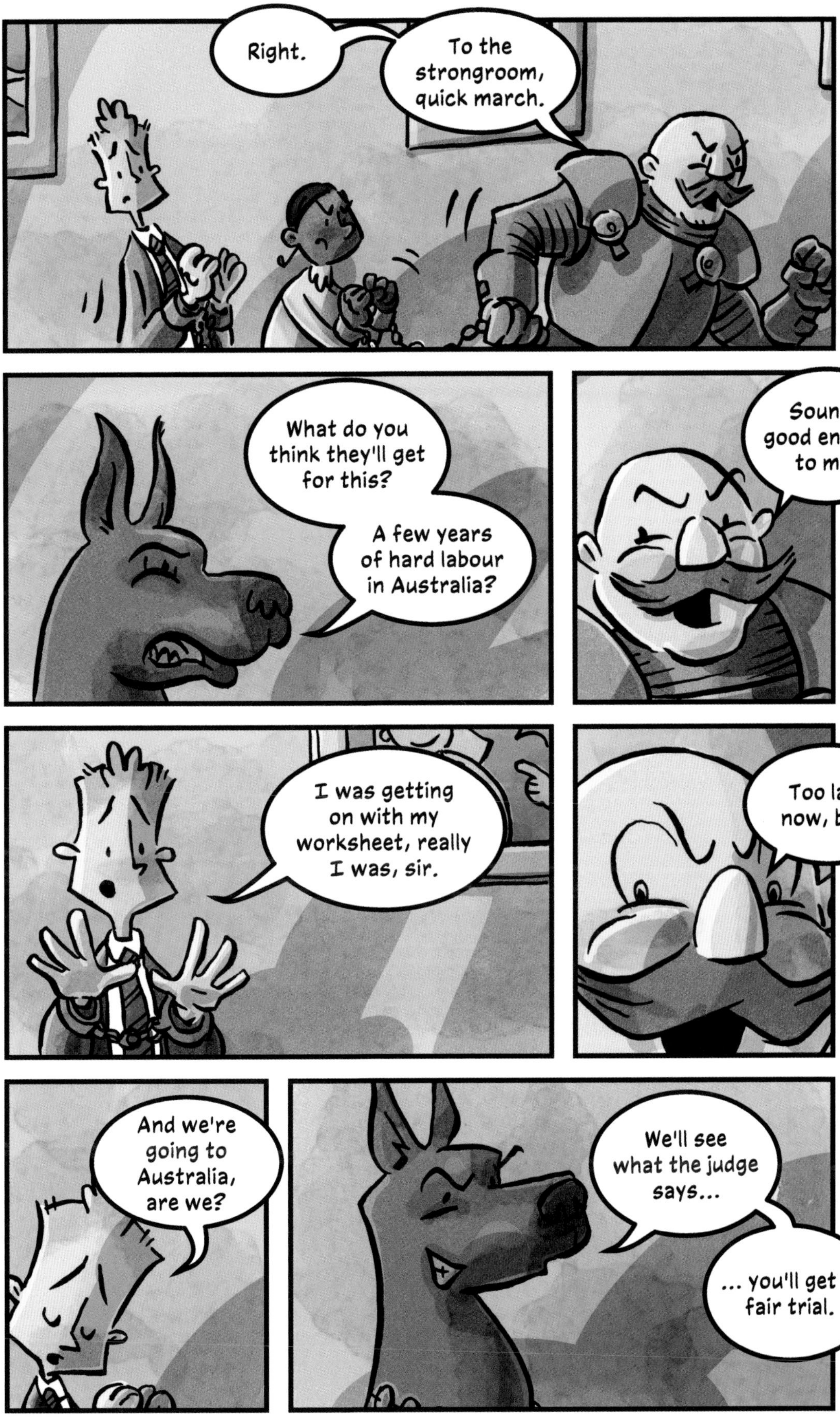
Right.
To the strongroom, quick march.
What do you think they'll get for this?
A few years of hard labour in Australia?
Sounds good enough to me.
I was getting on with my worksheet, really I was, sir.
Too late now, boy.
And we're going to Australia, are we?
We'll see what the judge says...
... you'll get a fair trial.

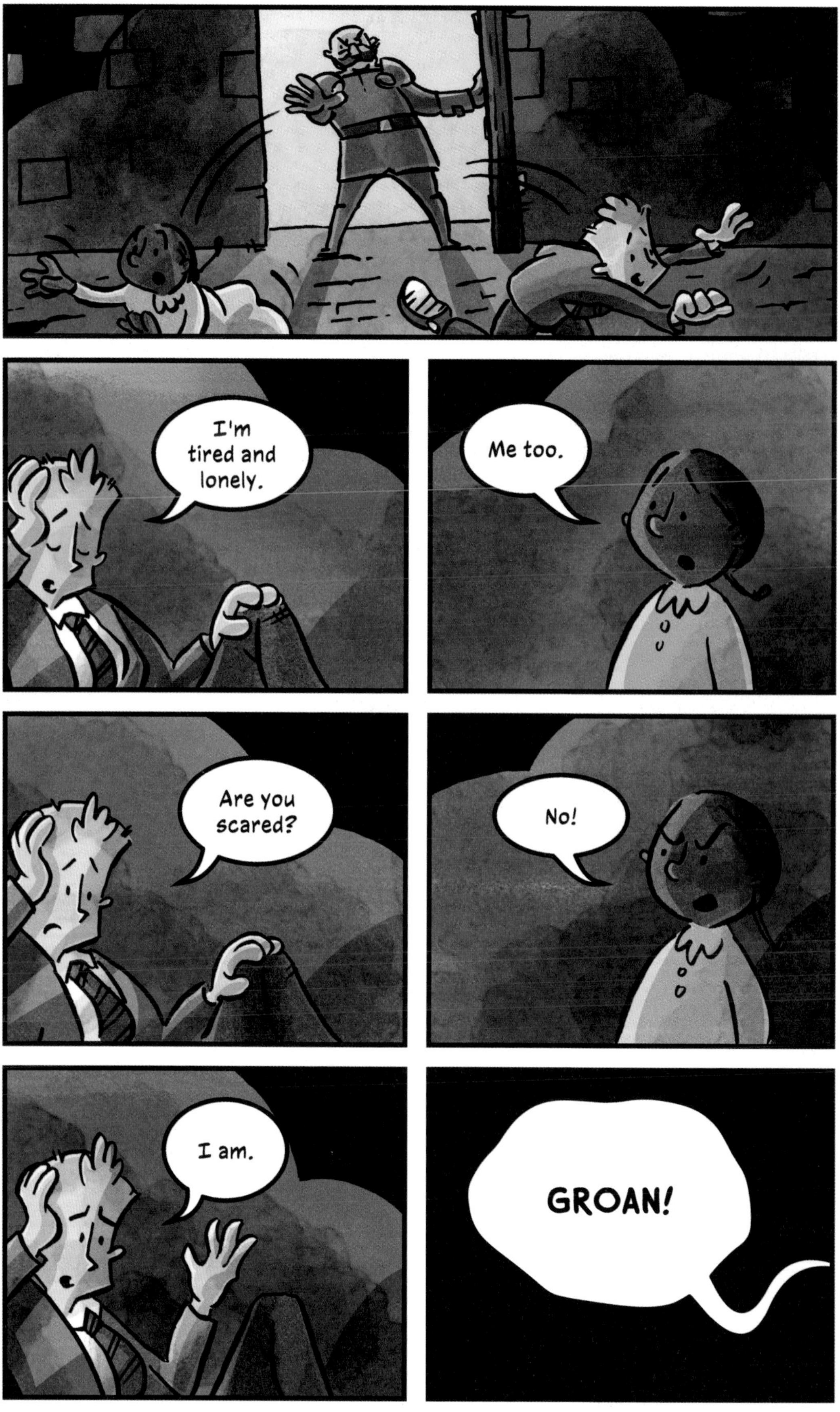
I'm tired and lonely.
Me too.
Are you scared?
No!
I am.
GROAN!

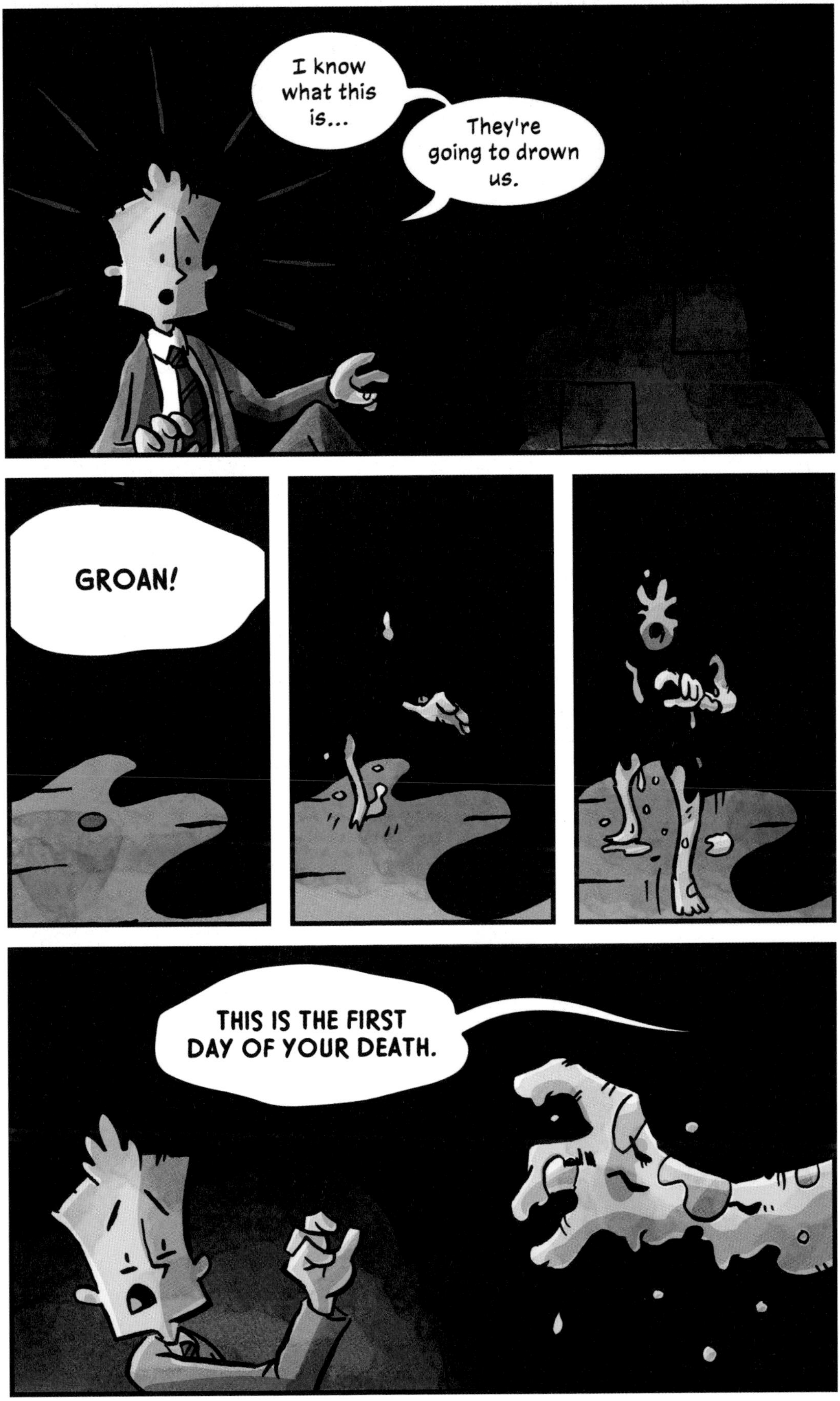
I know what this is...
They're going to drown us.
GROAN!
THIS IS THE FIRST DAY OF YOUR DEATH.

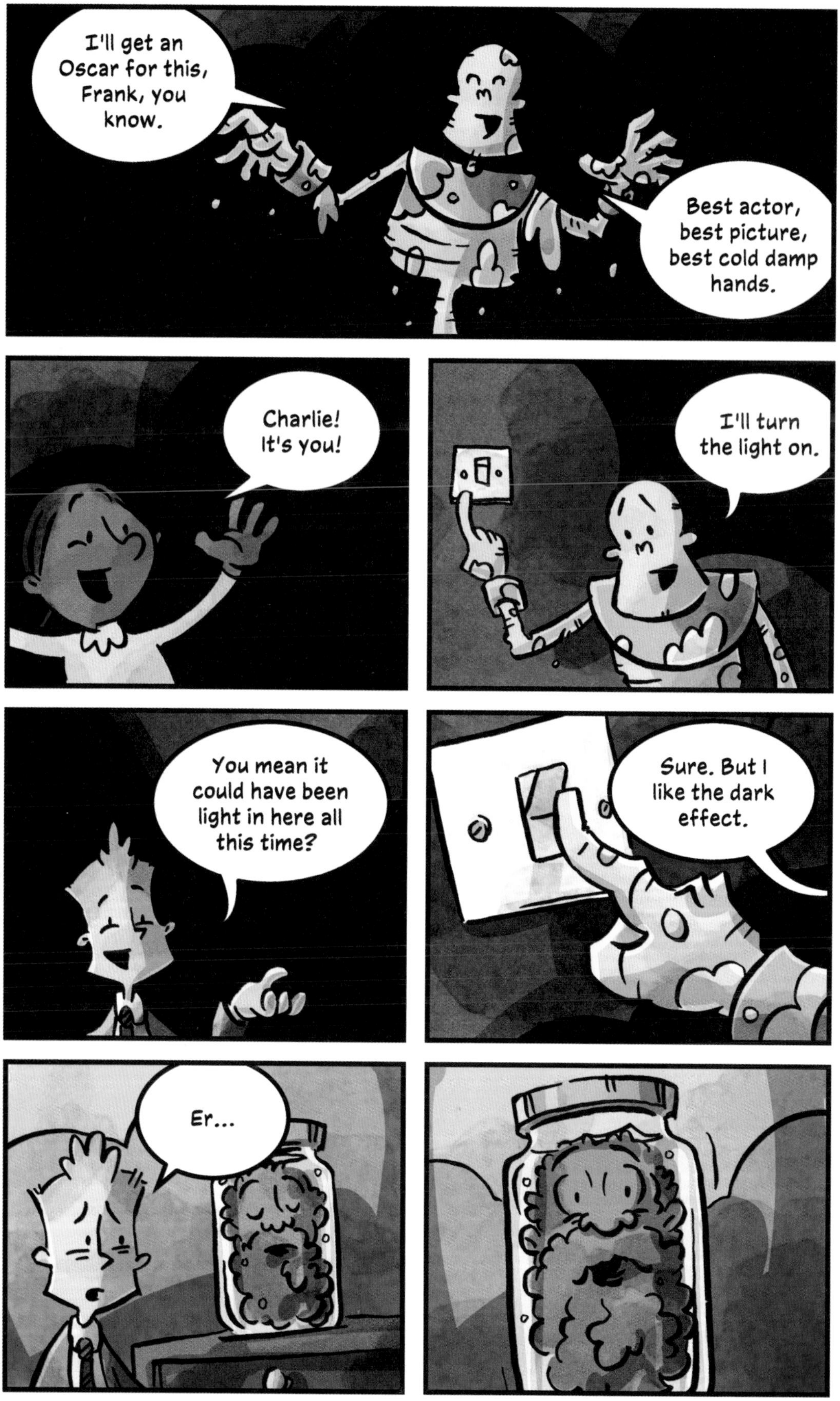
I'll get an Oscar for this, Frank, you know.
Best actor, best picture, best cold damp hands.
Charlie! It's you!
I'll turn the light on.
You mean it could have been light in here all this time?
Sure. But I like the dark effect.
Er...

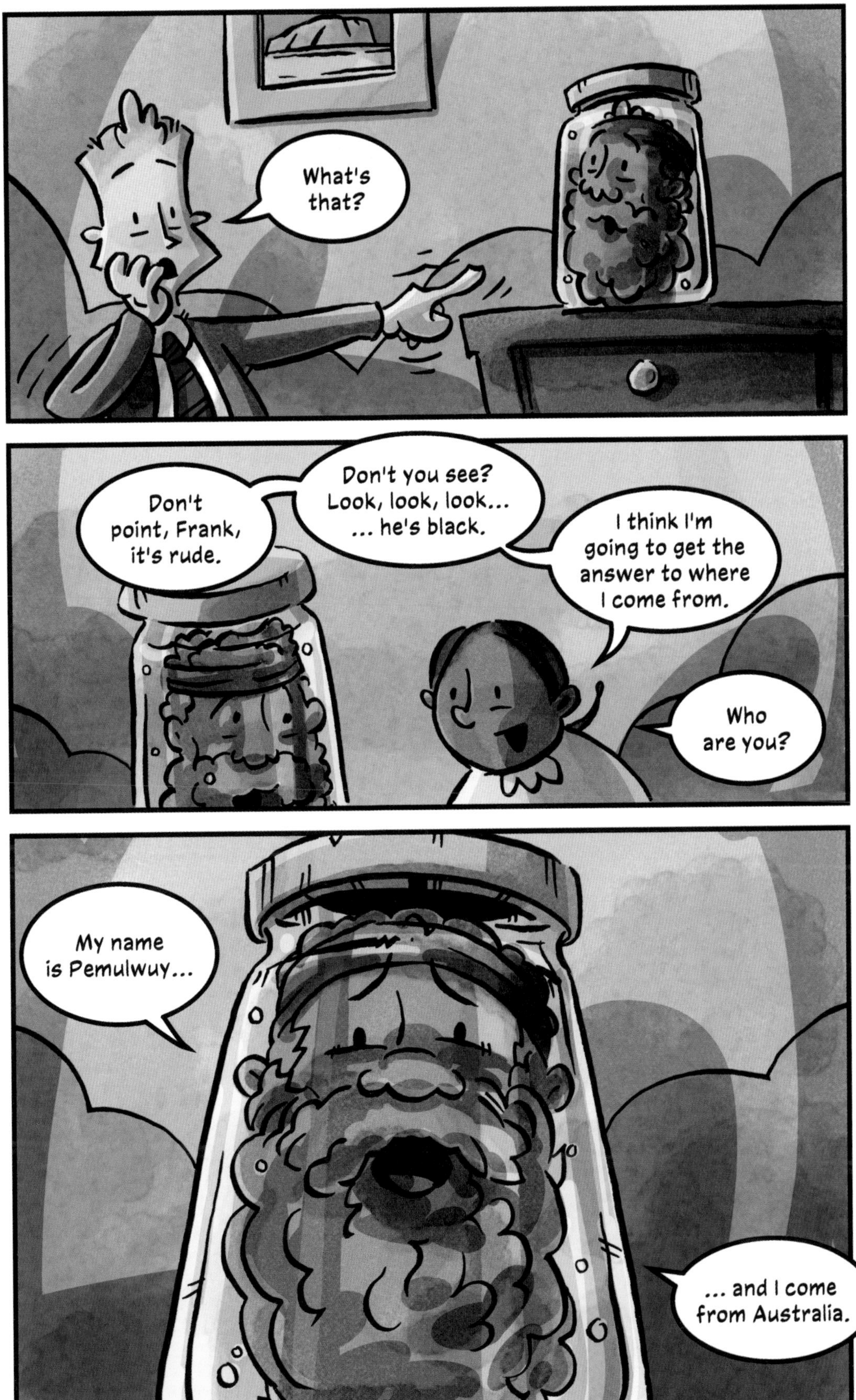
What's that?
Don't point, Frank, it's rude.
Don't you see? Look, look, look... ... he's black.
I think I'm going to get the answer to where I come from.
Who are you?
My name is Pemulwuy...
... and I come from Australia.

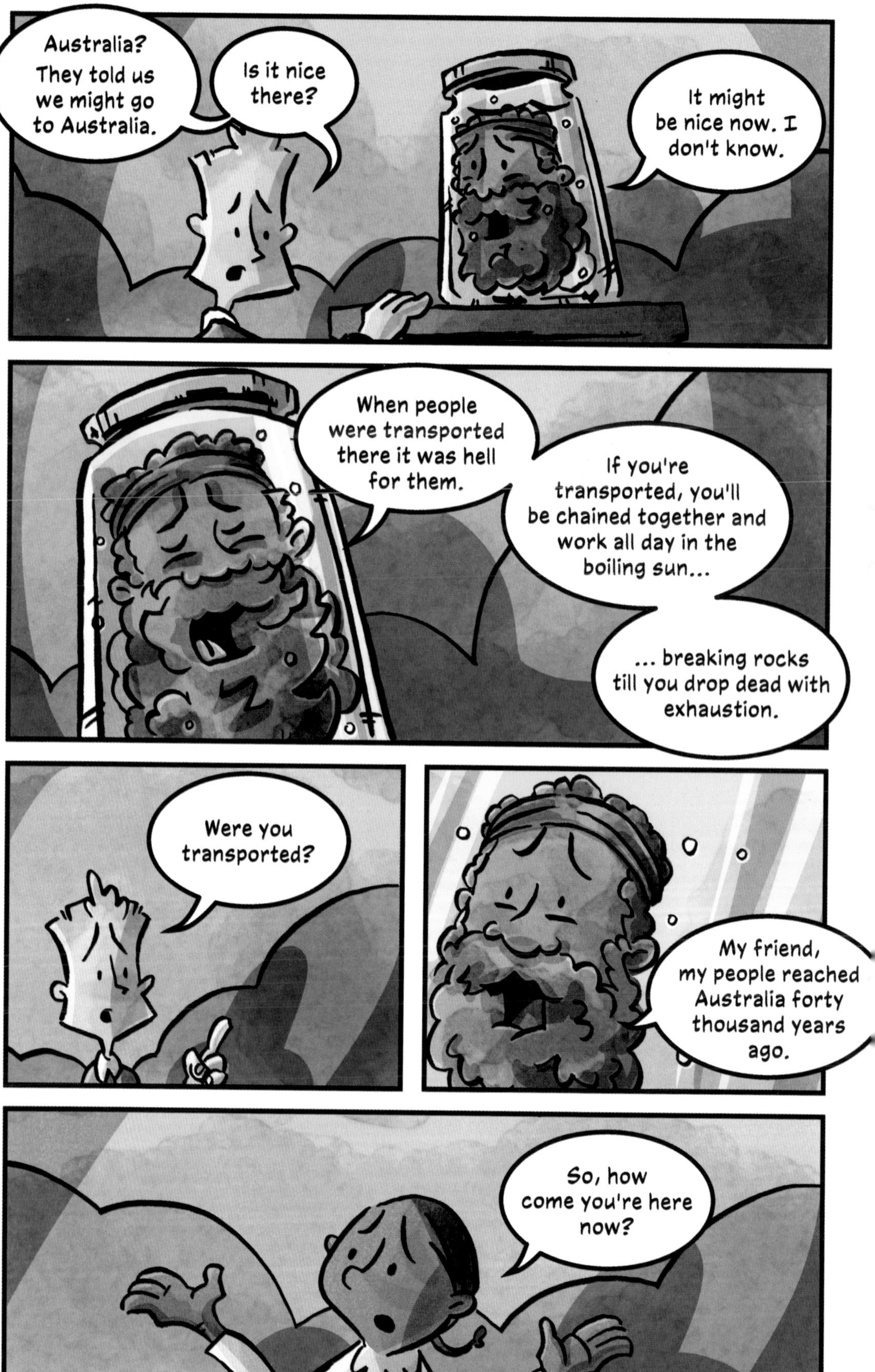
Australia? They told us we might go to Australia.
Is it nice there?
It might be nice now. I don't know.
When people were transported there it was hell for them.
If you're transported, you'll be chained together and work all day in the boiling sun...
... breaking rocks till you drop dead with exhaustion.
Were you transported?
My friend, my people reached Australia forty thousand years ago.
So, how come you're here now?

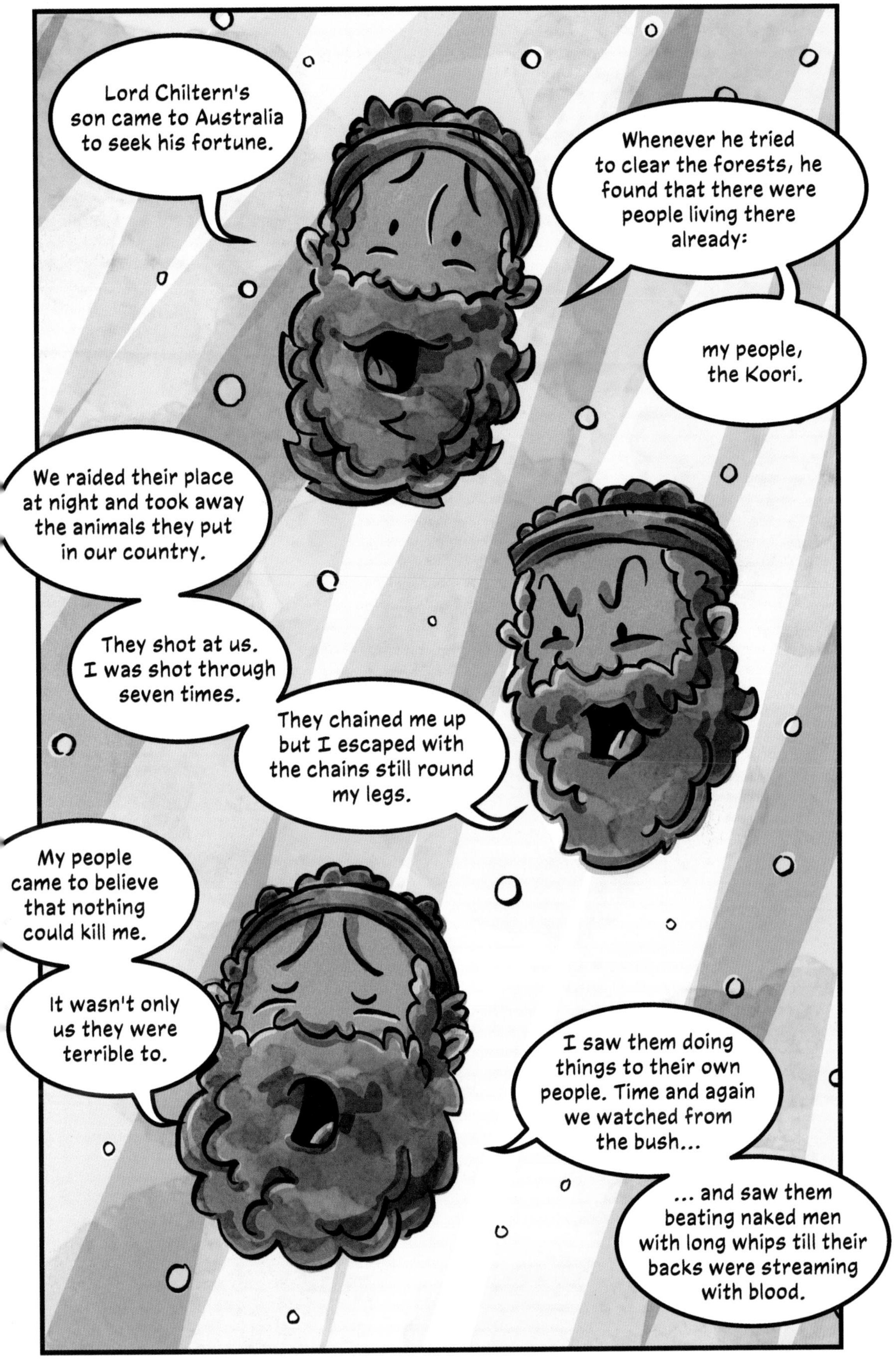
Lord Chiltern's son came to Australia to seek his fortune.
Whenever he tried to clear the forests, he found that there were people living there already:
my people, the Koori.
We raided their place at night and took away the animals they put in our country.
They shot at us. I was shot through seven times.
They chained me up but I escaped with the chains still round my legs.
My people came to believe that nothing could kill me.
It wasn't only us they were terrible to.
I saw them doing things to their own people. Time and again we watched from the bush...
... and saw them beating naked men with long whips till their backs were streaming with blood.

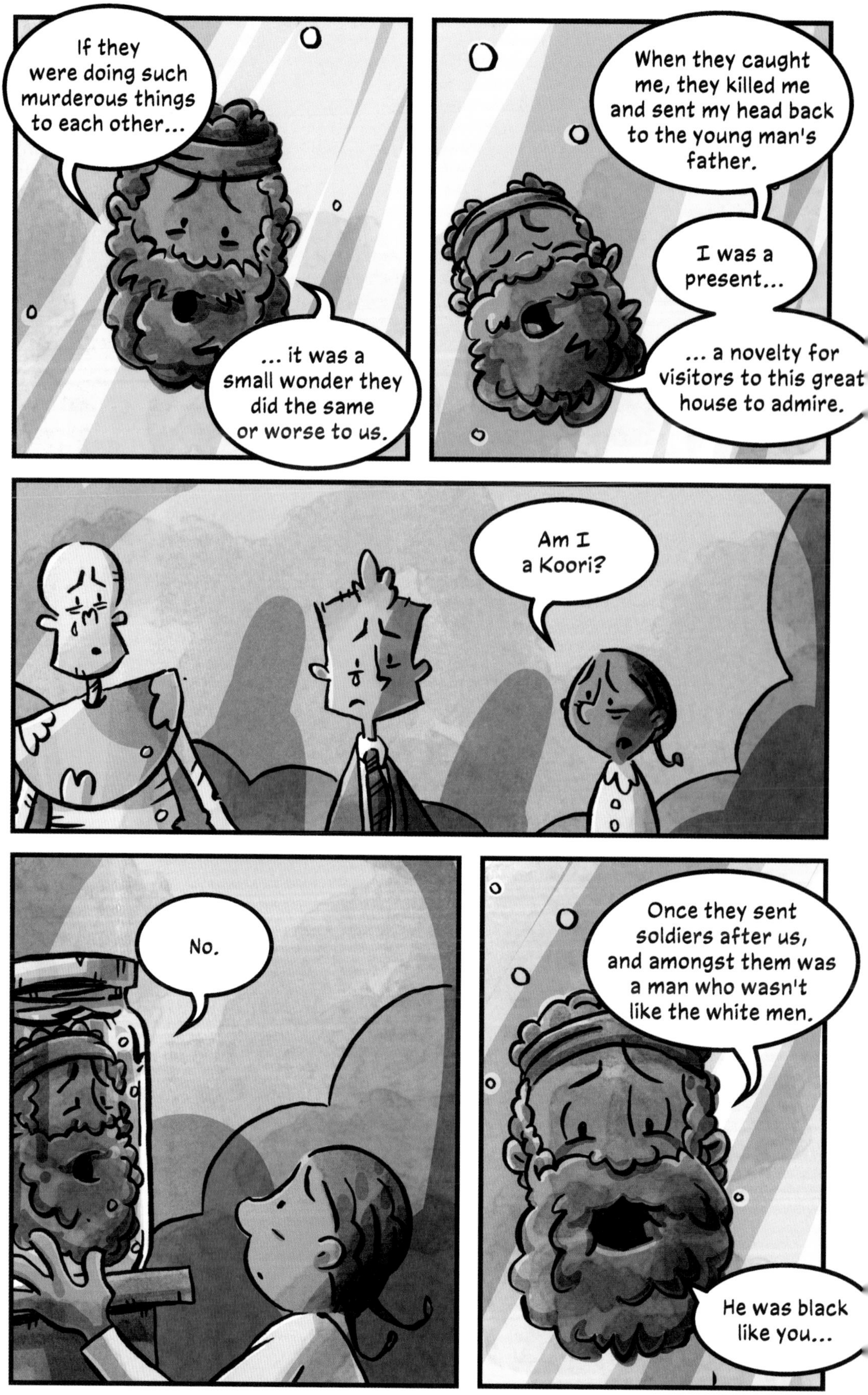

If they were doing such murderous things to each other...
... it was a small wonder they did the same or worse to us.
When they caught me, they killed me and sent my head back to the young man's father.
I was a present...
... a novelty for visitors to this great house to admire.
Am I a Koori?
No.
Once they sent soldiers after us, and amongst them was a man who wasn't like the white men.
He was black like you...

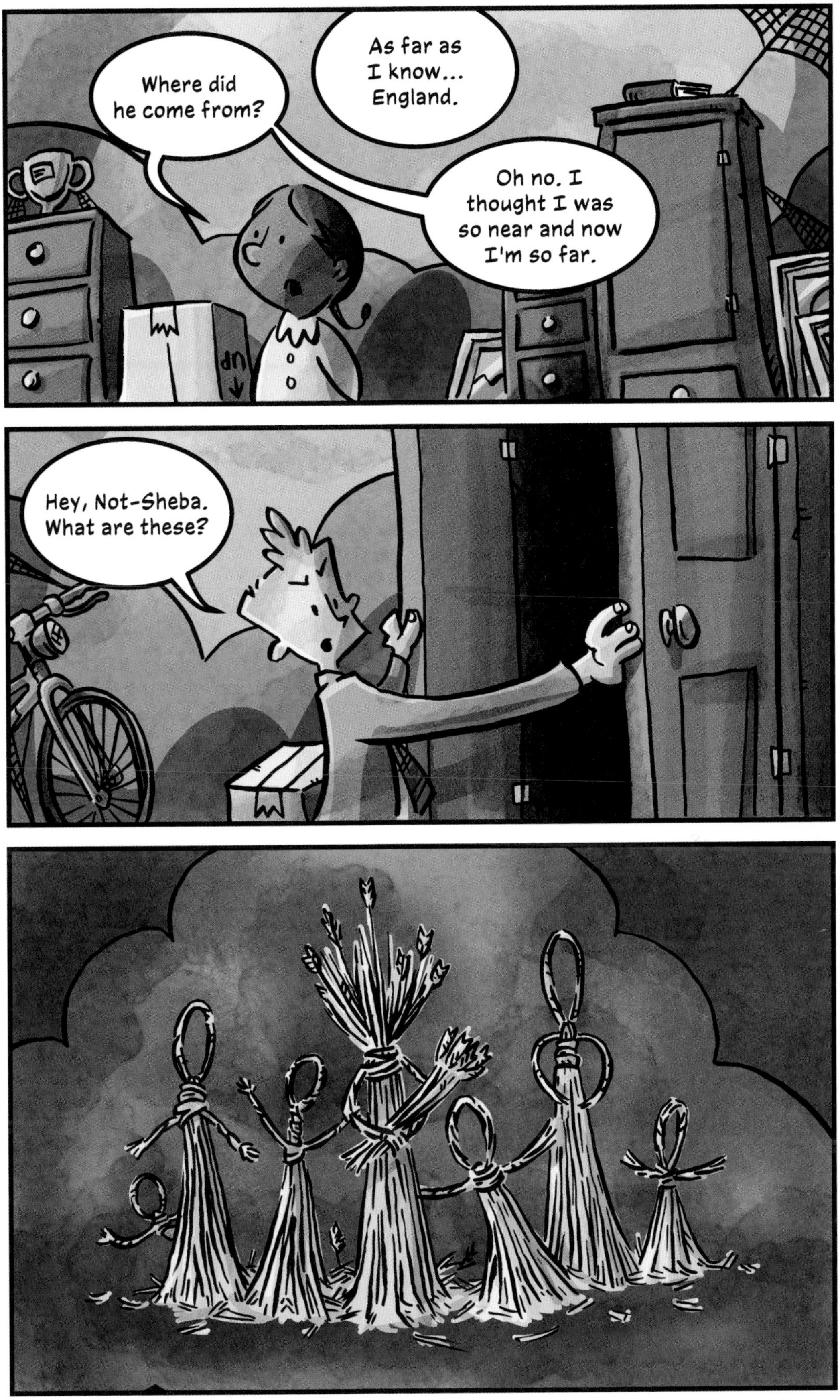
Where did he come from?
As far as I know... England.
Oh no. I thought I was so near and now I'm so far.
Hey, Not-Sheba. What are these?

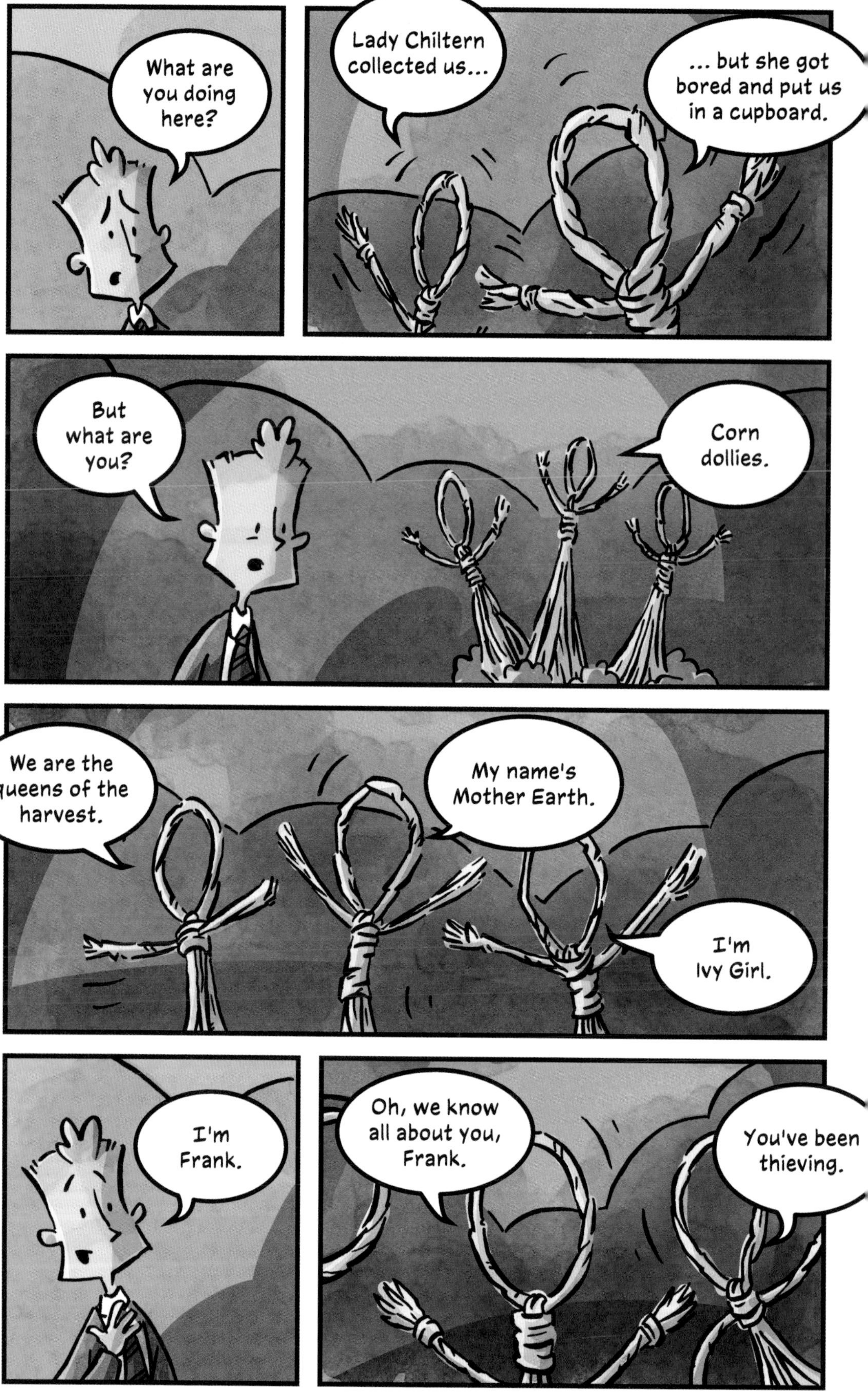
What are you doing here?
Lady Chiltern collected us...
... but she got bored and put us in a cupboard.
But what are you?
Corn dollies.
We are the queens of the harvest.
My name's Mother Earth.
I'm Ivy Girl.
I'm Frank.
Oh, we know all about you, Frank.
You've been thieving.

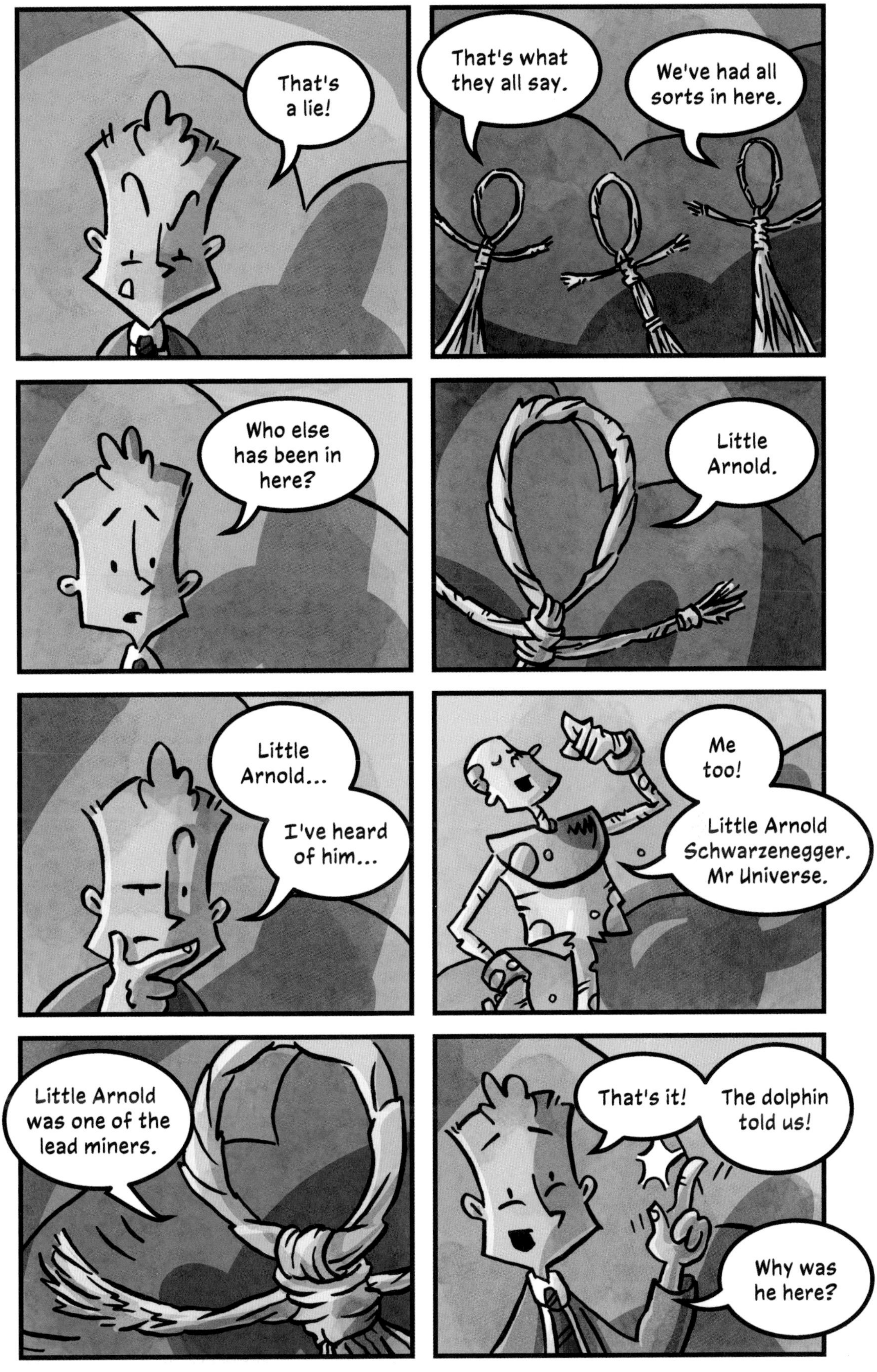
That's a lie!
That's what they all say.
We've had all sorts in here.
Who else has been in here?
Little Arnold.
Little Arnold...
I've heard of him...
Me too!
Little Arnold Schwarzenegger. Mr Universe.
Little Arnold was one of the lead miners.
That's it!
The dolphin told us!
Why was he here?

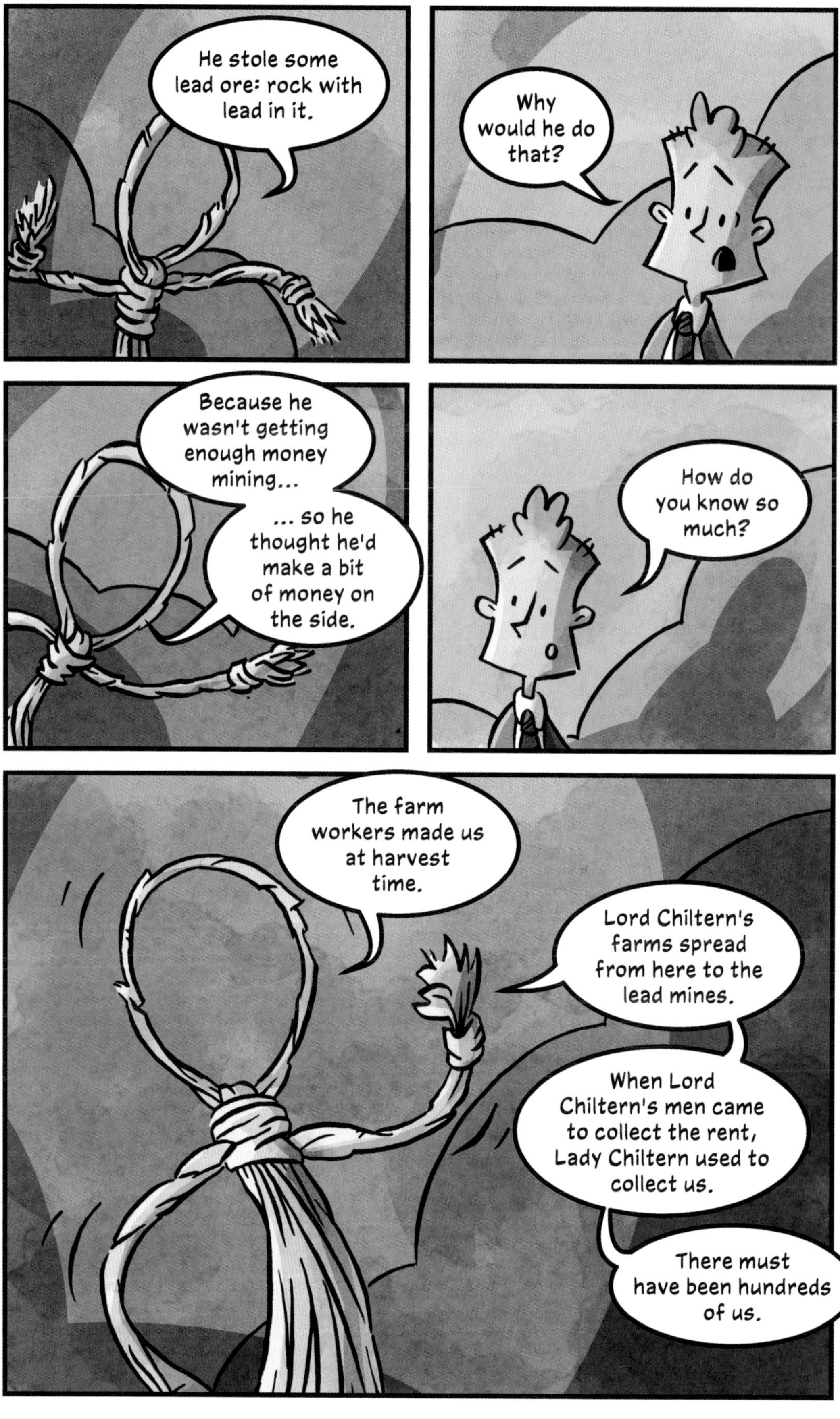
He stole some lead ore: rock with lead in it.
Why would he do that?
Because he wasn't getting enough money mining...
... so he thought he'd make a bit of money on the side.
How do you know so much?
The farm workers made us at harvest time.
Lord Chiltern's farms spread from here to the lead mines.
When Lord Chiltern's men came to collect the rent, Lady Chiltern used to collect us.
There must have been hundreds of us.

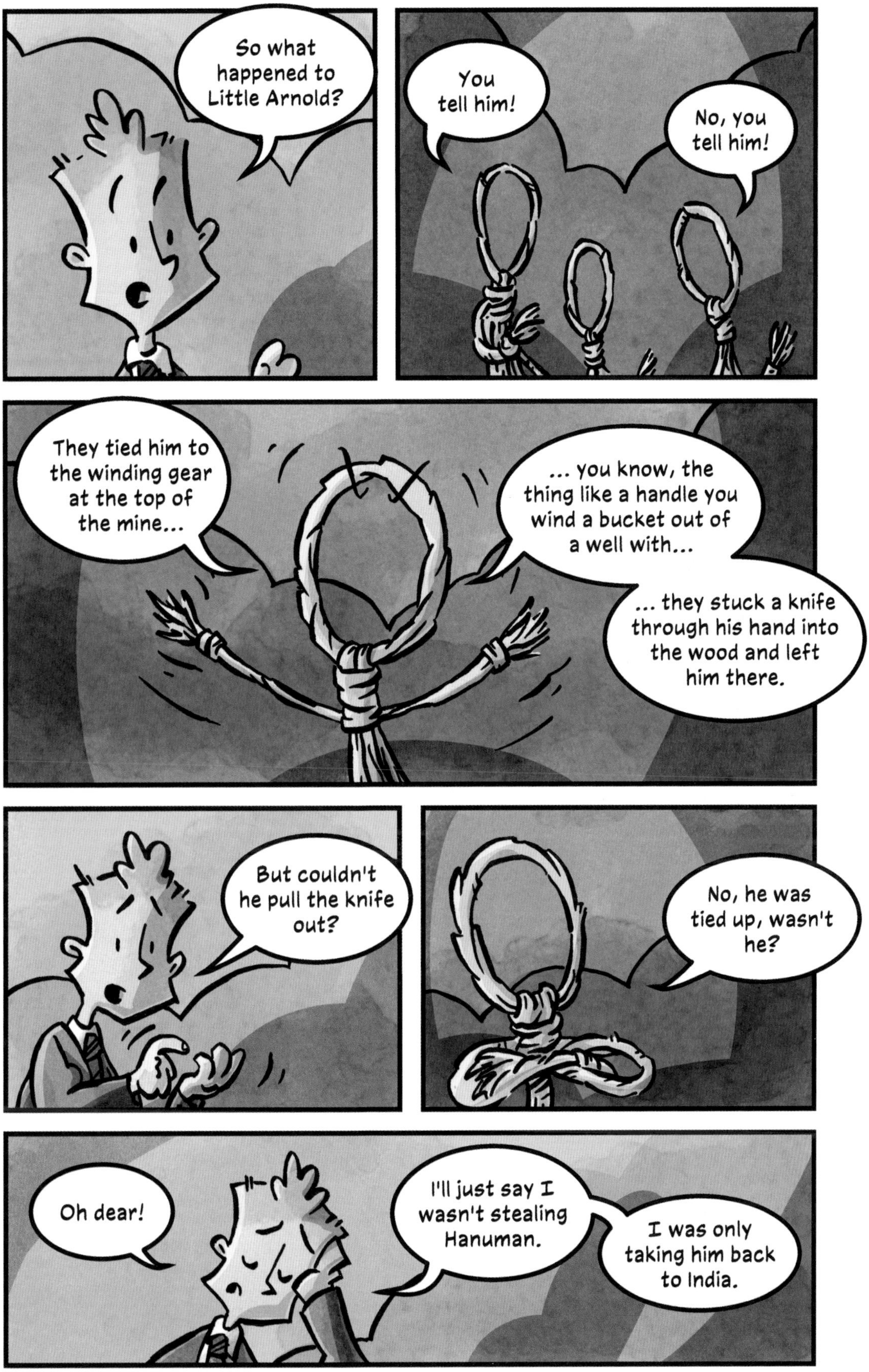
So what happened to Little Arnold?
You tell him!
No, you tell him!
They tied him to the winding gear at the top of the mine...
... you know, the thing like a handle you wind a bucket out of a well with...
... they stuck a knife through his hand into the wood and left him there.
But couldn't he pull the knife out?
No, he was tied up, wasn't he?
Oh dear!
I'll just say I wasn't stealing Hanuman.
I was only taking him back to India.

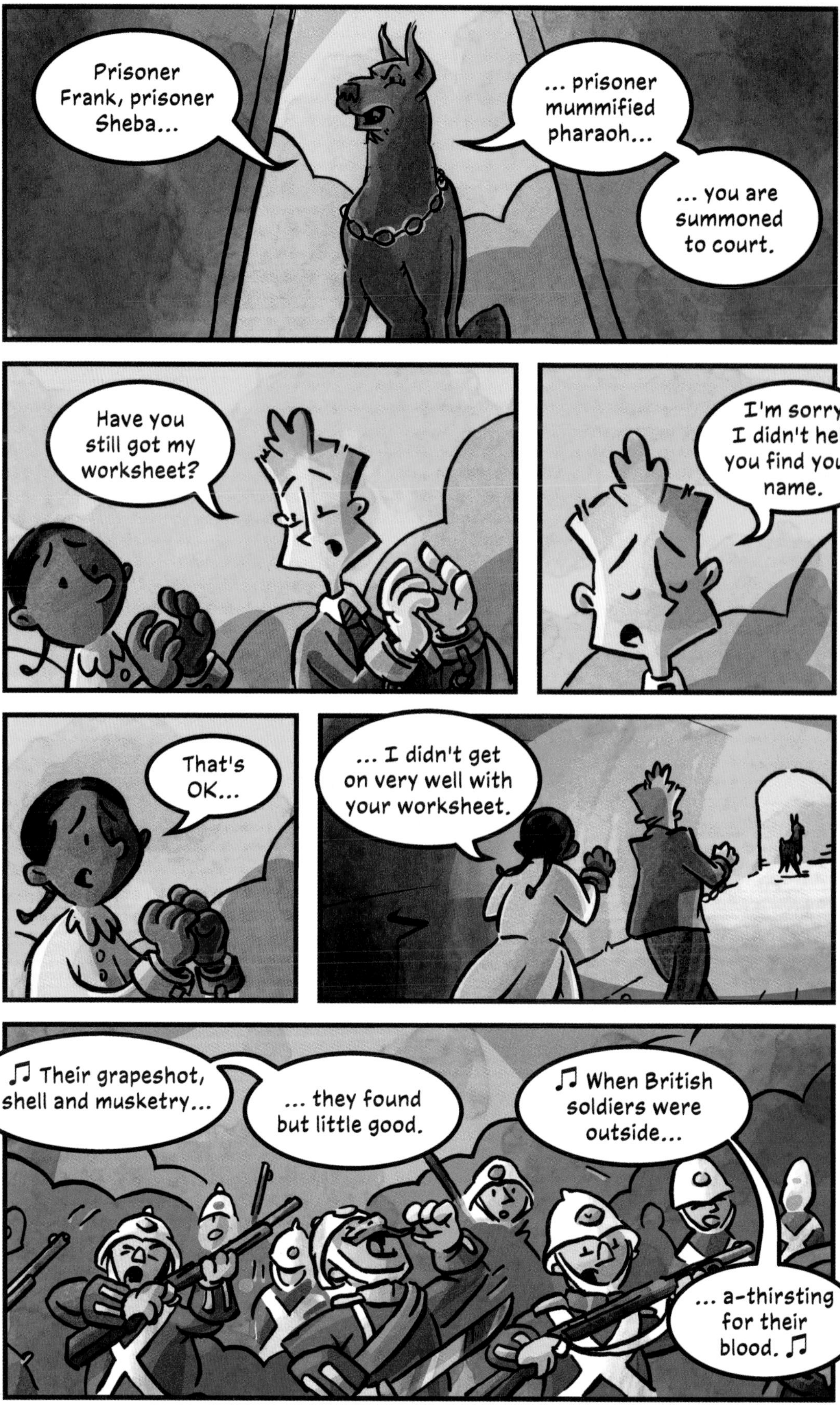
Prisoner Frank, prisoner Sheba...
... prisoner mummified pharaoh...
... you are summoned to court.
Have you still got my worksheet?
I'm sorry I didn't help you find your name.
That's OK...
... I didn't get on very well with your worksheet.
♫ Their grapeshot, shell and musketry...
... they found but little good.
♫ When British soldiers were outside...
... a-thirsting for their blood. ♫

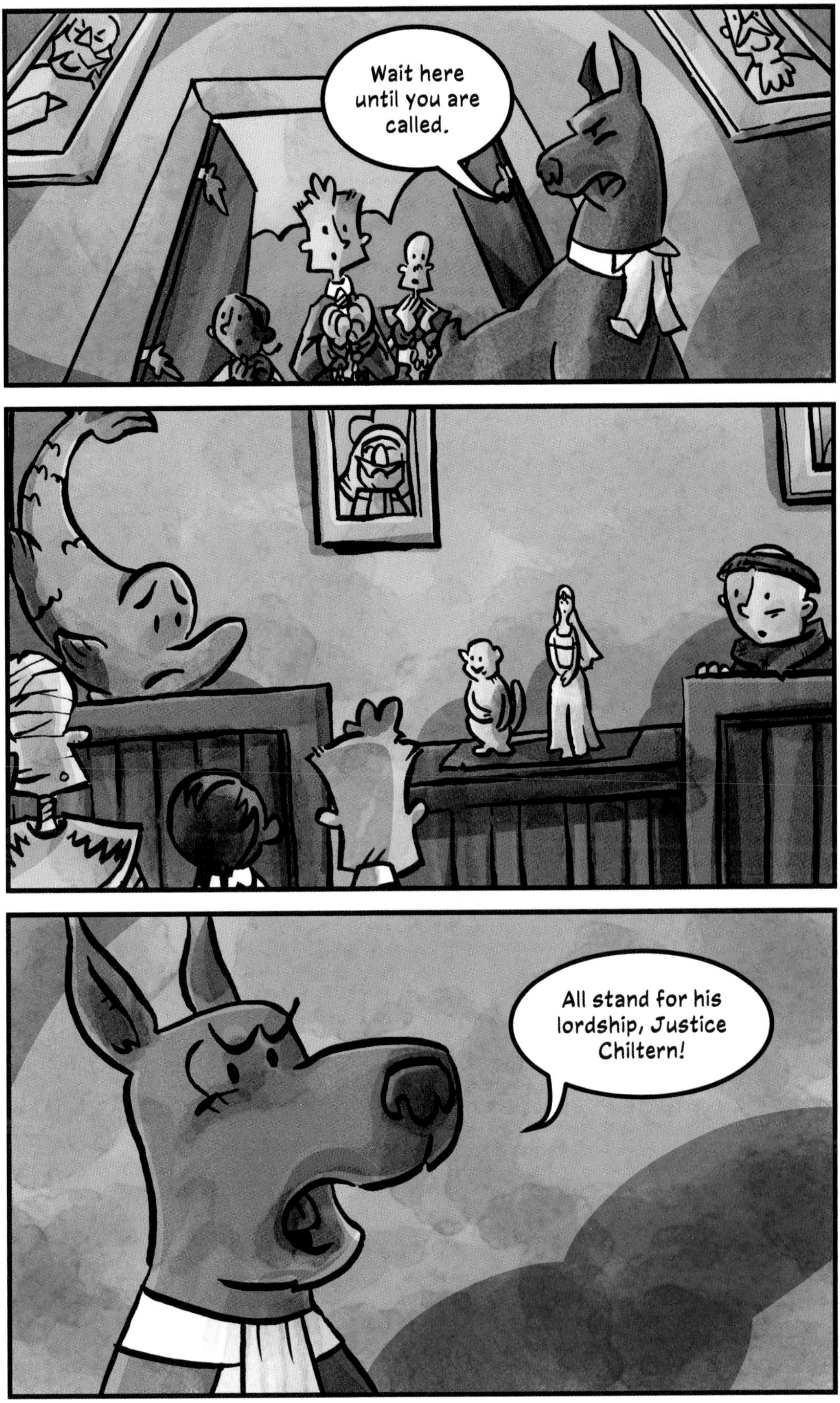
Wait here until you are called.
All stand for his lordship, Justice Chiltern!

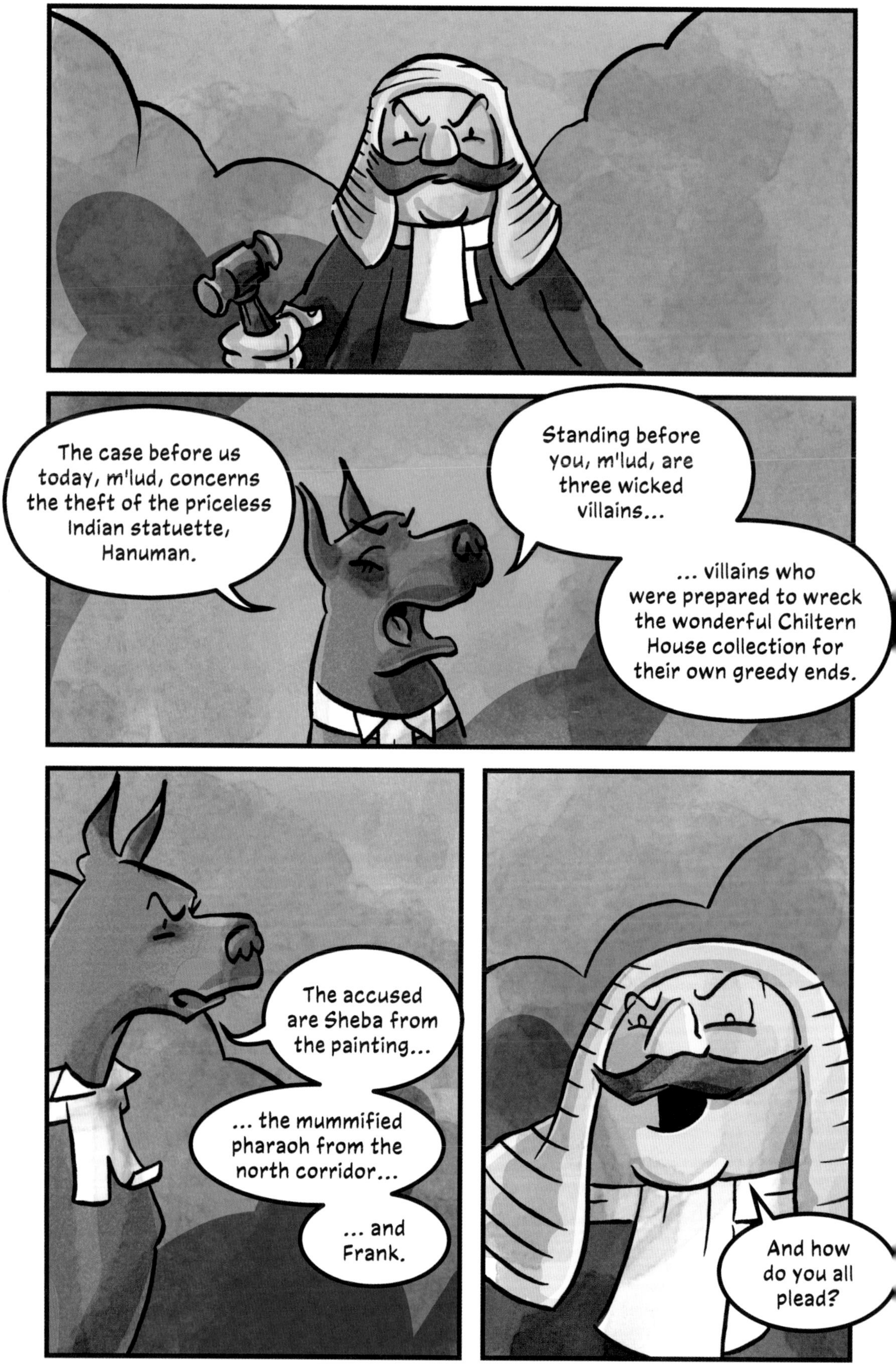
The case before us today, m'lud, concerns the theft of the priceless Indian statuette, Hanuman.
Standing before you, m'lud, are three wicked villains...
... villains who were prepared to wreck the wonderful Chiltern House collection for their own greedy ends.
The accused are Sheba from the painting...
... the mummified pharaoh from the north corridor...
... and Frank.
And how do you all plead?

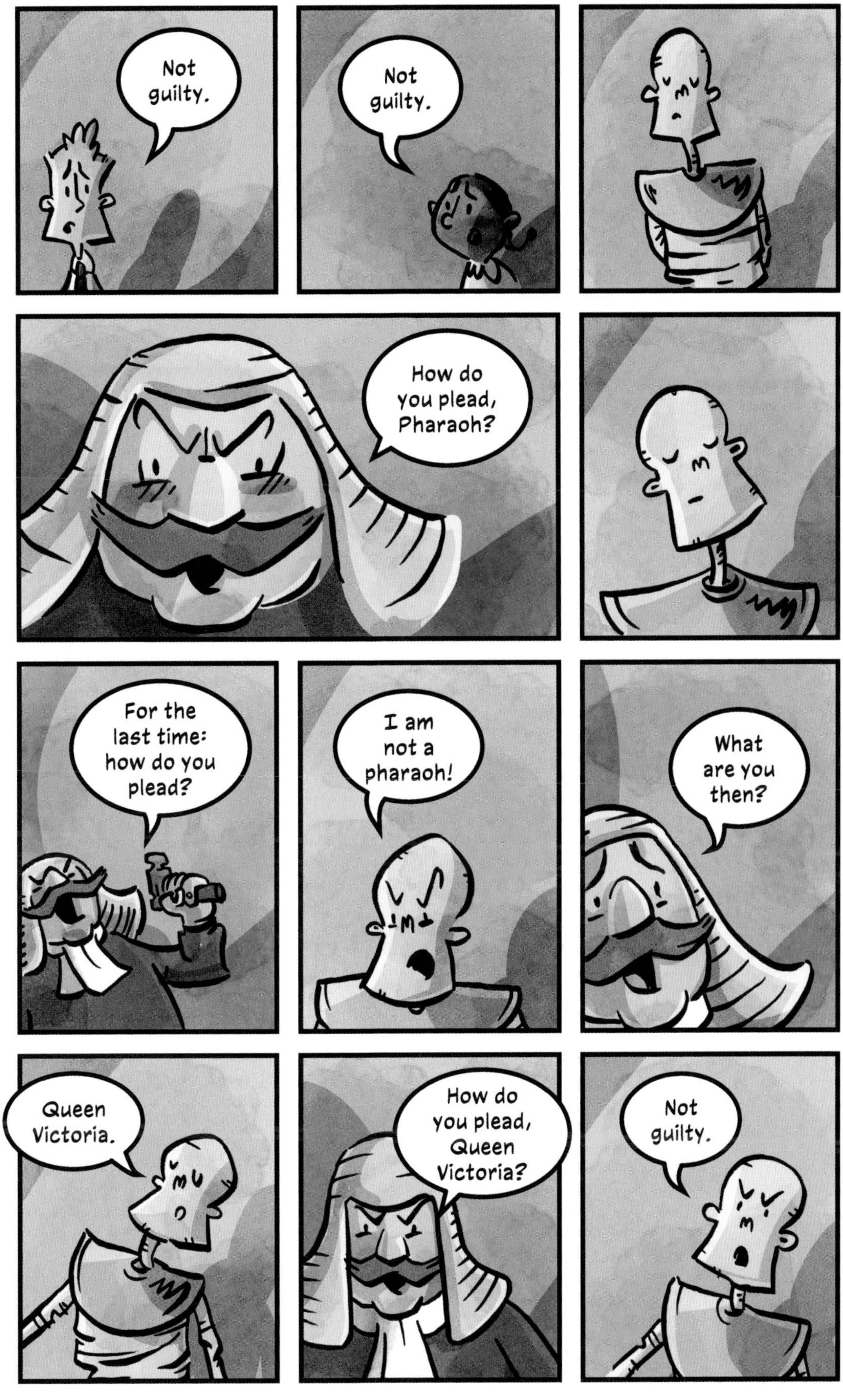
Not guilty.
Not guilty.
How do you plead, Pharaoh?
For the last time: how do you plead?
I am not a pharaoh!
What are you then?
Queen Victoria.
How do you plead, Queen Victoria?
Not guilty.

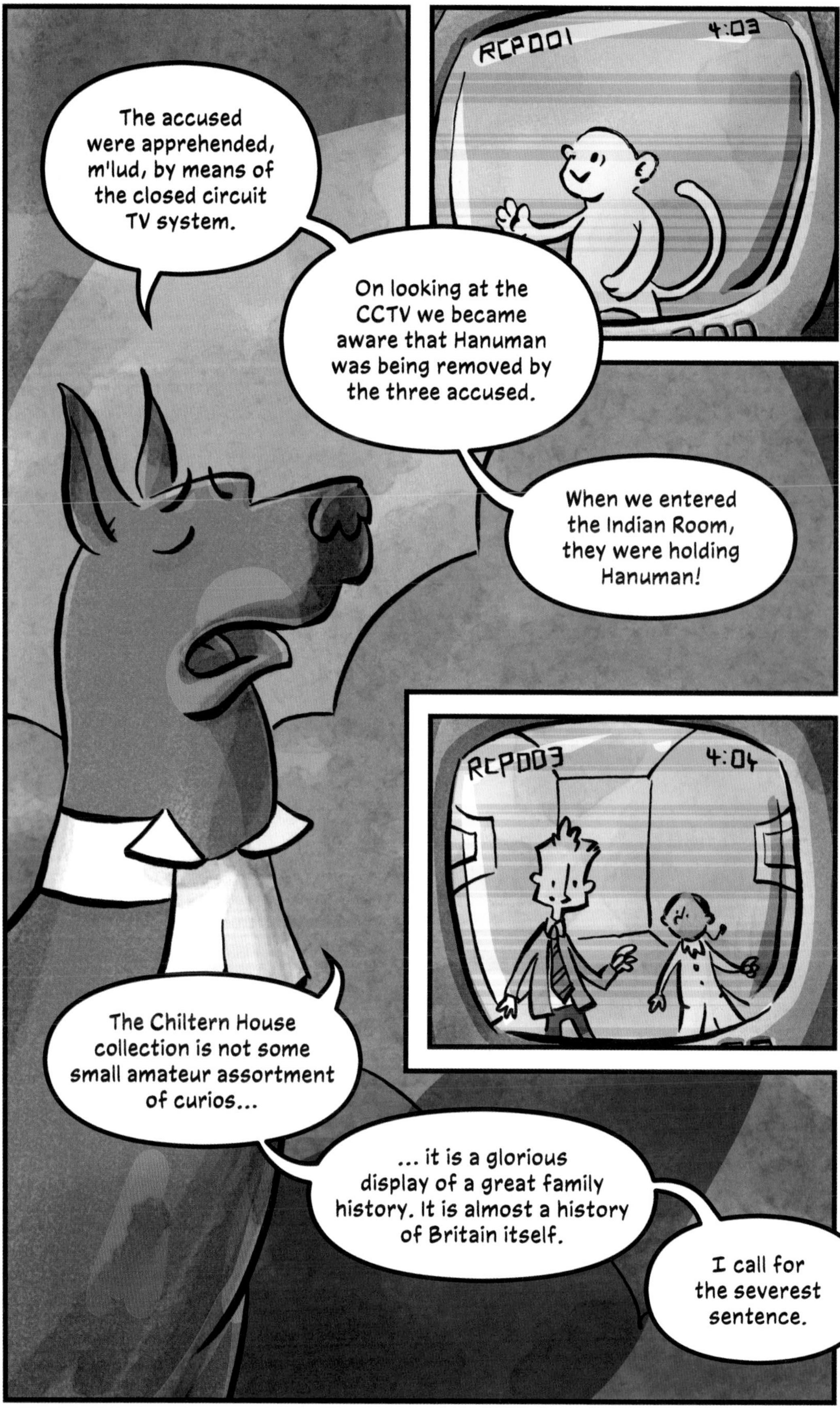
RCP001 4:03
The accused were apprehended, m'lud, by means of the closed circuit TV system.
On looking at the CCTV we became aware that Hanuman was being removed by the three accused.
When we entered the Indian Room, they were holding Hanuman!
RCP003 4:04
The Chiltern House collection is not some small amateur assortment of curios...
... it is a glorious display of a great family history. It is almost a history of Britain itself.
I call for the severest sentence.

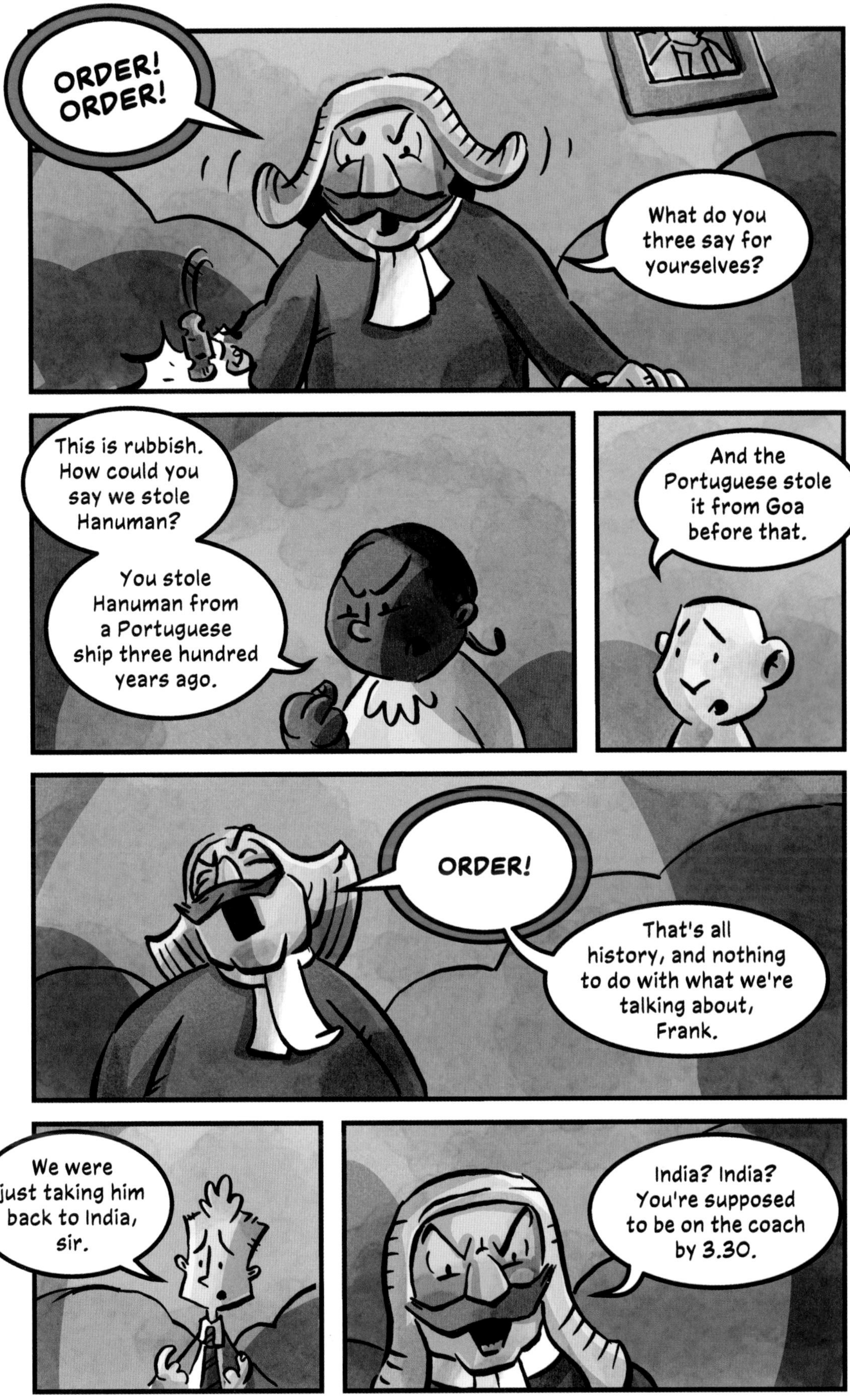
ORDER! ORDER!
What do you three say for yourselves?
This is rubbish. How could you say we stole Hanuman?
You stole Hanuman from a Portuguese ship three hundred years ago.
And the Portuguese stole it from Goa before that.
ORDER!
That's all history, and nothing to do with what we're talking about, Frank.
We were just taking him back to India, sir.
India? India? You're supposed to be on the coach by 3.30.

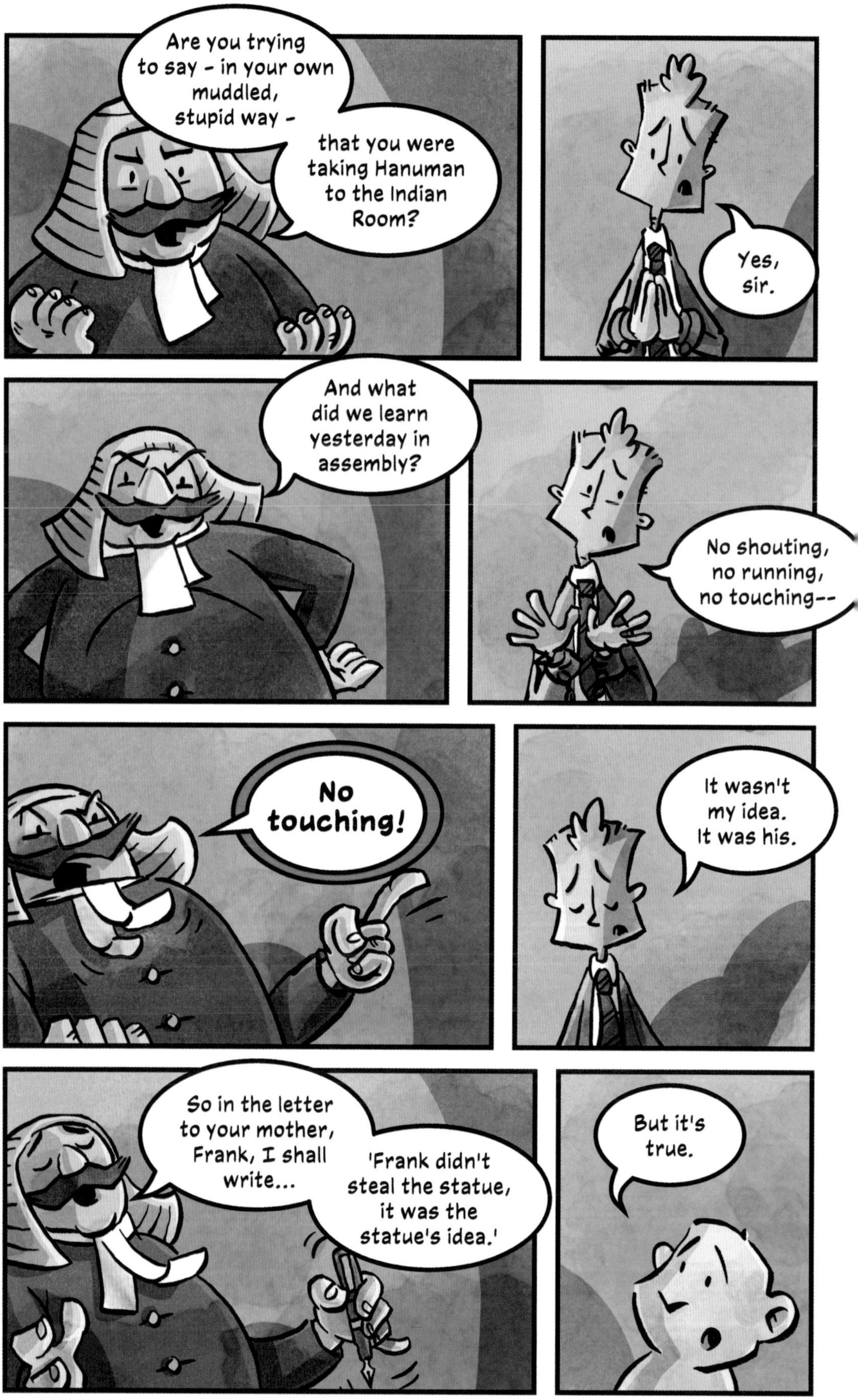
Are you trying to say - in your own muddled, stupid way -
that you were taking Hanuman to the Indian Room?
Yes, sir.
And what did we learn yesterday in assembly?
No shouting, no running, no touching--
No touching!
It wasn't my idea. It was his.
So in the letter to your mother, Frank, I shall write...
'Frank didn't steal the statue, it was the statue's idea.'
But it's true.

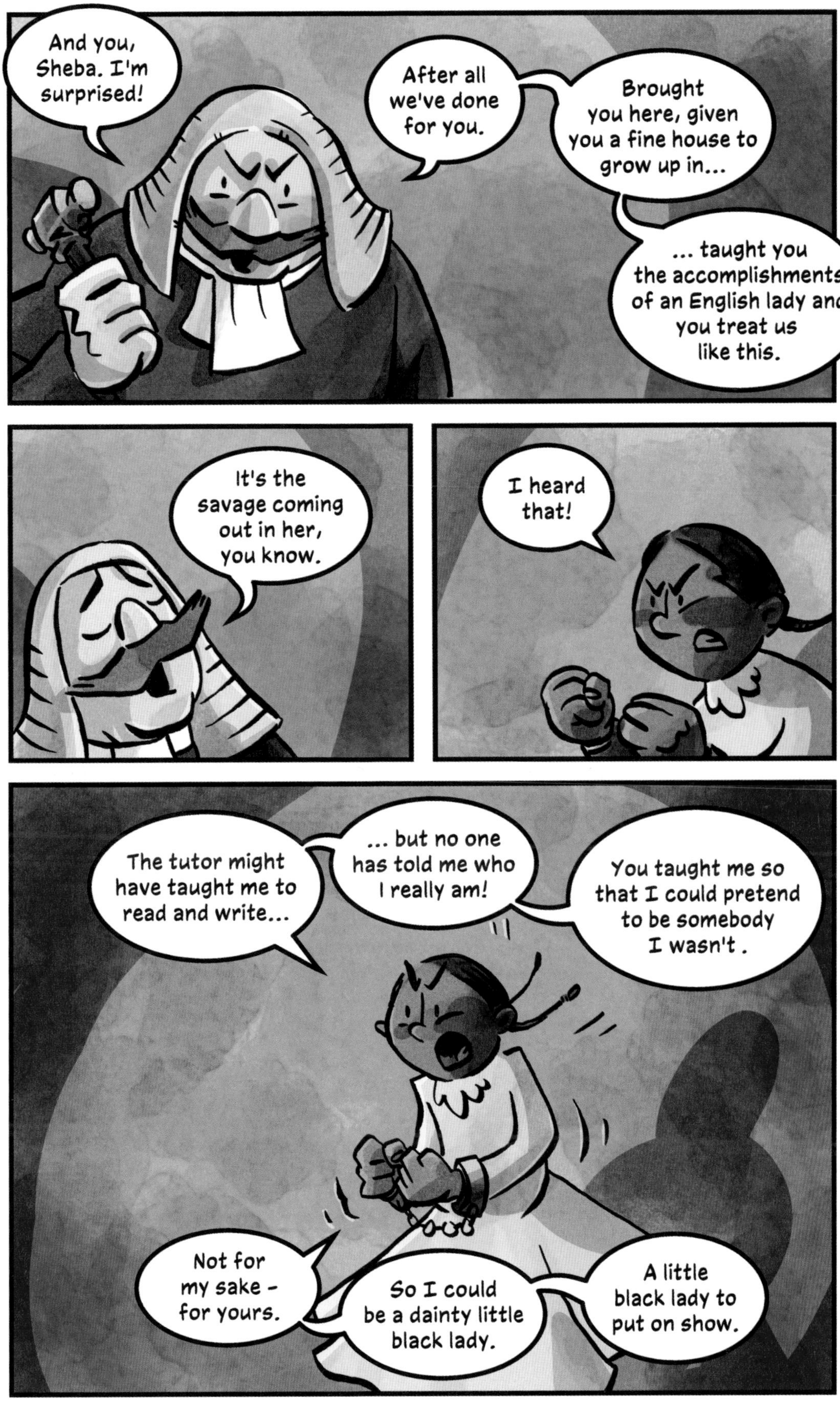
And you, Sheba. I'm surprised!
After all we've done for you.
Brought you here, given you a fine house to grow up in...
... taught you the accomplishments of an English lady and you treat us like this.
It's the savage coming out in her, you know.
I heard that!
The tutor might have taught me to read and write...
... but no one has told me who I really am!
You taught me so that I could pretend to be somebody I wasn't .
Not for my sake - for yours.
So I could be a dainty little black lady.
A little black lady to put on show.

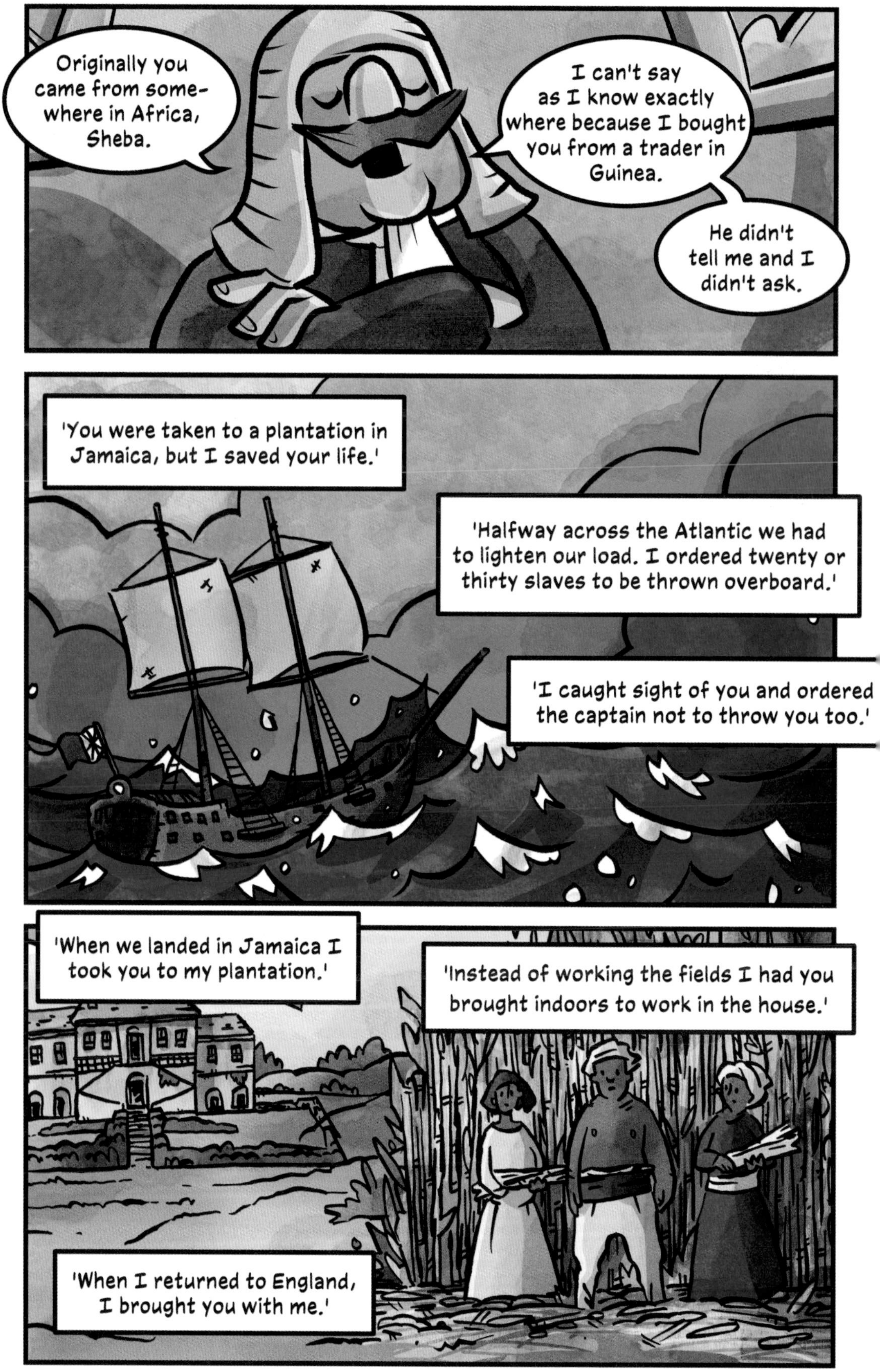
Originally you came from somewhere in Africa, Sheba.
I can't say as I know exactly where because I bought you from a trader in Guinea.
He didn't tell me and I didn't ask.
'You were taken to a plantation in Jamaica, but I saved your life.'
'Halfway across the Atlantic we had to lighten our load. I ordered twenty or thirty slaves to be thrown overboard.'
'I caught sight of you and ordered the captain not to throw you too.'
'When we landed in Jamaica I took you to my plantation.'
'Instead of working the fields I had you brought indoors to work in the house.'
'When I returned to England, I brought you with me.'

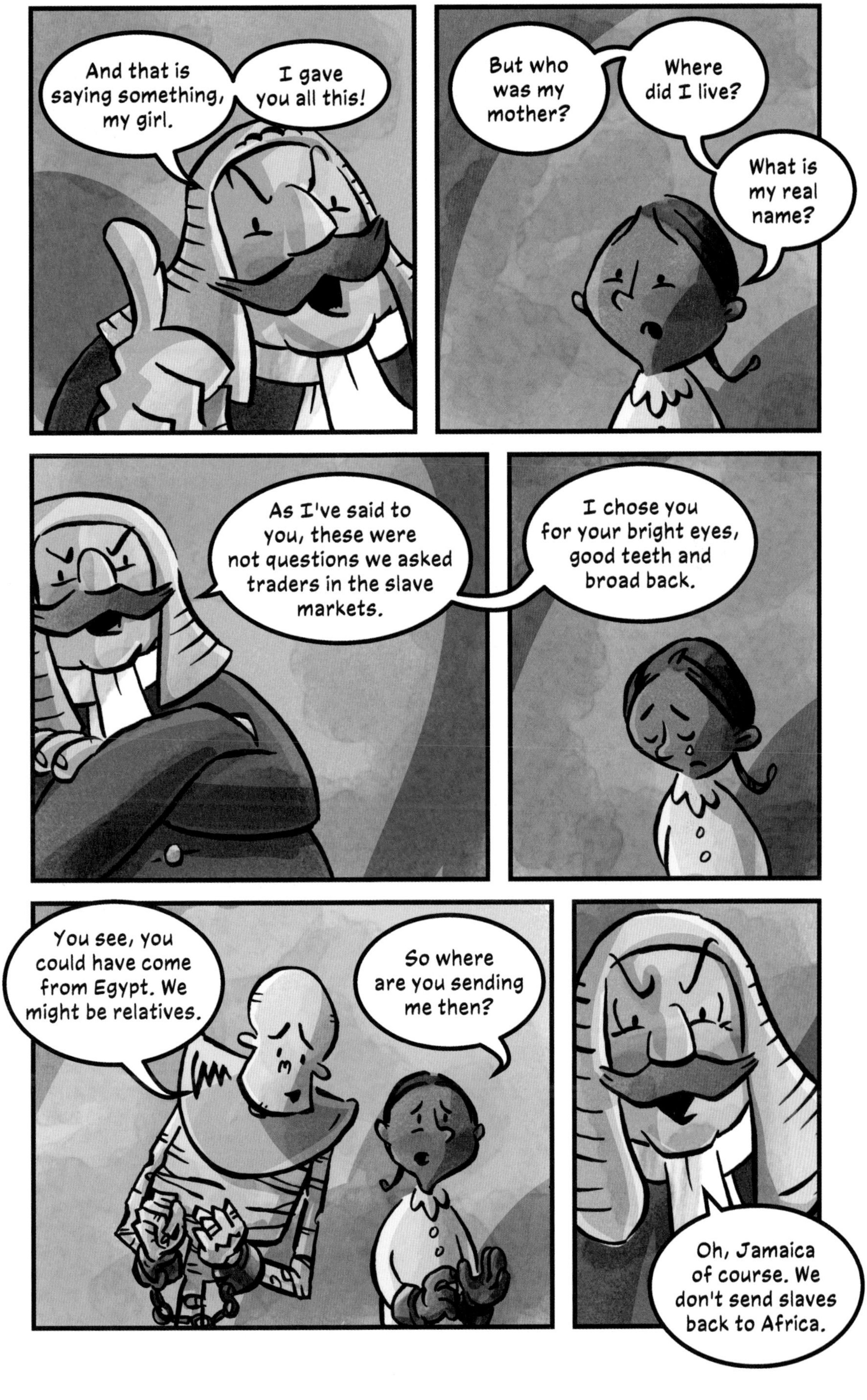
And that is saying something, my girl.
I gave you all this!
But who was my mother?
Where did I live?
What is my real name?
As I've said to you, these were not questions we asked traders in the slave markets.
I chose you for your bright eyes, good teeth and broad back.
You see, you could have come from Egypt. We might be relatives.
So where are you sending me then?
Oh, Jamaica of course. We don't send slaves back to Africa.

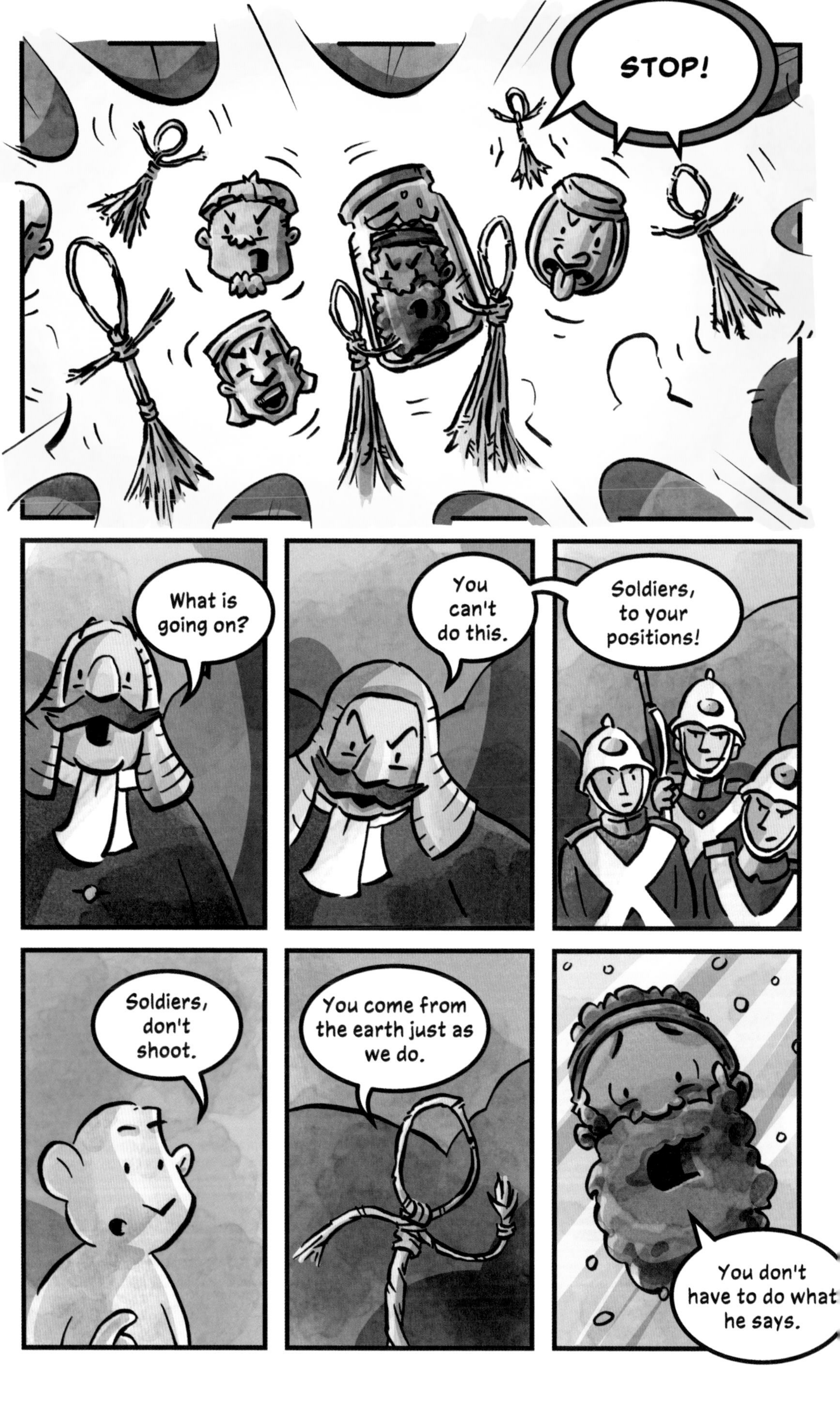
STOP!
What is going on?
You can't do this.
Soldiers, to your positions!
Soldiers, don't shoot.
You come from the earth just as we do.
You don't have to do what he says.

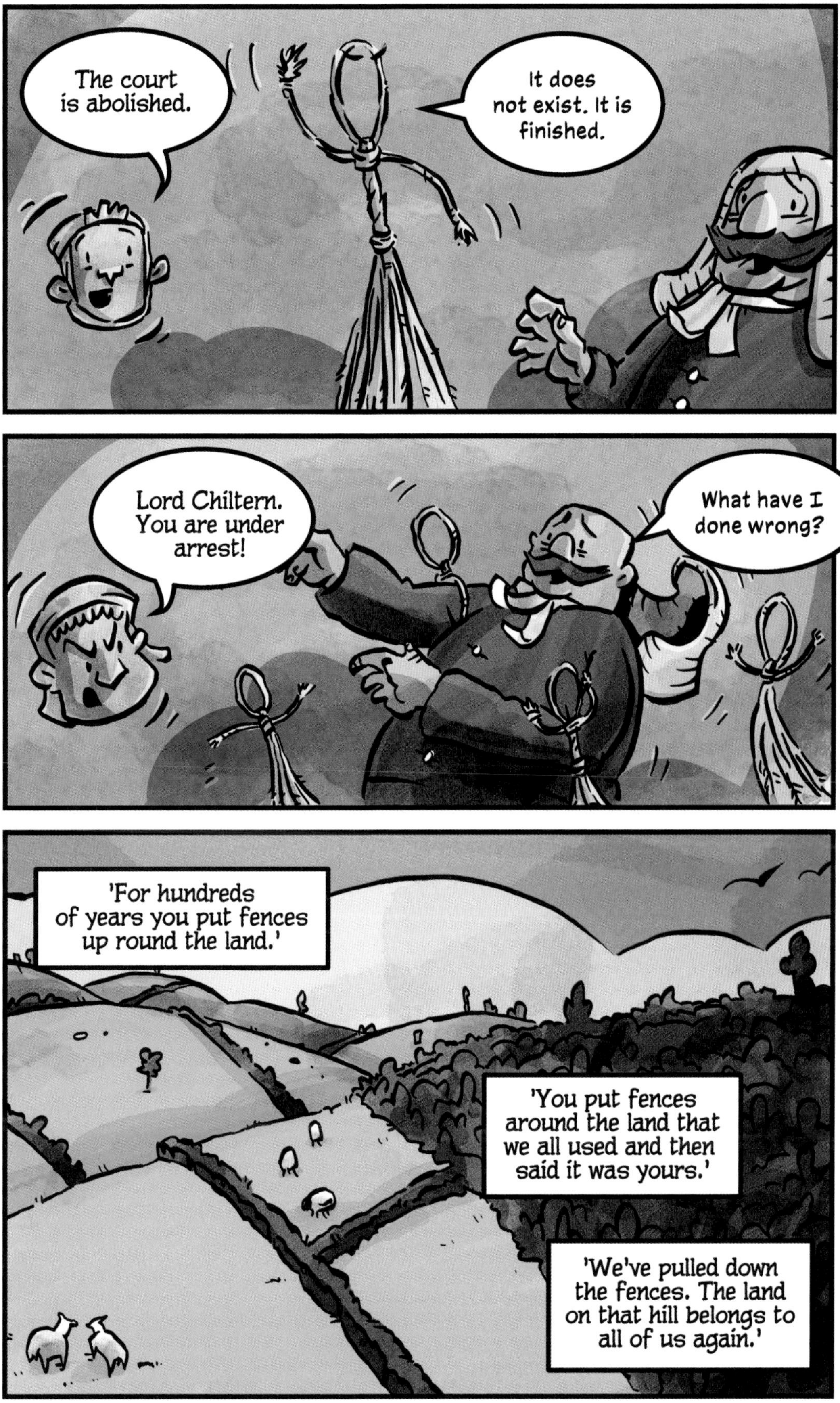
The court is abolished.
It does not exist. It is finished.
Lord Chiltern. You are under arrest!
What have I done wrong?
'For hundreds of years you put fences up round the land.'
'You put fences around the land that we all used and then said it was yours.'
'We've pulled down the fences. The land on that hill belongs to all of us again.'

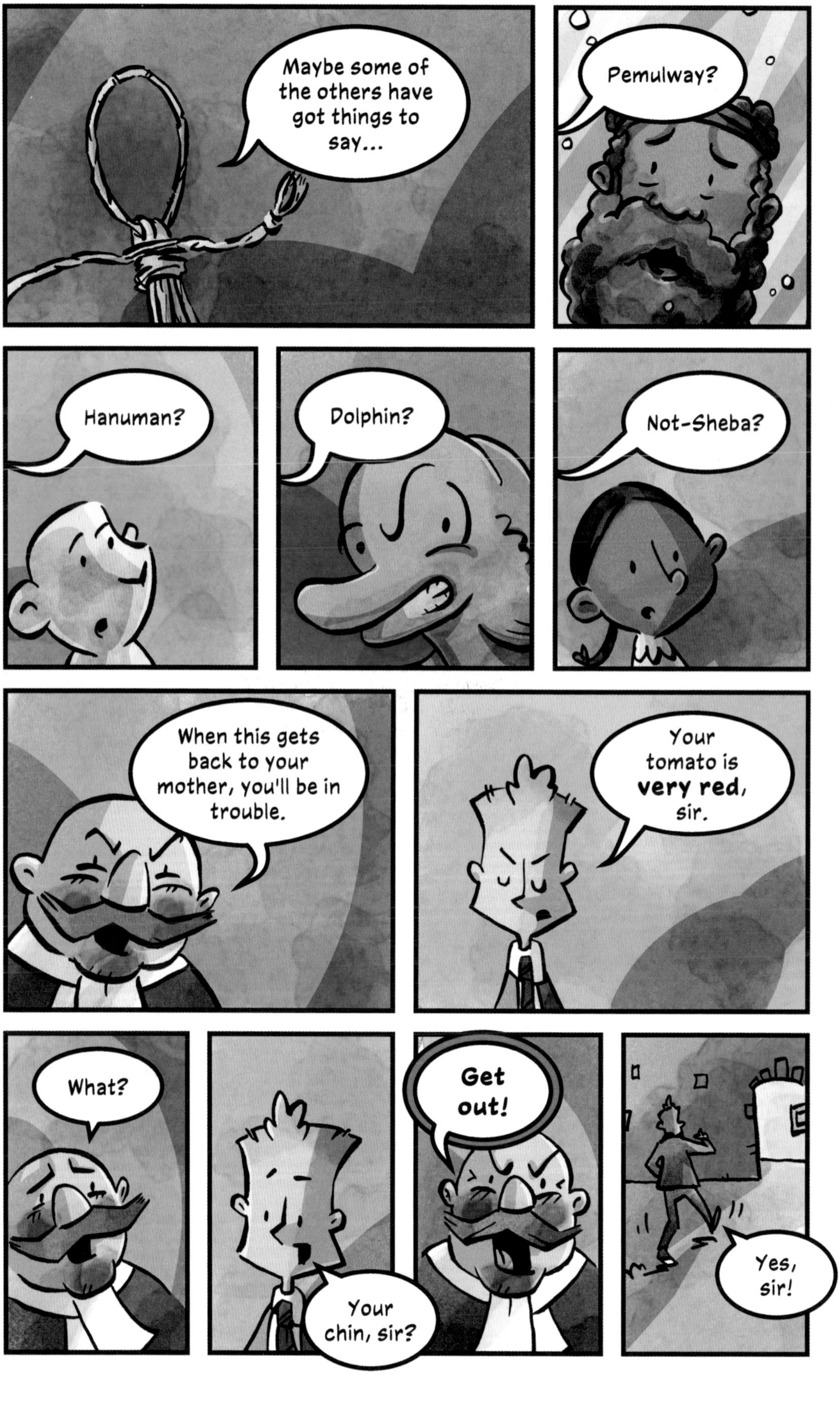
Maybe some of the others have got things to say...
Pemulway?
Hanuman?
Dolphin?
Not-Sheba?
When this gets back to your mother, you'll be in trouble.
Your tomato is **very red**, sir.
What?
Your chin, sir?
Get out!
Yes, sir!

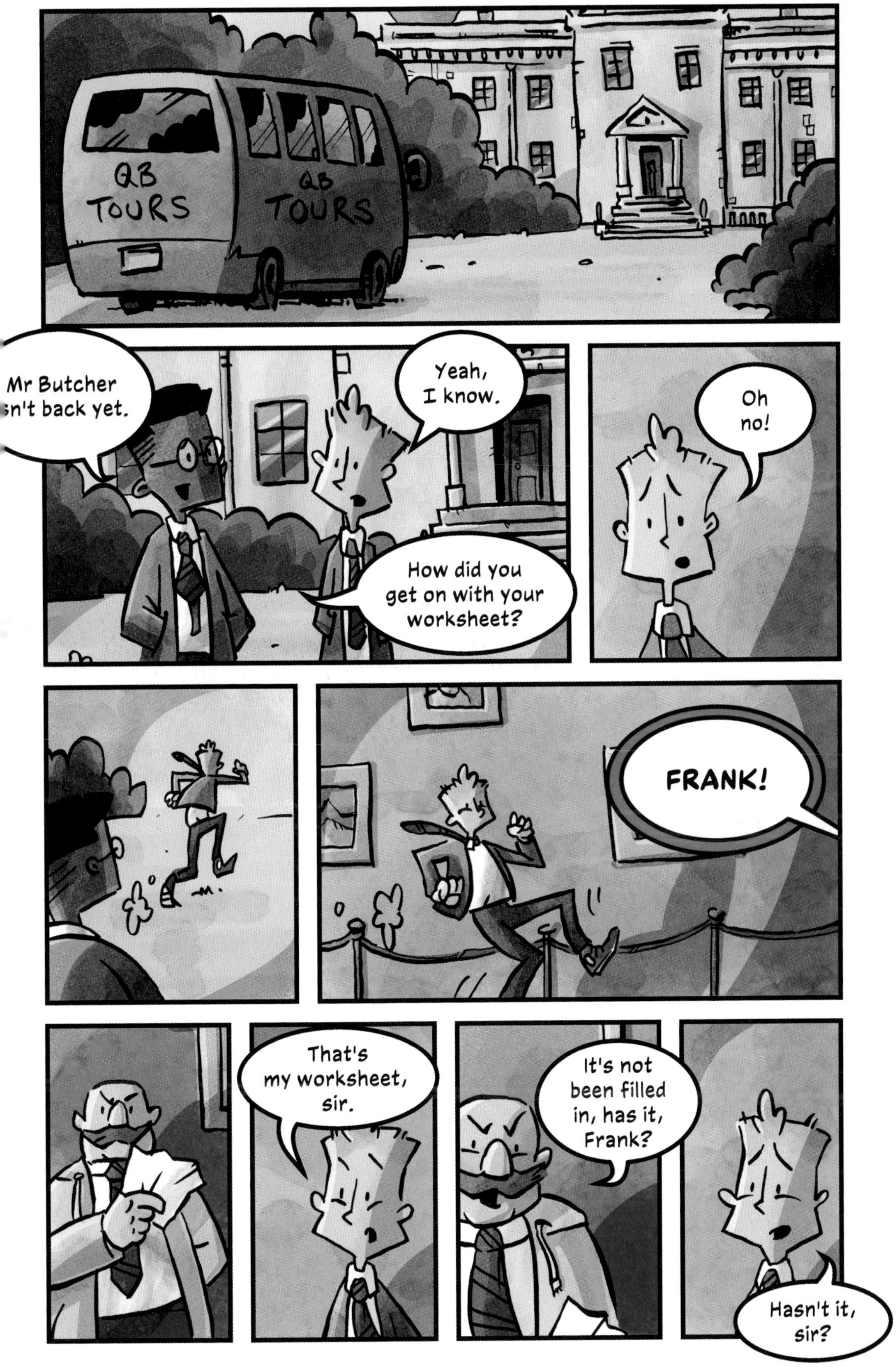
QB TOURS
QB TOURS
Mr Butcher
sn't back yet.
Yeah, I know.
How did you get on with your worksheet?
Oh no!
FRANK!
That's my worksheet, sir.
It's not been filled in, has it, Frank?
Hasn't it, sir?

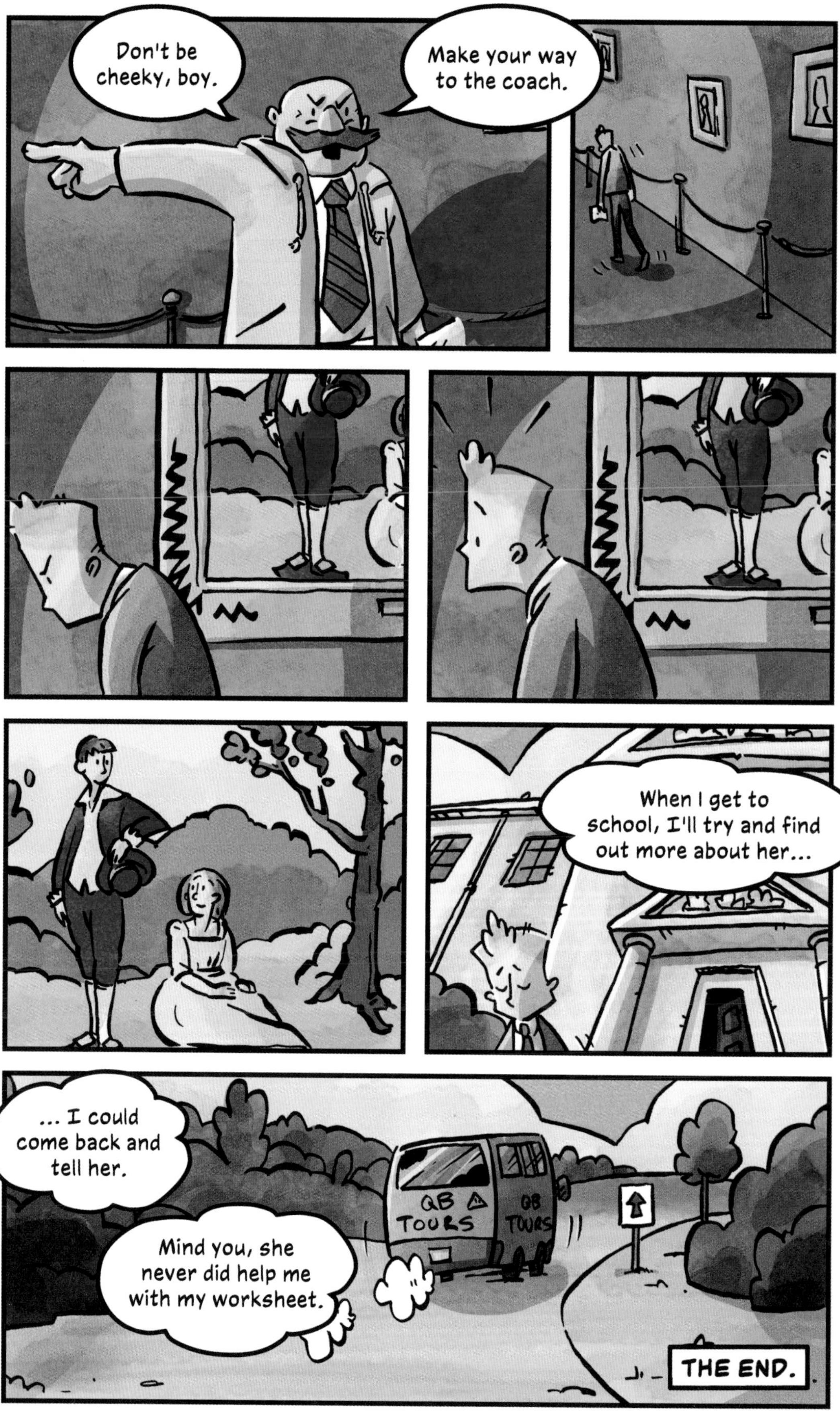
Don't be cheeky, boy.
Make your way to the coach.
When I get to school, I'll try and find out more about her...
... I could come back and tell her.
Mind you, she never did help me with my worksheet.
QB TOURS
QB TOURS
THE END.

A Note on the Author

Michael Rosen has written or edited over 200 books, and his most famous collaboration, *We're Going on a Bear Hunt*, has sold over 8 million copies worldwide. He has won numerous awards and from 2007 to 2009 was the British Children's Laureate. He broadcasts regularly on BBC Radio 4 and is a professor of children's literature at Goldsmiths, University of London. His YouTube channel, 'Kids' Poems and Stories with Michael Rosen', has over 600,000 subscribers and has had more than 100 million views.

A Note on the Illustrator

Cole Henley is an illustrator, recovering archaeologist and maker of websites based in Somerset. *You're Thinking About Tomatoes* is his first collaboration with Michael Rosen.

Acknowledgements

Michael:

This story began with me telling it to my son Joe when he was ten. At one point, one of the characters -- I can't say which -- died. He was so shocked and disappointed, I had to bring that character back alive.

The story itself touches on a theme that has become a topic of great interest: the British Empire, and the history of how Britain acquired its wealth. I think it's fantastic that it now has a graphic novel format, thanks to the artwork of Cole Henley. I hope that this really helps the story to be accessible to a wide range of audiences.

Cole:

Thanks to Lizzie, Cassie, DeAndra and all the team at Unbound who have brought this project to life and for giving me the nudges I have needed along the way.

To Ned for his help getting the idea over the starting line. To all our backers for their generous support and patience.

To my family for giving me the time, space and encouragement I needed.

But above all thanks to Michael and Joe for replying to a tweet, for providing the opportunity to work together and for trusting me with Frank, Charlie and Not-Sheba.

Unbound is the world's first crowdfunding publisher, established in 2011.

We believe that wonderful things can happen when you clear a path for people who share a passion. That's why we've built a platform that brings together readers and authors to crowdfund books they believe in -- and give fresh ideas that don't fit the traditional mould the chance they deserve.

This book is in your hands because readers made it possible. Everyone who pledged their support is listed below. Join them by visiting unbound.com and supporting a book today.

Sarah Akhtar
Bruce Alcorn
Alex Alex & Gabi
Hazel Alexander
Alexander and Myla
Clare Allen
Steve Allen
Nicola Alloway
Yasemin Allsop
Carol Anderson
Chloe Anderson
Claire Anderson
Igor Andronov
Elena Arevalo Melville
Jeanette Arregger
Debbie Arthur
Kat Ashburn-Scott
Nesher Asner
Jane Atkin
Michael Atkins
John Auckland
Daniel Avenal
Isla Axon
Peter Ayello-Wright
James Aylett
Samuel & David B
Arthur Bagnall
Jenny E Bailey
Kathleen Bakewell
James Baldwin
Gail Barnshaw
Ben & Rebecca Barrow
Gail Barton
Sarah Bartram
Tree Bartram
Al Barz
Anna Bayman
Eliza Beaman
Danielle Beaney
Naomi Beaumont
Carol Beck
Jenny Beck
John Beeching
Rowan Bell
Ronnie Bendall
Emma Bennett
Fiona Bennett
Phillip Bennett-Richards
Dom Benson
Julian Benton
Julie Bernstein
Patrick Beverley
Jurek Bijak

Pete Billingham

Heather Binsch

Fran Birch

Moli Birkinshaw

Alex Black

Gavin Bluck

Boaz Boaz and Amos

Oliver Bolland

Paul Bolland

Cath Booth

Jenny Bourne

Evan Bower

James Box

Eleanor Boyd

Conor Boyle

Gail Boynton

Isla Bradley

Laurie Bradley

Caroline Bradshaw

Andy Brereton

Joan Britten

Liz Broad

Adam Brouard

Louise Brown

Amelia-Anne Bruce

Lucy Brunnen

The Bunting Family

Eve & Violet Burke

Ali Burns

Marcus Butcher

Paul Butcher

Rosie Butler

Fiadh Butterly Payne

Siobhan Cairns

Ian Calcutt

Kate Campbell

Nikky Campbell

Sarah Campbell

Evie Campbell Balls

Monty Campbell Balls

Olivia Canham

Kit Cardinal

Victoria Cargill-James

Harri Carmichael

Ann Carrier

Ranjit Chagar

Chalkhill Primary School

Chi Chan

Benjamin Charles

Francis Theodore
    Charman

Paul Child

Beth Childs

Libby Clark

Richard Cleverley

Ruth Clougherty

Philippa Cochrane

GMark Cole

Maggie Cole

Paige Collingbourne

Callum Colraine

Kate Comiskey

Jacqui Connell

Luke Connell APFS DipCII
    CeFA

Gemma Connolly

Jennifer Connor

Illinois Cook

Mark R Cordell

Emma Corlett

Anna Cornelius

Sarah Cornelius

Katy Costello

Megan Cotter

Mat Coward

Tricia Cowdrey

Helen Cross

Lorraine Crossingham

Euan Crowther

Julia Croyden

Gabriel Dagmalm

Nathalie Dalton-King

Jane Davies

Jon Davies

Non Davies

David Dawson

Ian Dennis

Dan Dickson

Gary Dillon

Joanna Dirmikis

Sally Dodd

Stephen Dodd

Phil Dooley

Konnor Douglas

Matthew Douglas

Stuart Douglas Hunter

Jonathan Dransfield

Helen Duncan

Margot Duncan

Sue Dunn

Lochlan Dyas-Hamilton

Dylan Dylan and Rowan

Dave Eagle

Graham East

Pamela Edwardes

Nicola Edwards

June Ellerby

Ellie-Rose

Gavin Elliott

Niall Elliott Byrnes

Tilly Ellis Waring

Beatrice Empson

Ruby Evans

Maggie Eveleigh

Patrick Eyers

Jonathan Eyre

Michael Facherty

Hamilton-Pearce family

Patric ffrench Devitt

Seán Michael Fiddis

John Fielder

Alice Fillery

Monica Finch

Sophie & Alice Finlay

Lisa Fiske

Alex Fitch

Roger Flatt

Natasha Fletcher

For my son James
    Davidson, Love Dad

Charlie Fox

Mr & Mrs Fox

John Francis

Isabelle & Everlie Fraser

Luca Fukushige

Christina Gabbitas

Rachel Gallagher

Archie Galloway

Arthur J Galloway

Nicola Gamble

Sarah Garnham

Arthur Garth Smith

Verette and John Gatti

Stan Gavigan

Martin Genner

Peter George

Kim Gibson

Tom Gifford

Richard Gillin

Kate Glennon

The Goda Grandchildren

Deborah Good

Dan Goodwin

Ann Gorecki

Grace Grace and Henry

Nina Grant

Chris Gravell

Isaac and Freddie Gray

Neil Gregory

Susanne Griffin

Hannah Griffiths

Sarah and Andy Grigg

Lexi Grogan

Diana Guibord

Amber & Jamie Guise

Louisa Guise

EJ Guttzeit

EL Guttzeit

Charlotte Hacking

Seth Hall

Aegir Hallmundur

Cate Hamilton

David Hamilton

Jake & Eleni Hamilton

Matthew Hamm

Rod Hancox

Frank Handley

Noreen Harding

Summer Harding

Hector Hargrave

Kate Hargreaves

Ruth Hargreaves

Becca Harper-Day

Maria Harrington

Ann Harris

Pete Harris

Floss Harrison

A.F. Harrold

Ned Hartley

Monika Hartmann

Simon Haslam

Charlotte HB Mansfield

Mary Healy

Tina Helfrich

Chris Hemsley

Deryck Henley

Jason Henthorn

Mandy Hill

Nye & Abe Hodges

John Hodson

Fabio Holgado Lopez

Steve Hollingshead

Anne Hollows

Jane Hopwood

Sue Hornby

Jane Hostler

Rosie Houghton

Jo Howard

Lily Mae & Poppy Howard

Nicola Howard

Chris Huggins

Richard Humm

Sally Hunt

Harper Hunter Hux
    Crowley

Aran Hurley Harrington

Huxx & Loki

Alfie Ide

George Ivory-Bray

Sam Jackson

Paul Jameson

Alison Jenner

Anette Dal Jensen

Nicky Jerrome

Simon Jobling

Brion Johnson

Dan Johnson

Jenny Johnson

Rosie Johnson

Sidney Johnson Davidson

Alexander and Jefferson
   Jones

Jennifer Jones

Lisa Jones

Liz Jones

Nicolette Jones

Vikram & Annika Joshi

Jane Judge

Geoffrey Kahler

Oliver and Thomas
   Kawakami White

Jane Kay

John Kaye

Joshua Keetley

Steven Keevil

Chris Kehoe

Candace Kendall

Mary Kerr

Matthew Kerwick

Martin Kettle

Asad Khan

Dan Kieran

Elaine Kieran

Isobel Kieran

Eunji Kim

Lena Kimble

Lisa King

Teresa King

Clare Knight

Evgeniya Konnova

Richard Kuper

Abhilash Lal Sarhadi

Janet Lambrou

Zara Lamoreaux

Masön Lane

Sam Lane

Lara Lara + Thomas

Samuel Larsen Williams

Alyssa Larson

Patrick H. Lauke

Muriel Lavender

Roan Lavery

Hannah Lawrence

Jess Lawson

Ailbhe Leamy

Gaby Lees

Inayaili Leon

Samantha Lettington

Tom and Jack Lightley

Rossella Limongi

Christine Liston

Samuel Little

caroline Liversidge

Paul Robert Lloyd

Tilly Lloyd

Jim Lockie

Christine Lockwood

Tanya Logan

Loli

John & Christine Lomax

Sue Loosley

Emma Luckhurst

Lyla and Nola

Aimee Lyn

Bernadette Lynn

Craig M

Matt Machell

Drew Mackay

Kate Mackey

Hope & Ethan Mackie

Helen Maclagan

Andrea Malpica

Philippa Manasseh

Robert Maniam-Sirr

Helen Manners

Karen Mapplethorpe

Piper Maree White

Marie #YellowVests

Alyson Marlor

Wayne Marsh

André Marshall

Marston Vale Middle
   School

Rory & Margot Martin

Adam, Lewis & Ethan
   Matheson

Zhenya Matysiak

Rabiyah Mazhar

Joanne McBride

Trevor McCarthy

Lucy McCaul

Emma McCormack

Margaret McCormack

Marion McGillivray
   Harrison

Colin McGregor

Claire McLaughlin

Sam Mcloughlin

Karin McMullan

Gwen McNeil

Flora McPhail

Nicola McQuaid

Mary Megarry

William Menner

Kirsty Miller

Liz Miller

Peter Miller

Roberta Mitchell

John Mitchinson

Louise Moczulski

Charlotte Monaghan

Becky Moore

Frank Morgan

Sandra Morland

Daniel Morse

The Morson Kiddiwinks

Anna and Esme Morton

Chris Mosler

Ethan Mulder

Yasmeen Multani

Joseph William Mulvihill

Jane Murphy

Kate Murphy

Jennie Muskett

Kit Mycock-Overell

Phil Naldrett

Rachel Nash

Hanna & Oskar Navarro
   Staiger

Carlo Navato

Marie Nelson

Rowan Nelson

Andrew Neve

John New

Don Newton

Hilary Nicholl

Noah Noah & Jack

Archdeacon Eli "Wiggles"
   Norgate

Jan Norman

Xavier P. Nowicki

Lorraine O'Mahoney

Faye Ockelford

David Ogley

Gerry & Kath ONeill

Anthony Oram

John Oxton-King

Emilia Pacetta

William Francis Patterson

Stephen Peberdy

Chris Pennell

Jeff Perks

Michelle Peters at Bear
   Hunt Books

Andy Phillips

Olivia Phipps

Charlotte Pidgeon

Norah Piehl

Rowan Pike

Dawn Plumb

Beth Polak

Justin Pollard

Pamela Pollin

Grith Pope

Gene & Isaac Powell

Matt Powell

Collette Prentice

Siân Prime

Martin Pritchard

Debi Pudsey

Catherine Purcell

Laura Quigley

Malayka Rahman

Garry Ratcliffe

Elaine Rawlings

Julia Rees

Caroline Reid

Ezra Rendle

Sandra Rex

K.A. Reyna

Ethan RG

Richard and Florence

Anne Richards

Chris Richards

Rhoda Charlotte Richards

Sioned-Mair Richards

Katya Riley

Pierce J. Riley

Debby Roberts

Innes Robertson

Rachael Robinson

Stephen Robinson

Lisa Rodgers

Katy Roelich

Deborah Rosen

Gary Ross

Shannie Ross

Alex Rowe

Charlie Rowe

Alexander JG Roy

Edward HN Roy

Theo Ruffles

russellmarkolson

Maddie Ryan Tucker

Olivia Sack

SF Said

Anne Sarrag

Jessica Savage

Robin Schlinkert

Tomric Schueller Elmes

Gwyn Schulte

Edith Scott

Sylvie Scott

Caroline Sefton

Felix Selway

Nina Selway

Dick Selwood

Jeff Seneviratne

Emily Sexty

Ben (Storyus) Seymour

Philippa Shallcrasd

Rio Shanahan

Oliver and Zoe Sharp

Pennie Shaw

Azadi Sheridan

Marlen Siegert

Lorna Simes
Pete Sinclair
Robin Sissons
Keith Sleight
Susanne Small
Emmae Smart
Jane Smith
Jennie Smith
Jo Smith
Michael Smith
Tim Smith
Henry Smith & Edwin
    Schenck
Koyeli Solanki
Gaby Solly
Joe Somerville
Margaret and Ron
    Spriggs
Springfield Primary
    School
Rosanna Springham
Darcey Spruce
Edward Stace
Andrew Staff
Simon Starr
Katy Stoddard
Pat Stone
Oscar and Toby Strong
Frankie Sullivan Brown
Ian Swain
Susie Symes
Alden Gregory, Owen
    Gregory and Clare
    Symons
Aylah Tae Newman
Cynthia Tanner
Abby Taylor
Coral Taylor

Maisie Taylor
Sharon Taylor
Siobhan Taylor
Beth & Grace Tennant
Theo and Zachary!
Clara Lillian Thomas
Marcella Rose Thomas
John Thorpe
Toby Thurlow
Captain Tor West-Ley
Fiona Tough
Lucy Traves
Brighton Troetschel
Emmanuelle Troude
    Beheregaray
Ethan Tryon-Robson
Joana Tuixent Clarke
    Brey
James Turner
Phil Turner
William Charles Django
    Turner
Mhairi Tynan
Eduard Valle
Garry Vaux
Sarah Vernon
David Walker
Rebecca Walsh
Caro Warner
John Ross Warner
Freya Warren
Cassie Waters
Katie Watkins
Louis Watson
Elaine Waumsley
Alison Webster
Callisto Wenham
Gary West

Emma Wetter
Kathleen Whalen
Katy Wheatley
Ben & George White
Mhairi Whyman
Rob Wilkinson
Gemma Williams
Susan Williamson
Clare K Willison
Reuben Willmott
Alexa Wilson
Gavin Wilson
Otto Wilson
Mike Wingrove
Johnny Wolf Findlater
Walden Wong
Robert Wood
Amanda-Jane Woodland
Czarina Woodthorpe
Steve Woodward
David Wooldridge
Jane Woolley
Sue Wray
Alan Wright
Angelene Wright
Jackie Wthnall
Tony Wylie
Kate Yates